SUMMER CHILLS

SUMMER CHILLS

Strangers in Stranger Lands

Edited by
STEPHEN JONES

CARROLL & GRAF PUBLISHERS
NEW YORK

SUMMER CHILLS
Strangers in Stranger Lands

Carroll & Graf Publishers
An Imprint of Avalon Publishing Group, Inc.
245 West 17th Street
11th Floor
New York, NY 10011

AVALON
publishing group incorporated

The arrangement of this collection is copyright © 2007 Stephen Jones

First Carroll & Graf edition 2007

ISBN-13: 978-0-78671-986-0
ISBN-10: 0-7867-1986-9

9 8 7 6 5 4 3 2 1

Printed in the United States of America
Distributed by Publishers Group West

CONTENTS

ACKNOWLEDGMENTS

Special thanks to Will Balliett, Shaun Dillon, Dorothy Lumley, Mandy Slater, Val and Les Edwards, Jo Fletcher, and Michael Marshall Smith for all their help and support.

INTRODUCTION: HOLIDAYS IN HELL

Stephen Jones

Sometimes we all need a vacation. A chance to relax, to forget the daily grind and all our problems.

A couple of weeks of sitting in the sun. Playing on the beach. Touring foreign countries. Seeing the sights. In short, a chance to simply kick back and take it easy.

But what if something went wrong? I don't mean leaky showers or stomach upsets due to unfamiliarity with the local cuisine. I mean, what if something *really* went wrong?

What if you booked into a hotel that was hiding a deadly secret? Or you unknowingly visited an area held sacred by the locals? What if you did something to insult your hosts, picked up an object that you shouldn't have, or wandered off along some shadowy and mysterious alleyway . . .?

Anything can occur when you're in an unfamiliar location. And sometimes . . . it *does*.

So here are twenty stories about strangers in even stranger lands. From such age-old European cities as London, Paris, Venice, and Moscow, to exotic tourist locations like North Africa and South America . . . from the beaches of England, Greece, and Mexico to such unusual destinations as the Galapagos Islands and the Egyptian Pyramids, there are many dark and dangerous fates awaiting the unwary traveler.

The adventurous protagonists in these stories encounter everything from vengeful ghosts and ancient deities, to mythological creatures and nasty parasites. A British couple learn not to take what is not theirs . . . a charity worker discovers a patch of primal forest that seems to have a life of its own . . . a mountain cabin harbors something seductive and long-dead . . . a woman's secret assignation leads to a horrifying transformation . . . a collector of masks encounters a mythic shape-changer . . . and a pair of lovers find themselves caught up in a bizarre tradition between two living cities . . .

And when it's all over, then there are always your strange neighbors' photos of what they did on their holiday, or the corporate executive who stumbles upon a little old shop that makes maps of the imagination.

Take a journey with these twenty eminent writers into the dark lands, where anything may happen and most likely will. Travel to unfamiliar locations where the tour wanders off the beaten track, a small memento can cost you dearly, and the locals may not be quite as friendly as they first appear.

This is your guidebook to a world that is much bigger and more dangerous than you can possibly ever imagine. But as you read this volume by the pool, on the beach, in your hotel room or during your journey, just ask yourself this . . . can such places exist? And, if they do, maybe these stories are not fiction at all. Maybe these are thinly veiled descriptions of events that really happened to these careless explorers.

So, as you sit sipping your fruity cocktail and feel your skin prickling under a relentless sun, or find yourself investigating the local bazaars for interesting and unusual souvenirs, remember—you may not be quite as safe as you think . . .

—Stephen Jones
London, England
February 2007

SEEING THE WORLD
RAMSEY CAMPBELL

Ramsey Campbell's latest novel, The Grin of the Dark, *recently appeared from PS Publishing. He has completed a new supernatural novel,* Thieving Fear, *to be followed by* The Buried City.

Along with his columns in Video Watchdog *and* All Hallows *magazines, Campbell also now writes a column for* Dead Reckonings *magazine as well.*

"This was one of those tales that come upon me when a common experience turns in my mind to display its darker side," explains the multiple award-winning author. "I don't think I ever suffered badly from other people's holiday photographs, but now I have a digital camera (which makes even me into a good photographer) others may suffer from mine."

Just be thankful that you don't have neighbors like these . . .

At first Angela thought it was a shadow. The car was through the gates before she wondered how a shadow could surround a house. She craned over the garden wall as Richard parked the car. It was a ditch, no doubt some trick the Hodges had picked up in

Italy, something to do with their gardening. "They're back," she murmured when Richard had pulled down the door of the garage.

"Saints preserve us, another dead evening," he said, and she had to hush him, for the Hodges were sitting in their lounge and had grinned out at the clatter of the door.

All the same, the Hodges seemed to have even less regard than usual for other people's feelings. During the night she was wakened by Mozart's Fortieth, to which the conductor had added the rhythm section Mozart had neglected to include. Richard mumbled and thrashed in slow motion as she went to the window. An August dawn glimmered on the Hodges' gnomes, and beyond them in the lounge the Hodges were sitting quite as stonily. She might have shouted but for waking Richard. Stiff with the dawn chill, she limped back to bed.

She listened to the silence between movements and wondered if this time they might give the rest of the symphony a chance. No, here came the first movement again, reminding her of the night the Hodges had come over, when she and Richard had performed a Haydn sonata. "I haven't gone into Haydn," Harry Hodge had declared, wriggling his eyebrows. "Get it? Gone into hidin'." She sighed and turned over and remembered the week she and Richard had just spent on the waterways, fields and grassy banks flowing by like Delius, a landscape they had hardly boarded all week, preferring to let the villages remain untouched images of villages. Before the Mozart had played through a third time she was asleep.

Most of the next day was given over to violin lessons, her pupils making up for the lost week. By the time Richard came home from lecturing, she had dinner almost ready. Afterwards they sat sipping the last of the wine as evening settled on the long gardens. Richard went to the piano and played *La Cathédrals Engloutie,* and the last tolling of the drowned cathedral was fading when someone knocked slowly at the front door.

It was Harry Hodge. He looked less bronzed by the Mediterranean sun than made-up, rather patchily. "The slides are ready," he said through his fixed smile. "Can you come now?"

"Right now? It really is quite late." Richard wasn't hiding his resentment, whether at Hodge's assumption that he need only call for them to come—not so much an invitation anymore as a summons—or at the way Hodge must have waited outside until he thought the Debussy had gone on long enough. "Oh, very well," Richard said. "Provided there aren't too many."

He must have shared Angela's thought: best to get it over with, the sooner the better. None of their neighbours bothered with the Hodges. Harry Hodge looked stiff, and thinner than when he'd gone away. "Aren't you feeling well?" she asked, concerned.

"Just all that walking and pushing the mother-in-law."

He was wearing stained outdoor clothes. He must have been gardening; he always was. He looked ready to wait for them to join him, until Richard said firmly "We won't be long."

They had another drink first, since the Hodges never offered. "Don't wake me unless I snore," Richard muttered as they ventured up the Hodges' path, past gnomes of several nations, souvenirs of previous holidays. It must be the gathering night that made the ditch appear deeper and wider. The ditch reminded her of the basement where Harry developed his slides. She was glad their house had no basement: she didn't like dark places.

When Harry opened the door, he looked as if he hadn't stopped smiling. "Glad you could come," he said, so tonelessly that at first Angela heard it as a question she was tempted to answer truthfully. If he was exhausted, he shouldn't have been so eager to have them round. They followed him down the dark hall into the lounge.

Only the wall lights were on. Most of the light surrounded souvenirs—a pink Notre Dame with a clock in place of a rose window on the mantelpiece, a plaster bull on top of the gas fire, matches stuck in its back like picadors' lances—and Deirdre Hodge and her mother. The women sat facing the screen on the wall, and Angela faltered in the doorway, wondering what was wrong. Of course, they must have been gardening too; they were still wearing outdoor clothes, and she could smell earth. Deirdre's mother must rather have been supervising, since much of the time she had to be pushed in a wheelchair.

"There you are," Deirdre said in greeting, and after some thought her mother said "Aye, there they are all right." Their smiles looked even more determined than Harry's. Richard and Angela took their places on the settee, smiling; Angela for one felt as if she was expected to smile rather than talk. Eventually Richard said "How was Italy?"

By now that form of question was a private joke, a way of making their visits to the Hodges less burdensome: half the joke consisted of anticipating the answer. Germany had been "like dolls' houses"; Spain was summed up by "good fish and chips"; France had prompted only "They'll eat anything." Now Deirdre smiled and smiled and eventually said "Nice ice creams."

"And how did you like it, Mrs. . . . . Mrs. . . . ." They had never learned the mother's name, and she was too busy smiling and nodding to tell them now. Smiling must be less exhausting than speaking. Perhaps at least that meant the visitors wouldn't be expected to reply to every remark—they always were, everything would stop until they had—but Angela was wondering what else besides exhaustion was wrong with the two women, what else she'd noticed and couldn't now recall, when Harry switched off the lights.

A sound distracted her from trying to recall, in the silence that seemed part of the dark. A crowd or a choir on television, she decided quickly—it sounded unreal enough—and went back to straining her memory. Harry limped behind the women and started the slide projector.

Its humming blotted out the other sound. She didn't think that was on television after all; the nearest houses were too distant for their sets to be heard. Perhaps a whim of the wind was carrying sounds of a football match or a fair, except that there was no wind, but in any case what did it matter? "Here we are in Italy," Harry said.

He pronounced it "Eyetally," lingeringly. They could just about deduce that it was, from one random word of a notice in the airport terminal where the Hodges were posing stiffly, smiling, out of focus, while a porter with a baggage trolley tried to gesticulate them out of the way. Presumably his Italian had failed, since they understood hardly a word of the language. After a few minutes Richard sighed, realising that nothing but a comment would get rid of the slide. "One day we'd like to go. We're very fond of Italian opera."

"You'd like it," Deirdre said, and the visitors steeled themselves for Harry's automatic rejoinder: "It you'd like." "Ooh, he's a one," Deirdre's mother squealed, as she always did, and began to sing "Funiculì, Funiculà." She seemed to know only the title, to which she applied various melodies for several minutes. "You never go anywhere much, do you?" Deirdre said.

"I'd hardly say that," Richard retorted, so sharply that Angela squeezed his hand.

"You couldn't say you've seen the world. Nowhere outside England. It's a good thing you came tonight," Deirdre said.

Angela wouldn't have called the slides seeing the world, nor seeing much of anything. A pale blob which she assumed to be a scoopful of the nice ice cream proved to be St Peter's at night; Venice was light glaring from a canal and blinding the lens. "That's impressionistic," she had to say to move St Peter's and "Was it very sunny?" to shift Venice. She felt as if she were sinking under the weight of so much banality, the Hodges' and now hers. Here were the Hodges posing against a flaking life-size fresco, Deirdre couldn't remember where, and here was the Tower of Pisa, righted at last by the camera angle. Angela thought that joke was intentional until Deirdre said "Oh, it hasn't come out. Get on to the proper ones."

If she called the next slide proper, Angela couldn't see why. It was so dark that at first she thought there was no slide at all. Gradually she made out Deirdre, wheeling her mother down what appeared to be a tunnel. "That's us in the catacombs," Deirdre said with what sounded like pride.

For some reason the darkness emphasised the smell of earth. In the projector's glow, most of which nestled under Harry's chin, Angela could just make out the women in front of the screen. Something about the way they were sitting: that was what she'd noticed subconsciously, but again the sound beneath the projector's hum distracted her, now that it was audible once more. "Now we go down," Deirdre said.

Harry changed the slide at once. At least they were no longer waiting for responses. The next slide was even darker, and both Angela and Richard were leaning forward, trying to distinguish who the figure with the out-stretched arms was and whether it was shouting or grimacing, when Harry said "What do you do when the cat starts moulting?"

They sat back, for he'd removed the slide. "I've no idea," Richard said.

"Give the cat a comb."

"Ooh, he's a one, isn't he," Deirdre's mother shrieked, then made a sound to greet the next slide. "This is where we thought we were lost," Deirdre said.

This time Angela could have wished the slide were darker. There was no mistaking the fear in Deirdre's face and her mother's as they turned to stare back beyond Harry and the camera. Was somebody behind him, holding the torch which cast Harry's malformed shadow over them? "Get it?" he said. "Cat a comb."

Angela wondered if there was any experience they wouldn't reduce to banality. At least there weren't many more slides in the magazine. She glanced at the floor to rest her eyes, and thought she knew where the sound of many voices was coming from. "Did you leave a radio on in the basement?"

"No." All the same, Harry seemed suddenly distracted. "Quick," Deirdre said, "or we won't have time."

Time before what? If they were ready for bed, they had only to say. The next slide jerked into view, so shakily that for a moment Angela thought the street beyond the gap in the curtains had jerked. All three Hodges were on this slide, between two ranks of figures. "They're just like us really," Deirdre said, "when you get to know them."

She must mean Italians, Angela thought, not the ranks of leathery figures baring their teeth and their ribs. Their guide must have taken the photograph, of course. "You managed to make yourself understood enough to be shown the way out then," she said.

"Once you go deep enough," Harry said, "it comes out wherever you want it to."

It was the manner—offhand, unimpressed—as much as his words that made her feel she'd misheard him. "When you've been down there long enough," Deirdre corrected him as if that helped.

Before Angela could demand to know what they were talking about, the last slide clicked into place. She sucked in her breath but managed not to cry out, for the figure could scarcely be posing for the camera, reaching out the stumps of its fingers; it could hardly do anything other than grin with what remained of its face. "There he is. We didn't take as long as him," Deirdre said with an embarrassed giggle. "You don't need to. Just long enough to make your exit," she explained, and the slide left the screen a moment before Harry switched off the projector.

In the dark Angela could still see the fixed grin breaking through the face. She knew without being able to see that the Hodges hadn't stopped smiling since Harry had opened the door. At last she realised what she'd seen: Deirdre and her mother, she was certain, were sitting exactly as they had been when their record had wakened her—as they had been when she and Richard had come home. "We thought of you," Harry said. "We knew you couldn't afford to go places. That's why we came back."

7

She found Richard's hand in the dark and tugged at it, trying to tell him both to leave quickly and to say nothing. "You'll like it," Deirdre said.

"It you'll like," Harry agreed, and as Angela pulled Richard to his feet and put her free hand over his mouth to stifle his protests, Deirdre's mother said "Takes a bit of getting used to, that's all."

For a moment Angela thought, in the midst of her struggle with panic, that Harry had put on another slide, then that the street had jerked. It was neither: of course the street hadn't moved. "I hope you'll excuse us if we go now," Richard said, pulling her hand away from his mouth, but it didn't matter, the Hodges couldn't move fast, she was sure of that much. She'd dragged him as far as the hall when the chanting under the house swelled up triumphantly, and so did the smell of earth from the ditch that was more than a ditch. Without further ado, the house began to sink.

THE THREADS

CHRISTOPHER FOWLER

Christopher Fowler's latest books include Seventy Seven Clocks, Ten Second Staircase, White Corridor, *and* Old Devil Moon.

His 2003 book Full Dark House *won the British Fantasy "August Derleth" Award for Best Novel and was also a finalist for the Crime Writer Association's Dagger Award. The* Water Room *was short-listed for the CWA's People's Choice Award in 2004, and he won British Fantasy Awards for his short story "American Waitress" the same year and for his novella* Breathe *in 2005.*

"I was in North Africa not too long ago," Fowler recalls, "and am always struck by the strange behavior of Western tourists when faced with a radically different culture. People have become tentative and nervous since the blanket demonization of Islamic society. It doesn't help that Muslims have become so reliant on tourist cash, either, or that the two sides usually only meet in shops.

"I set myself three criteria: My story would center around one such meeting, it would not be xenophobic, and it would nod to the style of Paul Bowles."

In the story that follows, a British couple on holiday learn a harsh lesson about taking what is not rightfully theirs. . . .

"**I** don't know how people can bring themselves to live like this." Verity studied her surroundings in clear discomfort. She had perfected a way of standing with her fist on her left hip, legs apart, her fawn skirt stretched across her thighs, in a manner that unsettled the Muslims who passed around her. Even when she was well covered, she had a way of appearing faintly indecent if she chose it.

She wore heels, even though the earth floor was rutted and muddy. At the time of the morning the *souk* had yet to fill with tourists. Sunlight filtered through the overhead slats, casting matchstick stripes across the confluence of winding narrow alleyways. In front of each store sat a boy, usually aged somewhere between ten and sixteen. Too many kids with nothing to do, too many vendors selling the same things—shoes and bags and lamps—shopkeepers peering out of the shadows to collar passing trade. Outside of the *medina,* the warm dry desert air was starting to rise. Here it was still cool.

"It's a less evolved society, but not much worse for that," said her husband, Alan Markham. "They've a tendency to retreat to the safety of religious dogma which is rather touching but not especially harmful, except *in extremis.* And of course bribery is a recognized part of their culture. A service is performed and money changes hands—it's seen as completely normal here." He leaned in to smell the cardamom seeds and cumin powder that lay in the great raked trays of a shop. A young man popped up in an opened panel among the spices, so that he appeared to be buried to his shoulders. All of the vendors stood like this, at the center of their wares. "You have to strike a bargain that's less than half the original price they suggest. It's all part of the game. Give them too much and they'll have no respect for you. They're like children."

"Nothing looks very clean. Mind you, they have to wash five times a day, so I suppose that counts for something. The hotel has Moulton Brown shampoo in the bathroom, did you notice?" Verity tried not to be too judgmental, but always found it difficult.

Markham set off again, brushing aside the entreaties from the spice seller. Verity had difficulty keeping up. She had seen how most of the English tourists behaved, the wives clutching their husbands' arms as if expecting to be torn from their sides by madmen. The secret of enjoying North Africa, she felt, was not to be afraid of people simply because they were different. Somewhere far away from the *medina* were modern roads, shops and offices, although they were probably run with hopeless inefficiency. But here in the *medina,* this was how everyone wanted to imagine those yellow clay towns built on the edge of the Sahara, all back alleys and *burkas,* the call of the *muezzin,* the stench of the market.

She watched her husband waving away the vendors as he studied the storefronts with an anthropological eye. *One last chance to start again,* he had pleaded, *let's get out of London, just the two of us. Things will be better this time.* They needed to be; the money had all but dried up and she did not want to return to work, just to bail him out of another failed business. Truth be told, she no longer had much faith in him. These days, most of their conversations were really arguments that neither side could win.

Verity backed against a wall as a moped driven by a small boy hurtled past. Incredibly, he was holding fifteen cardboard trays filled with eggs between his body and the handlebars. On the way in from the airport they had passed a couple on motor scooters carrying a bed between them.

"In London you don't say a word when the restaurant bill comes to an absolute fortune, but here you'll haggle over a few pence just because they tell you to do it in the guidebook," she admonished, stopping to look at a handful of sickly chameleons climbing over each other in bamboo cages.

A huge-eyed brown child smiled up at her from behind the cages. She and her husband had not chosen to have children. She had seen how other people's had grown up, spoiled, rude, lost. The children here were different. They helped their parents, and appeared to enjoy doing so. Families were involved in the great adventure of living. They weren't shut away from each other.

"I know what I'm doing. If you want to buy silks, you have to be patient and let me do the negotiating. It's my job, after all. You at least used to have some respect for that. It was what brought in the money."

Alan Markham had cut away from the octagonal blue and white fountain that piddled feebly in the center of the *medina,* where the men washed their hands and feet at prayer-call, and was heading into the manufacturing quarters. Here there were virtually no women to be found, only boys with blackened, poisoned nails, hammering at curlicued spiderwebs of metal, bed-heads and chandeliers, and men with ruined lungs, seated cross-legged in the dense, dust-filled air of their workshops, chipping away delicate white triangles of plaster. Here, too, were the tanners and dyers, working beneath hanging pelts and skeins of crimson wool that were draped above them like the guts of great beasts.

"God, it stinks." Verity held her handkerchief against her nose.

"This is where we have to go, away from the tourist traps. You said you wanted to visit somewhere different." He shouted above the sound of blacksmiths hammering, backlit by sunsprays of sparks. It was as if they had stepped backstage, behind the artifice of tourist-friendly exotica, to where the real work was done. In one workshop a hundred crimson lanterns hung at different heights, bathing the walls blood red. Alan had bought and sold Anatolian and Kurdish silks for several years. He knew what was valuable, and what was rubbish. When he found the store he was looking for, he walked straight in, ignoring the sales pitch of the boy who had been left outside to hector passers-by.

As his eyes adjusted to the gloom, he examined the neatly folded stacks of rugs in burnt oranges and reds that had been stacked from floor to ceiling around the narrow shop.

"Tell me what you are looking for," said the middle-aged man with the gap in his white teeth, welcoming them. Markham's peppery hair and striped cuff-shirt had marked him as an Englishman. The shopkeeper was always earnest, but especially serious when he recognized potential in a customer. Selling was an art he had carefully studied for nearly fifty years. The Englishman was more than a casual browser trying to keep his wife amused. There was something in the way he turned and regarded the towers of cloth. The shopkeeper's boy was unrolling silk scarves in razor-blue and sunset red, but only the wife was bothering to cast her eyes over them. She seemed less comfortable than he, which was unusual. It was the women who tended to lead the way into his shop. Markham accepted a dark plum from a brass tray and sucked at it as he browsed.

"Upstairs?" he asked, indicating the floor above, his index finger raised. With a deferential nod, the storekeeper led the way up a narrow staircase lined with tablecloths. The room over the shop had no more than four square feet of space free at its center. Every other inch of space was filled with silks, tapestries, scarves, runners, and cloths graded by shade and shape, endlessly refolded and arranged. The lathe-and-plaster ceiling bulged threateningly inwards, making the room even smaller.

A tiny filigree table had been set out for mint tea. The boy appeared and poured three glasses, not from a great height, as waiters did for tourists, but with the spout lowered.

Markham was looking for something in particular. The air was full of tiny iridescent carpet fibers that turned in the shaft of sunlight angled from the single high window. Verity leaned back against the rolls of material, lifting the weight from her heels. It was December, a pleasant temperature, a good time to come here, but the heavy food exhausted her, and the arid air made her thirsty all the time. No wonder they valued their shade so much, designing their public buildings to capture and display the shadows in appealing arrangements. She eyed the glass of tea and decided not to risk the germs that might lie on the rim.

"This is for your wife," said the shopkeeper, waiting for the boy to unroll more fabrics, each brighter than the last.

"Oh, I don't know." Markham raised his leonine head and puffed out his cheeks, affecting an air of diffidence. "Something heavier, in blue perhaps . . . something more special."

The shopkeeper instructed the boy in Arabic, then followed him to find the cloth. Verity shot her husband a look, raising an eyebrow. He pursed his lips faintly. Code; *don't say anything.* He had seen something in the corner, and was moving toward it. Casually examined the material, pouting, pulling, rubbing.

"I like this one." She pulled out an indigo silk square with a scarlet rose at the center. Slender white tendrils snaked from its core to the outside edges.

"Put it down, it's tourist shit." He could be most dismissive of her tastes. He suddenly stopped examining the object of his interest, dropping his hand as the shopkeeper returned. She had seen him do this before, but never with such studied nonchalance. He had to be very excited about something to appear this bored.

He glanced at the bolts the boy and the old man unfolded before him, but she knew he was barely seeing them, even though he launched into a half-hearted negotiation for two sparkling ocean-green tablecloths.

"I think I need to discuss this with my wife for a minute," he told the shopkeeper in respectful French. The old man understood, nodded and withdrew downstairs.

Markham leapt back to the cloth he had seen and pulled it free, showing her, a slit tapestry of geometric designs in red, yellow and black. "Look at this. It's a Shahsevan Kilim from the Hastari area of Northwestern Persia, around 1900. They're normally about six by twelve but this one's a runner, a weft-substitution weave finished in cotton. God knows what it's doing here. There's a name in the corner. I've never seen anything of this shape and size in the catalogues, but it's quite authentic. It's worth a small fortune."

She could see the sweat beading above his ears. He was already wondering if there were others. Markham wiped his fidgety wet hands on his jacket. This was the equivalent of finding a signed first edition of *Bleak House* in a roomful of Jeffrey Archers. He called to the shopkeeper and went to work.

She had to grant him some grudging respect. He played the game very cleverly, slipping the cloth between a range of similar but worthless panels, offering to buy some little thing for his wife—would there be a discount if he bought several, this one, this one, perhaps *this one?* Carelessly casting them aside as if he didn't much care one way of the other—*pour amuser la dame.*

But it was not to be. The shopkeeper smiled politely and removed the one essential item, replacing it carefully on the stack, lapsing back into French with a wagging finger. *"Pas en vente, désolé."*

"But she likes it." Markham indicated his weary wife. *Don't rope me into this,* she thought. He gave a little shrug. "I think it's rather a nice little thing." He could not help looking back at the runner. The implication: *Too bad it's not for sale; your loss.*

The old man seemed to consider for a moment, but a cloud passed over his eyes, and he became intractable. Markham offered what he considered to be a good sum, then a little more, but only because he knew that the tapestry was worth a hundred times that amount.

Two American girls bustled into the tiny attic and acted as if no-one else was there, climbing over the bolts to pull down the surrounding stacks. To Verity's surprise, her husband suddenly clapped his hands and gave in with good grace. "Never mind then, just these silks. The big shawl for my wife, and these two as a gift for my mother."

The shopkeeper seemed relieved. He and the boy immediately started to prepare the purchase as Markham made way for his wife and another bundle toppled over behind them, cascading rainbows of satin down the staircase. Verity thought he would insist on bullying the price lower, but he did not. The boy was dealing with the American girls, and the old man was deftly tying ribbons over brown paper as Markham took another plum from the hospitality tray, leaving it in his mouth as he thumbed notes from his back pocket.

As they moved into the street outside, he took her elbow and guided her into the first turn-off. "Slow down—my heels," she said, but he kept up the pace. "Why didn't you use plastic to pay?" She knew something was up, and realized what it was when she saw the tip of the fabric protruding from his jacket. "You didn't steal it?"

"He had no idea of its value. It would have gone to waste up there, simply waiting to be attacked by weevils."

The sun was high in the market square. Fortune-tellers, street pharmacists, tumblers, acrobats, water-bearers and snake charmers were out in force. Markham and his wife made for the post office behind the colonnade, and queued in the hard bright hall beneath slow-turning fans as Markham repacked the item, folding it tightly into the brown paper parcel. He seemed uncharacteristically indecisive, breaking out of line at the last moment.

"What's the matter with you?" she asked. "If you're feeling guilty, take it back."

"I was going to post it home, but I'm thinking about customs." He tapped the package. "This is extremely valuable. And I don't feel guilty. I don't approve of returning antiquities, not if they're only going to be stored in some filthy old museum with poor security, or worse still in a tradesman's shop."

"Then let's go back to the *riad* and get some lunch. I'm hot and tired. I want a shower."

He was leading her out of the post office when she heard a sharp crack. He had bitten down on the plum stone. "Christ." He clutched his jaw and winced. "Jesus." The pain was bad enough to make him stop dead.

"You're making a fuss. Show me." It had sounded awful, like a cap exploding. She forced him to open his mouth. The stone had split an upper left molar clean in half. He shook her hand aside and spat blood on the ground. A piece of tooth came out with it. He let out a groan.

16

"How many times have I told you before? You had to go and—" She tried to keep her annoyance in check. "You should get the rest of the tooth taken out. They'll be able to find someone at the *riad*."

The girl at their hotel appeared unconcerned. "There are many dentists," she said.

"Well, where are they?" asked Verity with impatience, as if expecting one to walk through the curtained entrance to the reception office.

"In the square. I can arrange for a boy to take you—"

"In the square? No, no—" She had seen the ones in the square, seated cross-legged before pyramids of brown pulled teeth arranged on dirty squares of cloth. The higher the pile, the more successful they were considered to be. "My husband has broken his tooth. He needs to have all of the pieces removed or there could be an infection."

"Yes, yes, the square." The girl was trying to provide her guests with the best solution, but they seemed to want something else. She watched blankly as they headed off to their room, arguing with each other.

After half-an-hour of reading brochures and making incomprehensible calls, Verity rose from the bed and went to change her shoes. "Well, nobody else seems to be available, and if you're absolutely sure you can't wait until we get back to London, we'll have to do as she suggested," she said. "Come on, you won't be able to eat if we don't so something. Just have it cleaned up. You can get it replaced back in Harley Street."

"A street dentist, are you mad? Their practices are two hundred years out of date. Do you have any painkillers on you?"

"Did you see anything remotely resembling a pharmacy near here? We can try to find one, but don't look at me—I took my last Valium yesterday."

"All right, we'll go back to the square and I'll walk past, but I'm not going to use one if he's not clean."

They returned to the square to find three dentists still sitting cross-legged in the winter sunshine, patiently waiting for customers. Markham regarded each in turn before settling on the third, who was at least the most senior. "Might as well be this one," he said. "He's got the biggest pile of teeth in front of him."

The dentist gestured at his triangular footstool. When he smiled, he revealed a row of white teeth too peppermint-perfect to be real. "Don't be worried," he said in perfect English. "I have never lost a patient yet."

Markham seated himself while the dentist rinsed his hands with bottled water. Verity eyed the antique instruments spread out on his sheet with suspicion. She watched while the dentist pushed Markham's head back and made his examination. He soaked a white cotton pad in something from a fluted amber bottle and rubbed it over her wincing husband's gum. "To numb your mouth," he explained.

"He's right," Markham assured his wife, gape-mouthed, "it's already working."

"This is your wife?" asked the dentist chattily.

"Yes," Verity confirmed, stepping nearer.

"Perhaps you should go away for a few minutes. It is better."

"No, I'm perfectly fine. I don't get squeamish."

"I mean it is better for me."

"Oh." The local women were never seen on the streets unless they were shopping. Feeling vaguely affronted, Verity turned away and looked at the distant shops edging the *souk*.

Selecting a fearsome instrument that looked as if it had been designed to pull up floorboard nails, the dentist began to extract the pieces of Markham's broken tooth.

A few minutes later, he came across the square to find her. She was seated in the faded first floor café of the Hotel De Paris. "Fifty dirhams," he said, pleased with himself. "He wanted more but I didn't see why I should." He drew out a seat and looked around for a waiter.

"Show me," said Verity. "Oh, he's put a cap in there."

"Just a temporary replacement until I get back, to stop any germs from getting in. He got all the pieces out and cleaned up the wound, then dried it with some kind of herbal paste to stop infection. I daresay one could go to a homeopathy clinic in Mayfair and pay a fortune for the same thing."

"Well, you've changed your tune," she said with a rueful smile. "Half-an-hour ago you were calling him a savage."

"Then I'm prepared to admit I was wrong."

"Do you think you should be drinking anything?"

"He said it would be fine. I'm not at all numb. It wasn't like one of those injections that turns your face into a piece of slack meat for three hours." Still, he grimaced when he sipped a glass of chocolate.

They returned to the *riad*, read cheap paperbacks and lounged around until early evening, when they strolled out into the *medina* once more. Smoky stalls had been set up to serve evening meals of snail stew, lamb and pigeons pastry-baked in cinnamon and icing sugar, but most of the shops were still open, the same bored teens seated before stacks of slippers and leather handbags, stained-glass lanterns and mosaic vases. In clothing stores, sinister shop dummies cast from fifty-year-old moulds sported crooked dry wigs and faded fashion items.

Verity was bored. After a while, becoming endlessly lost in the back-streets of the *medina* was a very repetitive part of the exotic experience. She watched her husband tipping the guide book into the shafts of dying sun-light, trying to find a particular restaurant that had sign-posted itself by being more expensive and harder to find that any of the rest, and wondered when their mutual affinity for one another had divided, leaving them with this marriage of inconvenience.

He found the place. They ate *pastilla* beneath a vast wrought-iron chan-delier in a courtyard of topaz tiles, beside other Western couples who had run out of conversation. He was telling her about some colleague at work who was about to be fired when the food fell out of his mouth and he clutched the tablecloth so hard that their wineglasses shook to the floor, shattering. The waiters were solicitous, fearing the attack might be construed as food poisoning, and quickly helped him to his feet.

"What kind of pain is it?" she asked, trying to understand.

He was clutching his cheek on the side where the tooth had been removed. "Let me see," she pleaded, opening his mouth in the light of the restaurant foyer, but there was nothing beyond a little inflammation of the upper gum to indicate the source of the problem. Even so, she understood that it emanated from the replaced tooth. "I'm taking you back to that dentist," she insisted, knowing that the dentists had probably left their pitches for the night.

Back in the square, a pall of orange smoke hung over the great arena of food stalls. She was strong, and held him upright as they passed a row of lolling sheep heads laid out on a trestle table, their tongues protruding as if in mockery, their marbled eyes still and unflinching as flies danced across them. The area seemed less safe now. The colorfully costumed water-bearers had been replaced by loitering rent-boys and matchstick-chewing men with watchful eyes. Drums played somewhere, badly amplified scratch beats aimed at luring Westerners into an empty bar.

"We should never have come here," she said under her breath. "We should have taken accident insurance." He was growing heavy in her arms.

The dentists' pitches had been taken by hawkers selling cheap jewelry. A fight was breaking out nearby. She looked around. "I don't know—"

The teenaged boy was slouching at the counter of a small café, flicking nuts into his mouth, watching the world pass. He wore a dust-stained *burnous* and fez. When he spotted Verity he stood up and stepped forward.

"You are looking for the dentist. I see you today. Your husband." He mimicked a painful tooth.

"Yes, my husband—" she began gratefully, allowing him to slip from her arm to a chair. "He is in terrible pain. We must see the dentist at once."

"He has gone to my uncle for dinner, but I can take you there." He reached down and placed Markham's arm around his waist, pulling him up. "It is not far."

They headed back into the *souk,* Verity following with her husband's Panama hat gripped between her hands. The stores were lit with lanterns now. Fast food chefs were turning pungent chunks of fried meat on skillets, decanting them into folds of bread. There were more women around. They hurried through alleys filled with beetling dark *yashmaks,* keeping close to the walls in order to avoid being run down by mopeds. Verity had a vague idea that they were near the tanneries once more, but every street looked the same.

"Here, here." The boy led them into a store, then through the back into a second salesroom where the dentist sat drinking tea with his uncle.

"We meet again," said the uncle, a rotund man with a gap in his teeth, rising to give them room. Verity struggled to place his face and failed. "I sold you some silks. The dentist is my nephew, and this is his boy. We have been waiting for you."

She felt suddenly fearful, but Markham appeared not to understand. They had been deliberately returned here, she was sure, as part of some cruel plot. She wanted to be home, to be done with all this—*foreignness.* The dentist was nodding and smiling inanely, as if to confirm her worst thoughts.

"Come, let us show you the source of the trouble," said the shopkeeper, leading her husband to a stool. He pushed gently down on Markham's shoulders, maneuvering him into position so that the dentist could get a better look, then wedged his hand into Markham's mouth. His fingers tasted of old carpets. Markham tried not to gag.

"Good, good." The dentist smiled and nodded at his uncle. He reached into Markham's mouth and worked the cap loose, pulling it off and examining the inside. Her husband's groan of pain subsided into a whimper.

"Come, look." The dentist beckoned her, tipping the cap so that she could see. Unnerved, Verity found it difficult to approach him. Something inside the tooth appeared to be moving. When she saw them, her hand flew to her mouth.

"I want my tapestry back," said the shopkeeper. "All you have to do is return it to me."

"What is it?" asked Markham miserably. "What's wrong?"

"I don't know what they are," said his wife, unable to tear her eyes from the writhing crystalline threads that remained in the sticky blackness of the tooth cap. They looked like elvers, but finer, longer, like strands of living silk. With mounting dread she peered inside his mouth. The tiny worms had burrowed deep into the bloody, swollen cavity where his tooth had been, creating small mushroom-white boils. Silvery threads wriggled and vanished into livid flesh as the light from the overhead lanterns hit them. Markham released a terrible, rising howl of agony.

"We kill a sheep and grow them inside. They are parasites, very good for breaking down meat and making it tender. Too painful in someone who is still alive."

She saw now how the security system worked, how they were all connected, the girl in the hotel, the dentist, the boy at the bar, how they all knew and protected each other, guiding tourists from place to place, manipulating them. She saw how they punished transgressions. "For Christ's sake, Alan, will you explain to these people?"

Markham studied the shopkeeper with contempt. "I don't know what you're talking about," he persisted. She knew he would not admit to being wrong—he never did. He would not lose face, whatever the consequences.

"There is something you can take to kill them, and the pain will stop. It is very easy, and takes no more than a few minutes. If you don't, they will continue to breed—and to eat."

Markham tried to speak, but spluttered droplets of blood onto his chin.

"The tapestry," the shopkeeper repeated. The dentist and the boy stood beside him in solidarity.

"How dare you accuse me of something I haven't done," said Markham, his sense of outrage glinting through winces of agony. "I'm British, I don't steal from people."

"Please, Mr. Markham, this can easily be resolved." He had recalled the name from the credit card slip. "We are all civilized human beings."

"Civilized!" He spat the word back at them. "Is that what you call yourselves? You hide away your women while you sell us your trash at inflated prices, and we buy from you because we pity you. You think we want to take home this sort of crap?" He threw his arm wide at the display of dazzling silks, almost falling. "You force your children to weave your rugs and we buy them out of pity. Don't tell me you're civilized. You're nothing more than desert nomads who've been given calculators. You pray to Allah but you're working for the white man. Pigs and monkeys can be raised to do that."

The shopkeeper rose, indicating that the dentist and the boy should do the same. They gently ushered Markham and his wife back out of the shop, speaking across each other in Arabic. As soon as the couple were off the premises, they dropped the steel shutter with a slam.

The street was emptier now, and looked different. Verity supported him through the alleyways, but could not find the right route back. They moved deeper into the *medina,* where the streets were hardly lit at all, and the mud track became almost impassable in places. She lost track of the time. Markham was slowing down, his breath growing shallower.

She could no longer hold him upright. She let him rest, studying his face in the lamplight. His right eye was bloodshot and swollen. Tiny threads of red and white had traced themselves across the shimmering cornea. His slick skin had yellowed, as the worms drew their vitality from within, leaving dead cells behind as they burrowed.

A tiny woman in a billowing *chador* hurried past. Verity held up her hand to indicate that she needed help, but the woman darted out of the way, disappearing down a side alley.

Her skirt was stained with mud. She pulled the big shawl they had bought around her husband, wrapping his head tightly in it, and tied the other half around herself. Exhausted, they rested in the doorway of a derelict mosque, beneath the only street light, sliding slowly down into the shadows until they were sitting on their haunches. Markham was shaking hard now. He could no longer speak.

"Someone will come for us," she assured him, whispering gently. "There's nothing to be afraid of. Someone will come for us."

He rested his head on her shoulder and fell into a stupor. The overhead light went out. In the gloom of the African night, they looked for all the world like any of the other Muslim beggars in the market.

LITTLE DEDO

NANCY HOLDER

*Nancy Holder has sold approximately eighty novels, many of them set in
the* Buffy the Vampire Slayer *universe, along with 200 short stories,
essays and articles. Her latest book is* The Rose Bride, *a retelling of "The
White Bride and the Black Bride" by the Brothers Grimm.*

*She has received four Bram Stoker Awards, and has been nominated
for three more. A former trustee of the Horror Writers Association, she
lives in San Diego with her daughter Belle, their cats Kitten Snow Vampire and David, and their four hermit crabs—Mr. Crabbypants,
Vietnam, Athena, and Kumquat. She sleeps in her spare time.*

*"'Little Dedo' was the result of a trip to Paris that included Notre
Dame and Disneyland Paris," Holder reveals. "I sent the proof-read copy
to the editor of this anthology from Disneyland in Anaheim, during a
short vacation with my beloved daughter, Belle, and her best friend,
Haley, and her mom, Amy. We also met up with a dear friend of mine,
who skipped the roller coasters because she thinks she might be pregnant."*

*Which is just one of the concerns of the disturbed protagonist in the
following story . . .*

Before they had come to Paris, Jeanne had not understood the idea behind gargoyles. Their purpose, Sam had patiently (and patronizingly) explained, was to frighten away evil spirits. They perched among the spires and balustrades of dozens of medieval European churches, but it was the gargoyles of Notre Dame that had attracted the imagination of the world. She wondered if they truly were the most stupendous and ugly of all the ugly little gargoyles that adorned the holy places of Western civilization. The runes of Stonehenge were not the most spectacular, but they were the most famous.

Yet she still didn't quite understand how such squat, misfit creatures could keep evil at bay. How could you tell them apart from the things they were frightening away? She would have that magnificent golden angels or sweet, tiny fairies would be better at the job. The ugly would fear the beautiful, would they not?

Perhaps gargoyles were distractions. They fascinated the truly hideous because they were ugly enough to seem familiar. Something lovely would be too incomprehensible for things that had crawled up from the abyss. And while they were fascinated, St. George or whoever it was who slew evil things in medieval France (her namesake, Joan of Arc?) would charge in and destroy them.

Maybe that was why married couples fought about money, when what they were really struggling over was the survival of their individual identities. Or about their careers, when their actual objective was to stop themselves from killing each other.

Maybe that was why Sam seemed such a stranger now, so odd and different that he was beginning to frighten her. She touched her abdomen tentatively. With this new distraction, perhaps she was seeing her husband as he had been all along. They said that of women who married abusive men, that they just didn't see the evil inherent in them until they were beaten almost to death. Charmed by the beauty of a handsome smile, a bouquet of flowers, and so-called "encouragement" to forge a life of one's own, they dealt the death blow while you hovered staring at them, unable to look away as the mask melted and the putrescence glowed through the rotting layers.

She swallowed sick and sour bile and turned her attention to Sam's pointed finger. He must not know what she was thinking. There were no anchors here, nothing to save her from being cast adrift. She must not introduce the variable of marital disharmony into the thick Parisian fog of these weeks, this so-called celebration.

"Little Dedo," he said, and she followed his gaze. There he was, the ugly baby gargoyle, sucking his thumb of stone. Legend promised that he had been carved by a nun who had snuck into the cathedral in the dead of night and placed him among the grown-up gargoyles. The adults, poised and ready to take flight to loftier, more distant environs; the little monsters of protection, looming like attentive cats and dogs. At home, she and Sam had neither. Pets were too much trouble for yuppie couples such as they.

She wondered at a nun who would think of creating a baby gargoyle. A woman barred by choice, a woman who had denied herself what now lay inside Joan. The world's first career woman. Jeanne smiled unhappily, disliking the comparison but finding it apt. Despite all the talk of "balance" and the hipness of having children, it was still true that there was a mommy track and a success track in the world of law, which was now her field. This trip was to fete her graduation from law school. How could she tell Sam she was pregnant?

She thought of the horrible stories they had heard in England while touring the various country estates: of tiny skeletons curled in foetal positions tucked in the hollows of chimneys. The babies of servants not allowed to live, for their lusty shrieks would doom their mothers to being turned out as fallen women. Perhaps the nun had carved Little Dedo in memory of a child she had smothered in the nunnery, for herself or for a sister who had allowed the Devil to tempt her into enjoying the fullness of life . . .

27

"It's just like Disneyland," Sam grumbled, his voice making ghosts, as he put a coin in a box and picked up a candle. "You have to tip for everything."

Indeed. The two men who had escorted them to Quasimodo's bell had carried a yellow bucket to the tower. It was the job of Citizen #2 to sit on a stool and hold it out for your francs and centimes after Citizen #1 told you about the great bell and the poor old monster. You paid to buy candles to set before the statues of the saints dreaming of Heaven behind wooden gates while the gargoyles stared down at them.

You paid to pray to them.

She sagged. He was unhappy with everything. They had been a week in England, a week in France, and he had gotten crankier and edgier with each day. If he knew she was pregnant, he would be more than unhappy.

"It's not even the real cathedral. Half of it's been rebuilt."

"No," she disagreed, then let it go. She had dreamed of going to Notre Dame ever since seeing *The Hunchback of Notre Dame*—the original black-and-white film, not the remakes. The cathedral was everything she had wished for, the chiaroscuro romance of the vaults and ceilings, the dim coolness that touched your cheek like a faint but understanding friend. The stones speaking stories, and changes, and eulogies.

She and Sam were from southern California, where everything was new. It was astonishing to her that you could actually read a novel written in another century, then visit the places described there, and find them virtually unchanged. In Orange County, where they lived, the cathedral would have been a themed restaurant where "French" food was served—braised sirloin tips, omelettes, French bread and champagne. You could have purchased Quasimodo dolls. Disney might have arranged a tie-in deal, or sued the restaurant for appropriating what was, after all, a public domain property.

Jeanne had never found anything wrong with that. Her field was entertainment law. She had always loved the superficial amalgam of cultural "bits" with theme park structure. Why not build huge arenas and hire high school football players to joust one another in knightly garb? Why not charge kids a buck to pan for gold in an artificial river cleansed with chlorine? What did it hurt? Wasn't it the way the future would be, when everyone lived on space stations?

But suddenly, it was all wrong. Turned sideways; she flushed and shivered and remembered a time when she was so angry at Sam, incredibly furious, that she had driven herself to Disneyland. She had ridden the steamboat, and as it came along the island in the river, she stared at the fantastical shapes of New Orleans Square with a horrible vertigo and a sense that she had never been there before in her life.

"Finished?" Sam asked. There was an edge to his voice, as if he had come here only to placate her. As if somehow later, he would return with his learned colleagues and his discerning *amis,* who understood about gargoyles, and see the cathedral as it should be seen: quoting Hugo in the original, Rabelais and Moliere at his side.

"Yes," she said. "I'm done. "Let's go to Disneyland Paris."

He checked his watch. In Europe he had often looked at his watch, although they weren't following a set schedule.

"You don't have to," she flared. "I can go by myself."

He looked shocked. "I didn't say I didn't want to go."

"But you act like it . . . oh, never mind."

He peered at her as if inspecting her under a lens. "You're tired," he said. And the thing was, he was right. Being pregnant was a lot of work. She was tired and a little nauseated.

She wouldn't be able to go on all the rides at Disneyland Paris, and she wouldn't be able to tell him why.

She raised her chin. She didn't care. She was tired of doing things his way.

"I want to go now," she said firmly.

He inclined his head. *Noblesse oblige.* "Then of course we'll go."

"Don't do me any favors," she muttered, but he didn't hear her. He had proceeded ahead, holding court with imaginary judges and juries composed of people as clean-cut and erudite as the extras on an old *Perry Mason* episode.

He had gone to law school first, specializing in divorce cases. By the time it was her turn to go, life was comfortable for them. They had a large stucco house with wall-to-wall carpeting, *de rigueur* for an up-and-coming southern California career couple. It was not what Sam had grown up with. He was from the east, and his patrician other's house was genteel and old, with plaster walls and bare wood floors and plenty of bookcases loaded with first editions. Jeanne was sure her mother-in-law thought her son had married beneath his station, but the woman was far too well-bred to even hint at such a thing. Jeanne wondered what she would think of the baby.

She had already figured out how to get to the Happiest Place on Le Earth. It was the last stop on the line. It would take forty minutes. She knew how much the tickets would cost.

Yet Sam stopped in the underground station and double-checked everything, assuring himself that she hadn't made any mistakes.

"Little Dedo was cute, wasn't he?" she said, attempting small talk to hold her temper in check, regain the sensation of being in Paris, the wonder of it, the achievement. Sam had been before, many times. "Sort of a cupid gargoyle."

"Oh, yes." His supercilious smile set her teeth on edge.

"I know the story is probably bogus, but it's still fun to imagine some little nun sneaking him up there."

He practically winced at the word "bogus". As if they were the kind of people who didn't use language like that. She remembered an old *New Yorker* cartoon that tickled him: a chesty, pearl-drenched matron speaking to her husband, who looked like the younger brother of the little man in Monopoly. The woman said, "I wish we were the kind of people who ordered out for pizza."

"She's like my mother, isn't she?" he had said at the time, but even then, she suspected he admired people who didn't order out for pizza.

When he had gone to law school and she had slaved as an administrative assistant in the English literature department, they had eaten untold amounts of delivered pizza. They got whatever was on special, whatever you got with coupons. The purchase of his interviewing suit had been a major event in their lives, although he had murmured something about buying his prep school clothes on Oxford Street in London while she had written the check. Taking the wind out of her sails even then, devaluing the moment as she had flushed with pride at paying for something so vital to their survival, his twentieth-century armor. He had not taken a dime from his mother, and nothing had ever been said about that one way or another. She had no idea if she had offered funds and been turned down, or sat back to see if her son and his Orange County wife possessed the mettle to make it on their own.

Now, in Paris, they got on the train and Jeanne watched the stops. In southern California, anyone who could manage it had a car. If you took public transportation, you were suspect. You were either an economic bottom-feeder or an innocent tourist who would soon be on your way to the emergency room. They seemed like theme park attractions, unreal, as if they would simply take you around in a circle and deposit you back where you came from. As opposed to getting you somewhere you really wanted to go.

"We're here," she announced breezily, grabbing up his hand. "Let's hurry. It's late."

"I'm sure we'll have plenty of time," he said. Always ready with a counter-argument, always questioning whatever she initiated. He could win any debate. He would quiz her and trap her, and she knew soon she would stop going first, stop suggesting, and just wait to see what he thought or what he wanted.

She would be a terrible role model for the child.

She felt as if a bell were closing over her, the great bell of Quasimodo, and she would run around inside it for the rest of her life, a mouse.

For perhaps the last time, she ignored him and bolted ahead, tripping through the airy station toward the escalators.

Disneyland Paris! The entrance was enormous, with seemingly a hundred ticket booths waiting for their credit cards and wads of francs. She stood back and let Sam pay with the money that he had once assured her they had made together, although he had the high-powered job. She imagined herself taking her child to Paris not for Notre Dame but for Disneyland. A hotel stretched right over the entrance; at night you would be able to see directly into the park. What a treat!

Sam and his mother would find it incredibly common.

"Come on," she said desperately.

"You really are a kid," he said, but she could find no trace of affection in his voice.

But, Disneyland! Better than any kid could have imagined. It was different, it was bigger, and there was no one there. The French had not taken to Disneyland as the Americans and Japanese had in their respective countries. And the Germans, apparently, for whenever, they saw another living soul, which was not all that frequent, Jeanne heard German. She spoke pretty good German, but her command of the language of class, of the upper class—French—was weak at best.

She heard a little German child tell his mother, "I hugged Bugs Bunny." She chuckled, doubting an American child would make the same error, steeped in American pop culture as he or she would be.

As her baby—as Little Dedo—would be.

Again, the vertigo, the unreality, of Orange County and the Disneyland that thrummed there with a life unconnected to her own. The overlying blanket of unfamiliarity had traveled with her as she wandered into the shops, back out onto the streets. So mad at Sam, unbearably so, she had bought some perfume and daubed it onto her wrists, smelling it from time to time as if it were her own scent and that she was looking for reassurance that she was still herself, like a dog that sniffs its own feces. *I'm still here. I'm still what I am.*

Now, as Sam put his hand on her shoulder and peered at her with exaggerated concern, her heart catapulted into her throat and she fought the urge to run, or to smell him, to find his scent, and discover that this stranger was the young, eager boy who had loved her for the way she was.

"Sweetheart? Are you all right?"

He had said that before. And look what had happened to her. Her wrists—

—the scent not of perfume, but of blood—

They rode the rides, the pirates and the ghosts singing in French. She began to forget Sam was there. It was just she and Little Dedo on an exotic journey.

Then the park closed and the crowds made their way through the exit to the enormous boardwalk of restaurants and shops. It reminded her of the City Walk in front of Universal Studios in Los Angeles. Neon and clever architecture. She forgot Sam had been hurting her feelings all day and slid her hands around his arm.

"I'm hungry," she said, to have something to say.

"Just fifteen minutes ago, you said you weren't." Fifteen minutes ago there had been time for one more ride if they didn't stop to eat.

"Oh, Sam. I'm hungry," she said irritably, rudely.

"All right. All right. What would you like? More junk?"

"You're supposed to eat junk at theme parks."

He cocked his head, appraising her. "I'm only teasing."

No, he wasn't.

She chose a steak house only because it was expensive. The emerging dynamic between them frightened her: she, demanding and vindictive, childish, he paternal, grudging, the bestower of *largesse*. It would not be a healthy environment for a child.

And she saw then that she was making Little Dedo into the real Little Dedo, transferring her distress to him or her, making him the reason she was so unhappy. The gargoyle that keeps away the evil spirits, the ones who say, *You are helpless. You are trapped. This is the way it will be from now on.*

He ordered a bottle of wine without asking her if she wanted any; she drank none because of her pregnancy. He looked at her curiously; she said, "I don't want any," and she sounded petulant. Angrily, she announced, "I want dessert." When they got home, she must see someone, tell someone what was going on. Get help.

Flee.

"Honey?"

One word, a common word, spoken from the lips of this stranger, one of Sam's words.

"Are we the kind of people who say things like that?" she asked shrilly. The people at the next table over glanced in her direction.

And then everything turned sideways again, the maze of bells and winged monsters clanging and flapping around her. She was disoriented beyond jet-lag, beyond resignation, beyond anger.

"Honey?"

She blinked at this stranger, at this bell-ringer, and her body heaved. She stood up unsteadily. Was she having a miscarriage?

"I'll be right back. I have to go to the bathroom," she said.

She ran from him, found the W.C., raced in and checked her underwear. There was no blood.

She retched into the toilet. Morning sickness, a reassurance. She was no calmer. If anything, she was dizzy, hot, and cold.

She stayed in the sanctuary of the bathroom stall, her arms around herself, and began to rock back and forth. Perhaps if she pushed hard enough—

—Her eyes widened. What was she thinking?

Of gargoyles. Of hideous things pulsing inside her. Things gnawing through her, at her. Flying over the extent of her life and flapping away every good thing with their leathery wings because to others, those things were not good.

Not good enough.

"She just graduated from law school," she heard someone saying just outside the bathroom entrance. The voice frightened her because it was beautiful and because it should be familiar. "We're here to celebrate. This place is great, isn't it? Someday we'll have to come back here with our kids."

She dare not listen to Quasimodo ringing his bell. The ugly to frighten the uglier.

"Top in her class. She was under enormous pressure, but she did it."

Little Dedo, Little Dedo. That stranger's pride, so ugly. She pressed her stomach as the gargoyle baby moved inside. He shifted and rotated, descended, crawling toward her vaginal opening.

"She's trying to unwind. Jet-lag and all, you know. Sometimes traveling is an awful lot of hassle."

Hassle? Do we say hassle?

The wings were stuck; she grunted at the pain and leaned back against the toilet tank. Her forehead was bathed with sweat.

Don't leave me, Little Dedo. Don't leave.

I'll die.

I'll kill myself.

Sweat poured down her face. The bathroom whirled.

I hate law school. I want to quit.

Oh, honey, just hang in there. It's been your dream for so long.

His dream. His. Praying to saints in another language, not her language, her stucco tongue of theme parks and mangled French and her unbearable *bourgeois* upbringing.

White picket fence, Donna Reed, baking cookies.

High-rise office building, Ruth Bader Ginsburg, arguing in court.

The excruciating pain of birth exploded and radiated in all directions like talons, ripping everything to shreds, tattering, pressure, pressure, pressure . . .

. . . tattering her.

She bit through her lip.

How many bells had she rung? How many times had she climbed to the towers and sounded the alarm?

"Bit of Montezuma's revenge, I suppose." The stranger who was not Sam laughed gently. "That's what we call it in Tustin, where we live. Yes, very close to Disneyland. We go all the time. She's a real nut for Disneyland. I guess I am, too."

Not those kind of people. Not those kind.

Corporate suits. Impeccable manners. Prep schools.

She ground her top teeth against her bottom ones, incisors and molars. Blood streamed down her chin.

Then, in a rush of wind and emotion, Little Dedo flew from her body and flopped on his side. He was wet and slippery, an ashy grey. His limps moved erratically. He began to mew like a kitten. The blood from her chin dripped on his face. He made suckling motions.

She reached out her hands and touched him. He was warm, not ice-cold as she had expected. She slid her fingers beneath him and picked him up.

He blinked at her, recognized her. The bond was made.

Her blood dripped. She ripped open her blouse and put him to her breast. Though he had sharp teeth, he didn't bite. He only sucked. The feeling of being drained coursed pleasantly through her body.

"She's had a couple of really rough spots."

Leaves of absence.

Dr. Epperling.

Medications.

Pressure, pressure, pressure.

Just give it one more shot, baby. You can do it.

A knock on the door. "Jeannie? Honey? You okay, honey?"

One hand cradling Little Dedo, she clung to the toilet paper holder and pulled herself to a standing position. She pushed open the door and staggered into the bathroom. No one else was there, but someone gasped.

There was a window. She opened it, crawled out awkwardly on shards she had not previously noticed. The glass must have reopened the scars on her wrists. Blood ran like rain down the side of the building.

Little Dedo stopped sucking and looked up at her adoringly.

"My darling, my life," she murmured, and opened her own great leathery wings. She flapped them once, twice, and flew into the air, over the boardwalk, and Disneyland Paris, and Sam, and high-rise office buildings and Ruther Bader Ginsburg and custom suits and secretaries, and picket fences and minivans and flew like

mad

We're so proud of you; we're all so proud of you; you're going to make such a great lawyer.

mad

Her mother. It's so different now. In my day, you'd have a baby by now. Maybe two. Don't you want children? Soon you'll be too old.

Flew like mad

angry, cheated, confused, terrified, wishing, wishing

to the land of the gargoyles.

At once the others flapped their wings and swooped down on her, lifting her and Little Dedo up, up into the rampart of Notre Dame, past the bell tower to the turrets, to the cornices and the darkness. A little nun sat there, smiling beatifically, as if to say, *Welcome, sister.*

The gargoyles gently lowered her; her joints stiffening, her bones turning to stone; her blood congealing. In her arms she gathered Little Dedo, who was sucking his thumb.

She would never move again. She would never have to. It was finally, blessedly, over.

"Little Dedo," she whispered, her mind clear and bright. The stigmata of her wrists, the crown of thorns of misplaced ambition.

Last words, last thoughts.

The theme park called Paradise, the holy infant called Little Dedo. The martyred mother—

—the sacrifice of external ambition!—

—exalted.

Grâce à Dieu. God be praised, it is finished; she rose again among the other creatures of the air, of the magnificent golden, the beautiful, hearts of stone.

Shadows fell, but not on her.

Bells clanged, but she heard only the gathering of the fog, and the whispers of the saints.

Et voila, redemption eternal: Jeanne of the bells, of Paris, of the gargoyles.

THE DARK COUNTRY
DENNIS ETCHISON

Dennis Etchison's stories have appeared in numerous periodicals and anthologies since 1961. Some of his most best-known tales are included in the collections The Dark Country, Red Dreams, The Blood Kiss, The Death Artist, Talking in the Dark, *and* Fine Cuts. *A new collection of his short fiction,* Got to Kill Them All & Other Stories, *recently appeared from Cemetery Dance Publications.*

The following story won the World Fantasy Award in 1982 (tied with Stephen King), as well as the British Fantasy Award that same year—the first time one writer had received both major awards for a single work.

"'The Dark Country' was written after visiting a Mexican tourist town about sixty miles below the California border," explains Etchison. "I had just finished the final draft of a novel called Darkside—*the manuscript was dropped into the mail as I left Los Angeles—and I was eager to get away for some rest and relaxation in the sun.*

"This was my first time in Ensenada, and I could not help but record some of the vivid images I saw there. Leaving Los Angeles after months of intense work, I had arrived at Quintas Papagayo exhausted but still nervous about the final draft of Darkside, *not to mention some worrisome personal issues—the perfect ingredients for a heightened state of anxiety, even paranoia.*

"Twenty years later I began working as an editor for Mandalay Pub-lications in LA, at a bilingual magazine called Estylo. *One day I told the staff about my trip to Ensenada and the story I had written. They thought I was joking. Ensenada is not dark. It is not even the real Mexico, they explained, only the Baja Peninsula—a safe, benign destination for gringos. For them, the real Dark Country is the U.S., which they had found so strange and frightening when they arrived here. And of course they were right. It all depends on your point of view. To paraphrase Ray Bradbury, it is not necessary to stand on one's head to see the world in a different way. A tilt a few degrees to the left or right is all it takes . . ."*

For one man, a trip South of the Border leads toward a personal darkness. . . .

Martin sat by the pool, the wind drying his hair.

A fleshy, airborne spider appeared on the edge of the book which he had been reading there. From this angle it cast a long, pointed needle across the yellowing page. The sun was hot and clean; it went straight for his nose. Overweight American children practiced their volley-ball on the bird-of-paradise plants. Weathered rattan furniture gathered dust beyond the peeling diving board.

Traffic passed on the road. Trucks, campers, bikes.

The pool that would not be scraped till summer. The wooden chairs that had been ordered up from the States. Banana leaves. Olive trees. A tennis court that might be done next year. A single color TV antenna above the palms. By the slanted cement patio heliotrope daisies, speckled climbing vines. The morning a net of light on the water. Boats fishing in Todos Santos Bay.

A smell like shrimps Veracruz blowing off the silvered waves.

And a strangely familiar island, like a hazy floating giant, where the humpback whales play. Yesterday in Ensenada, the car horns talking and a crab taco in his hand, he had wanted to buy a pair of huaraches and a Mex-ican shirt. The best tequila in the world for three-and-a-half a liter. Noche

Buena beer, foil labels that always peel before you can read them. Delicados con Filtros cigarettes.

Bottles of agua mineral. Tehuacan con gas. *No returnable.*

He smiled as he thought of churros at the Blow Hole, the maid who even washed his dishes, the Tivoli Night Club with Reno cocktail napkins, mescal flavored with worm, eggs fresh from the nest, chorizo grease in the pan, bar girls with rhinestone-studded Aztec headbands, psycho-active liqueurs, seagulls like the tops of valentines, grilled corvina with lemon, the endless plumes of surf . . .

It was time for a beer run to the bottling factory in town.

"¡Buenos días!"

Martin looked up, startled. He was blinded by the light. He fumbled his dark glasses down and moved his head. A man and a woman stood over his chair. The sun was at their backs.

"¡Americano?"

"Yes," said Martin. He shielded his forehead and tried to see their faces. Their features were blacked in by the glare that spilled around their heads.

"I told you he was an American," said the woman. "Are you studying?"

"What?"

Martin closed the book self-consciously. It was a paperback edition of *The Penal Colony,* the only book he had been able to borrow from any of the neighboring cabins. Possibly it was the only book in Quintas Papagayo. For some reason the thought depressed him profoundly, but he had brought it poolside anyway. It seemed the right thing to do. He could not escape the feeling that he ought to be doing something more than nursing a tan. And the magazines from town were all in Spanish.

He slipped his sketchbook on top of Kafka and opened it awkwardly.

"I'm supposed to be working," he said. "On my drawings. You know how it is." They didn't, probably, but he went on. "It's difficult to get anything done down here."

41

"He's an artist!" said the woman.

"My wife thought you were an American student on vacation," said the man.

"Our son is a student, you see," said the woman. Martin didn't, but nodded sympathetically. She stepped aside to sit on the arm of another deck chair under the corrugated green fiberglass siding. She was wearing a sleeveless blouse and thigh-length shorts. "He was studying for his Master's Degree in Political Science at UCLA, but now he's decided not to finish. I tried to tell him he should at least get his teaching credential, but—"

"Our name's Winslow," said the man, extending a muscular hand. "Mr. and Mrs. Winslow."

"Jack Martin."

"It was the books," said Mr. Winslow. "Our boy always has books with him, even on visits." He chuckled and shook his head.

Martin nodded.

"You should see his apartment," said Mrs. Winslow. "So many." She gestured with her hands as if describing the symptoms of a hopeless affliction.

There was an embarrassing lull. Martin looked to his feet. He flexed his toes. The right ones were stiff. For something further to do, he uncapped a Pilot Fineliner pen and touched it idly to the paper. Without realizing it, he smiled. This trip must be doing me more good than I'd hoped, he thought. I haven't been near a college classroom in fifteen years.

A wave rushed toward the rocks at the other side of the cabins.

"Staying long?" asked the man, glancing around nervously. He was wearing Bermuda shorts over legs so white they were almost phosphorescent.

"I'm not sure," said Martin.

"May I take a peek at your artwork?" asked the woman.

He shrugged and smiled.

She lifted the sketchbook from his lap with infinite delicacy, as the man began talking again.

He explained that they owned their own motor home, which was now parked on the Point, at the end of the rock beach, above the breakwater. Weekend auto insurance cost them $13.70 in Tijuana. They came down whenever they got the chance. They were both retired, but there were other things to consider—just what, he did not say. But it was not the same as it used to be. He frowned at the moss growing in the bottom of the pool, at the baby weeds poking up through the sand in the canister ash trays, at the separating layers of the sawed-off diving board.

Martin could see more questions about to surface behind the man's tired eyes. He cleared his throat and squirmed in his chair, feeling the sweat from his arms soaking into the unsealed wood. Mr. Winslow was right, of course. Things were not now as they once were. But he did not relish being reminded of it, not now, not here.

A small figure in white darted into his field of vision, near the edge of the first cabin. It was walking quickly, perhaps in this direction.

"There's my maid," he said, leaning forward. "She must be finished now." He unstuck his legs from the chaise longue.

"She has keys?" said the man.

"I suppose so. Yes, I'm sure she does. Well—"

"Does she always remember to lock up?"

He studied the man's face, but a lifetime of apprehensions were recorded there, too many for Martin to isolate one and read it accurately.

"I'll remind her," he said, rising.

He picked up his shirt, took a step toward Mrs. Winslow and stood, shifting his weight.

Out of the corner of his eye, he saw the maid put a hand to the side of her face.

Mrs. Winslow closed the pad, smoothed the cover and handed it back. "Thank you," she said oddly.

Martin took it and offered his hand. He realized at once that his skin had become uncomfortably moist, but Mr. Winslow gripped it firmly and held it. He confronted Martin soberly, as if about to impart a bit of fatherly advice.

"They say he comes down out of the hills," said Winslow, his eyes unblinking. Martin half-turned to the low, tan range that lay beyond the other side of the highway. When he turned back, the man's eyes were waiting. "He's been doing it for years. It's something of a legend around here. They can't seem to catch him. We never took it seriously, until now."

"Is that right?"

"Why, last night, while we were asleep, he stole an envelope of traveler's checks and a whole carton of cigarettes from behind our heads. Can you beat that? Right inside the camper! Of course we never bothered to lock up. Why should we? Everyone's very decent around here. We've never had any trouble ourselves. Until this trip. It's hard to believe."

"Yes, it is." Martin attempted to pull back as a tingling began in his stomach. But the man continued to pump his hand, almost desperately, Martin thought.

"The best advice I can give you, young man, is to lock your doors at night. From now on. You never know."

"Thanks, I will."

"He comes out after the sun goes down." He would not let go of Martin's hand. "I figure he must hit the beach three-four in the morning, when all the lights are out. Slips right in. No one notices. And then it's too late."

Martin pretended to struggle with the books so that he could drop his hand. "Well, I hope you're able to enjoy the rest of your vacation." He eyed the maid. "Now I'd better—"

"We're warning everybody along the beach," said Winslow.

"Maybe you should report it."

"That don't do no good. They listen to your story, but there's nothing they can do."

"Good luck to you, then," said Martin.

"Thank you again," said the woman peculiarly. "And don't forget. You lock your door tonight!"

"I will," said Martin, hurrying away. I won't, that is. Will, won't, what did it matter? He sidestepped the dazzling flowers of an ice plant and ascended the cracked steps of the pool enclosure. He crossed the paved drive and slowed.

The maid had passed the last of the beachfront houses and was about to intersect his path. He waited for her to greet him as she always did. I should at least pretend to talk to her, he thought, in case the Winslows are still watching. He felt their eyes, or someone's, close at his back.

"Buenos días," he said cheerfully.

She did not return the greeting. She did not look up. She wagged her head and trotted past, clutching her uniform at the neck.

He paused and stared after her. He wondered in passing about her downcast eyes, and about the silent doorways of the other cabins, though it was already past ten o'clock. And then he noticed the scent of ozone that now laced the air, though no thunderhead was visible yet on the horizon, only a gathering fog far down the coastline, wisps of it beginning to striate the wide, pale sky above the sagging telephone poles. And he wondered about the unsteadiness in Mrs. Winslow's voice as she had handed back the sketchbook. It was not until he was back at the beach that he remembered: the pages he had shown her were blank. There were no sketches at all yet in the pad, only the tiny flowing blot he had made with his pen on the first sheet while they talked, like a miniature misshapen head or something else, something else, stark and unreadable on the crisp white sulfite paper.

He was relieved to see that the private beach had finally come alive with its usual quota of sunbathers. Many of them had probably arisen early, shortly after he'd left for the quiet of the pool, and immediately swarmed to the surf with no thought of TV or the morning paper, habits they had left checked at the border sixty miles from here. A scattered few lagged back, propped out on their patios, sipping coffee and keeping an eye on the children who were bounding through the spume. The cries of the children and of the gulls cut sharply through the waves which, disappointingly, were beginning to sound to Martin like nothing so much as an enormous screenful of ball bearings.

There was the retired rent-a-cop on holiday with his girlfriend, stretched out on a towel and intent on his leg exercises. There was the middle-aged divorcée from two doors down, bent over the tidepools, hunting for moonstones among jealous clusters of aquamarine anemones. And there was Will, making time with the blonde in the blue tank top. He seemed to be explaining to her some sort of diagram in the slicked sand between the polished stones. Martin toed into his worn rubber sandals and went down to join them.

"Want to go to a party?" Will said to him as he came up.

"When?"

"Whenever," said the blonde in the blue top. She tried to locate Martin's face, gave up and gazed back in the general direction of the southern bungalows.

There a party was still in progress, as it had been since last Wednesday, when Will and Martin had arrived. The other party, the one on the north side, had apparently been suspended for a few hours, though just now as Martin watched a penny rocket streaked into the sky from the bathroom window, leaving an almost invisible trail of powder-blue smoke in the air above the water. The skyrocket exploded with a faint report like a distant rifle and began spiraling back to earth. Martin heard hoarse laughter and the sudden cranking-up of stereo speakers inside the sliding doors. So the party there was also nearly in full swing again, or had never let up. Perhaps it was all one big party, with his cabin sandwiched like a Christian Science reading room between two pirate radio stations. He remembered the occasional half-dressed teenager staggering around the firepit and across his porch last night, grunting about more beer and did he know where those nurses were staying? Martin had sat outside till he fell asleep, seeing them piss their kidneys out on the steaming stones by the footpath.

"Bummer," said the girl seriously. Martin noticed that she was lugging around an empty twelve-ounce bottle. She upended it and a few slippery drops hit the rocks. "You guys wouldn't know where the Dos Equis's stashed, wouldjou?"

"*No es problema,* my dear," said Will, steering her toward the patio.

Martin followed. Halfway there the girl wobbled around and hurled the bottle as high as she could away from the shoreline. Unfortunately, her aim was not very good. Martin had to duck. He heard it whistle end-over-end over his head and shatter on the flat rocks. Will caught her under the arms and staggered her inside. Next door, a Paul Simon song was playing on the tape deck.

By the time Martin got there she was on her way out, cradling a bottle of Bohemia. Again she tried to find his eyes, gave up and began picking her way across the rocks.

"Take it slow," yelled Will. "Hey, sure you don't want to lie down for a while?"

Martin grinned at him and walked past into the high-beamed living room. The fireplace was not lighted, nor was the wall heater, but a faint but unmistakable odor of gas lingered in the corners.

"We better stock up on Dos Equis from now on," said Will.

"Is that her favorite?"

"She doesn't care. But we shelled out a deposit on the case of Bohemia. Dos Equis is no return."

Martin stood staring out at the island in the bay. The fishing boats were moving closer to shore. Now he could barely make out the details of the nearest one. He squinted. It wasn't a fishing boat at all, he realized. It was much larger than he had imagined, some kind of oil tanker, perhaps. "Guess what, Will? We're going to have to start locking the doors."

"Why? Afraid the *putas* are gonna OD on Spanish fly and jump our bones in the middle of the night?"

"You wish," said Martin. He sniffed around the heater, then followed the scent to the kitchen and the stove. "The gas pilots," he said. "It's the draft. You—we're—always going in and out. The big door's open all the time."

"Got a match, man?" Will took out a bent cigarette, straightened it and crumpled the pack. The table was littered with empty packs of cheap Mexican cigarettes, Negritos and Faros mostly. Martin wondered how his friend could smoke such garbage. He took out his Zippo. Will struck it with an exaggerated shaking of his hands, but it was out of fluid. He stooped over the gas stove and winked at Martin. He turned the knob. The burner lit. He inhaled, coughed and reached for the tequila. He poured himself a tall one mixed with grapefruit juice. "Mmm. Good for the throat, but it still burns a little."

"Your system runs on alcohol, Willy. You know that, don't you?"

"Don't all machines?"

"Myself, I could go for some eggs right now. How about you? What've we got left?" Martin went to the sink. It was full of floating dishes. "Hey, what the hell is it with the maid? We did remember to leave her a tip yesterday. Didn't we?"

"One of us must have."

That was it, then. That was why she had skipped them, and then snubbed him this morning. That had to be it. Didn't it?

The tape deck next door was now blaring a golden oldie by Steely Dan. Martin slid the glass door closed. Then he snagged his trousers from the back of a chair and put them on over his trunks. Started to put them on. They did not feel right. He patted his back pocket.

Will slid the door back open halfway. "You're serious, aren't you? Look at it this way. Leave it like this and the gas'll just blow on outside. Relax, man. That's what you came down here for, isn't it? After what happened, you need . . ."

Martin checked the chair. On the table were a deck of playing cards from a Mission Bay savings and loan, the backs of which were imprinted with instructions about conserving energy, a Mexican wrestling magazine with a cover picture of the masked hero, El Santo, in the ring against a hooded character in red jumpsuit and horns, and an old mineral water bottle full of cigarette butts. On the floor, lying deflated between the table legs, was his wallet.

"There's another reason, I'm afraid." Martin twisted open the empty wallet and showed it to his friend.

"Who in the hell . . . ?"

"Well, it certainly wasn't the maid. Look at this place." Outside, a small local boy came trudging through the patios. He was carrying a leather case half as big as he was. He hesitated at the cabin on the south side, as three teen-aged American boys, their hair layered identically and parted in the middle, called their girls out into the sun. "It must have happened during the night."

"Christ!" said Will. He slapped the tabletop. He reached for his own wallet. It was intact. "There. I was over there partying all night, remember? They must've passed by every place where anybody was still up."

The small boy opened his case and the American girls began poring excitedly over a display of Indian jewelry, rings and belt buckles and necklaces of bright tooled silver and turquoise. From a distance, an old man watched the boy and waited, nodding encouragement.

"You should have gone with me," said Will. "I told you. Well, don't you worry, Jack. I've got plenty here for both of us."

"No, man. I can wire my agent or—"

"Look," said Will, "I can even kite a check if I have to, to cover the rental till we get back. They'll go for it. I've been coming here since I was a kid."

I've got to get away from here, thought Martin. No, that isn't right. Where else is there to go? I've come this far already just to get away. It's hopeless. It always was. You can run, he told himself, but you can't hide. Why didn't I realize that?

"Here," said Will. "Here's twenty for now."

"Are you sure?"

"Don't worry about it. I'd better go see if the nurses got hit, too. Saw a bunch of people in a huddle down the beach a while ago." He drained his glass. "Then I'll make another beer run. The hell with it. We're gonna party tonight, God damn it! You going by the office, Jack?"

"Sure."

"Then you might as well report it to the old lady. I think she's got a son or a nephew in the federales. Maybe they can do something about it."

"Maybe," said Martin, cracking open a beer. He could have told Will that it wouldn't do any good. He stopped in at the office anyway. It didn't.

He wandered on up the highway to Enrique's Cafe. On the way he passed a squashed black cat, the empty skin of it in among the plants, the blood-red flowers and spotted adder's tongues and succulents by the roadside. The huevos rancheros were runny but good. When he got back, Will's four-wheel drive was still parked under the carport. He took the keys and made the beer run into town himself, police cars honking him out of the way to make left turns from right-hand lanes, zigzagging across the busy intersections of the city to avoid potholes. He bought a case of Dos Equis and, for forty cents more, a liter of soft, hot tortillas. As the afternoon wore on he found himself munching them, rolled with butter and later plain, even though he wasn't really hungry.

That evening he sat alone on a bench by the rocks, hearing but not listening to a Beatles song. ("Treat Me Like You Did the Night Before"), the smoke from his Delicado wafting on the breeze, blending with wood smoke from the chimneys and rising slowly to leave a smear like the Milky Way across the Pleiades. It's time for me to leave this place, he thought. Not to run away, no, not this time; but to go back. And face the rest of it, my life, no matter how terrible things may have turned back home since I left.

Not Will, though; he should stay awhile longer if he likes. True, it was my idea; he only took the time off at my suggestion, setting it all up to make me comfortable; he knew I couldn't take any more last week, the way things were up there. He's my friend. Still, he was probably waiting for just such an excuse in order to get away himself.

So I'll call or wire the agency for a plane ticket, give them a cock-and-bull story about losing everything—the truth, in other words. It was the truth, wasn't it? I'll say the trip was part of the assignment. I had to come down here to work on some new sketches for the book, to follow a lead about headstone rubbings in, let's see, Guanajuato. Only I never made it that far. I stopped off for some local color. Charge it against my royalty statement . . . I'll talk to them tomorrow. Yes, tomorrow.

Meanwhile, there's still tonight . . .

But I should tell Will first.

He resumed walking. There was a fire on the breakwater by the Point. He went toward it. Will would be in one of the cabins, partying with a vengeance. Martin glanced in one window. A slide show was in progress, with shots that looked like the pockmarked surface of another planet taken from space. He pressed closer and saw that these pictures were really close-ups of the faces of newborn seals or sea lions. Not that one, he thought, and moved on.

One of the parties he came to was in the big cabin two doors north of his own. That one was being rented, he remembered, by the producer of a show in the late seventies called *Starship Disco*. Martin had never seen it.

An Elvis Costello tape shook the walls. A young card hustler held forth around the living room table. A warm beer was pushed into Martin's hand by a girl. He popped the beer open and raised it, feeling his body stir as he considered her. Why not? But she could be my daughter, technically, he thought, couldn't she? Then: what a disgusting point of view. Then: what am I doing to myself? Then it was too late; she was gone.

Will was not in the back rooms. The shelf in the hallway held three toppling books. Well well, he thought, there are readers down here, after all. Then he examined them—*By Love Possessed* by Cozzens, *Invitation* to Tea by Monica Lang (The People's Book Club, Chicago, 1952), *The Foundling* by Francis Cardinal Spellman. They were covered with years of dust.

He ducked into the bathroom and shut the door, seeing the mirror and razor blade lying next to the sink, the roll of randomly-perforated crepe paper toilet tissue. There was a knock on the door. He excused himself and went out, and found Will in the kitchen.

"*¡Dos cervezas,* Juan!" Will was shouting. "Whoa. I feel more like I do now than when I got here!" With some prodding, he grabbed two cold ones and followed Martin outside, rubbing his eyes.

He seemed relieved to sit down.

"So," began Martin. "What did you find out? Did anyone else get popped last night?"

"Plenty! One, the nurses. Two, the bitch from San Diego. Three, the— where is it now? Ojai. Those people. The . . ." He ran out of fingers. "Let's see. Anyway, there's plenty, let me tell you."

The ships were now even nearer the shore. Martin saw their black hulls closing in over the waves.

"I was thinking," he said. "Maybe it's time to go. What would you say to that, man?"

"Nobody's running scared. That's not the way to play it. You should hear 'em talk. They'll get his ass next time, whoever he is. Believe it. The kids, they didn't get hit. But three of those other guys are rangers. Plus there's the cop. See the one in there with the hat? He says he's gonna lay a trap, cut the lights about three o'clock, everybody gets quiet, then bam! You better believe it. They're mad as hell."

"But why—"

"It's the dock strike. It happens every year when there's a layoff. The locals get hungry. They swoop down out of the hills like bats."

Just then a flaming object shot straight through the open front door and fizzled out over the water. There was a hearty "All r-r-ight!" from a shadow on the porch, and then the patio was filled with pogoing bodies and clapping hands. The night blossomed with matches and fireworks, 1000-foot skyrockets, bottle rockets and volleys of Mexican cherry bombs, as the party moved outside and chose up sides for a firecracker war. Soon Martin could no longer hear himself think. He waited it out. Will was laughing.

Martin scanned the beach beneath the screaming lights. And noticed something nearby that did not belong. It was probably a weird configuration of kelp, but . . . he got up and investigated.

It was only this: a child's broken doll, wedged half-under the stones. What had he supposed it was? It had been washed in on the tide, or deliberately dismembered and its parts strewn at the waterline, he could not tell which. In the flickering explosions, its rusty eye sockets appeared to be streaked with tears.

A minute after it had begun, the firecracker war was over. They sat apart from the cheering and the breaking bottles, watching the last shot of a Roman candle sizzle below the surface of the water like a green torpedo. There was scattered applause, and then a cry went up from another party house down the beach as a new round of fireworks was launched there. Feet slapped the sand, dodging rocks.

"Do you really believe that?"

"What?"

"About someone coming down from the hills," said Martin. *Like bats.* He shuddered.

"Watch this," said Will. He took his bottle and threw it into the air, snapping it so it flew directly at a palm tree thirty feet away. It smashed into the trunk at the ragged trim line.

Instantly the treetop began to tremble. There was a high rustling and a shaking and a scurrying. And a rattling of tiny claws. A jagged frond dropped spearlike to the beach.

"See that? It's rats. The trees around here are full of 'em. You see how bushy it is on top? It never gets trimmed up there. Those rats are born, live and die in the trees. They never touch down."

"But how? I mean, what do they eat if—?"

"Dates. Those are palm trees, remember? And each other, probably. You've never seen a dead one on the ground, have you?"

Martin admitted he hadn't.

"Not that way with the bats, though. They have to come out at night. Maybe they even hit the rats. I never saw that. But they have mouths to feed, don't they? There's nothing much to eat up in the hills. It must be the same with the peasants. They have families. Wouldn't you?"

"I hate to say this. But. You did lock up, didn't you?"

Will laughed dryly. "Come on. I've got something for you. I think it's time you met the nurses."

Martin made a quick sidetrip to check the doors at their place, and they went on. They covered the length of the beach before Will found the porch he was looking for. Martin reached out to steady his friend, and almost fell himself. He was getting high. It was easy.

As they let themselves in, the beach glimmered at their backs with crushed abalone shells and scuttling hermit crabs. Beyond the oil tankers, the uncertain outline of the island loomed in the bay. It was called Dead Man's Island, Will told him.

He woke with the sensation that his head was cracking open. Music or something like it in the other room, throbbing through the thin walls like the pounding of surf. Voices. An argument of some kind. He brushed at the cobwebs. He had been lost in a nightmare of domination and forced acquiescence before people who meant to do him harm. It returned to him in fragments. What did it mean? He shook it off and rolled out of bed.

There was the floor he had pressed with his hand last night to stop the room from spinning. There was the nurse, tangled in the sheets next to him. He guessed she was the nurse. He couldn't see her face.

He went into the bathroom. He took a long draught of water from the faucet before he came out. He raised his head and the room spun again. The light from the window hurt his eyes—actual physical pain. He couldn't find his sock. He tottered into the other room.

A young man with blown-dry hair was playing the tape deck too loudly. The sound vibrated the bright air, which seemed thin and brittle, hammering it like beaten silver. There was the girl in the blue tank top, still seated next to the smoldering fireplace. An empty bottle of Damiana Liqueur was balanced against her thigh. Her eyes were closed and her face was stony. He wondered if she had slept that way, propped upright all night. On the table were several Parker Brothers-type games from stateside: *Gambler, Creature Features, The Game of Life*. A deck of Gaiety Brand nudie cards, with a picture on the box of a puppy pulling a bikini top out of a purse. Someone had been playing solitaire. Martin couldn't remember.

There was a commotion outside.

"What's that?" he said, shielding his eyes.

"Talking Heads," said the young man. He showed Martin the tape box. "They're pretty good. That lead guitar line is hard to play. It's so repetitious."

"No, I mean . . ."

Martin scratched and went into the kitchen. It was unoccupied, except for a cricket chirping somewhere behind the refrigerator. Breakfast was in process; eggs were being scrambled in a blender the nurses had brought with them from home. Martin protected his eyes again and looked outside.

There was Will. And there were three or four tan beach boys from the other party. And the cop. He wasn't doing his leg exercise this morning. They were having an argument.

Martin stumbled out.

"But you can't do that," one of them was saying.

"Stay cool, okay, motherfuck? You want the whole beach to know?"

"You think they don't already?"

"The hell they do! We drug him over out of the way. No one'll—"

"No one but the maids!"

"That's what I'm *saying*. You guys are a bunch of jack-offs. Jesus Christ! I'm about *this* close to kicking your ass right now, do you know that?"

"All right, all right!" said Will. "That kind of talk's just digging us in deeper. Now let's run through the facts. One—"

Martin came up. They shot looks at each other that both startled him and made him unreasonably afraid for their safety as well as his own. They stopped talking, their eyes wild, as if they had gobbled a jar of Mexican amphetamines.

Will took him aside.

"We've got to do something!" said the one with the souvenir hat. "What're you—?"

"Hold on," said Will. "We're all in this together, like it or—"

"I'm not the one who—"

"—Like it or not. Now just try to keep a tight asshole another minute, will you, while I talk to my friend Jack? It's his neck, too."

They started back up the beach. Will propelled him ahead of the others, as to a rendezvous of great urgency.

"They got him," said Will.

"Who?"

"The thief, whoever he was. Poor bastard. Two guys from next door cornered him outside our place. Sometime around dawn, the way I get it.

Apparently he fell on the rocks. He's dead. They found me here a little while ago. Now—"

"What?"

"—Now there's no use shitting bricks. It's done. What we have to do is think of a way to put ourselves in the clear—fast. We're the strangers here."

"We can make it look like an accident," said the one in the hat. "Those rocks are—"

"Accident, hell," said the security cop. "It was self-defense, breaking and entering. We caught him and blew him away. No court in—"

"This isn't the USA, you dumb shit. You know what greaser jails are like? They hate our guts. All they want's our money. This buddy of mine, he got . . ."

And so it went till they reached the porch, the surrounding beach littered with the casings of burnt-out rockets, vomit drying on the rocks, broken clam shells bleaching between the rocks, the rocks like skulls. And here blood, vivid beyond belief even on the bricks of the patio, great splotches and gouts of it, like gold coins burnished in the sun, a trail that led them in the unforgiving light of day to the barbecue pit and the pile of kindling stacked in the charcoal shade.

Martin knelt and tore at the logs.

And there.

The body was hidden inside a burlap sack. It was the body of the boy who had come by yesterday, the boy who had wanted to sell his jewelry.

He felt his stomach convulse. The small face was scraped raw, the long eyelashes caked and flaking, the dark skin driven from two of the ribs to show white muscle and bone. A great fear overtook Martin, like wings settling upon him, blocking out the sun. He folded under them momentarily and dry-heaved in the ashes.

Will was pacing the narrow patio like a prisoner in a cell, legs pumping out and back over the cracking cement, pivoting faster and faster at the edges until he was practically spinning, generating a hopeless rage that would not be denied but could not be released. His hands were shaking violently, and his arms and shoulders and body. He looked around with slitted eyes, chin out, lips drawn in, jaws grinding stone. Far down the beach by the Point an elderly man came walking, hesitating at each house and searching each lot. He was carrying a leather case.

Will said, "You kicked him to death, didn't you? You stomped this child until he was dead." Then, his voice a hiss, he began to curse them between his teeth with an unspeakable power and vileness. The one in the hat tried to break in. He started shouting.

"It was dark! He could've been anyone! What was he doing creepin' around here? He could've been—"

But Will was upon him, his arms corded, his fingers going for the throat. The others closed in. People on the beach were turning to stare. Martin saw it all as if in slow motion: himself rising at last to his full height, leaping into it a split-second before the others could grab hold, as he fell on their arms to stop the thumbs from Will's eyes, to break Will's hands from the other's throat. Everything stopped. Martin stepped between them as the young one fell back to the flagstone wall. Martin raised his right hand, flattened and angled it like a knife. With his left he cupped the back of the young man's neck, holding it almost tenderly. The young man's eyes were almost kind. They were eyes Martin had seen all his life, outside recruiting offices and Greyhound bus depots the years over, and they were a law unto themselves. He brought his right hand down sharp and hard across the face, again, again, three times, like pistol shots. The tan went white, then red where he had slapped it. For a moment nobody said anything. The old man kept coming.

They passed motorcycle cops, overheated VWs, Jeeps, Chevy Luvs, Ford Couriers with camper shells, off-road vehicles with heavy-duty shocks and, a mile outside of town, a half-acre of pastel gravestones by the main road. Martin fit as best he could among the plastic water jugs, sleeping bags and Instamatic cameras in the back seat. The boys from next door were piled in with him, the one in the hat in front and Will at the controls of the four-wheel drive.

The twenty-mile access road behind Ensenada wound them higher and higher, pummeling them continuously until they were certain that the tie rods or the A-frame or their bodies would shake loose and break apart at the very next turn. The lane shrank to a mere dirt strip, then to a crumbling shale-and-sandstone ledge cut impossibly around the backs of the hills, a tortuous serpentine above abandoned farmland and the unchecked acreage between the mountains and the sea. Twice at least one of the wheels left the road entirely; they had to pile out and lay wild branches under the tires to get across fissures that had no bottom. Martin felt his kidneys begin to ache under the endless pounding. One of the boys threw up and continued to retch over the side until Will decided they had gone far enough, but no one opened his mouth to complain. After more than an hour, they set the hand brake at the start of a primitive downslope, blocked the wheels with granite chips and stumbled the rest of the way, numb and reeling.

The silence was overpowering. Nothing moved, except for the random scrabbling of lizards and the falling of individual leaves and blades of grass. As they dragged the sack down to the meadows, Martin concentrated on the ribbon of dirt they had driven, watching for the first sign of another car, however unlikely that was. A small, puddled heat mirage shimmered on the dust, coiled and waiting to be splashed. A squirrel darted across the road, silhouetted as it paused in stop-motion, twitched its pointed head and then ran on, disappearing like an escaped shooting gallery target. Great powdered monarch butterflies aimlessly swam the convection currents; like back home, he thought. Yes, of course; I should have known. Only too much like home.

"Dig here," said Will.

The old wound in Martin's foot was hurting him again. He had thought it would be healed by now, but it wasn't. He rocked back wearily on one heel. A withered vine caught at his ankle. It snapped easily with a dull, fleshy sound as he shook free. He took another step, and something moist and solid broke underfoot. He looked down.

He kicked at the grass. It was only a tiny melon, one of dozens scattered nearby and dying on the vine. He rolled it over, revealing its soft underbelly. Too much rain this season, he thought absently; too much or too little, nourishing them excessively or not enough. What was the answer? He picked it up and lobbed it over their heads. It splattered on the road in a burst of pink. Watermelons, he thought, while fully formed seeds pale as unborn larvae slithered off his shoe and into the damp grass. Who planted them here? And who will return for the harvest, only to find them already gone to seed? He stooped and wiped his hand. There was a faint but unmistakable throb and murmur in the ground, as though through a railroad track, announcing an unseen approach from miles away.

"What are you going to do, Jackie?"

Martin stared back at Will. He hadn't expected the question, not now.

"It's like this," said Will, taking him to one side. "Michael, for one, wants to get back to his own van and head on deeper into Baja, maybe San Quintin, lay low for a few days. He wasn't registered, so there's no connection. Some of the others sound like they're up for the same, or for going north right away, tonight. Kevin's due to check out today, anyway."

"And you?"

"Don't know yet. I haven't decided. I'll probably stay on for appearances, but you do what you want. I wouldn't worry about the maid or anyone coming by to check up. Anyway, we hosed off the patio. Nobody else saw a thing, I'm sure. The girls don't know anything about it."

There was a grunt. The sack, being lowered, had split open at the seams. Hands hurried to reclose it.

"What's that?"

Will grabbed a wrist. A silver bracelet inlaid with polished turquoise glittered against a bronze tan in the afternoon light.

"I—I bought it."

"Sure you did," said Will.

"I brought it with me on the trip. Ask my girl. She—"

Will stripped it off the arm and flung it into the shallow grave. "You want to get out of this alive, kiddo? That kind of work can be traced. Or didn't you think of that? You didn't think, did you? What else did you steal from him while you were at it yesterday? Is that why he came back last night? Is it?"

"Lookit, man, where do you get off—"

"We all hang together," said Will, "or we all hang together. Get it?"

He got to his knees to close the sack. As an afterthought, he reached deep and rifled the dead child's pockets for anything that might tie in with Quintas Papagayo.

His hand stopped. He withdrew a wad of paper money which fell open, a flower on his palm. A roll of American dollars, traveler's checks, credit cards.

"Hey, that's—"

"I had eighty bucks on me when—"

Martin joined him in examining the roll. The checks were signed NORMAN WINSLOW. Two of the cards, embossed on the front and signed on the back, read JACK MARTIN.

"Knew I was right!" said the one in the felt hat. "Fuck if I wasn't! Lookit that! The little son of a bitch . . ."

Martin straight-armed the wheel, running in darkness.

He reminded himself of the five-dollar bill clipped to the back of his license. Then he remembered that his wallet was flat, except for the credit cards. Motorcycle cops passed him like fugitive Hell's Angels. He kicked on the lights of his rented car and thought of the last news tape of the great Karl Wallenda. He had been running, too, though in wind, not fog, toward or away from something.

Did he look back, I wonder? Was that why it happened?

. . . Heading for the end, his last that day was weak. Or maybe he looked ahead that once, saw it was the same, and just gave up the ghost. No, not Wallenda. For him the game was running while pretending not to—or the other way around. Was that his private joke? Even in Puerto Rico, for him the walk was all. *Keep your head clear,* he wanted to tell Wallenda. For that was how it finished, stopping to consider. But Wallenda must have known; he had been walking for years. Still he should have remembered . . . Martin put on his brights, gripped the steering wheel and made for the border.

He turned on the radio, found an American station.

It was playing a song by a group called The Tubes. He remembered the Trivoli Night club, the elevated band playing "Around the World" and "A Kiss to Build a Dream On." He remembered Hussong's Cantina, the knife fight that happened, his trip to the Blow Hole, policia with short hair and semiautomatic rifles. The housetrailers parked on the Point, the Point obscured by mist. The military guns with silencers.

The doll whose parts had been severed, its eyes opening in moonlight.

Shaking, he turned his mind to what lay ahead. He wanted to see someone; he tried to think of her face. Her eyes would find his there under the beam ceiling, the spider plants in the corners growing into the carpet, the waves on Malibu beach, the Pleiades as bright, shining on what was below: the roots between the rocks, the harbor lights like eyes, the anemones closed inward, gourds and giant mushrooms, the endless pull of riptide, the seagulls white as death's heads, the police with trimmed moustaches, the dark ships at anchor . . .

He came to a bridge on the tollway. Ahead lay the border.

To his right a sign, a turnoff that would take him back into Baja.

He sat with the motor running, trying to pick a direction.

THE ANGUISH OF DEPARTURE

ROBERTA LANNES

Roberta Lannes is a native of Southern California, where she teaches high school fine and digital art. Her first horror story was written and sold in Dennis Etchison's UCLA extension course "Writing Horror Fiction" and appeared his 1985 award-winning anthology, The Cutting Edge.

Since then, her short stories, essays, and articles have been published widely, and she has every intention of completing a novel as retirement from teaching approaches.

"In the summer of 2006," explains the author, "my husband and I spent a glorious, but brief time in Venice, Italy, staying in a secluded hotel, far from the tourists, shops, and commercialized glamour.

"While walking to dinner using directions given to us by the hotel, we got lost. I was sure which way we should go, but my husband hung back as I hurried on, and for half a minute I was on a dark street alone. The panic had nearly set in when he found me and we continued on to the restaurant. During dinner we talked about what a horror story it could have become had we been separated, unable to find our way to each other. And so 'The Anguish of Departure' took shape right there, over the piatto dolce *and* grappa!"

During a trip to Venice, a woman becomes obsessed by her heritage as a dark family secret is revealed. . . .

T he Venice Marco Polo airport was no longer visible as the Ali Laguna motorboat maneuvered the choppy waters of the Canale della Guidecca towards the Canale di San Marco. Colin spooned himself around Franca in the early autumn afternoon as she leaned over the teak railing. The breeze pushed her auburn curls into his face. He pulled some of her hair out of his mouth and nuzzled her neck, spoke into her olive skin.

"What'd you say?" Franca arched her back and half-turned to him.

"I said 'I love you'." He waited.

Franca gave him her profile as she grinned into the golden light. "I can't believe we're really here! The place where my grandmother was born, my grandfather, my great-great grand *everyone*. I wish my father was here. He always wanted to see where his parents came from."

"If only . . ." Colin leaned away from Franca, stared down at the orange plastic seat, so uninviting after so many hours sitting in airports, on planes, in taxis. "We could never have afforded to bring him when he was alive."

Franca grasped her hair into one hand and looked at him. Her eyes were sad, disappointed in a way Colin had become too well-acquainted "Yes, it's ironic that it's his inheritance we're spending to see *his* Venice on our anniversary. Well, a little corner of the money. When I think of how hard he worked to build his wealth yet never gave himself the things, the experiences he could have had when he was alive . . ."

Her tone shut him up. Four years since her father died; their lives had changed dramatically with the inheritance. Yet she was still bitter Colin had not measured up to him—the sainted Marino Guardini. How had he been enough for her those six years before? How had Marino's death changed things so drastically? Stop this, he told himself, you're here to enjoy yourself. It's our anniversary. A celebration.

She pulled herself away, moving through the travelers to the bow. He watched her leaning out, hair fluttering; an ancient masthead, proud. A gaunt old man in his Sunday suit sitting beside her grasped Franca's arm. He pulled himself up slowly, jostled by the choppy ride. He leaned close, spoke to her. His eyes were rheumy, his lined face dotted with dark moles; his pomaded white hair gleamed in the light. Franca shook her head. The man held her arm and continued to speak. Franca smiled, nodding, appeasing, surely understanding almost nothing. Colin looked away as the motorboat pulled up to a station.

The motorboat was nearly empty by the time they reached their stop at Vallaresso. Franca stepped carefully toward Colin as the boat rocked and bumped the short pier. The old man sat with his hands in his lap, watching Franca. Colin waved at him as he took Franca's arm and led her to their luggage. The old man blinked, then covered his face with a handkerchief, as if hiding tears.

"What did that man say to you?" Colin shifted his rolling case behind him.

Franca yanked at her bag, juggling an overstuffed backpack. "God, why did I pack so much? We're only here a week!"

"Franca, what did that old man say? He spoke to you for quite a while."

She kept her back to him. "He spoke Italian. I tried to understand him, ask if he spoke any English, but he only knew a few words. And you know how much Italian I know. I was just being nice . . . listening. I thought of my grandfather . . . what he must have been like. I guess he thought I was Italian. I mean Venetian. A native. *Satisfied?*"

Colin pouted. How he wanted this trip to be the thing that changed them, put them back together, or just put the last four years into the *rough patch* category old marrieds spoke of in their seventies.

"Let's find out where our little apartment is." They'd rented a home via the Internet. The price was surprisingly modest, but Franca wanted authenticity, not luxury.

Colin delegated navigating to Franca. She insisted men knew nothing of directions, and were too proud to ask, so it fell upon the female to get them where they were going. She stood surrounded by the raven-black cases, in front of the Maritime Building holding a street map. She'd taken a pen and drawn a line along the streets leading to the home, as if making her way through a maze in a children's magazine.

"Okay, follow me."

The tourists parted as they trundled their cases along the streets. He was amazed at the closed-in, narrow streets, the clear difference between the tourists, who avoided eye-contact, and the locals who met his stare and seemed to beckon, 'step inside', 'eat', 'shop'. He felt oddly disturbed by the lack of the familiar; sounds like traffic, horns honking, the space in which conversation and footfalls echoed and reverberated were exchanged for hushed voices, camera shutters clacking, seagulls squawking, and water lapping at stone. As they crossed awkwardly with their luggage over bridges, the sounds were truncated, stilled by the closeness.

Franca suddenly stopped. "Okay, it looks like we cross over this square here . . .," she pointed to an open area the size of a small garden off which streets branched in every direction. "Then go down Calle dietro le Scuole and turn left towards the waterway." Colin saw the street sign. She was amazing. It was one of so many things about Franca he admired.

He'd looked hard for things to keep him from bolting after she'd changed. Once she'd gone into mourning for her father she became a stranger. In all the time Colin had known her, she'd regarded her father with pained indifference. After all, due to his remarkable absence or neglect, he was a man she'd known little. Turning away from Colin, she embraced the ghost of Marino and her family's history, finding intimacy with the dead beyond that which she'd ever lavished on Colin. It crushed him. In the hope that this trip would release her from this fixation, Colin prayed something would happen to trigger it. Anything. He just wanted his wife back. Or be set free of the pain.

He saw Franca across the square and hurried after her.

The apartment faced the narrow street at one side, and water at the bridge. It was smaller than it looked on the Internet, and grungier. Tall and long in shape, like a train car flat, the ground floor was a damp-smelling entry with a storage room on one side, stairs and a sitting area, and a corridor to the door on the water where long ago the original family must have set off on a gondola or their own boat for shopping and visits to the cemetery on San Michele. The first floor was a parlor with a balcony overlooking the canal, a wide dining room, and kitchen. The bedrooms were upstairs. The attic had been made into a bedroom for children, but sealed boxes, each labeled in Italian, topped the beds and covered the floor.

Franca took the bedroom facing the canal. Colin felt his hopes squashed. Why hadn't he stood on the landing as they peeked into both rooms and said, "Let's take the big room?" Instead, he watched her pull her case, fling her backpack onto the sagging double bed and say, "This will do me."

He turned into the room with two twin beds flanking a storage locker for a nightstand. At the far end were two long windows facing more long windows thirteen feet across the street. Bookcases lined the walls leading to the windows. The one softness in the room was an overstuffed lounging sofa beside a tea table. The room smelled of wheat paste, dust, and mold, damp, aging paper and leather bindings.

As he stood opening the window, he swallowed a sob. He might as well be on his own. A house in the countryside with acres of green, copses of trees, streams and grazing cows was more his thing. In their first six years together, they had both enjoyed the solitude and each other with holidays in Ireland, Scotland, Wales. Museums and churches were rare diversions before. Since Marino's death, Franca's preferred lots of them. If she could be near anything old, ancient—especially Italian—she felt invigorated.

When they met, she'd been a sample maker for a major designer. Her world was modern literature, hip clothing, clubs, and fancy parties. It was he who had given her an appreciation for antiques, for things with a past. While he revered such treasures—antiquities, art—he had his fill of them on the job as a museum conservator and restorer. Living in a city filled with buildings, old and new, shops and bustling crowds, he longed for time away from all that.

He started with Franca's voice from the other room. "We need to find a market so we can stock the kitchen. Do you have the information the Kumaris sent us about where to shop?"

"Can't hear you!" That would draw her in, then she'll see what a slum his room was and tell him to join her.

Her bare feet slapped at the stone floor and stopped on his doorway. She peered in. "This is lovely! Look at all those books! You should feel right at home . . ." His frown made her pause. "What? Don't you like it?"

"Franca, it's fine, but this is our anniversary. I want to sleep *with* you. Not in the kid's room."

"I'll snore and keep you awake. Why should it be any different while we're on holiday?" She hated him waking her constantly to stop her nasal buzzing in the night.

"Because I won't care if I feel less rested. I'm on holiday." He thought, 'do I have to beg my own wife to allow me in our bed? Have we really lost each other and just can't see it?'

"Fine!" Her false gaiety annoyed him. She'd rather sleep alone knowing he was nearby, but not *there*, where it mattered. "But the room's small. We can keep our bags in here."

The sun was setting as they struggled back up the stairs with far too many groceries. Franca was ecstatic with the adventure of being near so many things of her grandparent's. Her chatter was filled with pointing out each building, street, marketplace she remembered hearing about as a child. Colin coiled deeper inside himself. It confounded him that her happiness could be so totally removed from him, from sharing their anniversary, sharing anything.

Franca set about cooking dinner as Colin uncorked a bottle of Chianti. The warm nutty taste along with the Parmeggiano-Reggiano she shaved on a plate, pleased him more than it did at home. He put *Carmen* on the CD player, sat back and closed his eyes. He wanted to get into this holiday, feel the sense of place. The aromas filling the room helped.

"I think the pasta is done. The fish is baking. Here." Franca set a plate for Colin on the long dining table.

"Smells delicious . . . garlic!" He sat down, poured her another glass of wine.

"I used the recipes I brought along. Grandmother's. Bought just what was on her shopping lists she saved with each recipe. I hope it tastes just like it did to my father when he ate it." She drew in the scent then forked the fettuccini to her mouth.

Colin tasted it. It was *too* much garlic. It was almost painful to eat, burning his tongue. The tomatoes had been sun dried or pressed in salty oil. It all tasted extreme, as if designed for someone with a numbed palate. He pretended to like it. Franca was enjoying it so much.

The fish was better, but drenched in butter and capers, with just enough parsley to cut the relentless brininess. Colin ate mostly crunchy bread with wine.

Franca took the dishes to the sink and began rinsing them. "Now I'd like nothing better than a gelato. How about we walk down the streets until we find some?"

"Sounds good. I'll wait on the bridge until you're done. I want to watch the gondolas with the lights." Franca grinned at him then. A familiar, five years ago grin. From her heart. It softened him.

A singing gondolier's voice filled the narrow canal as Colin leaned on the bridge railing. The air was filled with cooking odors, dirty water, and the varnish on the well-kept gondolas. Dogs barked and people shouted at each other in the apartments along the canal. For a time, no one else walked along the street, over the bridge. It was just Colin and Venice. And he got it. The magic. They would go into Piazza San Marco tomorrow, go into the Basilica, Doge's Palace. Have lunch and listen to the small orchestra playing to the tourists and pigeons.

"Hey, where are you?" Franca came up beside him and he jerked.

"Thinking about tomorrow, as a matter of fact. The Museo Diocesano d'arte Sacra, lunch in the Piazza? You being happy to be here. Me, happy to be here." He reached out to her and pulled her close. She leaned into him.

"That sounds great. Later this week, I want to go to some of the smaller churches, search their records for my family. The old grandfather said . . . ," she stopped herself, corrected, "well, from what he said I *thought* he told me I could find others through the records the churches kept. My grandfather donated a lot of money towards restoration, father once said. It might be more likely to find someone who was active in the church if he was generous. Don't you think?"

She asked me a question, Colin thought. She wants me included! "Yes, it would be the same here as at home, all of Europe, I imagine. Let's ask around tomorrow, see if we can get some idea of a specific place to start."

Franca put her arms around him. "Oh, Col, I'm so glad we're doing this. I feel them here. All of them; even my father." She put her hands to his face and looked him in the eyes. "I know the last few years with me have been far from happy for either of us. But coming here, I feel like I am going to find some kind of release from my sorrow. I don't know how or what. I don't make sense to myself much these days. But I need to be here."

"I know, Franca. I'm beginning to understand it more each hour we're here. We're going to learn so much. Maybe more than just about your family. About us."

She shrugged. "I hope so. I actually feel hopeful for the first time in . . . I can't remember . . ."

He kissed her then. She kissed him back. Really kissed him, as she had before she lost her father. The shouting came from gondolas and friendly passersby. "Amore!" and "Bacio!" "Amantes!" "Fidanzati!" They stopped, embarrassed, smiling.

That night, they made love for the first time in years. They both cried when they finished, then fell into deep, sweet sleep.

Colin got up to use the toilet early in the morning. Franca was quietly snoring beside him as he rose. The smell of their bodies, sex, the lingering scents of dinner, the apartment itself made him giddy. Standing at the urinal, he found the utter silence oddly loud. He wondered if he had ever been anywhere so quiet, except in the countryside.

He started down the steps to the bedroom when heard the sound of a window falling closed in the other bedroom. He padded in. It was too dark to see anything. He pressed the light switch and a little table lamp came on. He walked to the windows and tried to recall if he had left the window open when he had been in the room earlier. Perhaps it had been open and when the night air cooled, the frame shrank and the window shut. Yes, that had to be it.

He looked up across the street into the windows opposite. At first he thought he saw patterned curtains drawn, but when they moved aside, he realized someone was watching him back. He waited, then realized he was in silhouette with the light behind him, and he saw more of his own reflection than outside. He went to the lamp and switched it off.

Returning to the window, he could more easily see an old man standing a foot or so back from the window. He wore a patterned robe, his hands shoved into the pockets. In the darkness, all that was obvious was the thick pomaded white hair and rheumy eyes. The man from the motorboat Ali Laguna! His heart thudded wildly. Was it an accident he was there? Did Franca know? Colin was suddenly frightened for them.

He returned to bed, curling around Franca, but sleep came only in fits and starts.

They lingered in the Doge's Palace until three, and then went into the Piazza to sit down and listen to the music, have a lunch. Franca asked questions about the art, why some were kept in cold rooms and wondered how restorers created pigments to match those mixed hundreds of years before. Colin couldn't recall her asking about his work much after they had known each other a few months. In the beginning, she was tireless in her curiosities. It boded well for a new beginning.

The sun peeked between thickening lofty clouds, a chilly breeze blew, and the pigeons clustered near the tourists who fed them. Colin drank his espresso as Franca gabbed on about wishing she could see the real David statue. His eyes took her in as he glanced around the square. It was there, under the blouson awning, he saw the old man again in his Sunday suit.

"Look, Franca. Your old friend from the motorboat. He's standing just behind you across the piazza." Colin nodded. She turned slowly, casually. When she saw him, she stiffened. "Wha . . . what's he. . . ." She turned back to Colin, her face paler. "I didn't think . . . why would he be . . . do you think he's watching us?"

"*You* talked with him. What do *you* think?"

Franca turned defensive. "I . . . I have no idea, Colin. Really. He said almost nothing in English. I got about a tenth of what he said. Maybe he understood me when I told him I was here to learn about my family on my father's side. I might even have mentioned our name. Maybe he knows we're tourists and . . ."

"And that's why he's watching us? I think there are far too many tourists for him to have decided on us. You. Maybe you were too friendly. Italians misconstrue things."

Franca snapped at him. "What do you know of Italians, Colin? You barely knew my father, never met my grandparents, and besides a few Italian paintings that you've worked on, haven't made an attempt to know."

"Your grandparents were dead, Franca. Your father rarely made an effort. But, I know you. You *are* Italian even if you never saw Italy until now. It's in your cells, your history." Colin cupped his hand over his mouth, exhaled roughly through his fingers, then folded his arms across his chest. "I meant that a woman being open, friendly, signals interest and men move toward her, sometimes with more intensity than a woman wants."

"Oh, so my listening to the little old man meant I wanted him to follow me all over Venice? Next you'll tell me he's moved into the apartment across from ours and watches us through our windows." She gestured wildly towards sunlight glinting off so many glass panes.

Colin felt his face go red, then the blood leave. "Oh." He swallowed hard. "How could you know that? I didn't tell you."

Franca's face changed from angry to scared, then frowning, skeptical, and finally she smirked. "Oh, very funny, Colin. You got me. I'm supposed to be frightened and fall into your arms so you can protect me from the skinny little old man." Then she laughed coldly.

"You think I'm joking. This is all a ruse to suck you in? I'm scared witless." He told her about the window, seeing the man across the way. The look on Colin's face, his color gone, must have given her pause because she lost the smirk. "Maybe it's all coincidence, maybe you said something more to him than you thought. Either way, I don't find his presence comforting."

She weighed Colin's words, looked back to see the man had gone. "Well, our fighting scared him away, so maybe he's not such a threat after all."

He shook his head. "Let's forget it. We were having a good time."

"*Were*. My feet hurt. I want to go back to the apartment."

"Fine." Colin waved the waiter over to pay the cheque.

Franca stood. "I'm going on ahead. I'll leave the marked map for you. See you there."

Before he could address her, the waiter was there with the cheque. She set the street map down and hurried off.

Colin stopped in a little shop selling reproduction paintings of Renaissance work. The Plague masks, harlequin dominos, and fancy parade scepters hung from the low ceiling. He admired the deft brushwork in a *faux* Caravaggio, and picked up a small painting of a monk. He pictured it on the

73

wall in his library at home and bought it impulsively. The saleswoman handed him another painting and insisted he purchase it as well.

This painting was dark, with a scene of a woman having given birth, the baby swaddled beside her on the bed. The saleswoman explained that the midwives, nurses, and family surrounded the bed, lamenting the infant's death as the mother lay pale, in shock. A cat cried up at the bed and the eyes of a bird perched high in a cage gleamed sinisterly from the darkened corner. It was unpleasant and the last thing Colin would want.

"Take this one. Your wife, she will like it." The shop-keeper pushed the painting at him, her face grim, knowing.

"My wife likes modern art. She hates anything before the nineteenth century." He wondered why he was telling the shopkeeper. The woman spoke English well enough to sell to Americans, but getting into an art discussion was foolish.

"Yes, but this one is special. For her. It mean something for her. Take it. If she does not like, bring back. I give you money back."

Colin grinned. He knew Franca would hate it, but he took it, too.

Franca sat in the kitchen with a glass of wine. Colin set the wrapped paintings on the table.

"Do your feet feel better?" He felt hopeful. Glad.

"After a bottle of Chianti, everything feels better." She looked at the brown-paper wrapped paintings. "What did you buy?"

"Paintings. One for you, one for me. The woman who sold them to me insisted you would like this one, but I am not going to show it to you until the end of our trip. I want it to be the last of many anniversary gifts."

"Show me yours, then." She stood, sidled up beside him.

Colin showed Franca the monk. She knew immediately where he would put it in his library. Colin found it a little disconcerting that she didn't pressure him to see her painting. No matter, she seemed pleased for him.

"You know, this monk looks a little like you. The shiny pate, the long aquiline nose, the serious look." She elbowed him to show she was teasing. He was sensitive about losing his hair. "And my father would have loved it, too. Sometimes, I think I married you because he admired you so much. Your reverence for things of value, antiques and things. Not like me, my love of the modern, and the ephemeral, like her—my mother." She looked on the verge of tears.

"Admired me? We probably spent a total of twenty hours together in seven years."

"But my father hated small talk, insincerity, fatuousness. He was an excellent judge of character. Look at his empire, the people he chose to build it with him. You never engaged him in idle chit chat. Dinners we spent with him, you discussed antiquities, commodities; argued the merits of archaic standards, the definition of success. And you looked at me as if I was more than a beautiful, young, rich man's daughter. You talked about me as a partner, someone you delighted in. You never hit a false note with him. He trusted you with me implicitly. He told me that when I called and said you'd proposed. He said, 'Marry him, ciccina. He will take you wherever you need to be in life.' I think he thought you were like him, that you would take the time he never did with me."

Colin embraced her. "I love you." And she kissed him, suddenly. Hard.

They made love there, on the floor, scraping knees and bruising elbows, laughing and teasing each other. Venice was affecting her, him. The trip was turning out to have been a brilliant idea.

In the night, Colin felt Franca get out of bed. He rolled onto the warm sheets where she'd been sleeping and fell back asleep. When he woke up, she had not returned. The sun was glittering off the canal and reflecting onto the ceiling. It was morning.

Expecting her to be in the other bedroom, he padded in. One of the small beds had been turned down and it was clear she'd crawled into it in the early morning. He felt the sheets. Cold. He turned to the tall windows and saw that the curtains in the window of the apartment across the way were parted, open. One tall window in the long room where Franca had slept was open as well.

The daylight was dim, rusted golden. He went to the window and watched. He saw figures moving about deep in the room, but only guessed the white-haired old man was there. Colin's stomach growled. Breakfast seemed a good idea. Franca would be in the kitchen.

The table was left as it had been the night before, but the package with Franca's painting had been opened. The painting leaned against a candle-holder. Did that mean she'd liked it? Colin shouted out for Franca, but he got no response. Panic rushed through him, then he reminded himself how close they had been. Intimate. If she went out, she'd soon be back.

He made himself eggs with prosciutto and rosemary and one of the many cheeses they'd bought. He ate staring at the painting of the family in mourning, wondering if buying it had been a bad idea.

Two hours passed and Franca had still not returned. He went back up to the double room and stood by the tall window. Nothing happened for a long while. Then suddenly, he saw the old man. He was wearing a smoking jacket, puffing on a cigarette. He went right to the window and turned to face Colin. He grinned a little, as if he was listening to something pleasant, his eyes traveled off, gazing into the distance. Then he saw Franca behind the old man.

She came to the window and sat on the ledge. She was in a dressing gown, one Colin hadn't seen before, and her wavy hair was tied up, as if she was about to go into the bath. She spoke to the old man and he nodded twice. Colin leaned out the window and barked her name.

"Franca!" He waited for a reaction. None. He yelled again. Not even the old man responded. The panic he'd dismissed before filled him. How could she be less than five yards away with an open window and not hear him?

He dressed quickly and raced down to the ground floor and out onto the street. He searched for the door to the apartment directly across, but could find none. He guessed the entrance was on the other side and rushed down the street to the first left turn and began running. It seemed the street went on for far too long before he could turn left again. When he did, he found himself on a larger street facing a square near the Rialto. There were many entrances along the street, one to the fondamento that lead into an inner series of passages.

Once inside the tangle of tiny streets branching into dead ends and the canal on one end, Colin knew he was completely lost. He pictured the strong lines on the map Franca had laid out for them, back at the apartment. He had to get back and retrieve it. At least then he could see where these crazy little avenues lead. He turned to go back the way he'd come in.

It was a longer passage way than the one he'd just taken in, and it lead not onto the larger street and the Rialto, but into a dark alley behind a building. He hoped it was the building where the old man lived. He knocked on a door, rang the bell of the first building. No one answered. On to the next. A young dishwasher opened the door and Colin could see into the back end of a restaurant. The boy spoke little English.

Colin continued knocking, ringing, asking anyone who answered if an old man lived in the house. And Old Italian man, white hair. No one seemed to remember such a man. Desperation made Colin frantic. He asked one woman where the police were, but she found Colin's frenetic mention of officials disturbing and shut the door on him.

The sun was higher as Colin moved deeper into the maze of streets. He was sweating and crying. A German tourist asked him if he was lost. He nodded. The man pointed behind him and said, "San Marco, that way." Colin thanked him profusely and hurried in that direction.

Eventually he found himself in the square. The familiar billowing awnings, lunching tourists listening to the band, pigeons cooing calmed him. He could find his way back to the apartment from here. He felt suddenly silly, a fool. He was sure he had rushed out and missed a note Franca had left him somewhere. All of this mad hunting would have been for nothing. He headed back.

She was sitting on the bed with unwrapped packages; scarves hung over the metal foot board, a pair of red low-heeled shoes perched on a pillow. "God, you look awful."

Colin stared at Franca, incredulous. "I've just been all over Venice looking for you. I found you gone when I woke up. The painting . . . you'd opened it. *You were gone.* I saw you in the apartment across the way, but when I tried to find entry, there was none. So I . . ." He stopped when he saw she was busy examining a pair of earrings, unflapped.

"Oh, the hell with it. Why did I even come along? You aren't the least bit interested in sharing this with me, making this an anniversary trip. It's all about your family, and . . ." he pointed at the bed, "shopping!" He walked out of the room, then stuck his head back in. "I'm going to have a bath." As he turned back into the hallway, he saw she was looking at him strangely. As if she wasn't sure she'd seen or heard him at all.

He could hear her moving about, cooking, as he let the warm water soak into him. He felt shivery and full of unease. She called up to him twice offering wine. He ignored her, hoping she'd come up anyway. Finally, he got out, dried himself, and put on a pair of jeans and T-shirt.

Franca was sitting at the table, drinking wine and picking at a tampenade with some crusted bread. The painting he'd bought her was still propped up. She was staring at it.

"The woman at the shop said you would love this painting, but how she would know that I haven't a clue."

"I *do*. The two men standing by her bedside look like my father and grandfather. The woman in the bed looks like my mother. I can't see the infant. Is it me?" She sounded listless, far away.

"Really. I didn't look at it. I just bought it . . . I don't know why." He sat down beside her, poured himself a glass of wine.

When he really looked at it, he saw the more youthful face of Marino Guardini, and beside him, the white-haired old man; taller, not so lined, nor eyes so deep-set and rheumy. Colin had seen only photographs of Franca's mother. She'd left when Franca was ten, died when Franca was twenty years old, but the face did look much like her.

"Did the woman who sold it to you know my family?" Franca looked up at him, innocent, child-like.

"How could she, Franca? She didn't know me from any other tourist. She just made a smart sales move. She got me curious."

Franca blinked, touched her fingers to the painted surface. "I don't know . . . it's as if someone took a photograph of my mother when I was born and put my father and grandfather, grandmother there, then painted it."

Colin sensed Franca was going away from him again, her heart and mind bound to her family's past. The painting, which couldn't be of her birth, was triggering a freefall into a very dark place. Colin's throat closed, his breath went shallow.

"The child in this painting is dead, Franca. It might seem familiar, but it's . . . I don't know. Creepy as hell." He tried to suck in a deep breath. A strangled squeak came out.

She finished off her fourth glass of wine and calmly poured another, filled Colin's glass. "You've never heard the story of when I was born." She stood, held the painting against her waist. "They thought I was dead. My mother had lapsed into a diabetic coma during childbirth and I refused to emerge, so my grandmother had reached in and pulled me out. She thought she'd strangled me, or I was stillborn. The family gathered, thinking us both dead. I was wrapped in bunting and set beside her. Supposedly, my grand-father threw himself on the bed, put his hands on me and said a prayer in tongues. The midwife thought he was mad . . . tried to pull him off. When he let go of me, I cried. Loudly. My mother never felt a bond with me. Maybe it was the coma. She never recovered completely . . ."

79

Colin took the painting, put his arms around her. "I understand why this painting means something to you. But if it's going to depress you more, perhaps we should return it. The woman said she would give me back the money."

Franca growled, grabbing for the painting before Colin could set it down. "No! It's mine! I want to keep it. I don't care if it isn't my family, isn't real. There's something about it . . ."

Colin shook with the cold sweat running down his back, prickling his skin with gooseflesh. "Okay. It's yours."

They sat drinking late, neither much for conversation. Colin carried Franca to bed when it was clear she was too drunk to manage the stairs, but he couldn't fall asleep. The story of her birth, the painting that so accurately depicted it, frightened him. The foreboding of loss clenched his belly. And a nagging itch of fear grew as the minutes passed. Finally, he got up and wandered into the other bedroom, to the window. The apartment across the way was dark, the shutters closed. Relief.

He turned to the doorway. Franca spoke in her sleep.

"No. No! I won't go. I didn't die. I'm here. *Here.*"

He went to check on her, his heart thumping wildly. She was snoring, words going to gibberish. She tossed and turned. The room was redolent with the stink of their wine breath, sweat drenched with anxiety and sorrow. Reluctant to get back into bed with her, he went to the other room, pulled down the blankets and crawled in. He fell deeply asleep; so soundly, he missed the light going on across the street, slicing between the shutters, the amber glow bleeding into the street.

The first thing Colin sensed when he woke was the chilly air and the silence like total submersion in water. He had to mentally swim through it until he felt awake. He sat up. Two sharp yellow shards of light from the tall windows slashed across the bedroom, falling to the foot of the beds. He was compelled to follow them to the windows.

Pulling the blanket up around him, he rushed toward the mid-morning light, yanked the window open and leaned out. The air was sun-warmed. He looked into the facing windows, shutters open. Figures moved slowly, deliberately, as if staging for a play, finding their places. The old man stood at the window, his back facing Colin, his hand moving to unheard music, directing the scene. Colin blinked. Was that Franca holding something as she leaned against a table? Was that her father beside her? He shouted across the street.

"Franca!" A sob rose in his throat. When he said her name again, it was in a wail.

The old man turned; not as if he'd heard Colin, but casually, as if idly looking down onto the street. Colin froze. Would he see him, hear him? Colin was weeping now, wiping his face with the blanket. Then the old man locked eyes with Colin. He expected a malevolent sneer or maniacal laughter, but the old man smiled warmly and nodded. He said something, then turned away.

Colin ran from the window into their bedroom. He stared at the impression on their bed, the blankets curled and twisted to the side. He threw himself on it, put his face in her pillow, but her scent was not there. Looking about the room, he saw her backpack and case were missing. He threw on his jeans and T-shirt and rushed down to the kitchen.

There were no dirty dishes, no remnants of two people drinking wine, eating bread and cheese. He opened the small refrigerator. There was a bowl of grapes, two bottles of white wine, and some cheese, none of it from their grocery trip. Colin sat down at the table where both paintings still sat against the candlesticks, two stories being told.

Colin spent the rest of his stay in Venice searching the streets after the *polizia* seemed at first suspicious that his wife had gone missing, then mystified, and when they could find only a one-way ticket for a Franca Guardini-Tanner, sad for this pathetic man. Surely she had taken a lover and had planned to stay with him, not the husband. They assigned a phlegmatic detective to Colin's case, but he seemed to feel there was something not right with Colin.

Twice Colin thought he saw the old man with white hair. The second time, he approached, asked in a desperate panic where Franca was, but the old man spoke no English, seemed irritated by this stranger's questioning, and dismissed Colin with a wave of a silk handkerchief.

Colin retreated each night to the apartment and wept. He called his sister, told her what had happened, but by her response, Colin knew she thought he'd gone off the deep end. When he hung up, he believed, too, that he had. He stared at the paintings, wishing them gone and his wife's return.

The last night, he walked aimlessly, stopping at bridges, remembering how they had found a brief period of closeness. When he looked into the dark water, he saw her there, a peaceful Ophelia splayed just beneath the surface. Passing windows, he saw her beside him in his reflection—a ghost.

The shop where he'd bought the paintings seemed to appear where he stood. The woman inside was helping a tourist decide on a mask. He watched her. She turned, motioned for him to come inside.

He was paralyzed. All he could do was think about leaving in the morning without his wife. Perhaps, he thought, he couldn't go with her still missing. His hands shook. He felt feverish, stunned with grief. Then he walked into the shop, his body lighter, more sure.

Colin picked up a few paintings from the floor where they sat. There was one identical to his monk, only three times as large as his, a country villa surrounded by grape orchards, two of cats with wide wise faces. A large piece with smaller paintings leaning against it piqued his interest. He set the smaller paintings aside.

"You like this one?" She was behind him. The tourist had gone.

It was a family sitting around a dinner table holding wine glasses up in a toast. Food was heaped on plates; the room was just like the parlor across from Colin's apartment. Some of the faces were familiar. From the painter's vantage point, behind the people were the two long parlor windows of the rented apartment. Colin knelt down. In one of the windows behind the family was a man leaning out, wrapped in a blanket, his mouth open, calling out. It was Colin.

"That's . . . her family. Me, in the window." The woman touched his elbow. Her fingers felt hot, as if he'd leaned into an iron. He flinched away.

"You buy this painting, yes? It go with other paintings. Tell whole story."

Colin swallowed hard. Static filled his head. He shivered. It would make sense somehow. Someday. It had to.

"Yes," he told her, "I'll take it."

THE CAVE

BASIL COPPER

Basil Copper became a full-time writer in 1970. His first story in the horror field, "The Spider," was published in 1964 in The Fifth Pan Book of Horror Stories. *Since then, his short fiction has appeared in numerous anthologies, been extensively adapted for radio and television, and collected in* Not After Nightfall, Here Be Daemons, From Evil's Pillow, And Afterward the Dark, Voices of Doom, When Footsteps Echo, Whispers in the Night, Cold Hand on My Shoulder, *and* Knife in the Back.

Along with two nonfiction studies of the vampire and werewolf legends, his other books include the novels The Great White Space, The Curse of the Fleers, Necropolis, The Black Death, *and* The House of the Wolf. *Copper has also written more than fifty hardboiled thrillers about Los Angeles private detective Mike Faraday, and has continued the adventures of August Derleth's Sherlock Holmes-like consulting detective Solar Pons in several volumes of short stories and the novel* Solar Pons versus The Devil's Claw *(actually written in 1980, but not published until 2004).*

In the following tale, a walking tour of Austria leads to a terrifying encounter with something ancient and deadly. . . .

"Fear is a strange thing, and yet a comparative thing," said Wilson. "It means something different to you, something again to me. Temperament has so much to do with it; one man is afraid of heights, another of the dark, a third of the illogical in life."

The small group in the dining club stirred and gazed expectantly. Nobody answered. Encouraged, Wilson went on.

"In fiction anything to do with the illogical, the mysterious, or the macabre has to be stage-managed. The mise-en-scène is set about with darkness, storms, scudding clouds, and all the apparatus of the Victorian Gothick novella. Life isn't like that and fear often comes, as the Bible says, at noonday. And this is the most frightful type of fear of all."

I put down my newspaper and Pender followed suit. The half dozen or so of us in the room gathered about the big central mahogany dining-table, facing Wilson in his comfortable chair by the fire.

"I remember a particular instance which fitted no pattern imposed by logic," said Wilson, "and yet it was a perfect example of the terror by noonday. I had it at first-hand from an unimpeachable witness. It was simply that Gilles Sanroche, a middle-aged farmer, went stark-raving mad in the middle of a wheatfield, at noonday, in perfect August weather, on a hillside above Epoisses in Central France. It was not sunstroke, there was nothing in the field, and in fact the affair would have been an absolute mystery but for one thing.

"The man was able to babble about 'something in the wheat' and there were three witnesses who came forward to say that they had seen great waves of wind following a fixed pattern in the corn surrounding the unfortunate man. And there was no wind at all on the day in question."

Wilson paused again to see that his words were taking effect. No one ventured an opinion, so he resumed his apparently disconnected musings.

"There's a mystery for you, if you like. And what drove Sanroche insane in broad daylight on a beautiful day in a French cornfield has never been discovered. But the local people spoke of 'the Devil snarling and prowling in the wind' up and down the valleys, and in fact a mediaeval inscription speaks to that effect in one of the local churches.

"There is a germ of truth in the superstitions of these country folk and they talked, in a picturesque phrase, of the 'fence of the priesthood being thin' in that part of France. I was much taken with this simile, I must say; it was as though the physical presence of the clergy were spread in a living chain through the mountains and valleys of the country, literally fencing out the Devil.

"Whether the Devil actually appeared to Gilies Sanroche I have no idea; he may have thought he did. But there is no doubt in my mind that fear took away his sanity that hot August afternoon. In one of his stories some-where, de Maupassant strikingly illustrates the effect of fear on the human mind. He describes a night in a mountain hut—a night of appalling fear for the occupant—but dawn finds a logical explanation. The hideous face at the window was merely the narrator's dog and the remainder of the story was supplied by the atmosphere of the lonely hut and the man's own terror.

"I was greatly impressed with this story when I first read it as a young man," Wilson continued, "and I have often returned to it since, as it strik-ingly parallels an experience of my own—also in the mountains—which again, though unexplainable, communicated to me the most fearful sensa-tions of my life. The difference in my case being that though I myself saw or experienced very little in the way of concrete happenings, the facts underlying the experience were very terrible indeed, as subsequent events made clear."

There was by now a deep and expectant silence in the room, broken only by the hardly discernible crackling of the fire. Fender hastily passed the whisky decanter to me, refilled his own glass, and we then gave our undi-vided attention to Wilson who sat, one hand supporting his head, gazing fixedly into the fire.

"I had gone on the second of a series of long walking tours in the Austrian Tyrol," he said. "All this was many years ago. I was then a young man of about twenty-nine years, I should say; strong, well built, untiring after eight hours' walking over rough country. Sound in wind and limb in every way and not at all imaginative or given to morbid fancies or anything of that kind.

"I enjoyed long holidays in those days and I expected to spend at least two months in the exhilarating atmosphere of those great mountains. I was in good spirits, in first-class condition after three weeks' hard tramping, and in addition I was in the early stages of love.

"I had met the girl who was later to become my wife in Innsbruck the first day of my holiday, and when our ways parted a week later, I had arranged to meet her again some weeks after. In the meantime I intended to explore some of the more remote valleys and photograph the carvings in a number of the older churches.

"I had spent the greater part of one day slogging my way up an immense shoulder of foothill, stumbling on scree, and awkwardly threading up through dense forests of pine and fir. By late afternoon I became painfully aware that I had little idea of my whereabouts. The village I had been making for that morning should have been, according to my map, down the next valley but I could see nothing but the green tops of the pines marching to the horizon. It seemed obvious that I had passed the valley entrance in making my long circuit of the shoulder; I had little alternative than to press on farther up the hill or camp where I remained. I was ill-equipped for the latter; I had few provisions and not much more than a ground sheet and a couple of blankets strapped to my back.

"It did not take me long to make up my mind. There were quite a few more hours of daylight left and once I had quit the shadows of the forest and regained open country I should be walking in the sunshine. I decided to see what awaited me at the summit of the foothill; in the meantime I spent ten minutes resting, smoking, and admiring the view. I found half a packet of chocolate in my pocket and fortified by this went forward up the last half mile, if not with élan, at least with more cheerfulness.

"I was pleased to find with the thinning out of the trees at the top, that I had chanced on a small road which evidently led from one valley to another. It was little more than a cart track but nevertheless a heartening sign of civilization, and with the help of my map I was able to orientate myself. I soon saw where I had gone wrong and assumed, correctly, that the road I had found would take me over to the next village to the west of the one I had originally intended making for.

"I was glad to be out of the sombre gloom of the forest, and the upland road with its air of height and spaciousness, together with the sun which danced on the ground ahead of me, completely restored my spirits. I had walked for over an hour, and the road again began to descend into a valley, when I eventually saw the wooden spire of a tall church piercing the roof of the pines below me. A minute or two more and a sizeable community of thirty or forty houses spread itself out in the evening light.

"But as I descended to the village I caught sight of a large sign at the roadside: Gasthof. Set back from the road were heavy wooden gates, which were flung open. A drive corkscrewed its way upwards and a few paces round the corner I could see a large hotel of the chalet type, its pine construction gleaming cheerfully in the fading sunlight. The trim grass in front was kept in bounds by a blaze of flowers. The whole place had a magnificent view of the valley below and it was this, as much as the prospect of saving myself a walk, that decided me to put up here for the night.

"Though the accommodation would probably be expensive, it would be worth it for the view alone. Alas, for my hopes. A stout, Brünnhilde type of woman, her blonde hair scraped back in a large bun, who appeared in the hotel foyer in response to my repeated ringing at the outer door, shook her head. Nein, she said, the guesthouse was closed for the season.

"Here was a blow. Worse was to come. The woman, who seemed to be some sort of caretaker, explained in bad English, prompted by my halting German, that the hotels in the village were closed also—it was the end of the season. I could try but she very much doubted if I would be successful. There were only two hotels and she herself knew that the proprietor of one had closed and taken himself and his family off for their own holiday in Switzerland.

"By this time the woman had been joined in front of the hotel by a brace of savage wolfhounds, who kept up menacing growls. I was glad I had not encountered them in the grounds and said as much to the woman, who gave me a wintry smile. What was I to do, I asked. She shrugged. My best hope was to try one or two houses where families took in occasional boarders. I could obtain advice from the police station.

"I thanked her and was already retracing my footsteps along the drive when she recalled me with a word. She apologized; she didn't know what she had been thinking of. If I didn't mind another short walk in the forest she was sure Herr Steiner could offer me accommodation. It would be of a simple sort. . . . She shrugged again.

"She pointed out a path which twisted between the hotel flower beds and descended steeply through the inevitable pine trees. I gathered the place was half inn, half private residence, run by a middle-aged German couple. In the season it acted as a sort of overflow annex to the hotel, as it was only a quarter of a mile away, though quite secluded. Herr Steiner had an arrangement with the hotel over sending him guests; there was a monetary aspect and he was no doubt pleased of the extra custom for his own remote establishment. The woman apologized once again; she came from another district and was deputizing for her sister, otherwise she would have remembered the guesthouse earlier. I thanked her once more. She told me then that the road I had found earlier looped just before it reached the village and met Herr Steiner's establishment. I could either take the path from the hotel grounds or go along the road.

"I made my farewell and decided to take the road. The dark path looked uninviting, the sun was sinking, and the thin tinkling of water from far distances lent a melancholy aspect to the evening. Besides, I had no wish to meet the wolfhounds in some lonely clearing, so I waved the woman good-bye.

"In another five minutes I had descended the road, found the fork she spoke of, and then, a couple of hundred yards farther on, was rewarded by lights shining through the trees. It was now dusk and the noise of water was louder. I threaded a moss-grown path and saw a substantially built gasthof, of the traditional chalet pattern, with carved porch and vast, overhanging eaves.

"Herr Steiner and his wife Martha, the couple who owned the gasthof, were an amiable pair and made me welcome, late in the season though it was. The husband, a man of late middle age, tall, stoop-shouldered, with a drooping ginger moustache, was much given to sitting by the kitchen fire by the hour, reading all the news in the ill-printed local newspaper, holding up the sheet close to the eyes and studying the small print with the aid of a pocket magnifier.

"He seemed to go through every scrap of information it contained, including the small advertisements, and it was always with regret that he at last closed the lens with a snap, disappointed that there was nothing further to read. His wife was quite elderly, at least fifteen years older, I should have said, reserved and quiet. She flitted like a shadow in the background but nevertheless it was flitting to some purpose for her establishment was impeccably clean, the meals punctual and of excellent quality.

"I was only with the Steiners three days, but it did seem to me as though some trouble lurked at the back of Steiner's eyes, and once or twice I caught him, when he thought himself unobserved, in a curious posture, his newspaper dropped unnoticed to his knees, his head on one side, as though he were listening for someone or something.

"For in truth, though their establishment was within such a short distance of both the village and the more imposing establishment higher up the hill, it appeared both lonely and isolated, mainly due to the over-hanging hillside which cut it off from the main hotel, and to the thickly overgrown woodland with which it was surrounded.

"This made the place seem damp and melancholy, and on my first evening, pushing open the shutters of my bedroom window, the impression given by the falling of water from somewhere below, in the silence of the night, affected my heart with a profound sadness. In all other matters, how-ever, I saw nothing untoward. The Steiners were reasonably cheerful land-lords, the terms moderate, the food of the best, as I have said, and all in all I counted myself fortunate to have such a headquarters while I continued on my walks and explorations of the neighbourhood.

"I had proposed staying for a week, but events conspired to make this impossible, as you will see. On my first morning at the Steiners I set out soon after breakfast to reconnoitre the neighbourhood. I decided to leave the village until later and concentrated on the thick shelf of woodland on which the lower guesthouse was built.

"This ran slanting across the mountainside and eventually came out onto a cliff-like plateau. Below was a superb panorama of the village and the forests beyond; above, more forest and the uplands on which the large hotel stood. It was a day of bright sunshine and it was with considerable contentment that I left the last of the trees behind and was able to walk freely on mossy undersoil, split here and there by outcrops of rock. I wan-dered in this way for an hour or more until I at length came out on a pre-cipitous bluff and was rewarded by a magnificent view of the entire valley.

"It was as I was coming away, half drugged by the beauties of the scene, that my eye was arrested by a patch of bold colour in the landscape. This was unusual in this region of dark greens of pines and fir, and the russet hue irritated my mind, so that I turned aside my steps and went to see what it was. An unpleasant shock then, in that time and place, my thoughts quite unprepared for such a thing, to find that what had attracted my eye was the scarlet of blood.

"Great splashes and gouts were spread over the rocks and it was with considerable alarm that I followed a short trail. A few yards away, on the other side of a large boulder, lay the corpse of a young goat, evidently not long dead. I must say I looked about me with considerable unease, for I had at first thought the creature might have fallen from the rocks. I then plainly saw I had been mistaken and that the animal's throat had been torn out, and its breast viciously savaged.

"This was evidently the work of some large and dangerous animal, and I make no apology for stating that I broke off a heavy tree branch and armed in this fashion set back on my walk to the guesthouse. On the way I met a man, who from his dress seemed like a shepherd, and told him of my discovery. He went pale and swore at some length.

" 'We have been troubled with this beast for some time,' he said, so far as I could make out from his heavy German accent. He told me too that even cattle had been dragged off from herds in the vicinity over the past few months. He thanked me and said he would warn the municipal authorities.

"I was glad to arrive back to find the usual peaceful atmosphere in the guesthouse. My lunch was just coming up to the table, Herr Steiner as usual, reading by a fire which simmered in the great kitchen range.

"There being no other guests in the hotel, I chose to have my meals in the great beamed kitchen with the Steiners, and they were cheerful company in the evenings. My landlord had quite a good command of English, so conversation was not the strain it might have been for me.

"I set to with eagerness, for the walk had sharpened my appetite. The main course over, I sipped my beer contentedly, and fell into conversation with Herr Steiner. But when I mentioned the matter of the dead goat it had an unlooked-for effect. Steiner turned quite white and sat with his mouth open, staring at me. I was rescued from this somewhat embarrassing moment by a loud crash in the background. Frau Steiner had gone to fetch the dessert and there was the bowl shattered on the floor of the kitchen.

"What with apologies, moppings up, and the preparation of a fresh dessert, the incident passed over. When we again returned to it at the end of the meal, Steiner remarked, with an obviously simulated ease, that there had been some ravages among livestock by a beast which local hunters had so far failed to kill. He had been taken aback, he said, by the fact that the goat may have been from their own herd, but this could not be so as they were completely enclosed in the meadow below the house.

"I accepted this explanation, not wanting to appear over-curious, but I remained convinced in my own mind that Steiner was lying. The old couple's alarm was too great for such an incident as they had suggested, but the matter was their concern, not mine, and there I was prepared to leave it. But the business continued to fret my mind and after lunch, somewhat ashamed of my overprecipitate retreat from the area where I had found the goat, I set out to explore once again. On the way through the outbuildings surrounding the Steiners' establishment, I caught sight of the block where the old man had been chopping up firewood, and, almost without thinking, seized the small hand axe which stood on the block, and thrust it into my belt.

"It would make a useful weapon if need be and it boosted my morale no end. I eventually found my way back to the scene of my unnerving experience; the patch of blood was still there, dried and black in the sun, but the goat had disappeared, removed no doubt by the foresters. Or had the beast which killed it, disturbed by my appearance, hidden and retrieved its prey after I had returned to the inn? That was an even more disturbing thought and it was with a valour that surprised myself, that I took out my axe and started a circular search to see if the dead beast had been dragged off.

"I was not at first successful. The bleeding had stopped and there was only an occasional splash. But then I was rewarded by a wavering line in the dust, apparently made by the goat's hind legs. It had been dragged back in the direction it had already traversed in its dying struggles. I felt a slight tickling of the hair at the base of my neck when I saw these faint scratch marks, and I must confess I looked round me sharply in every direction and tightened my grip on the axe.

"Though I am no expert tracker, the marks seemed to prove that the beast concerned could not be a very big one, as it would otherwise have carried the goat clear of the ground. My experiences in India proved my point, for I have seen a tiger carry a full-grown bullock clear of the ground, its enormous strength capable of tremendous leverage, once its jaws were firmly fixed in the centre of the bullock's back.

"But nothing stirred in all the wide expanse of foothill, apart from the soft movement of the branches of the trees, and the sun continued to pour down onto a beneficent world. The scratching on the earth gradually ceased and eventually, when thick grass was reached, the trail petered out. But I had already noted the general direction in which the goat was being dragged and I continued to push on towards a region of cliffs and rocky outcrops in the distance as I felt the end of my search might well lie there.

"I had by now gone about two miles and when I eventually reached my destination the sun had sunk a considerable distance in the sky, though not enough to give me any anxiety, as there were several hours of daylight left. I felt I could remain on this spot about an hour and a half, for under the circumstances and not knowing with what type of beast I might be dealing, I judged it prudent to gain the inn over the long forest road while daylight lasted.

"And yet the end of my journey was almost an anticlimax. There was no sign of a trail, which had long disappeared, neither could I see any trace of the goat, as I studied the terrain from the pinnacle of a rocky hillock. I walked a little closer to the frowning cliffs facing me and after a while found myself in a small gorge. I gripped the axe tightly as I rounded the last corner and discovered it was a cul-de-sac. There was no trace of anything having passed, which was not surprising, as the valley floor was almost entirely composed of solid rock.

"I was about to retrace my steps when I spotted the dark entrance of a cave, half seen beyond the lip of a mountainous pile of boulders and rubble.

As I approached I saw that it was of vast size. The gloomy entrance went up perhaps forty feet into the solid cliff above, which ended in an overhang. In front of the cave was a belt of sand and I stood for a moment, shading my eyes, attempting to penetrate the deep shadow beyond. I could see nothing from where I stood.

"I hesitated a moment longer. There was no sound anywhere; not even a bird's cry broke the stillness, and the paternal sun shone blandly down, gilding everything in a limpid golden light. I grasped the axe again and then went forward in a rush, rather more hysterically than I had intended. This brought me almost to the cave entrance; the shadow lay not more than six feet away and with this proximity came a layer of dank air.

"It was a strange feeling, almost like stepping into a bath of cold water. The sun warmed my back but on my face and all the front of my body fell the dampness and mouldiness of decay. My last steps had also taken me to one side and I could now see the carcase of the goat lying half-in, half-out of the shadow. The head had been eaten, but the rest of the body was intact. I saw something else too; scattered in the gloom of the cave mouth were a few bones of small animals, morsels of flesh. I recognized a thigh bone of something and farther back a rib cage.

"Still militant, I went forward again and then my axe fell to my side. Once within the shadow, the clamminess and coldness completely enveloped me. I saw nothing more, nothing moved, but I sensed, rather than saw, that the cave went back to vast depths into the earth. And I knew then that I could not, to save my life, venture into it and retain my sanity. With this knowledge came relief. I was able to take four paces backwards—I dare not turn my back on the place—and once again stood in the freshness of the sunshine.

"It was then that I heard the faintest scratching noise from the interior of the cave and I realized with a certainty that something was watching me. My nerve almost snapped, but if I gave way to panic, it would be fatal. I had the strength and fortitude to retain my hold on the axe, my one frail defence against the terror that was threatening to master me, and step by step, walking backwards I progressed from that sinister place into sanity.

"I had got almost to the area where the grass met the first rocky outcrops some hundreds of yards away, and a ludicrous sight I must have been to any observer, when there came the final incident which broke my nerve. It was nothing by itself, but it seemed to paralyze my will and send a scalding thrill of terror down into my entrails.

"From somewhere within the area of the cave came a low, dry, rasping cough—it wasn't repeated and there was nothing exceptional about it—but the terrible thing to me was, that it was like the furtive, half-stifled throat clearance of a human being. Something went then; I could not face that sound again and I whirled on my toes and flailing with the axe before me I ran for my life, with stark fear at my heels, until the blood drumming in my head and the wild thumping of my heart at last forced me to collapse onto a rock half a mile from the area I had just quitted.

"The sun was by now a good way down the sky. Nothing had followed me, but I still had a longish walk through the forest, so after a short breather I set out again, albeit more sedately, until I at last came to the inn and the safety of my own room.

"I was late down to supper that evening. I had debated long with myself over the wisdom of revealing what I had discovered to the Steiners. Their reactions of the morning had been so extreme that I feared what might be the outcome. In the event I waited until Frau Steiner had retired, then I tackled her husband. He sat smoking his pipe in the kitchen as usual, politely waiting until I had finished my after-dinner brandy, so that he could clear away.

"Though his face turned an ashen colour, he was surprisingly calm and we discussed for some time the implications of my discovery. He told me that he would let the civil authorities know the following morning; no doubt they would arrange for a shoot to take place if the depredations among goats and cattle continued. I had naturally made nothing of the more sombre side of the matter. I merely told him I had found the cave and that it did seem to me that it might be the lair of the beast responsible for cattle killing.

"But there still remained the problem of Herr Steiner's manner. Both he and his wife had given me the impression that they were well aware of the strange and sinister creature that was taking such a toll of the livestock; that they were secretly afraid and they themselves had no intention of initiating any action against it. It may have been, I felt, turning it over in my mind yet again in my bedroom later that evening, that they had a similar experience to myself. Remembering the incident of the cave and the whole atmosphere of these dark and stifling woods, I could not say that I particularly blamed them.

"Anyway, it was no business of mine; I was merely a passing stranger and expected to be on my way shortly. Though I was extremely comfortable at their inn, I had had my fill of walking recently and was inclined to linger. It was pleasant to know, as one trudged back in the twilight of these great woods, that a pleasant meal was awaiting one, with friendly faces and a good bed assured. Fortified by these and similar thoughts I soon slept.

"Next morning I decided to take a stroll down into Grafstein; it was similar to a thousand other small villages of its type scattered about Central Europe—a huddle of timbered homes, a small central *platz,* the whole thing pivoting on the large, splendidly carved fourteenth-century church, the town hall, the two hotels, and an arcade or two of shops, some unfortunately modernized to take advantage of the tourist trade.

"While I was in the village I enjoyed a really excellent coffee and pastries at the only coffee shop and then called in at the small police station. Here I reported the matter of the goat and the cave to the local sergeant. He thanked me for my cooperation, and I showed him the location on his large-scale map, but I did not gather from his manner that the matter was regarded as of any great importance, or that anything would be done about it in the immediate future. This sort of thing was a commonplace in the forests thereabouts, he told me.

"I looked in at the church before going back to my own guesthouse for lunch. I had brought my camera and busied myself by taking some closeups of the really magnificent carvings; the pastor was away, I was told, but I had readily obtained permission from his housekeeper, for the small intrusion my photo-making would incur. The skill of these old carvers, most of them anonymous, was really incredible, and once more I was thrilled and uplifted by the beauty and elaboration of their work.

"I finished the spool in my camera with half a dozen shots of the finely carved details of the front row pews, immediately facing the altar. They represented, so far as I could make out, scenes from the Book of Job, but one of them gave me something of a shock. It was a most unpleasant carving, of most exquisite workmanship, but the result was malevolent and forbidding in the extreme. I expect you all remember the gargoyles on Notre Dame and the way these old stone-masons had given vent to their expression of the powers of darkness that surrounded them.

"Well, this was something of the same kind, but intensified for me a hundredfold. It may have been the darkness and quiet of the old church, but I found my hands trembling as I went to set up my camera for a time exposure. The carving represented some disgusting creature with a misshapen head; incredibly emaciated, it stood erect, most of its body mercifully hidden in what I took to be reeds or grasses.

"Its long neck was disfigured by large nodules of immense size, the teeth were curved and sharp, like a boar, the eyes like a serpent. In its two, clawlike hands it held the body of a human being. It had just bitten off the head, much as one would eat a stick of celery, and the carver had cleverly managed to suggest that the creature was in the process of spitting out the head before making a start on the meal proper.

"I cannot tell you what nausea this loathsome creature inspired in me; it seemed almost to move in its frame of dark wood, so brilliantly had the carver, an artist of some genius, depicted his subject. In the flat terms which I have just used, it is impossible to convey my impressions of that moment.

But loathsome or not, I knew that I had to have the carving on film and that when I returned to England I should want to find out more about it.

"So I hastily completed my preparations for the picture, pressed the catch, and waited for the clicking of the time-exposure mechanism to cease before dismantling my tripod and equipment. As the mechanism died and the exposure was made, there was a loud noise somewhere at the back of the church. This startled me for some reason, but I thought that perhaps the verger, or whatever his German equivalent might be, had come in to see that all was well.

"However, the interruption caused me considerable unease and I hastily packed up my gear and made my way back up the aisle of the church and into the open air. To my surprise, there appeared to be nobody else in the building, neither could I see any reason for the noise. Nothing appeared to have fallen down in the church; but I was late for lunch and hurried out of Grafstein and back to my hotel.

"During the afternoon I wrote some letters and apart from a short excursion down to the village to post them in the early evening, did nothing else of note that day. I lay down in my room for an hour or two before supper; when I got up again it was quite dark and I felt I had overslept. But a glance at the luminous dial of my wristwatch was enough to reassure me that the time was only half-past eight. We did not eat usually until nine or half-past, so I had plenty of time.

"I had not switched on the light and I stood at the window for a moment, looking down into the valley. It was a beautiful moonlit night and the pine forests spread out below me, with the spire of the church sticking up far beneath, looked like an old cut by Dürer.

"I was about to turn away when I heard the big sheepdog of the Steiners start barking down at the side of the hotel; I opened the window and looked out, but could see nothing. The dog was still growling, and then I heard the faintest crackling rustle in the undergrowth surrounding the hotel. The dog did not follow the noise but suddenly began to make a high, howling whine and then I heard Steiner come out with curses and cuff the dog, shouting to it to go back indoors.

"The noise continued for a few moments, farther away now, a faint abrasive, sinister rustling like someone or something making its way with definite aim and purpose. It slowly passed away over the ridge and the night was silent again. Considerably troubled about this, though I could not really say why, I eventually made my way down to supper.

"The meal, as usual, was excellent, and sitting in the warm, high-beamed kitchen with the firelight dancing on gleaming brass and pewter, I once again counted myself fortunate in my accommodation and we passed a jolly evening. Tonight, for some reason or other, I had spread out on another part of the huge central table my route maps, notes, and other material for my research, and after supper it was my wish to continue work on this.

"It was now about half-past ten and I busied myself in clearing up the material, preparatory to taking it up to my room. Frau Steiner had gone to bed, but my host, who as usual remained with me to smoke and read his paper, would have none of this.

" 'Work there,' he said jovially, motioning me to leave my things where they were. I protested that my notes and route-preparations might take me until midnight. He merely said that he was going to bed anyway and that if I would see that I switched off the lights before I came up, I could stay there as long as I liked.

"This suited me nicely. The autumn nights were chilly and the warm atmosphere of the kitchen was preferable to that of my own room; apart from this, Herr Steiner pushed a plate of cakes and sandwiches, together with half a bottle of beer towards me, giving me a broad wink as he left. Thus it was that I came to be working in the kitchen of the Gasthof on that night, the only person on the ground floor.

"The dog was locked up somewhere in the outbuildings at the rear and to all intents I was alone in the world. One curious feature of the establishment was the fact that the kitchen door was never locked, winter or summer, as long as the Steiners were in residence. The main entrance and a door on the other side of the guesthouse were scrupulously locked every night, but for some reason, the kitchen door was excluded from this.

"It was true, it faced the main road and the village rather more conveniently than did the hotel entrance proper, though I could not quite see the point of this. The real explanation that offered itself to me was that the only means of securing the kitchen door was by a massive baulk of timber which fitted into two metal clips set either side of the door frame. Possibly because of the trouble involved in lifting this into place every night and removing it each morning, the Steiners had let the custom lapse. And for some other reason they had omitted to have the door fitted with an ordinary lock.

"Anyway, there I was, working away quietly, enjoying the warmth of the fire and the simple excellence of the food and the beer. I completed my notes and had got well on with the details of my route for the next part of my holiday. By this time it was approaching midnight and I had begun to feel a certain tiredness coming on.

"I stretched myself and went to poke up the kitchen range fire into a blaze again, when I became aware of a faint noise. I listened intently. The sound did not emanate from inside the inn but from the outside. It was too subtle to make out at first. It was not the tinkle of running water nor the footsteps of a passing villager. I looked at my watch again and realized it was far too late in any case for these simple folk, who sought their beds early, to be about.

"Walking on tip-toe, so that I could still hear perfectly—though why I did this was somewhat obscure to me—I crossed the kitchen and stood near the window. The noise came again, a moment or two later, unpleasantly like the rustling I had heard in the wood earlier, when looking from the upstairs window.

"I do not know if you can picture my situation, and it is a difficult scene to recapture, sitting as we are in the middle of London this evening. The rustling, or scratching, call it what you will, was agonizingly slow and deliberate, and it came to my mind that it would be similar to that made by a badly crippled person walking with the aid of two sticks. There was a moment of silence, followed shortly by the scratching noise, like two sticks being dragged painfully across the ground. At that moment, the dog gave an agonizing howl from the back of the hotel somewhere.

"That just about finished me, I can tell you, tensed up as I was. Far from being a reassurance, it meant that the dog knew there was something foul and unnatural outside which wanted to get in. As this thought came to me, I looked wildly at the door, with the obvious intention of locking it. I am not normally a nervous or timid sort of man, but something had got hold of me that evening and I was not my usual self.

"The baulk of timber was obviously too big and heavy to manoeuvre into place without a lot of noise, and besides, something kept me rooted to the spot, so that I seemed incapable of action.

"The electric light still burned on, comfortingly modern, etching everything in bright relief. I had stood to one side of the window, so that my shadow could not be seen, but I felt that whoever—whatever—was outside, very well knew who was there. And I would not, for any money you can name, have turned out the light, for reasons too obvious to go into.

"As the scratching noise was repeated, and, as it seemed to my hypersensitive nerves, even nearer, I looked around again for a weapon of some sort, but without success. There was a long moment of silence and then, from outside the house, came the foul, low sort of snuffling cough I had heard in the cave. The dog gave another whine that set my jagged nerves aflame and there was a creak as the big old wooden latch of the door commenced to lift.

"I was galvanized into action then. I did not know what might be outside but I only knew that I should become insane if I met it face to face. I threw myself at the door and put all my weight on the latch, forcing it downwards. The pressure was not resisted, but a moment or two later I found it rising, with irresistible force. For a horrifying second or so the door actually opened an inch, perhaps two, then with the strength of fear I hurled it closed and clung to the latch with all the weight of my body.

"Once more I felt it being raised, despite all I could do to stop it. But now I had got my feet jammed against a brick in the irregular stone floor and I exerted all my strength to prevent what was outside from coming in. I was still terribly afraid but something of that first appalling fear, which saps all will power from the brain, had left me, and as I was forced fractionally back, I cast looks about me for aid.

"Then I saw the beam lying in the angle of the wall, not more than four feet from me. I crashed the door back into its framework, and jamming my foot against the bottom, I seized the huge piece of wood and with the strength of terror man-handled it towards me. My foot slipped on the floor as the door pressed in on me, and the end of the beam, rasping across the kitchen wall, upset a large brass warming pan which fell down to the stone floor with a tremendous crash. I think this is what saved the situation, for hitherto this insidious struggle in which I had been engaged, had been fought implacably, in silence.

"The door gaped wide for a moment, but then the dog, aroused by the crash commenced barking angrily; and at the same instant Herr Steiner, woken by the noise, shouted down the stairs. Light sprang on in the upper-storey, and as the pressure on the door melted away I fell against it and slammed the beam home in the metal stanchions with almost hysterical strength. Then I fell onto the kitchen floor, all the purpose gone from my legs.

"I will not weary you with the scene that followed; the amazed and ter-rified appearance of the Steiners; the temporary insanity of the dog; the pouring of brandy down my throat; my disconnected story to the innkeeper and his wife. Needless to say none of us slept for the remainder of the night; we piled the heaviest furniture we could find against all three doors—even this took considerable resolve under the circumstances—and it was as much as I could do to carry out my part of the undertaking.

"Never have I felt such fear as I encountered that night; it turned my limbs to water, sapped all my willpower; it took all the strength of character I possessed to double-rivet my soul back into my body, if you can understand such a term. After I had recovered myself a little—a false recovery, as it turned out, engendered largely by the brandy—Steiner and I secured all the doors and windows, as I have said. Then we retired to the topmost room of the house, leaving every light in the building burning. Steiner had the excellent idea of scattering the staircase with copper pans and utensils, so that we should have prior warning of anything moving towards us up the stairs.

"He then took three enormous sporting rifles—one more like a blunder-buss—with him, and we all three locked ourselves in the bedroom with the stoutest door. We had more than four hours to wait until dawn—it was by now about half-past one—but since the commotion in the kitchen when I fell to the ground there had mercifully been no further sound from out of doors.

"We passed a wretched time, talking in half-whispers and starting at the slightest sound outside—from the night wind to the faint tapping of a branch upon a topmost windowpane. After my explanation, we did not refer directly to the situation, but approached it by oblique routes, and I was more than ever convinced that the Steiners knew more than they were willing to tell.

"Once I heard his wife mumble, 'But they have never come this far before,' and then her husband clamped his hand over her arm and she lapsed into silence. For my part, I was alone with the terrible truth of the situation; for which among God's creatures has the wit and intelligence to lift a door latch in the manner of a human being? An ape or monkey perhaps? Perhaps. But ridiculous to think of such a thing in these forests.

"Another type of animal such as a deer might lift a door latch by accident, when its horn caught underneath, but the thing which had been on the other side of the door had lifted the catch easily, much as a human being would; and there had been a terrible force and purpose in the pressure which had accompanied that silent and sinister incursion into my reason. And I had been convinced from the beginning that no human being was responsible.

"I gave it up at last and slept brokenly, sitting in a corner of the room, my back against the wall, my head on my upraised knees, clutching one of Steiner's antiquated rifles. Dawn came at about six o'clock, and though I was not awake to see it, when I did become aware of it I have never been so thankful, not even during the war years. The sounds of everyday came up to us with increasing clarity; the chant of a rooster, the grunting of pigs, the little, fussy noises of hens, and then, eventually, the reawakened bark of the old sheepdog, his fears of the night dispersed.

"But it was not until past seven o'clock, that we dared stir downstairs. We first opened windows on every side of the house but could see nothing alarming. Then a creaking farm cart passed, with a man riding on top and another walking by the shafts, and this shamed us so much, particularly as the Steiners were usually abroad looking after their livestock before six, that we all three went downstairs at once, albeit we were talking and making rather too much noise.

"The lights still burned, the copper pans were undisturbed; all was as it had been, even down to the unquestioned fact of the warming pan which I had knocked down in my superhuman efforts to get the door barred. While the Steiners set the kitchen to rights and prepared the breakfast, I mustered my courage to unbar the door and set foot outside. I must say that I waited until I heard the approach of another cart, and then with a sort of tottering bravado hefted the massive beam to the ground and stepped out into the sunlight.

"My nightmare of the evening before might never have been. I breathed in the fresh morning air, said good-day to the two fine fellows on the cart, and then received my second shock of the last twelve hours. There had been no fantasy in the strength which had resisted mine an inch-door panel away from me, and neither was there in the curious prints of the thing which had stood without the door. I stumbled and almost fell.

"Picture if you can, the prints which met my eye that autumn morning in the foothills of those Alps. I am certain that little similar has been seen since the dawn of time. There was nothing more than two holes which stood before the door. The impressions, which were quite small, were about six inches apart. They looked more like the imprints of the ferrules of a walking stick, except that they were both slightly elongated and oval in shape. I stared at these two slots in the ground until I thought I should go mad.

"No God-created beast could have made such imprints, and as I fell back from the door I saw that there were further sets; advancing to and retreating from the inn back along the forest path I had taken on my walks to the area of the cave. Faint scratch marks linked the sets of prints."

There was a long silence in the room, as Wilson broke off his narrative and sat looking into the depths of the fire.

"The prints of a deer, perhaps?" Pender eventually suggested nervously, as Wilson showed no sign of resuming his story.

He shook his head impatiently. "Impossible. I know the slots of a deer, man, as well as I know my own face in the glass. I said the prints were complete sets of two; in other words the thing, or whatever it was, was standing on its hind legs—or its only legs for all I know—while attempting to open the door.

"I followed the tracks back for a short way, a very short way, for they gradually faded out. And then perhaps I did a rather foolish thing, in the light of what happened afterwards. For in a fit of angry panic I went down the path and deliberately erased the last trace of those devilish tracks with my heavy walking boots.

"However, I felt I owed a very real duty to the Steiners and I spent most of the morning trying to dissuade them from stopping at the inn; I even tried to give them hints about the tracks I had seen, but the words wouldn't come properly. Naturally, the old couple wouldn't dream of giving up their home of a lifetime to move away at their age.

" 'But, Herr Wilson,' said the old man, 'be reasonable. It is our living.' He had quite a point there, but it didn't dissuade me from asking them to go, for I was mortally afraid for the couple. They had been extraordinarily kind to me in the short time I had known them. But I saw it was no use in the end, though I did suggest that they buy a couple of wolfhounds like those at the hotel above and—before all—have a good set of bolts fitted to the kitchen door.

"Steiner almost gave himself away at the last for he looked at me almost as though he would burst into tears, and said. 'Bolts are no good, in the end, against such things.' Then he saw the look on his wife's face and became silent; it was his last word on the topic and he never referred to it again. Naturally. I had no desire to remain any longer at the Gasthof where I had passed such a night; I had packed in the morning. The Steiners quite understood, but it was with a heavy heart that I said good-bye to them in the early afternoon, shouldered my rucksack, and set off through the forest once again.

"I made one last attempt before I left and said, 'At least see that the village mounts a hunt and cleans out that cave.' He looked at me in a sorrowful manner and waved good-bye. His last words to me were, 'Thank you, mein Herr. We know you are only trying to be helpful.' I had rerouted my trail, to pass at least eight miles to the west of the cave, so I set off down into the village and resumed my walking tour, the remainder of which was uneventful—insofar as it touches the core of this story, that is."

Wilson paused again and silently drained his glass. "You need not worry that I shall leave the story unfinished," he said. "There is a sequel and a terrible one, though by rights I should have left the thing where it was. But all the rest of my holiday I kept thinking about the old couple, the loneliness of the guesthouse, that cursed cave and the nature of the events which had given me such a dreadful night.

"I made the mistake of going back and thereby added guilt to my remembered fear, I made a slight detour on my way home to England and stopped off for a day on the way through. I was accompanied by three other people who don't concern the story, though one, as I have indicated already, was to concern me for the remainder of my life. I left them at the cafe and walked up the well-remembered hill to the hotel. On the way I met the sergeant of police and a lot of activity; cars and so forth coming down.

"I asked him what was the matter and he said, quite quietly and simply, that the old couple had been murdered; in the most brutal and sadistic fashion imaginable. They had been literally torn to pieces after barricading themselves in a bedroom, and—most foul detail of all—had been decapitated; the heads were never found. I thought of the carving in the church and felt sick. This terrible event had happened only two days before; the forests had been combed, but to no avail. We had by this time walked back down to the small police station, for I now had no wish to continue up the hill. I thought of the events of three weeks earlier and began in my mind the first of a hundred thousand regrets.

"And yet I was angry with the police, and the Steiners too, if I analyzed my own feelings; I asked the sergeant, rather roughly in the circumstances, whether he had taken my advice about the cave. Had they, in fact, organized a shooting party to kill the beast that I supposed lurked within it? The beast that might, in fact, be responsible for the Steiners' death?

"He looked at me stammering, his face quite pale. Nothing had been done, of course; the matter had been entirely overlooked—the village and the police particularly, had the murders to think of. But with typical German efficiency he immediately set about organizing a hunting party and two hours later a heavily armed posse of about forty expert shots streamed out of the village.

"I should have gone with them, but somehow I could not face it; the death of the Steiners had quite knocked me out; but we—that is, myself and my three friends—were put up for the night by one of the village families. The party, who, of course, knew the cave area well, returned long before nightfall. The sergeant, when I saw him again, was curiously reticent. It was, he said, a bad place.

"The men had not ventured far beyond the entrance; the labyrinth stretched for miles, they had been told; they were fetching dynamite in the morning, and an Army expert over from the garrison town, to block the entrance. He looked at me apologetically, as though I were about to accuse him and his colleagues of cowardice. But I could not say I blamed him. Had I not done exactly the same? And that is what they did. Brought down the entire mountainside and bottled in the thing or whatever it was; I kept in touch by letter and so far as I can learn the countryside has remained untroubled."

Wilson broke off once more to recharge his glass. "Which brings the wheel full circle," he said. "The problem of fear. Fear such as I have never experienced in my life, and which I could not possibly face again. To this day I could not tell you why. Yet I saw nothing, unless you count two slots in the ground. And I felt little, except that tremendous pressure on a door; I heard little, except a muffled cough and some faint scratchings in the night. Little enough for a student of the macabre. Yet something devilish killed the Steiners."

"And you know nothing beyond that?" queried someone else, who sat in shadow beyond me.

"Only theories," said Wilson, lifting his head in the brindled firelight. "I developed my rolls of film when I got back home. All were perfect except one, inside the church, which was a complete blank, with never a trace of a picture. And I am sure you will know the picture I mean. But if my theory is correct it would explain their attitude."

There was a long silence again.

Then, "Pass the brandy, Pender," I said, rather more sharply than I had intended.

SURVIVAL OF THE FITTEST

SCOTT EDELMAN

Scott Edelman (the editor) currently edits both Science Fiction Weekly, *the Internet magazine of news, reviews, and interviews, and* Sci Fi, *the official print magazine of the Sci Fi Channel. A former editor of* Science Fiction Age, Sci-Fi Entertainment, Sci-Fi Universe *and* Sci-Fi Flix, *he has been a four-time Hugo Award finalist for Best Editor.*

Scott Edelman (the writer) has published more than fifty-five short stories in magazines and anthologies such as The Twilight Zone, Science Fiction Review, Fantasy Book, Crossroads: Southern Tales of the Fantastic, MetaHorror, Moon Shots, Mars Probes, *and* Forbidden Planets. *Upcoming stories will appear in the anthologies* Aim for the Head, A Dark and Deadly Valley *and* The Mammoth Book of Monsters, *plus the magazine* PostScripts. *He has twice been a HWA Bram Stoker Award finalist in the category of Short Story.*

"My wife and I went to the Galapagos Islands in 2001," recalls Edelman, "having made plans that we were going to fulfill that particular life-long dream as a way to celebrate our 25th anniversary.

"Once there, I came as close as I'm ever going to get to visiting a prehistoric world. I was surrounded by dozens of species that exist nowhere else on Earth. A number of the scenes from 'Survival of the Fittest' have been snatched from memories of that trip, and I hope to go back again

someday to gather new memories, and who knows, inspiration for a future story."
Sometimes we can't let go, even after death. . . .

As Marc headed toward a landing on Española Island, a wave thrust his rubber raft skyward, almost spilling him into the sea. He tumbled back, and the stretch of beach strewn with boulders momentarily vanished from view. A woman sitting across from him had to drop her camera bag onto the bottom of their zodiac and grab his shoulder to keep him on board.

As she steadied him, he thanked her with words that were only partially coherent. He grasped more tightly at the rope that ringed the lip of their raft, and became aware that his face had suddenly flushed from more than just the Galapagos sun. He hadn't yet gotten used to being touched since Melissa had died, and the sudden contact had surprised him more than his near capsizing.

He looked away from their guide, Rafael, and the other eight tourists with whom he was squeezed in the zodiac, and gazed back at the ship anchored behind them. That would help him avoid having to speak further to the woman, or so he hoped. She seemed pleasant enough, with a welcoming smile and bright eyes that seemed slightly startled, whether or not she was, but it wouldn't do for him to get distracted from his purpose here. He stared up at the frigatebirds who paced them, hoping she'd turn away from him.

Which meant that when their raft touched the shore, it came unexpectedly. Melissa would have been amused. She'd often told him that he always seemed to be looking back from where he'd come rather than ahead to where he was going. As the bottom of the raft bumped gently where the water stopped and the beach began, Marc had to wave off another one of the woman's outstretched hands.

He scrambled into shallow water that almost reached his knees and walked several yards up to where the sand was warm and dry. Rafael handed him a towel from a waterproof sack, and as Marc rubbed his legs, he realized that the lumps he'd earlier seen scattered along the beach had not been boulders. They began to move.

The closest sea lions turned lazily to gaze at him, their necks elongating as they sniffed him out. Hundreds of them were dripped along the sand, dotting the shore until it curved away out of sight.

Rafael led their small group along that beach, leaving behind others who were climbing out of the next rafts that followed to make landings behind them. He reminded them of how they were supposed to behave, relating the rules they'd all been told at the previous night's welcome dinner. Their group was supposed to stay together, always either landward or seaward of the creatures, as sea lions got nervous if they thought themselves surrounded. No matter how cute they seemed, never attempt to touch them, lest you pass your scent on to a pup and the mother then abandons it. Beware the aggressive beach master, the huge bull who would charge to protect his herd if he sensed they were being threatened.

As they walked along, following exactly where Rafael led to avoid disturbing the nests of turtles and birds, the other tourists discussed these rules, and shared what they knew of the life cycle of sea lions. So many facts filled the air that the guide almost seemed unnecessary, except as a presence to shame them into their best behavior.

Marc had nothing to contribute. He'd arrived among these islands unprepared, and couldn't even recall what little they'd been told during their crash course the night before.

He'd never thought of himself as an ignorant man, but the other passengers made him feel like one. It wasn't their fault, or even his. He was just never meant to be in this place. This trip was not a fulfillment of his dream; it had been Melissa's, always and only Melissa's. But still, he blamed himself for not having tried to understand her dream better before embarking on it for himself. All he understood were his own unwelcome dreams, the ones that had begun not long after her death, and what those dreams represented.

He paused and let the group pull away from him, stopping to watch a particularly huge blob of a sea lion attempt to roll over. It wriggled clumsily, sand crystals sparkling down its length. It truly didn't care that he was there, and that amazed him. Melissa had always told him that the Galapagos Islands were as close as one could get in this life to the Garden of Eden. Maybe it could have been that to him once, if they'd come here together, but now that she had been taken from him, it no longer held out that kind of promise.

"They're beautiful, aren't they?"

Marc turned to see that the woman who had righted him on the raft was standing just behind him. He nodded, not knowing quite what to say.

"They may look clumsy now," she continued, "but in the water, it's like they're doing ballet. You'll see."

Marc looked ahead self-consciously to the rest of the group from which they'd become separated, then felt ridiculous at his nervousness. He owed it to Melissa to continue acting as if she hadn't taken his soul with her.

"I'm afraid that once I get into the water," he said, "you'll find that I'm just as clumsy as I am now."

"My name is Barbara," she said, her smile returning.

"I'm Marc," he said.

"Nice to meet you, Marc," she said, and held out her hand. He hesitated taking it, but before his indecision could become too obvious, a shout came from where the rest of the group had clustered. Rafael was waving the two of them forward, and pointing to what seemed to be a dark smudge at his feet.

"I guess we should see what that's all about," said Marc, turning away from Barbara with a sense of relief.

When he caught up with the others, he found them ringed around a low, bloody mound about a foot and a half in diameter. Rafael told them that it was a placenta, and that since it hadn't yet been pecked into invisibility by birds, that meant the mother and her pup were surely close by. He instructed them all to spread out and to keep their eyes open.

"Isn't this exciting?" asked Barbara.

Others lifted binoculars to their eyes, or framed the vista with their cameras, and Marc had brought neither. Yet he was the one who spotted the pair first, hidden where they had crawled behind the short grass that lined the beach. He didn't speak up to alert the others, just walked slowly and quietly up to them and watched. The mother lay on her back, exhausted, while the pup wriggled franticly against her in search of a nipple. As with the other sea lions Marc had seen so far, neither cared that he was there. Humans appeared to be like air or water to them.

He knelt in the grass, and stared into the mother's moist eyes from no more than a yard away. Did she know, he wondered, how lucky she was to be alive, how lucky she was that her child had survived? He doubted she had that capacity. Most humans even lacked it, treating a successful birth as a certainty instead of as a gift.

The pup finally found a nipple just as the others caught up with him. They murmured, oohing and aahing while Rafael related the facts of life as they existed in the Galapagos, but Marc barely heard what they had to say, lost as he studied the mother and child, lost as well with the mother and child he himself had lost. He didn't pull away from the spectacle until Melissa rested her hand on his shoulder and gently asked him why he was crying so.

He stood abruptly, shrugging off her touch. He couldn't think of any answer that would make sense, so he walked quickly and silently back to the rafts that were shuttling those who'd had enough for the day back to what would be their home for the next week. He sat on the sand and awaited his rescue, staring off at the tiny ship in the distance, a ship that until the day before he had known only from the brochures Melissa had been showing him for years, brochures to which he had paid too little attention until it was much too late to matter.

That night, instead of lingering in his cabin as he had during meals ever since the ship had pulled away from Baltra to begin their visits to the smaller islands, and only eating at the last moment when the dining room was about to close so he could avoid too much contact with the other passengers, he left his cabin just as dinner began and the first crush of people arrived. He spotted Barbara from across the room and approached her before anyone else could.

"May I?" he asked, pointing at the empty seat beside her. She was alone at a table meant for four. She seemed surprised to see him. Or maybe, he reminded himself, that was just her eyes.

"Certainly," she said. Her smile, when it appeared, changed her face, making her look younger.

Marc sat, and decided he needed to speak quickly, just in case others did decide to join them. He owed her an apology, which were difficult enough without an audience.

"About this morning," he said.

She stopped him with the touch of her hand to his.

"No need to say anything more," she said. "I know what it's like when you've been alone too long. You can sometimes forget what it's like to be with other people."

"How do you know that?" he asked.

"Do you think I'd have empty chairs around me if I didn't know?" she said. "I know. I've had losses of my own. I'm like you, Marc. It was Marc, wasn't it?"

He pulled his hand away, ostensibly to spread the napkin on his lap and straighten the silverware.

"I don't feel as if it's been too long," he said, remembering the most recent dream of the night before, filled with Melissa's disappointed eyes, and her angry words. "I don't know that I'll live long enough for it to ever seem too long."

"I know," she said, but Marc knew by her words, by her concerned yet impossibly casual tone, that she couldn't, not really. She'd led a normal life, and her losses has been normal losses, and the price she had paid had been a normal price.

"And it's possible that it will always feel that way," she continued. "But that doesn't mean that you have to live like a hermit. I didn't know your wife, but whoever she was, I'm sure she wouldn't have wanted you to live that way."

"No," said Marc. "No, she wouldn't have."

What he didn't say, what he couldn't say, was that he knew to a certainty that his wife didn't want him alone, because every night, night after night, Melissa made *sure* that he didn't lead the life of a hermit. Because a hermit had no visitors, living or dead, right? Being alone, being truly alone, might have been a better end.

"How did you lose her?" Barbara asked quietly, surprising him with her forthrightness. She was a woman who obviously measured the limited time ahead as carefully as she counted out the wasted time behind.

He was silent longer than was probably polite while he tried to decide whether he should answer her question. He'd never really had much cause to speak to anyone of it before. All their parents were dead, and they'd had no children. At least, none that had lived. What friends they'd had as a couple were mostly brought to the relationship by her, and once the tragedy occurred he'd dodged their phone calls until they simply drifted away. So he had no experience with speaking of the unspeakable. Just in obsessing over it.

And dreaming of it.

Before he could reach a decision, a young couple, garbed in khakis and happy in their ignorance, came up to the table, their hands entwined, and asked whether they could join them, looking from Marc to Barbara and back again. There was no way that Marc could speak of what was hidden beneath his surface in front of them. But he couldn't bring himself to say no, not when the happiness being thrust in front of him was so rare. And besides, there was still another week ahead of him on the ship if he truly felt like baring his soul. So Marc gestured them on, and Barbara waved at the empty chairs.

As Marc had expected, the couple—the woman, Kandi, all giggles, and the man, Carl, all coy smirks—were indeed newlyweds, in the Galapagos for their honeymoon. After the introductions, talk turned to their exhausting day spent exploring the island.

"That big round puff ball was the cutest thing, wasn't he?" said Kandi, once the appetizers had arrived and she had speared her first shrimp and was twirling it in cocktail sauce.

"Which big, round puff ball was that?" asked Barbara. Marc could sense her amusement, but Kandi seemed immune to it.

"They all looked the same to me," said Carl, with a laugh. "A puff ball is a puff ball is a puff ball."

Marc was pleased to discover that they knew as little of the history of this place as he did, though their ignorance was born of different reasons. They were here for the snorkeling, and because everything was so cute, and to make love beside portholes that looked out upon a different sky and an unfamiliar sea. Marc was here because this place had mattered once to someone he loved, and he felt that he owed this visit to her, that in coming here, he could . . . what? Say goodbye? Leave his heart behind so it wouldn't have to break each morning when he woke to an empty bed and a remembered absence? No, he wasn't really sure why he was here, only that it seemed like a thing that was overdue and must be done, with the exact reasons to be filled in later.

Barbara was the only one among them who seemed to have bothered to show up accompanied by the facts.

"Oh, no," she said. "A bird *isn't* a bird isn't a bird. You'll see that as we move on. Each island's species are uniquely different. You've read your Darwin, haven't you?"

Carl shook his head while holding up his hands in surrender, then turned to look sheepishly at Marc.

"Admit it, Marc," he said with a grin. "You haven't either."

"You've got me there," said Marc.

"When it comes to things like that," said Carl, "the wives are always more interested than us, right? Husbands don't have to sweat those kinds of details."

"'Husbands?,'" said Marc, confused. "You think . . . we're married?"

He looked to Barbara, then turned away quickly when it became clear that she was less concerned by the error than by his alarm over it.

"I'm so sorry," said Carl. "I just assumed—"

"So tell me more about this big puff ball of a bird as you call it," Barbara interrupted to ask Kandi. Marc was grateful that Barbara had turned the focus elsewhere, and he sensed she knew it.

"It was about as big as a Thanksgiving turkey," said Kandi. "Big and fat and round as a bowling ball. And the amazing thing is that it was stuffed like a turkey, too, so stuffed that you could almost hear it slosh. I wish I could remember what the cutie was called, but I'm no good at things like that. I could show you a picture of it if that helps."

Before Kandi could retrieve her digital camera from her lap, Marc and Barbara spoke at the same moment, with the same words, though with vastly different tones.

"It was an albatross," they each said.

"Are you *sure* you two aren't married?" asked Kandi.

Barbara patted Marc's hand before he could respond, and he found that he didn't mind her touch quite so much this time.

"That was a baby albatross we saw," continued Barbara. "It spends all of its young life on that one spot, while its parents fly off to sea to hunt and bring back fish to feed it. The one we saw probably had two gallons of fish oil inside it, getting ready for its growth spurt, for the day when it will have an eleven-foot wingspan."

"Wow," said Kandi. "I'm just glad we saw it when it was still cute."

Marc hadn't thought it was cute. All Marc had thought, after Rafael had pointed it out and identified it, was, *so that's an albatross.* Since Melissa had died, Marc had thought of himself as carrying one, but he'd always kept that thought in the realm of metaphor, never believing that he'd ever actually see one, no matter how many times Melissa had probably mentioned them. Maybe that's why he had to come here, to discover that they weren't always so frightening as all that. Sometimes they were just little balls of fat. Maybe someday his could grow wings and fly away . . .

When the time came for desert, the newlyweds begged off and vanished. Marc surprised himself by hanging on. He'd only planned on coming down long enough to apologize, and there were implications, after all, to lingering conversations over coffee. But Barbara acted as if there weren't any, and just gestured at the disappearing couple.

"Honestly," she said. "They have no idea, do they?"

"No," said Marc, and he was surprised to find that he was the one smiling this time.

"Were we really once so young?" she asked.

"Not me," said Marc. "I can't remember *ever* being young."

"So we're back to the doom and gloom again," she said.

"Where else?" he said. "That's where I live."

"I think," she said, "that there was something you wanted to tell me."

This time, given the opportunity, he didn't hesitate. He began to tell her everything. He didn't think he'd even ever told *himself* everything before. How he'd lived a life of loneliness until he and Melissa had met. How they'd found each other at an office party, and fallen instantly in love. How she'd longed to visit this place, but could never afford it, and how they decided to splurge and go into debt for their tenth anniversary. How they were surprised by an unexpected pregnancy, one that they'd welcomed. And how instead of ending up with a child, Melissa had sickened, and nothing, not surgery, nor drugs, nor radiation, nor prayer had worked.

And then, how he was alone again, and how he'd stayed alone, for the five long years since.

"Our fifteenth anniversary is coming up," Marc said. "It's in just a few days."

"You poor thing," said Barbara. "You sound haunted."

He was stung by her use of that word. It felt like a slap. He'd never thought of the clouds that hung over him and the dreams that came with them in that way. But now that Barbara had mentioned it . . .

"Can I trust you with a secret?" he asked, realizing then that whenever someone asked that question, they usually knew the answer before the question was even asked.

"Of course," said Barbara, leaning into him. "We only met last night, I know that, but still, I feel as if we've known each other for years."

Marc had no memory of having met Barbara the night before at the welcome party. Until that morning, she'd been lost in a blur of faces he never expected to know better. But he felt he should tell her, should tell *someone* of the dreams and what he was here to do about them.

But then the waiter coughed at his shoulder, and he looked up to see that he and Barbara were the last guests in the dining room, and the staff was hoping to close up for the night. It had been years since Marc could remember time having passed so quickly. Usually, it crawled, because he was carrying Melissa on his back. Perhaps in talking about her with someone else, he had managed to put her down for at least a moment.

As the staff put out the table settings for the next morning's breakfast, Marc walked with Barbara into the passageway outside the dining area.

"Now what?" asked Barbara, as they took the stairs up to the deck.

"I was just thinking," Marc said. "Carrying an albatross can be exhausting."

"You can choose to put it down," she said.

"No," he said, as they paused by the railing to look out at the sea. "I don't think I'm capable of making that choice."

"Then you can at least choose to let someone else carry it with you," she said, patting his arm and then leaving it there. "You're not the only one who's been made to live a life alone. And we weren't made to live that way. That much we can choose."

"Yes," said Marc, covering her hand with his own. "Yes, you're right."

They watched the setting sun until it had vanished completely, and it wasn't until much later that he realized that he'd only been thinking of Melissa intermittently, rather than constantly. As they continued talking in the darkness, Barbara did not bring up the as yet unspoken secret he had tried to offer, and Marc did not attempt to revisit the matter. Whatever unexplored potential might exist between them, he still had to go through with his plans, and if anyone was going to get in trouble for them, he wanted it to be only him.

Back in his cabin, Marc eyed his narrow bunk with suspicion. It had been a pleasant evening, the first such after a long desert of loneliness, and he didn't want the dreams that would surely come to wash it away. He hoped to stay awake as late as he possibly could.

He sensed that he could have spent the night with Barbara if he chose. She could have delayed the restless sleep that awaited him. But it wasn't yet time for that. He knew that he had to put down one burden before his hands could be free to pick up anything else.

The only distraction he was going to allow himself that night were the guidebooks he'd brought, Melissa's guidebooks, which he'd barely opened up until then. He'd felt that all he needed to know about this place he already knew. Melissa had been a good teacher, even though he had been a lousy student. But it had been an exhausting day, and so he fell asleep sitting in bed with books scattered across his lap, staring at Melissa's scribbled notes in their pages and thinking of how they had once been across her lap.

And then Melissa was there in the cabin.

She did not come to him with scary faces or menacing gestures, none of what he once had thought would accompany a ghost. She was just sitting there, tucked in bed beside him as she once had always been. Her eyes were sad, and at the same time, a little afraid.

"Don't do it," she said, as casually as if she were asking him what he wanted for breakfast.

Her voice brought back such memories as nearly made him weep, but at the same time he felt a spark of guilt, guilt for what he'd earlier been contemplating about Barbara.

"Nothing happened," he said to his dead wife. "Nothing is going to happen. You don't have to warn me."

She shook her head. Did she not believe him? He had never lied to her before.

"Don't do it," she repeated, more urgently this time.

"I won't, Melissa," he said. "Please . . . I didn't come here for anyone else but you. I waited too long to do it, I know that. I should have come earlier. But I'm here to make amends."

She lunged for him then, grabbing his wrists. An electric shock coursed through him at her touch that both frightened and exhilarated him.

"Don't do it," she said once more, pulling him toward her for a kiss.

But he woke before their lips could touch.

The bed was empty, the cabin dark. In the quiet of the small room, he felt her absence more than ever.

He looked forward to the end of his journey here, when he would set them both free.

• • •

Marc had only seen a few flamingos in his life before, and those had either been in a cage or on a neighbor's lawn. But the marsh on Floreana Island held hundreds of them that were neither imprisoned nor plastic.

Barbara stood beside him as he marveled at the flock. Through some unspoken agreement, they had ended up on the same raft when the passengers gathered to disembark at their latest island. And when they'd come ashore, they'd continued together walking side by side on the path inland as she shared trivia with him about this bird and that tree. Though he sensed he shouldn't use that word when he thought about it, because from the passionate manner in which she spoke, it was anything but trivia to her. When Eduardo, their guide for that day, complimented Barbara on her knowledge, Marc felt an unexpected pride he knew he shouldn't have allowed himself to feel.

Standing there, looking out at the flock that seemed to stretch as far as he could see, reaching the base of mountains that vanished upward into mist, he recognized that he was feeling less oppressed.

"I wonder if albatrosses are jealous of flamingos," he said, surprising himself. Barbara clasped his hand then and gave it a little squeeze. He squeezed back, not letting go, refusing to give credence to the previous night's dream warnings.

What would Kandi and Carl say if they should see them now? Marc was glad those two were off as part of another group, because he didn't want to make his feelings concrete enough to verbalize an answer.

Eduardo next led them to a wooden barrel stuck in the sand. He told them that whalers had used it in the eighteenth century to leave messages for each other, and that in modern times, that custom continued, albeit altered. And with a different barrel, of course.

Eduardo stuck his hand into an opening in the barrel and pulled out a handful of postcards. He passed them to those who stood closest to him, and explained that they were supposed to take a look at the destination and deliver them personally if possible, that is, if the recipient happened to live close to their home. In that way, they would help carry on and be a part of the whalers' tradition.

Barbara slid a few postcards from her shoulder bag and tossed them into the barrel for someone else to deliver in the future.

"No one you want to write?" she asked him.

"No one left to write," he said. He'd already told her how and why, so he didn't explain again. But being reminded of reality, his buoyant mood was gone.

As the postcards slipped from hand to hand so they each could examine them, Marc reached out for the stack held out to him, not really in the mood to take part in the ritual, expecting to pass them unread quickly on to Barbara to pass on to the next outstretched hand. But something made him glance down just as she was about to take them from him. Written across the top card in large letters were the words "Don't do it." He froze as Barbara grabbed the stack, and wouldn't let go.

The postcard's recipient was unnamed, and the message was unsigned, but the handwriting . . .

The handwriting was Melissa's.

"What's wrong, Marc?" asked Barbara, giving the stack a little tug.

"It's just the sun," he whispered, turning the card over and over in his hands, a photo of dolphins appearing and disappearing again. But each time, the handwriting remained. "I think I've had a little too much sun. That's all."

Marc casually removed the top card and made a show of fanning himself, giving the rest of the handful to Barbara. When she looked away while passing the stack on to the next in the circle, he slipped the card into a pocket. By the time she looked back at him, he'd made up his mind.

"I think I need to go back to the ship now," he said, turning back toward the path that had brought them there.

"I'll go with you," she said, starting to follow.

"No," he said, stopping her. "Don't let me take you away from this. It's something you've been dreaming of for years. We'll catch up at dinner."

But they didn't catch up at dinner. Back at the ship, Marc told the purser that he wasn't feeling well and asked if a sandwich could be sent to his cabin. He leaned the postcard against an ice bucket on the dresser of his small room. He paged through the guidebooks that he had been eying the night before, looking at Melissa's scribbles in the margins. There could be no doubt that the notes and the card had been written by the same person. He slid a suitcase out from under his bed, and retrieved a shoebox which he placed on the dresser next to the card. He drummed his fingers on the box's lid, but could not bring himself to open it.

"What is it that you want, Melissa?" he said. "What does 'Don't do it' *mean*? Don't do what I came here to do? Don't do what I never anticipated coming here to do? It was just dinner, Melissa, and a walk along the beach. I'll never be able to replace you. So what are you trying to tell me?"

There was no answer, but then, he didn't think that he really expected one, because since her death, she had only spoken to him in dreams.

He was interrupted in his pleading by a knock at the door. It was only the purser with his sandwich. But he couldn't bring himself to eat, and so instead he tucked directly into bed. He hoped that he would dream of Melissa, and that in the dream she would more explicitly tell him what he was to do, but for the first time in half a decade, she did not visit him.

Marc woke in the middle of the night, disoriented and drenched in sweat. The air in the room had grown stuffy, and his covers had been kicked to the floor. He needed fresh air, and from the ship's rocking as it made its way at speed to the next day's island, he knew that there'd be plenty of it up on the deck.

He dressed again and then made his way down narrow passageways, seeing no one. At this time of night, as he circled the deck with a stiff wind in his face, the vessel seemed deserted. Which was just as well, because if he had seen anyone, what would he have said to them?

If he saw Barbara, what would he say to her?

That his dead wife had sent him a postcard warning him against her? Or perhaps, that his dead wife had warned him against doing what he'd come to do on the final day of the trip? How could he possibly say such things? Share what was really going on in his head and the ship's doctor would likely restrict him to quarters.

Better to say nothing. Better to do nothing. Better to treat the other passengers like the strangers they really were. Better to take a step back from Barbara, go back to treating her the way he'd been treating people ever since Melissa had died—pleasantly, politely, and kept at arms length. There was safety in that, the safety he needed to accomplish his mission.

The moon was only a quarter full, but still cast enough light for him to see the billowing waves as the ship cut through them. The island that waited ahead of them was only visible in the distance as an absence of stars along the horizon. Another time, another life, Marc could have considered such a vista romantic. But no longer. Now the stars and the sea only reminded him of the fact that he'd once had someone to share them both with, but did no longer.

As he neared the prow, he noticed a glow coming from the bridge, so he wasn't entirely alone at that hour. Someone, of course, had to be steering the ship smoothly (well, somewhat smoothly, he told himself as he moved along unsteadily) to his destiny. He peered in as his path took him by, but did not pause, hoping to get past without conversation, but then the door slid open, and the captain stuck out his head.

"Couldn't sleep?" the man asked, the glow of the instrument panels providing more light than did the moon.

Marc nodded.

"You're in luck tonight," he continued. "Go up front and take a look down. In a few minutes, you're going to have something special to brag about to the others."

Marc did as the man suggested, interested more in continuing his solitude than in gaining any conversational gambit for the following day, even though he could use something else to speak of besides postcards, and what was to come. He stood at the prow, nothing more ahead of him but the rhythmic breaking of the waves, which were hypnotic in their randomness, and made him realize that he was still tired. Sleep no longer brought him rest, and sometimes he thought the more sleep he got the less rested he was. But nothing unusual was occurring, regardless of what the captain had promised, so he thought perhaps he'd better head back to bed to at least try.

But then he could see straight lines raking the chaos of the sea, as if missiles had been fired at the ship from an array of unseen enemies, and soon the area directly beneath him was filled with dolphins. They all faced in the same direction, speeding forward, getting an extra boost from the motion of the ship. It was a game to them, the dolphin version of a roller coaster, he imagined. Marc had seen that behavior before during the day, but these dolphins were different—they glowed as they broke the water, awash in an eerie green light. They seemed happy somehow, and though he knew it was silly to ascribe anthropomorphic feelings to animals, as some of them leapt into the air in front of him, to him their mouths almost seemed curved upward in smiles.

He turned back and looked up at the captain, who waved and then gave him a thumb's up. Marc waved back. He hoped that was enough of a thank you for the gift of what he'd seen. But he'd had enough for one night. For all he knew, the dolphins could go on until dawn like this. It was time to abandon them so his head could hit his pillow once more. He'd need his energy the next day to properly avoid the others.

But then, as he gave one last look below, a dolphin transformed. Melissa was now down in the midst of them, Melissa glowing as she swam along in the waves, Melissa happy instead of lost in the various miserable emotions she showed him in his dreams. He called out her name and leaned as far as he could over the lip of the prow without tumbling into the water himself.

"What do you want?" he shouted, but he doubted she could hear him over the roar of their passage. "Melissa, talk to me! What are you doing here? What are you trying to tell me?"

She gave him no answer, just sped along, seeming to ignore him, and it wasn't until the other dolphins broke away, their playtime over, and headed back to their homes, that Melissa took a brief look up at him, only to dive suddenly below the surface, vanishing, taking the green glow with her.

"Come back, Melissa!" he cried. "Come back!"

But the sea was empty once more, his heart was empty once more, and nothing he could say could change that. As he stumbled past the bridge on the way back to his cabin in a daze, the captain stuck his head out once more.

"Amazing, isn't it?" he said, grinning. "The algae in this area is phosphorescent, and at night, when the dolphins break it with their snouts . . . well, you saw the result."

"Yes, I saw," said Marc. "Thank you."

He hurried back to his room, where he discovered that the postcard was gone. But the shoebox, and what lay within, still remained. He cried beside the open package until the morning came, then fell asleep sitting at the desk and stayed asleep until he was woken by a knock at the door.

"Marc, are you in there?" came Barbara's muffled voice. "Are you all right?"

He removed his shirt so he'd have an excuse to keep Barbara out of the room, then opened the door a crack and peered out.

"I brought you some food," she said, holding out a covered plate.

"Oh, hello, Barbara," he said, without much energy. He hoped that she'd blame his lack of enthusiasm on his feigned illness, and not take it personally. He didn't want to hurt her, though he knew that he probably would, and that when she looked back on this trip, if she thought of him at all, she would probably blame herself, no matter how he handled the uncomfortable situation.

"How are you feeling?" she asked.

"Woozy," he said, opening the door slightly wider so he could take the plate. "I'm not really up to talking."

He peered beneath the plate's covering to find eggs, bacon, and a croissant. It was what he had eaten the day before, and he was amazed that she had noticed. And a little regretful as well. It meant that her pain would be that much greater.

"Maybe it will help you get your strength back."

"I appreciate it," he said, keeping the door firmly between them. "But I'd better get back to bed."

"Feel better," she said. "We'll be docking at Santa Cruz Island today. You won't want to miss Lonesome George. It's going to be a big day."

"I don't think I'll be able to make it," he said, but when he saw the disappointment play across her face, added softly, "We'll see."

He thanked her again and quietly closed the door before he could be drawn into further conversation. He set the plate on the desk, but didn't get around to eating. There was no way that he could eat when he was this excited.

Barbara had been correct. Today *was* going to be a big day.

Marc peered furtively out through his porthole at the harbor of Santa Cruz Island. Unlike the other islands of the Galapagos, which were mostly uninhabited, a small city had grown up there. It was difficult to believe that this was where his journey would end. That soon there'd be no more dreaming.

He watched as zodiac after zodiac headed for the small dock to shuttle passengers ashore to visit the Charles Darwin Research Center and Puerto

Ayora, the latter really more village than city. He couldn't identify each tourist as the rafts pulled away, fattened by life preservers and topped by floppy hats to protect them from the sun. Barbara, ever enthusiastic, was surely on one of the first few of them. So once the rush had cleared, he placed the shoebox in his waterproof backpack and headed for the ladder that would load him into the zodiac. His delay had helped him just as he had planned, because there was no longer much of a line. He ended up among a small group of stragglers he did not recognize, and their raft ended up being only half full. He felt relieved. There'd be no attempts at conversation that day, and they would not be looking to him for companionship once ashore for their self-guided tour.

As he stepped off onto the dock, he knew that he should head straight for the cemetery. He felt the tug of it deep in his heart, but after years of delay, after having left this promise unfulfilled for so long, he felt that Melissa would understand a wait of another hour.

He boarded a small shuttle bus for the Charles Darwin Research Center, and ignored the beauty of the ride, lost in his own thoughts. The backpack was heavy in his lap, heavier than it should be for what it carried, but he dared not put it down. What if through his inattention it was stolen? What would he do then? There would be no end to Melissa's story, nor to his own. So he closed his eyes and clutched the bag tightly until they arrived at the facility.

However interesting the other displays might have been, he walked past all of them. Only one exhibit held meaning for him now, and so he headed straight for the enclosure that contained Lonesome George. Most of what Melissa had told him and Barbara had repeated had vanished from his mind, but Lonesome George had stayed, just as it had stayed in this place, and stayed and stayed, seemingly immortal. Marc remembered what they had called it, the last of its kind, and perhaps that fact stuck with him because he somehow knew that someday he, too, would be the last of his kind. There was something romantic about it, and something tragic, too, and when Marc thought of himself he didn't know which word best described him.

He leaned over the barrier to look at the large tortoise munching on a cabbage. He couldn't remember the name of the island from which it had been plucked as the last survivor, but he could remember that it was at least one hundred years old, if not older. It had spent most of its life alone, hopeful for a mate, but never finding one, rejecting the females of other species who were presented to him in the hopes that at least a part of his genetic makeup would live on. It didn't look depressed about its circumstances, but then, with a tortoise, who could tell? Marc knew that if he were faced with such a situation, he would make a choice.

He had a choice to make now. But with no other possible way of ending this, did it really deserve to be called a choice?

He left the station and returned to the town. He passed the restaurants by, even though he had gotten hungry and regretted not at least nibbling at Barbara's offering, and passed the souvenir stands as well, because he wasn't planning to take anything from this place, but instead leave something behind.

The small cemetery was unlike other cemeteries he had been forced to visit in his lifetime. He could almost call it cheerful. The stones and markers had a primitive, personal feel to them, many adorned with mosaics of broken glass and pottery shards. Custom had allowed the mourners to express themselves, unlike the uniformity he was used to back home, where fitting in held the highest priority. As he admired the display with one part of his mind, another part was scouting for the best place to do what he needed to do. Though he'd always realized that it would all end here, he'd forgotten that a cemetery, even a small one, was not specific enough a destination. He had to find exactly the right patch of ground, and quickly. His backpack continued to be heavy beyond its weight, and he needed to put it down.

As he wandered the grounds, attempting to sense that perfect spot, he had little company. Whether it was due to the day of the week or just the time of day, there were no mourners here, just an occasional tourist like himself wandering through, no one who might find his own presence curious or interfere with his plans. No one invested enough in the place to bother to stop him.

He took his time, eying each marker in turn, seeking a sign, and instead finding only names that he could not easily pronounce, and dates that reminded him that life was short and cruel. Eventually, he spotted a stone engraved with the image of a tortoise crawling along the ground, a dolphin arcing high over its head, and he thought, this is the place. This is where it should happen. The tortoise was who he was, who he had been before he met Melissa, plodding along, and now it was who he was after Melissa, lonely. The dolphin was Melissa herself, always leaping high, as she had the other night, reaching out to him, glowing, giving him, he now realized, a sign.

He had to do it here.

He slipped the shoebox from his backpack and knelt before the marker. He could barely believe this would all be over soon. His fingers shook as he lifted the lid.

When he saw what was revealed inside, he tumbled back. Resting atop what he had brought with him was the postcard that had been delivered to him on Floreana Island. "Don't do it," the card still said, only this time, scribbled beneath that earlier inscription were the words, "Please, Marc."

And it was signed, "Love, Melissa."

He slumped to the cool earth and wept.

"What do you want from me, Melissa?" he said between sobs. "I'm only trying to finally do what you wanted. I'm sorry it took so long. I'm only trying to do what I promised you I'd do."

When enough tears had passed that he was once more able to function, he lifted the shoebox into his lap and felt the cool and familiar metal inside.

"It can't go on like this," he said. "It just can't."

He turned his head, and found himself eye to eye with the leaping dolphin of the grave marker. It seemed to be smiling, the way Melissa had been when he'd last seen her, swimming through the surf in the night. He traced the curve of its flank with one finger, and smiled himself.

A scuffling in the dirt nearby broke his concentration, and he looked up to see Barbara walking through the cemetery. She hadn't noticed him there yet. He hurriedly put the lid back on the box and stood, brushing the dirt from the seat of his pants. She noticed him as he popped up above the stones.

"There you are, Marc," she said hesitantly. "I was just about to head back for the ship when one of the guides told me that you were feeling better. *Are* you feeling better?"

"I think I am," he said.

"Did you manage to see everything you wanted to here?" she asked.

"I think I have," he said, shifting the backpack easily from one shoulder to the other. "Let's go. It's time to get back to the ship."

Once on board, Marc no longer hid in his cabin, but instead joined the others for the rest of the day's meals. After dinner, one during which he did his best to keep all conversation light, he walked the deck with Barbara as the ship started its passage to their next and final island.

He sat beside her in a deck chair, and while they stared off together at the sunset, he found the strength to begin an apology to her for the way he had been acting.

"I'm sorry," he said, but found that he could only follow those two words up with silence, instead of the words he really wanted to say.

"You certainly are," she said sharply, then softened a bit. "What's been bothering you? You started to tell me the other day, but then . . ."

Her words drifted off, and this time, she was the one who let the silence linger. They sat quietly until the sun was gone, and then without another word, she was gone. He did not blame her. Unless you are with someone who can tell you everything, why bother to stay?

He returned to his room, but did not sleep. He waited until the middle of the night, and then went up to the bridge. This time, instead of trying to speed by, he popped in to sit with the captain for a moment.

"Will they be back again tonight?" he asked.

The captain shook his head.

"Doubtful," the man said. "We won't be passing anywhere near that area. Sorry."

But Marc did not believe him. He *could* not believe him. Tonight it would all be over. He felt as sure of that as he'd ever felt of anything. So he excused himself and went to the prow. He peered over, down into the surf, where he saw nothing beyond the surface of the impenetrable sea.

He waited, barely able to breath.

"I'm going to do it," Marc said. "I'm going to do it whether you tell me I should or not. It all ends right now."

As he reached into his pack, the dolphins came, streaking toward him like arrows aimed at his heart. They frolicked and glowed below, and there in the midst of them . . .

"Melissa," he whispered. She leapt up, spinning, iridescent, and paused to smile at him before tumbling back into the sea. He removed the shoebox from his pack, and opened it, so that the smooth metal within glowed in what remained of the moonlight.

"Is this what you really want?" he asked.

She leapt again, so high that it almost seemed she would not stop, and as she reached the apex of her arc, Marc unscrewed the urn's lid. He tilted the urn, and what remained of Melissa's body sprinkled down into the surf, and then what remained of her soul plunged into the midst of it. One by one, the dolphins left, until there was only Melissa. She smiled at him, and then slowly vanished beneath the waves.

There was a jerk at his arm, and Marc turned to see that the captain was beside him. He realized then that the man had been shouting, but he'd been unable to hear any of it. The man cupped his hands between his mouth and Marc's ear.

"You're not allowed to do that," the man yelled.

"I know," said Marc, staring down to where the ship broke the waves below. "But I had to do it anyway."

The captain did not stop Marc as he put the urn in his backpack. As Marc swung the bag over his shoulder, he felt something in his shirt pocket, something that hadn't been there earlier. It was the postcard again, only this time, it bore no writing, only the imprint of a pair of lips. Melissa's lips.

Marc pressed them to his own, and as he said goodbye, the wind ripped the card from his fingers and tossed it high into the air, where it hung for a moment against the moon like a distant albatross passing in the night.

Tomorrow, he would have to tell Barbara all about it.

Tomorrow, he would have to tell Barbara everything.

THE LANDLOCK

ELIZABETH MASSIE

Elizabeth Massie lives in the Shenandoah Valley of Virginia with illustrator Cortney Skinner. A two-time HWA Bram Stoker Award winner, she is the author of Sineater, Wire Mesh Mothers, Twisted Branch *(as "Chris Blaine"), and other books. Her latest novel is entitled* Homeplace.

"My mother and sister spent several weeks in Belize with a church group," Massie explains, "helping rebuild school walls that had been destroyed during a hurricane. They both came back with vivid stories of a beautiful land with summer weather so hot and humid, a person not used to it could quickly lose an otherwise pleasant personality.

"I was intrigued with the tales, especially those of the Caribs, people who seemed to carry with them the ancient secrets of a lush and primeval land. I hope someday to visit Belize myself . . . though I shall not travel into the forests alone."

Which is exactly what an American charity worker does in the story that follows . . .

This land is an embryo, its surface shifting constantly, being molded and contorted in an attempt to find the true and pure form to which it will return. Trees stretch against the damp, dense air, fronds shimmering, bark glistening. Creatures stir the loamy ground, restless and aware. The sea strokes its shores, studying the subtle variations it creates, watching for perfection to be achieved.

And I watch the land. Without the patience of the sea, with the restlessness of the land creatures. I watch and wait. I wonder if the land will ever truly find what it seeks. It is trapped within the soiled, poisoned world of its mother as much as I am trapped by my own folly. The land is a dauntless, vengeful infant; I am a reluctant pilgrim of my species. God let the pilgrim die. I was not born for this.

Our plane touched down in Belize on June 24th. My flight-mates, fellow teachers from Pittsburgh's Henry Clay High School, were itchy and excited, straining against their seat belts, hands cupped to the small windows, watching as the thick green of the jungle rose to meet the descending aircraft. I was in an aisle seat, looking at my hands, swallowing down the suffocating sense of claustrophobia that had been crawling up and down my throat since our Air Belize jet had taken off from Miami. I didn't share my companion's enthusiasm for our mission. It was a fine enough idea, for those who cared. Mary Booker, our sociology-world cultures teacher, had come up with the idea, modeling the premise after a student-sponsored charity drive held in our school, a fund-raiser entitled "Youth Helping Youth." Mary, an active member of a Pittsburgh United Methodist Church, had heard of the plight of a certain high school in Belize City. A hurricane had washed across the city, trashing fragile homes and caving in the eastern wall of the school. Couldn't teachers serve as an example here? Mary argued. Her church would raise the travel expenses for those who would go and serve as workers for two weeks in the coastal city, putting noses to the block pile and rebuilding the wall. "Educators Helping Educators."

It hadn't taken me long to decide to go, though it wasn't a magnanimous desire to help others that got me to sign up. I needed in a most desperate way to escape the oppressive garbage pit of my American City and of my vast, polluted country. My body needed escape for its survival. My emotions were still raw after my husband had decided that his computers and his lovely business partner offered more promise to his life than what I'd previously given. And so I looked for a peace that my fellow humans could not offer. At first, I journeyed through our state parks and natural preserves. I spent each weekend hiking, kayaking, camping, seeking solace in the beauty that was nature without people. Yet in spite of propaganda to the contrary, I could not find a single spot of wilderness that was not desecrated by a scrap of paper, a tossed beer can, a cigarette butt, a used condom or plastic grocery bag.

And so I lied my way into the group of dedicated missionaries, seeking instead of a chance to build a universal bridge via a school wall, a chance to spend time in an untarnished, primal land. I could see no harm in my lie. Most living things will seek equilibrium when tipped too far out of balance.

The plane thumped once, bounced, and settled its wheels on the runway of the airport. The remains of the Miami airport hotdog dinner made an effort to defy gravity, then settled again, uneasily in the base of my stomach. The plane slowed, circled, stopped. Stewardesses, uniformed smartly in blue, popped from their seats and began assisting passengers with overhead baggage. The door opened; Mary ushered her missionaries down the crowded aisle toward the streak of sunlight.

I remember, as a child, watching *The Wizard of Oz*. Dorothy's house, crashing to earth in a swirl of black and white; Dorothy opening the door to Oz, and coming face to face with a bright shock of dazzling color. Exiting the plane was a disturbing reversal. The interior of the plane had been modern, clean. What I saw as I stepped onto the steel-framed port-a-steps was a vision of blandness, of dusty weeds strangled in blacktop, tarpaulin-shrouded jeeps and tanks, sagging wire fencing, a small heat-ravaged building. A single hanger sat by the far end of the runway, with several aged, single-engine craft tethered about its side like ungainly lawn ornaments. Gathered along the gate that opened to the terminal-shack were wide-eyed natives, old men and women, peeking over the top, children gawking through the wire.

"The airport is entertainment," Mary told us as we trudged to the gate. "They come for miles for this. Very little television, even in the city." She laughed. The other teachers joined in, cutting curious glances at the natives. I looked away. I had not come to be watched. I'd had my fill of people, both at school and in my crowded Pittsburgh neighborhood. I needed aloneness. Surely this land would provide it. A rush of impatience coursed through my veins.

Our taxi ride to the city took us winding through the flatland, heading south. The sun was setting, falling behind the buzzing forest and distant mountains to the west. The six of us were wedged so tightly we could not move to look around, but there was little to see in the growing darkness. Shadows stretched long over the road, punctuated with small, dark, skittering things. Every few moments something would pop beneath the tires. Our driver, who supplemented his Spanish with a fairly understandable English, explained that it was crab-mating season, and the noises under the wheels were hapless male crabs, moving *en masse* in search of females. Again, Mary laughed. I wanted to pull my feet from the floor. I said: "Can't we dodge them?" "Oh, Laura," Mary chided, and the driver laughed along with her.

Belize City was larger than I imagined, but I was not surprised at its size. Every country has its human sludge pit; every nationality needs its gathering place, its watering hole. It was the unspoiled, unpopulated outlying land

140

that had called to me. We circled through the city, with cheap street lamps strobing our taxi at random intersections. We passed night-empty markets, shops boasting jewelry and mahogany carvings, elaborate Episcopal churches, simpler structures for the city's Mennonites and Presbyterians, past colonial homes and long streets of flimsy shacks atop stilts, cinderblock banks, Chinese and Lebanese restaurants, gatherings of people on dark corners, arguing and shaking their fists at each other. We then drove past the newer part of the city, by Yankee-style clothing stores, tourist agencies, and past an elite European hotel, The Belizean. The driver slowed so we could have a good look at the architecture and the well-dressed patrons milling around. He seemed proud of this addition to his city. I was unimpressed. We arrived at the school's compound just after 9:30 P.M. and my small bed in a communal dorm room was a welcome bit of human design.

We rose at 7:00 the next morning, and ate a breakfast of bread and fried plantains prepared by the school's cook and Diane, one of our own. After that we took a look at the destroyed wall. It resembled a cannon-blasted war remnant, with little left but mounds of dusty and cracked block. A truck-bed of new block sat inside the coils of barbed wire along the street. Three natives were at the wire, staring in looking as though, if given the chance, they would clear out any unwanted scraps in the schoolyard when our backs were turned. Plastic buckets of dry mortar awaited water. Mary assigned positions; George and Phil sorted through the piles of block separating unbroken pieces from the broken. Mary, Andrea, and I walked the thirty-five foot length of the wall, testing remaining chunks for soundness. Much of what we touched we pulled free and tossed aside; we then took old towels and brushed off crumbled mortar from the wall. As we worked, several more city-dwellers joined the first, and watched us from the barbed wire, grinning, talking, pressing so closely it was a wonder they did not leave hunks of their flesh on the barbs.

Diane served lunch at noon, giving us the chance to come out of the sun and into the shade of the school's dining room. We ate fish and tiny, barely-yellow bananas. George joked about the natives.

"We ought to let them help, " he said. "We would probably end up with some elegant Mayan sacrificial platform on top of the wall. Nice change of pace from your ordinary wall."

"And it could be useful for student discipline problems," replied Phil.

Diane plopped a scoopful of fish onto Phil's head, and he chuckled.

After lunch we were given two hours to rest. While the others napped in the dorm, I decided to take my first journey south, out of the city, in search of wilderness. I considered taking a taxi, but my funds were low. And so I donned a loose T-shirt and pair of shorts and set off on Kraal Road. The salty heat took hold of my throat, drying it, making the mere act of swallowing a useless reflex. It was no wonder to me why most of the natives did little or nothing in the early afternoon. The few who traveled around me appeared to be heading home, their eyes weary of the day already.

The road was covered in ground shell and gravel, making for uncomfortable footing. There were dead lizards and insects stirred into the road dust, as if even this tropical heat was in a subtle, cruel struggle for dominance over nature.

Kraal ended abruptly, and intersecting it was smaller road. I checked my map. This was Fawber Street, primarily residential, and it bore east several blocks and then south to the edge of town. As I turned left, two children playing beneath the ungainly bulk of their shack saw me, and with a squeal of delight, ran after me. I turned my gaze from them, not wanting to encourage. Yet they came, nearly colliding with me, grabbing my belt loops to slow them down. They were dark children, smelling of the same fish I had eaten for lunch.

"Hammus moonay gah?" one of them said. I looked at her. She was a Carib, her face pretty and damp, her teeth blackened stubs. Her brother was shorter, wearing only frayed jeans and the same spiked-tooth grin.

"Hammus moonay gah?"

I did not understand Carib. I waved the children away, and they skipped back several steps, but when I began walking, they trotted up behind me again.

"Hammus?"

I quickened my steps, passing other house-topped stilts, passing skinny dogs and trash spinning in the hot breeze. Other children saw us, and they left the shadows to follow. One small boy dragged an obscene plaything behind him on a bit of string; a dead parrot.

They were at my back and to my sides now, all chanting at me. A gust of wind stirred the gravel at my feet. I coughed. The children laughed. I walked faster. Little fingers plucked at my belt loops. Hands patted my hips and shoulders. My sleeve was tugged.

"Go away," I said. The children moved, several coming around to my front. They skipped backward, just beyond my feet, their faces bright in the sweltering air.

"Hammus moonay gah?"

The children behind me touched my neck, patting at the clasp of my chain necklace. The ones to my side stroked my arms. Those to the front slowed. I slowed also, a sudden rash of chills racing along my spine. I could hear their secret laughter, and the slapping of brown tongues against the diseased roofs of their mouths. My neck shuddered but the fingers returned like hungry flies.

The children in front of me stopped. Mouths opened wide; black, rancid pits. Those beside me clamped my arms in a quick, powerful motion. I thought that my death was here, death as food for starving human waste.

The tallest boy before me raised a bone-thin finger, and pointed it at me. His eyes narrowed into threatening slits. "Hammus gah?" I stepped backward. There was the squeak and protesting whine of a child behind. The tall boy did not flinch. His finger moved closer to my face.

"Hammus?"

My necklace was loosened and fell away from my throat.

And then came a bellowing shout, and the boy dropped his finger. He turned in the direction of the sound. All the small faces tightened, and then registered a shock of fear. They ran off, scuttling into the darkness beneath the shacks. I stood, watching after them, squinting, trembling violently.

In the center of the road stood an old woman. Her hands were on her hips, her feet planted apart, her head hanging low, as though it had been glued to the front of her neck. Her chin stuck out defiantly. I could not see her eyes, as the brim of her straw hat threw a streak over her face. But she was looking at me. I could feel it as surely as I could feel the taunting trickle of sweat carving a path between my shoulder blades.

"Littles give you trouble?" she said. Her voice was like volcanic grit.

"Yes," I said. I licked my lips, but they remained dry.

"You Yankee." It was not a question.

"Yes. "

"Why you out now in heat? You need rest from sun."

I shrugged.

The woman came closer. "I hear littles out here bother you. Littles worse and worse with each batch, eh? But that true in every place. Many, many bad littles. Less and less good littles. But I hear you. I rest but come out to help. You thank me? "

"Sorry. Thank you." My heart was thundering. It felt as if my lungs were sweating.

The woman tipped her head back and smiled. She was of Indian descent. Her eyes were visible now, friendly coal chips.

"You not on tour. Where your group?"

I motioned vaguely north. "I'm with a group rebuilding the Methodist school wall."

"Ah ha ha!" she laughed. The grating sound made my own throat hurt. But the laugh was genuine, with no malice. "You mean that? You want to do it?"

"Yes," I lied.

"Ah ha ha! You come with me. My home there. Come, I give you drink in this hot day." Turning, she noticed the necklace in the dirt and snatched it up. "Come."

She then crossed the road to the dead grass of the roadside. I watched her, perplexed but curious. She stopped and looked back, beckoning, then continued beneath a stilt house, crossing the rear yard and beneath another. I hurried after, compelled by gratitude, intrigue, and my vanishing necklace.

The woman's house was also on stilts. She climbed the splintery steps into an open doorway. I hesitated at the bottom. I looked around the rusted jeep beneath the shack, checking for more children. Seeing none, I climbed in after her.

The interior of the single room was greyed with shadow and grime. There was an oppressive smell of sweat and old meat. It was stuffy, but not as intense as the heat outside. The windows were small holes, bamboo shutters turned and fastened to the inside. Peculiar dried fruits hung on long strings like beaded curtains. Small, motionless geckos clung to the walls. The only furnishings were woven mats and wooden shelves. The shelves were bowed under the weight of books, jars, tasteless wooden figurines and knick-knacks.

The woman ladled water from a pail and handed the cup to me. I smiled faintly and pretended to drink. She poured a cup for herself and drank heavily. She put the cup on the mat beside her and studied me. "I am Pilar. You?"

"Laura. Lyles. "

She nodded. "You want smoke? Got good Yankee ones."

"No, thank you."

Pilar shrugged and slid a tin from the shelf, popping the top and removing a fat White Owl. "Ah, yes," she said.

145

I pretended to drink again.

"You rich, yes?"

"Oh, no."

"You come to Belize on plane. You didn't not swim here." She lit the cigar. The name reflected on her face, then puffed out.

"Well, yes I flew. But it was a free flight. I'm here with teachers from the States. Our way was paid by a church back in Pittsburgh."

Pilar exhaled slowly. "Why you do that? Build up school?"

Mary's pat answer found its way to my lips. "Educators helping educators."

Pilar laughed, an explosive grunt. Ash sprayed from the cigar tip. "You not that silly! I see your face out on road. Smart face, you got. You not here to fix school."

She was right. The backs of my hands went cold.

Pilar leaned in to me. "You know no one beats land, sea, storms. The war grows so much now. People sad, bad soldiers. Can't win."

A gecko darted across the floor near me. I pretended another sip of water. The cup smelt of body oils. "I didn't actually come for the building project, no," I said. "I came to get away from things, to find solitude for a time. To see nature in a purer form. It's so foul back home. I do help build, but I'm going to use my free time to explore the forest."

"Yes?" Pilar smiled.

I smiled then.

"I should show you something," Pilar said. She pulled a cracked man's wallet from the pocket of her dress. My necklace fell out with it but she did not notice. From the wallet came a black and white photo. She put it into my hand.

"My son. Pretty man, yes?"

I nodded. The photo was nearly as cracked as the wallet, but the man in it was young. They were obviously related. "Where is he?"

Pilar reached out and patted my face. In the heat, her hands were cool.

"Want to see forest, yes? I know it. I can show you. Let you be alone as you wish. See special forest in the beauty it is. Tell me when you not build?"

"Early afternoon hours. Early evening hours."

"No matter. You come when you come. I be here. Then we go."

"All right," I said. I wasn't sure I wanted someone to go with me. For to see the land alone was to find the land alone. But for some reason, I trusted her.

I rose and stepped to the doorway.

"Oh, don't forget this nice thing," said Pilar. She was holding out my necklace. "Take."

"Keep it," I said. "It's the least I can do."

Pilar's face seemed to lighten. Her eyes widened in sheer pleasure. She slipped the necklace into her pocket with the wallet. "It's the least I need, you see?"

I didn't, but I nodded, and stepped out into the brightness. Behind me, Pilar began humming softly.

I did not walk the city again until Thursday. The second and third days of work involved the beginning of construction, and I was left exhausted. I grabbed a nap with each free moment I was given. The work and heat seemed to affect the cheerfulness of the others as well. Joking became strained and pointed. The number of spectators had doubled since the first day, adding an irritating pressure to our job. The natives snacked and called to us through the fencing. I thought of my school, and the jeering calls of students in the halls. I thought of DC, and the jeering calls of bums in the Metro stations.

On Thursday, I forced myself to go out again, even though the thought of sleep had a hypnotic appeal. The solace of the forest was an appeal even stronger. I borrowed Diane's sunglasses and went south.

I found Pilar on Fawber, in the shade of a house, cigar smoke curling about her face like a dingy thread of old cotton.

"We go," she said simply. I followed her to her shack, and we climbed into the old jeep.

Pilar lit a new cigar. "You want to see land. You so sure land want to see you?"

Before I could come out with an appropriate, indignant reply, she chuckled and gave the accelerator a heavy-footed jab. We were off in a spray of shell grit.

We were in the forest less than twenty minutes after leaving Pilar's home. We drove, bouncing like a cork over fallen limbs and bold roots. I couldn't grasp what I was seeing, but Pilar didn't seem concerned. She bit the stub of her cigar and plowed ahead. The windshield protected us from the majority of slapping branches, but our arms were scraped by those that were able to make quick sneak attacks. Pilar talking over the engine and around the cigar as we drove.

"Forest here is old. But we will see the new soon. And it don't like me. I no good person to it. I understand, too. I smoke, make a stink. Also I one time make money with my husband trapping in forest, selling furs. But my son was a good little. Became good man. Land never knew he was coming."

"Never knew he was coming? I don't understand," I shouted.

"You good person, too, so I think," Pilar continued as if I'd said nothing. "We see if land can feel you on its skin."

In that instant we came out into a clearing. The sun was staggering. I shaded my eyes above the sunglasses. Pilar drove several yards into the clearing and cut the motor.

"See? See here?" she said.

I looked. The clearing was a long, rather narrow strip of grassy meadow, with a hill to the right, and the silvery flash of the sea to the left. Across the clearing was what caught my attention, however. It was more forest, but not like that through which we had just traveled. I slipped from my seat and stood beside the jeep, mesmerized.

I had never seen a primeval jungle, as it exists only in the faint genetic memory of modern mankind. Yet here it was before me, a great wall of life, brilliantly painted against the horizon as if by a Master Impressionist: greens upon blues upon reds upon yellows. Gigantic trees wavered boastfully, throwing sun-sparks from their leaves and fronds. Vines, thick and woody, embraced the tree trunks with lovers' grips, and the grasses and flowers below the trees trembled, suggesting a bounty of exotic animals. I could smell the forest even from where I stood. It was a strong smell of newness, of freshness, of greenness. Stronger even than the gasoline stink of the jeep and the stench of Pilar's cigar.

I had found what I was afraid did not exist. I took a step forward.

Pilar leaned from the jeep and caught my arm. "Let me talk first."

I frowned at her over my shoulder. I did not need her talk now.

Her grip tightened. She climbed from the jeep and dropped the cigar into the grass. I stubbed it out.

"This land here is more beautiful, more different. That why you come."

I nodded.

"Land here like new skin under old. Like baby still in mama, you see?"

"No." I stretched my shoulders. They were sore from building and our rough ride.

"War will end with this new land. It grows larger always. Very slowly, but it grows. What is time to land? This is its revenge.. In thousands year, maybe millions, it will win."

"Let me go," I said. I jerked my arm. Pilar's fingers dug deeper.

"Land cannot lose this war. Any man it feels, it will kill."

"Stop it!" I jerked again, freeing myself. I turned toward the forest, striding forward with long steps through the crackling grasses.

It was not the voice but the sight that stopped me. Pilar cried out in anger, and came rushing by me in a blur of brown dress and straw hat. Her arms flailed about madly. Several wild birds darted from the protection of the grass in front of her. She stopped ten yards in front of the forest and spun back around, facing me. Her finger rose, as threateningly as that of the boy days earlier, and jabbed at me.

"You smart, good person!" she screamed. "But right now you act like bad one! You don't listen, you don't learn. How you be careful if you don't understand? You think I show you? Huh?"

"Damn it, Pilar."

"I show you, then. I show you."

"Pilar—"

She whipped around to face the forest. There was hesitancy, and in the brief photo-image I was struck with the ridiculousness of the human form against the beauty of nature. Then Pilar gathered herself, tightening shoulders, tipping head back, and took a step forward. Then another. Then another.

I thought it was a snake, for the swiftness and the fluidity was serpentine, and the cold deadliness was startling. It slithered from a tree and dropped into the brush, then with the sound of wind in winter, raced toward Pilar. Grass flattened under its weight. Pilar did not move.

"Get away!" I screamed.

Pilar didn't move. The great snake roared forward, lifting its head at the last moment. A head that was not a head, but a smooth woody knob, split open to reveal a wide maw of ragged and vicious splinter-teeth.

Pilar jumped back. The snake-thing reached its full length and was snapped back with a soft creaking. It lay in the grass. I stood, staring in horror. Pilar stood beside me, panting, wiping sweat from the brim of her hat.

"Land know me. I no good person. My husband came into this new land and he not come home no more."

The snake-thing withdrew, sliding quietly backward, rewinding itself, then pulled back up onto the tree from which it fell, becoming entwined with the trunk and branches; a simple jungle vine.

"Oh, my God," I said.

"Now you," said Pilar.

"We've got to get out of this place!"

"No, you go now. You want to see land pure and free of humans. Go see now if you are fit for it."

I looked at Pilar, dumbfounded.

"Less and less good people in world, you see. One day, all littles will be bad, grow up bad. If any mankind to survive, we must find good ones to save them."

"You're not making sense!"

Pilar pointed at the vine, now harmlessly laying on the tree. "That make sense, yes? You want to see beauty? Yes. I want to know if land can feel you? Yes. Go now. Go slow. See for yourself."

The forest seemed to sigh, and then tremble. I thought I could hear it grow; could hear it step forward several inches. A beautiful insect, wings sapphire nets, buzzed from the trees, circled out over the clearing, and then flew back into the forest.

I moved forward. Nothing stirred. I slowed, but continued to walk. No vines fell, no evil branches reached for me. I heard Pilar behind me. "Oh yes, be careful."

I nodded. And walked, past the point where Pilar had stood, into the shadowed grass at the edge of the forest. I stopped and stood, listening, waiting. It was as though I had come unnoticed. As though Pilar were the only human there.

"Ah ha ha! " laughed Pilar. "It is true! Good one, you are. I know it! Go now and enjoy. I wait at the jeep."

I looked at her and she grinned, jabbing a new cigar into her open mouth and lighting it with a dramatic, self-congratulatory flick of a match.

Mary was angry at my lateness, but it did not surprise me. It did not concern me, either. I had seen what she might never see. I had walked the new land and felt its unspoiled vitality. I had spent well over an hour roaming the forest, and had come out to find Pilar asleep. We had returned to the city as night was falling, and Mary swore that she had been ready to send the police in search of me. I felt sorry for Mary then, in all her trivial concerns, and went to bed to sleep in peace.

I went to the forest again on Saturday. Pilar drove me and again, stayed in the jeep to smoke and doze. The forest had grown a bit more. Would it be a thousand years until it reformed the world? A million? This was on Pilar's mind, but not mine. Was there a genuine war going on between humanity and nature? I didn't know or I didn't care. It was enough to see that nature had decided to stand strong. I explored more deeply this day, taking time to study the lowliest spider, to watch the drops of dew evaporate from an orchid leaf. Animals didn't run from me or to me, but grazed or slept or rooted unawares. I felt like a god, a spirit apart and yet a part.

It was nearing noon when I found the grisly display.

I'd been following a tree frog when I collided into the skull. It was human, its bone white and clean, its eyeholes black and staring east. I straightened and shivered. The skull was wedged low into the branches of a small tree. I stepped around the tree to see a circle of others, each adorned with a white human skull. In the center of the circle was a large flat stone, etched with a crude writing of some ancient language. A burial spot, I thought. My heart jumped, thinking of Pilar and the vine. A graveyard, perhaps, of those who'd not been good, who had ventured into this new place and had been corrected harshly?

I turned from the graveyard and moved north again, toward the clearing, finding it easy to dismiss the skulls in the wonder of the woods. Mosquitoes hummed in my ear and continued on, not settling down for a meal. Lizards lumbered across my path, sunning sporadically in the patches of sunlight, feeling no threatening vibrations from my footfalls.

Sunday was church, and the congregation of the compound's chapel honored the builders with a banquet and party. I feigned sickness and stayed in my room. Mary brought me a piece of spiced turtle and laughed when my face did actually turn a shade whiter.

Monday morning, we were at work again. The native crowd was greater than it had been before. There was a wall of faces—brown, reddened, flattened faces all pushed into the wire fence. Eyes rolled, watching our progress. When a block was dropped, a match of laughter was lit that coursed through the spectators like a fuse. Tongues and fingers alike pawed through the fence in our direction. There was no breeze at all. The air was stagnant, dammed by the human wall.

Phil and Mary cursed beneath their breath as they worked the block onto the mortar. Andrew and George were tight-lipped. And I was ready to quit. It was here, as it had been at home. Gawkers, watchers, worthless lives, with nothing to give but foulness, sucking life from the world, filling nothing but space.

"Crap." The trowel slipped through Mary's sweaty fingers. "Thank God we're finished in four days."

Andrea cleared her throat, clearly irritated.

Suddenly there was a shrieking in the crowd. Bodies began moving back and forth against each other like maggots beneath a layer of rotting skin. And then something burst from the crowd and hurled over the fence.

We all stopped our work and turned toward it. The voices in the crowd were instantly hushed. It was a small spider monkey, its coat crusted with mud, its eyes wide. It stood, transfixed in terror in the forest of human beings.

We blinked at it. It stared back.

I thought, *How did this creature survive this city?*

Mary said, "Stupid animal." She picked up her trowel and threw it. The metal caught the side of the monkey's head and the animal fell over, dazed, onto the dirt.

"Ha!" laughed one of the crowd.

Mary walked over and picked up both the trowel and the monkey. She glanced back at us, delivering a wicked wink then went to the fence. Fingers grappled in her direction. Teeth chattered noisily.

"Bad thing!" said one native. "Get in way of work!"

"Bad, bad," said one old woman. "Make a bother when work should go on."

Mary laughed for the first time in hours, and the sound was dark, evil. I thought of the children on the road, of the chopped and burned and scarred land of my own country, of the haughty smile of the lovely business partner when Steve told me our marriage was over. I clutched my stomach, overwhelmed.

"Give me bad thing." A dark hand shot out over the wire and took the monkey by the neck. Another hand followed, grabbing the trowel. The crowd backed up a fraction. The monkey was dropped to the ground. The trowel came whistling down. With three chops, the monkey was dead. The crowd cheered. The mutilated monkey was held up for inspection.

"No more bad thing stop work!" called the man holding the animal.

My work mates chuckled and shook their heads.

"No more bad thing," echoed Mary.

I did not realize where I was going until I fell, panting and retching, at the base of Pilar's steps, and she was muttering: "War not pretty, no?"

She said nothing more, but gave me warm tea and a hug that felt like Mother Earth herself, solid, comforting, ageless. I thought I saw the flash of my necklace in the corner of my darkening vision, but then I slept.

I slept.

I slept.

Darkness followed light and there was nothing again. Sounds came and then faded. There was earth, then sky, then earth. Spike-toothed children reached for me and through me. A bloody, butchered monkey climbed a barbed wire fence, chanting: "Hammus more? Hammus more?" My necklace floated before my face; I tried to move away from it as it morphed into a writing vine and then back to the necklace. I couldn't move. My head was against something soft but ungiving. The necklace came closer. I moved my hands to stop it; they were caught and held down, and someone said, "Must find good ones to go for us."

"Go where?" I whispered.

My eyes opened. "Go where?" I said. Above me were unfamiliar faces and stars and my chain necklace waving in the darkness.

"Ah, good one is awake now. Bless her. She ready to go for us."

I turned toward Pilar's voice. She was kneeling beside me, her face almost featureless in the light of a campfire. We were in the clearing. I could smell the new forest nearby.

I was lying on the ground. I tried to sit up, but was held down by the strangers around me.

What was happening?

"Pilar," I said, "my head hurts."

"Not so very much, I think. And not for long. Soon you go with other good ones into the many years ahead. You be our pilgrim. You go for us. When war is over and land has won revenge, you come out again and it be a very good thing."

I tried to sit up but was not allowed. Then I struggled, thrashed, but the hands kept me prone. A needle-prick came then into my lower arm. Warmth rushed, uninvited, into my bloodstream. My muscles fell into an enraged stillness.

"This is Paulo," said Pilar. A large face loomed over me, grinning. It was he who held my necklace. "Paulo a good one, like you. Is man of much magic and power. You like his tea, eh? Made of your essence, of little bit of your spirit in the pretty thing you give me. Paulo see your spirit and know you are truly good one. He make you ready for journey."

Journey?

Paulo nodded, then his eyes rolled up into the sockets revealing only the whites. He jingled the necklace and mumbled softly. A drop of saliva fell from his lips onto my face. I couldn't move away. Paulo touched my face with the necklace, and then with his hand. And suddenly, there was a knife gleaming in the night.

I screamed.

"Oh, no, no," said Pilar, compassion in her voice. "No reason to fear. My son there already, and other good ones from other times. We save them, put them into landlock until fight is finished."

I screamed.

"You know less and less good ones born in the world these days. Someday, will be no good ones at all. Land will kill them all. Will chew them into nothing. Then what of mankind?

So we save what good ones we can. When land is pure again and happy, souls of good ones will come free from the landlock. Free to enter any animal. Evolution will begin again. But world will be paradise for them, since they unfelt by land. Will be kings and queens in new world."

"No, don't! Don't do this to me!"

The knife touched me; instantly all feeling drained from my flesh. Paulo grinned, muttering. The knife entered me, moving easily through my skin, the cartilage, the bone. Paulo smacked his lips. He lifted my head to the murmurs of approval of the others. I rolled my head about, seeing my body below, my blood bathing the grass, turning it black. Pilar kneeled, rocking, clasping her hands together in rapture.

"Queen in new land," she whispered. "If I was only a good one to go with you."

Paulo stood, holding my head reverently. He gave Pilar my necklace. She slipped it about her neck and kissed it.

Paulo took me into the new forest. To the circle of trees and skulls and the flat stone of strange carvings. He skinned my head and removed my eyes; but with his magic my vision remained. I could see tears on his cheeks as I was placed in the low branches of a small tree. "There-there," he said. "I be here soon, too." He retreated then. And the brush did not complain at his feet. The insects did not fret. The animals were not startled nor deterred. He was not there to them.

We were the good ones.

I watch the land. For how long, I do not know. Is it a week now, a year, or a thousand? Is it the screams of the bad I hear, dying beneath the lush and blood-thirsty warrior seeking revenge, or those of the good, enraptured in honor or betrayed into service? I watch and wait. And I think. I think about our coming time of freedom. I think about revenge. My revenge. I did not ask to be a queen. I was tricked into this hideous service.

I think revenge will bring satisfaction, and so I think of it. I dream of it and savor it. The thought of cutting and burning and scarring is not so terrible now. I will spoil the new evolution. Perhaps my thoughts will reveal me to the land, and will, happily, be my death. And if not, I have time for plans. Such plans. You see?

Ah ha ha.

RICHARD RIDDLE, BOY DETECTIVE, IN "THE CASE OF THE FRENCH SPY"

Kim Newman

Kim Newman is the author of The Night Mayor, Anno Dracula, The Bloody Red Baron, Dracula Cha Cha Cha *(aka* Judgment of Tears: Anno Dracula 1959*), and* Life's Lottery, *amongst other novels. His short stories are collected in* The Original Dr. Shade and Other Stories, Famous Monsters, Seven Stars, Unforgivable Stories, Where the Bodies Are Buried, Dead Travel Fast, *and* The Man from the Diogenes Club.

A winner of two HWA Bram Stoker Awards, the British Science Fiction Award, the British Fantasy Award, the Children of the Night Award, the Fiction Award of the Lord Ruthven Assembly and two International Horror Guild Awards, he has also written and edited a number of nonfiction books, including Horror: 100 Best Books *and* Horror: Another 100 Best Books *(both with Stephen Jones).*

"Lyme Regis, in the county of Dorset, is perhaps best-known as the setting for John Fowles' prematurely post-modern Victorian novel The French Lieutenant's Woman," *Newman reveals. "Fowles was a famous, if mysterious local resident and lived quite near my fictional Orris Priory. In the 1970s, I spent many weekends around the little coast town, where my father had a boat.*

"This story draws on my own memories of pottering around Lyme and

the famous anecdote of the Hartlepool monkey. The story goes that, during the Napoleonic Wars, a ship sank off the coast of the Northern fishing town. The sole survivor was a monkey dressed in a miniature sailor's uniform. The locals, having never seen a Frenchman, took the monkey for a spy, tried the unfortunate creature, and hanged it, prompting citizens of rival towns to taunt Hartlepool natives to this day with a jeer of 'who hung the monkey?'"

Fans of H. P. Lovecraft's "Deep Ones" may also find a surprise awaiting them in this children's detective adventure. . . .

I: WMJHU-OJBHU DAJJQ JH QRS PRBHUFS

"Gosh, Dick," said Violet, "an ammonite!"

A chunk of rock, bigger than any of them could have lifted, had broken from the soft cliff and fallen on the shingle. Violet, on her knees, brushed grit and grime from the stone.

They were on the beach below Ware Cleeve, looking for clues.

This was not strictly a fossil hunting expedition, but Dick knew Violet was mad about terrible lizards—which was what "dinosaur" meant in Greek, she had explained. On a recent visit to London, Violet had been taken to the prehistoric monster exhibit in Crystal Palace Park. She could not have been more excited if the life-size statues turned out to be live specimens. Palaeontology was like being a detective, she enthused: working back from clues to the truth, examining a pile of bones and guessing what kind of body once wrapped around them.

Dick conceded her point. But the dinosaurs died a long, long time ago. No culprit's collar would be felt. A pity. It would be a good mystery to solve. The Case of the Vanishing Lizards. No, The Mystery of the Disappearing Dinosaurs. No, The Adventure of the Absent Ammonites.

"Coo," said Ernest. "Was this a *monster*?"

Ernest liked monsters. Anything with big teeth counted.

"Not really," Violet admitted. "It was a cephalopod. That means "head-foot.""

"It was a head with only a foot?" Ernest liked the idea. "Did it hop up behind enemies, and sink its fangs into their bleeding necks?"

"It was more like a big shrimp. Or a squid with a shell."

"Squid are fairly monstrous, Ernest," said Dick. "Some grow giant and crush ships with their tentacles."

Ernest made experimental crushing motions with his hands, providing squelching noises with his mouth.

Violet ran her fingers over the ammonite's segments.

"Ammon was the ram-headed God of Ancient Egypt."

Dick saw Ernest imagining that—an evil God butting unbelievers to death.

"These are called 'ammonites' because the many-chambered spiral looks like a the horn of a ram. You know, like the big one in Mr. Crossan's field."

Ernest went quiet. He liked fanged monsters, giant squids and evil Gods, but had a problem with *animals*. Once, the children were forced to go a long way round to avoid Mr. Crossan's field. Ernest had come up with many tactical reasons for the detour, and Dick and Violet pretended to be persuaded by his argument that they needed to throw pursuers off their track.

The three children were about together all the time this summer. Dick was down from London, staying with Uncle Davey and Aunt Maeve. Both were a bit dotty. Uncle Davey used to paint fairyland scenes for children's books, but was retired from that and drawing only to please himself. Last year, Violet showed up at Seaview Chase unannounced, having learned it was David Harvill's house. She liked his illustrations, but genuinely liked the pictures in his studio even more.

Violet had taken an interest in Dick's detective work. She had showed him around Lyme Regis, and the surrounding beaches and countryside. She wasn't like a proper girl, so it was all right being friends with her. Normally, Dick couldn't admit to having a girl as a friend. In summer, it was different. Ernest was Violet's cousin, two years younger than her and Dick. Ernest's father was in Africa fighting Boers, so he was with Violet's parents for the school holidays.

They were the Richard Riddle Detective Agency. Their goal: to find mysteries, then solve them. Thus far, they had handled the Matter of the Mysterious Maidservant (meeting the Butcher's Boy, though she was supposed to have a sweetheart at sea), the Curious Affair of the Derelict Dinghy (Alderman Hooke was lying asleep in it, empty beer bottles rolling around his feet) and the Puzzle of the Purloined Pasties (still an open case, though suspicion inevitably fell upon Tarquin "Tiger" Bristow).

Ernest had reasoned out his place in the firm. When Dick pointed the finger of guilt at the villain, Ernest would thump the miscreant about the head until the official police arrived. Violet, Ernest said, could make tea and listen to Dick explain his chain of deduction. Ernest, Violet commented acidly, was a dependable strong-arm man . . . unless the criminal owned a sheep, or threatened to make him eat parsnips, or (as was depressingly likely) turned out to be "Tiger" Bristow (the Bismarck of Bullies) and returned Ernest's head-thumping with interest. Then, Dick had to negotiate a peace, like between Americans and Red Indians, to avoid bloodshed. When Violet broke off the Reservation, people got scalped.

It was a sunny August afternoon, but strong salt wind blew off the sea. Violet had tied back her hair to keep it out of her face. Dick looked up at Ware Cleeve: it was thickly wooded, roots poking out of the cliff-face like the fingers of buried men. The Tower of Orris Priory rose above the treetops like a periscope.

Clues led to Orris Priory. Dick suspected smugglers. Or spies.

Granny Ball, who kept the pasty-stall near the Cobb, had warned the detectives to stay away from the shingle under the Cleeve. It was a haunt of "sea-ghosts". The angry souls of shipwrecked sailors, half-fish folk from sunken cities and other monsters of the deep (Ernest liked this bit) were given to creeping onto the beach, clawing away at the stone, crumbling it piece by piece. One day, the Cleeve would collapse.

Violet wanted to know why the sea-ghosts would do such a thing. The landslide would only make another cliff, further inland. Granny winked and said "never you mind, lass" in a highly unsatisfactory manner.

Before her craze for terrible lizards, Violet had been passionate about myths and legends (it was why she liked Uncle Davey's pictures). She said myths were expressions of common truth, dressed up to make a point. The shingle beach was dangerous, because rocks fell on it. People in the long ago must have been hit on the head and killed, so the sea-ghost story was invented to keep children away from danger. It was like a BEWARE THE DOG sign (Ernest didn't like this bit), but out of date—as if you had an old, non-fierce hound but put up a BEWARE OF DANGEROUS DOG sign.

Being on the shingle wasn't really dangerous. The cliffs wouldn't fall and the sea-ghosts wouldn't come.

Dick liked Violet's reasoning, but saw better.

"No, Vile, it's been *kept up,* this story. Granny and other folk round here tell the tale to keep us away because *someone* doesn't want us seeing what they're about."

"Smugglers," said Ernest.

Dick nodded. "Or spies. Not enough clues to be certain. But, mark my word, there's wrong-doing afoot on the shingle. And it's our job to root it out."

It was too blowy to go out in Violet's little boat, the S.S. *Pterodactyl,* so they had come on foot.

And found the ammonite.

Since the fossil wasn't about to hop to life and attack, Ernest lost interest and wandered off, down by the water. He was looking for monster tracks, the tentacle-trails of a giant squid most likely.

"This might be the largest ammonite ever found here," said Violet. "If it's a new species, I get to name it."

Dick wondered how to get the fossil to Violet's house. It would be a tricky endeavor.

"You, children, what are you about?"

Men had appeared on the beach without Dick noticing. If they had come from either direction along the shore, he should have seen them.

"You shouldn't be here. Come away from that evil thing, at once, *now.*"

The speaker was an old man with white hair, pince-nez on a black ribbon, an expression like someone who's just bit into a cooking apple by mistake, and a white collar like a clergyman's. He wore an old-fashioned coat with a thick, raised collar, cut away from tight britches and heavy boots.

Dick recognized the Reverend Mr. Sellwood, of Orris Priory.

With him were two bare-armed fellows in leather jerkins and corduroy trousers. Whereas Sellwood carried a stick, they toted sledge-hammers, like the ones convicts use on Dartmoor.

"Foul excrescence of the Devil," said Sellwood, pointing his stick at Violet's ammonite. "Brother Fose, Brother Fessel, do the Lord's work."

Fose and Fessel raised their hammers.

Violet leaned over, as if protecting a pet lamb from slaughter-men.

"Out of the way, foolish girl."

"It's *mine,*" she said.

"It's nobody's, and no good to anybody. It must be smashed. God would wish it . . ."

"But this find is important. To *science.*"

Sellwood looked as if that bite of cooker was in his throat, making his eyes water.

"Science! Bah, stuff and nonsense! Devil's charm, my girl, that's what this is!"

"It was alive, millions of millions of years ago."

"The Earth is less than six thousand years old, child, as you would know if you read your scriptures."

Violet, angry, stood up to argue. "But that's not true. There's *proof*. This is . . ."

Fose and Fessel took their opportunity, and brought the hammers down. The fossil split. Sharp chips flew. Violet—appalled, hands in tiny fists, mouth open—didn't notice her shin bleeding.

"You *can't* . . ."

"These so-called proofs, stone bones and long-dead dragons," said Sellwood, "are the Devil's trickeries."

The Brethren smashed the ammonite to shards and powder.

"This was put here to fool weak minds," lectured the Reverend. "It is the Church Militant's sacred work to destroy such obscenities, lest more be tempted to blasphemy. This is not science, this is sacrilege."

"It was mine," Violet said quietly.

"I have saved you from error. You should thank me."

Ernest came over to see what the noise was about. Sellwood bestowed a smile on the lad that afforded a glimpse of terrifying teeth.

Teeth on monsters were fine with Ernest; teeth like Sellwood's would give him nightmares.

"A job well done," said the Reverend. "Let us look further. More infernal things may have sprung up."

Brother Fose leered at Violet and patted her on the head, which made her flinch. Brother Fessel looked stern disapproval at this familiarity. They followed Sellwood, swinging hammers, scouting for something to break to bits. Dick had an idea they'd rather be pounding on something that squealed and bled than something so long dead it had turned to stone.

Violet wasn't crying. But she was hating.

More than before, Dick was convinced Sellwood was behind some vile endeavor. He had the look of a smuggler, or a spy.

Richard Riddle, Boy Detective, would bring the villain to book.

II: Trs Ndps ja qrs Dggjhbqs Dhhbrbfdqjm

Uncle Davey had let Dick set up the office of the Richard Riddle Detective Agency in a small room under the eaves. A gable window led to a small balcony that looked like a ship's crow's-nest. Seaview Chase was a large, complicated house on Black Ven, a jagged rise above Lyme Bay, an ideal vantage point for surveying the town and the sea.

Dick had installed his equipment—a microscope, boxes and folders, reference books, his collection of clues and trophies. Violet had donated some small fossils and her hammers and trowels. Ernest wanted space on the wall for the head of their first murderer: he had an idea that when a murderer was hanged, the police gave the head as a souvenir to the detective who caught him.

The evening after the fossil-smashing incident, Dick sat in the office and opened a new file and wrote *Trs Ndps ja qrs Dggjhbqs Dhhbrbfdqjm* on a fresh sheet of paper. It was the R.R.D.A. Special Cipher for *The Case of the Ammonite Annihilator*.

After breakfast the next day, the follow-up investigation began. Dick went into the airy studio on the first floor and asked Uncle Davey what he knew about Sellwood.

"Grim-visage?" said Uncle Davey, pulling a face. "Dresses as if it were fifty years ago? Of him, I know, to be frank, not much. He once called with a presentation copy of some verminous volume, printed at his own expense. I think he wanted me to find a proper publisher. Put on a scary smile to ingratiate. Maeve didn't like him. He hasn't been back. Book's around somewhere, probably. Must chuck it one day. It'll be in one of those piles."

He stabbed a paintbrush towards the stacks which grew against one wall and went back to painting—a ship at sea, only there were eyes in the sea if you looked close enough, and faces in the clouds and the folds of sail-cloth. Uncle Davey liked hiding things.

When Violet and Ernest arrived, they set to searching book-piles.

It took a long time. Violet kept getting interested in irrelevant findings. Mostly titles about pixies and fairies and curses.

Sellwood's book had migrated to near the bottom of an especially towering pile. Extracting it brought about a bad tumble that alerted Aunt Maeve, who rushed in assuming the whole of Black Ven was giving way and the house would soon be crashing into Lyme Bay. Uncle Davey cheerfully kicked the spill of volumes into a corner and said he'd sort them out one day, then noticed a wave suitable for hiding an eye in and forgot about the children. Aunt Maeve went off to get warm milk with drops of something from Cook.

In the office, the detectives pored over their find for clues.

"Omphalos Diabolicus, or: The Hoax of 'Pre-History'," intoned Dick, "by the Reverend Daniel Sturdevant Sellwood, published 1897, Orris Press, Dorset." Uncle Davey said he paid for the printing, so I deduce that he is the sole proprietor of this phantom publisher. Ah-hah, the pages have not been cut after the first chapter, so I further deduce that it must be deadly dull stuff."

He tossed the book to Violet, who got to work with a long knife, slitting the leaves as if they were the author's throat. Then she flicked through pages, pausing only to report relevant facts. One of her talents was gutting books, discovering the few useful pages like a prospector panning gold dust out of river-dirt.

Daniel Sellwood wasn't a proper clergyman any more. He had been booted out of the Church of England after shouting that the Bishop should burn Mr. Darwin along with his published works. Now, Sellwood had his own sect, the Church Militant—but most of his congregation were paid servants. Sellwood came from a wealthy Dorset family, rich from trade and shipping, and had been packed off to parson school because an older brother, George, was supposed to inherit the fortune—only the brother was lost at sea, along with his wife Rebecca and little daughter Ruth, and

Daniel's expectations increased. The sinking of the *Sophy Briggs* was a famous maritime mystery like the *Mary Celeste* and Captain Nemo: thirty years ago, the pride of the Orris-Sellwood Line went down in calm seas, with all hands lost. Sellwood skipped over the loss in a sentence, then spent pages talking up the "divine revelation" which convinced him to found a church rather than keep up the business.

According to Violet, a lot of folk around Lyme resented being thrown out of work when Sellwood dismantled his shipping concern and dedicated the family fortune to preaching anti-Darwinism.

"What's an omphalo-thing?" asked Ernest.

"The title means 'the Devil's Belly-Button'," said Violet, which made Ernest giggle. "He's put Greek and Latin words together, which is poor Classics. Apart from his stupid ideas, he's a *terrible* writer. Listen . . . 'all the multitudinarious flora and fauna of divine creation constitute veritable evidence of the proof of the pellucid and undiluted accuracy of the Word of God Almighty Unchallenged as set down in the shining, burning, shimmering sentences, chapters and, indeed, books of the Old and New Testaments, hereinafter known to all righteous and right-thinking men as the Holy Bible of Glorious God.' It's as if he's saying 'this is the true truthiest truest truth of truthdom ever told truly by truth-trusters'."

"How do the belly-buttons come into it?" asked Dick.

"Adam and Eve were supposed to have been created with navels, though—since they weren't born like other people—they oughtn't to have them."

This was over Ernest's head, but Dick knew how babies came and that his navel was a knot, where a cord had been cut and tied.

"To Sellwood's way of thinking, just as Adam and Eve were created to *seem* as if they had normal parents, the Earth was created as if it had a pre-history, with geological and fossil evidence in place to make the planet appear much older than it says in the Bible."

"That's silly," said Ernest.

"Don't tell me, tell Sellwood," said Violet. "He's a silly, stupid man. He doesn't want to know the truth, or anyone else to either, so he breaks fossils and shouts down lecturers. His theory isn't even original. A man named Gosse wrote a book with the same idea, though Gosse claimed *God* buried fossils to fool people while Sellwood says it was the Devil."

Violet was quite annoyed.

"I think it's an excuse to go round bullying people," said Dick. "A cover for his real, sinister purpose."

"If you ask me, what he does is sinister enough by itself."

"Nobody did ask you," said Ernest, which he always said when someone was unwise enough to preface a statement with "if you ask me". Violet stuck her tongue out at him.

Dick was thinking.

"It's likely that the Sellwood family were smugglers," he said.

Violet agreed. "Smugglers had to have ships, and pretend to be respectable merchants. In the old days, they were all at it. You know the poem . . ."

Violet stood up, put a hand on her chest, and recited, dramatically.

> *"If you wake at midnight, and hear a horse's feet,*
> *Don't go drawing back the blind, or looking in the street.*
> *Them that ask no questions isn't told a lie,*
> *Watch the wall, my darling, while the gentlemen go by.*
> *Five and twenty ponies, trotting through the dark,*
> *Brandy for the parson, 'baccy for the clerk;*
> *Laces for a lady, letters for a spy,*
> *And watch the wall, my darling, while the gentlemen go by."*

She waited for applause, which didn't come. But her recitation was useful. Dick had been thinking in terms of spies *or* smugglers, but the poem reminded him that the breeds were interdependent. It struck him that Sellwood might be a smuggler of spies, or a spy for smugglers.

"I'll wager "Tiger" Bristow is in this, too," he said, snapping his fingers.

Ernest shivered, audibly.

"Is it spying or smuggling?" he asked.

"It's both," Dick replied.

Violet sat down again, and chewed on a long, stray strand of her hair.

"Tell Dick about the French Spy," suggested Ernest.

Dick was intrigued.

"That was a long time ago, a hundred years," she said. "It's a local legend, not evidence."

"You yourself say legends always shroud some truth," declared Dick. "We must consider *all* the facts, even rumors of facts, before forming a conclusion."

Violet shrugged. "It is about Sellwood's *house,* I suppose . . ."

Dick was astonished. "And you didn't think it was relevant! Sometimes, I'm astonished by your lack of perspicacity!"

Violet looked incipiently upset at his tone, and Dick wondered if he wasn't going too far. He needed her in the Agency, but she could be maddening at times. Like a real girl.

"Out with it, Vile," he barked.

Violet crossed her arms and kept quiet.

"I apologize for my tactlessness," said Dick. "But this is vitally important. We might be able to put that ammonite-abuser out of business, with immeasurable benefit to *science.*"

Violet melted. "Very well. I heard this from Alderman Hooke's father . . ."

Before her palaeontology craze, Violet fancied herself a collector of folklore. She had gone around asking old people to tell stories or sing songs or remember why things were called what they were called. She was going to write them all up in a book of local legends and had wanted Uncle Davey to draw the pictures. She was still working on her book, but it was about Dinosaurs in Dorset now.

"I didn't make much of it, because it wasn't much of a legend. Just a scrap of history."

"With a spy," prompted Ernest. "A spy who came out of the sea!"

Violet nodded. "That's more or less it. When England was at war with France, everyone thought Napoleon . . ."

"Boney!" put in Ernest, making fang-fingers at the corners of his mouth.

"Yes, Boney . . . everyone thought he was going to invade, like William the Conqueror. Along the coast people watched the seas. Signal-fires were prepared, like with the Spanish Armada. Most thought it likely the French would strike at Dover, but round here they tapped the sides of their noses . . ."

Violet imitated an old person tapping her long nose.

". . . and said the last army to invade Britain had landed at Lyme, and the next would too. The last army was Monmouth's, during his rebellion. He landed at the Cobb and marched up to Sedgmoor, where he was defeated. There are *lots* of legends about the Duke of Monmouth . . ."

Dick made a get-to-the-point gesture.

"Any rate, near the end of the 18th century, a man named Jacob Orris formed a vigilance patrol to keep watch on the beaches. Orris's daughter married a sea-captain called Lud Sellwood; they begat drowned George and old Devil's Belly-Button. Come to think, Orris's patrol was like Sellwood's Church Militant—an excuse to shout at folk and break things. Orris started a campaign to get "French beans" renamed "Free-from-Tyranny beans", and had his men attack grocer's stalls when no one agreed with him. Orris was expecting a fleet to heave to in Lyme Bay and land an army, but knew spies would be put ashore first to scout the around. One night, during a terrible storm, Orris caught a spy flung up on the shingle."

"And . . .?"

"That's it, really. I expect they hit him with hammers and killed him, but if anyone really knows, they aren't saying."

Dick was disappointed.

"Tell him how it was a *special* spy," said Ernest.

Dick was intrigued again. Especially since Violet obviously didn't want to say more.

"He was a sea-ghost," announced Ernest.

"Old Hooke said the spy had *walked* across the channel," admitted Violet. "On the bottom of the sea, in a special diving suit. He was a Frenchman, but—and you have to remember stories get twisted over the years—he had gills *sewn* into his neck so he could breathe underwater. As far as anyone knew round here, all Corsicans were like that. They said it was probably Boney's cousin."

"And they killed him?"

Violet shrugged. "I expect so."

"And kept him *pickled,*" said Ernest.

"Now that *isn't* true. One version of this story is that Orris had the dead spy stuffed, then hidden away. But the family would have found the thing and thrown it out by now. And we'd know whether it was a man or, as Granny Ball says, a trained seal. Stories are like limpets on rocks. They stick on and get thicker until you can't see what was there in the first place."

Dick whistled.

"I don't see how this can have anything to do with what Sellwood is about now," said Violet. "This may not have happened, and if it did, it was a hundred years ago. Sellwood wasn't even born then. His parents were still children."

"My dear Vile, a century-old mystery is still a mystery. And crime can seep into a family like water in the foundations, passed down from father to son . . ."

"Father to *daughter* to son, in this case."

"I haven't forgotten that. This mystery goes deep. It's all about the past. And haven't you said that a century is just a heartbeat in the long life of the planet?"

She was coming round, he saw.

"We have to get into Orris Priory," said Dick.

III: BA BQ WDP SDPY QJ ABHO, BQ WJTFOH'Q IS *RBOOSH*

"Why are we on the shingle?" asked Ernest. "The Priory is up there, on top of the Cleeve."

Dick had been waiting for the question. Deductions impressed more if he didn't just come out with cleverness, but waited for a prompt.

"Remember yesterday? Sellwood seemed to turn up suddenly, with Fose and Fessel. If they'd been walking on the beach, we'd have seen them ages before they arrived. But we didn't. Therefore, there must be a secret way. A smugglers' tunnel."

Violet found some pieces of the fossil. She looked towards the cliff.

"We were facing out to sea, and they came from behind," she said.

She tossed her ammonite-shard, which rebounded off the soft rock-face.

The cliff was too crumbly for caves that might conceal a tunnel. The children began looking closely, hoping for a hidden door.

After a half-hour, Ernest complained that he was hungry.

After an hour, Violet complained that she was fed up with rocks.

Dick stuck to it. "If it was easy to find, it wouldn't be *hidden,*" he kept saying.

Ernest began to make helpful suggestions that didn't help but needed to be argued with.

"*Maybee* they came up under the sea and swam ashore?"

"They weren't wet and we would have seen them," countered Dick.

"*Maybee* they've got invisible diving suits that don't show wetness?"

"Those haven't been invented yet."

"Maybee they've invented them but kept it quiet?"

"It's not likely . . ."

"But not *impossible,* and you always say that 'when you've eliminated the impossible . . .'"

"Actually, Ernest, it *is* impossible!"

"Prove it."

"The only way to prove something impossible is to devote your entire life to trying to achieve it, and the lives of everyone to infinity throughout eternity, then *not* succeed . . ."

"Well, get started . . ."

". . . and that's *impractical!"*

Dick knew he was shouting, but when Ernest got into one of these *maybee* moods—which he called his "clever spells"—everyone got a headache, and usually wound up giving in and agreeing with something they knew to be absurd just to make Ernest shut up. After that, he would be hard to live with for the rest of the day, puffed up like a toad with a smugness that Violet labeled "very unattractive", which prompted him to snipe that he didn't want to attract anyone like her, and her to counter that he would change his mind in a few years, and him to . . . well, it was a cycle Dick had lived through too often.

Then Violet found a hinge. Two, in fact.

Dick got out his magnifying glass and examined the hinges. Recently oiled, he noted. Where there were hinges, there must be a door. Hidden.

"Where's the handle?" asked Ernest.

"Inside," said Violet.

"What's the use of a door it only opens from one side?"

"It'd keep out detectives, like us," suggested Violet.

"There was no open door when Sellwood was here," observed Dick. "It closed behind him. He'd want to open it again, rather than go home the long way."

"He had two big strong men with hammers," said Violet, "and we've got you and Ernest."

Dick tried to be patient.

He stuck his fingers into a crack in the rock, and worked down, hoping to get purchase enough to pull the probable door open.

"Careful," said Violet.

"Maybee . . ."

"Shut up, Ernest," said Dick.

He found his hand stuck, but pulled free, scraping his knuckles.

There was an outcrop by the sticking point, at about the height where you'd put a door-handle.

"Ah-hah," said Dick, seizing and turning the rock.

A click, and a section of the cliff pulled open. It was surprisingly light, a thin layer of stone fixed to a wooden frame.

A section of rock fell off the door.

"You've broken it now," said Ernest.

It was dark inside. From his coat-of-many-hidden-pockets, Dick produced three candle-stubs with metal holders and a box of matches. For his next birthday, he hoped to get one of the new battery-powered electrical lanterns—until then, these would remain R.R.D.A. standard issue.

Getting the candles lit was a performance. The draught kept puffing out match-flames before the wicks caught. Violet took over and mumsily arranged everything, then handed out the candles, showing Ernest how to hold his so wax didn't drip on his fingers.

"Metal's hot," said Ernest.

"Perhaps we should leave you here as look-out," said Dick. "You can warn us in case any *dogs* come along."

The metal apparently wasn't *too* hot, since Ernest now wanted to continue. He insisted on being first into the dark, in case there were monsters.

Once they were inside, the door swung shut.

They were in a space carved out of the rock and shored up with timber. Empty barrels piled nearby. A row of fossil-smashing hammers arranged where Violet could spit at them. Smooth steps led upwards, with the rusted remains of rings set into the walls either side.

"'Brandy for the parson, baccy for the clerk'," said Violet.

"Indubitably," responded Dick. "This is clear evidence of smuggling."

"What do people smuggle these days?" asked Violet. "Brandy and tobacco might have been expensive when we were at war with France and ships were slow, but that was ages ago."

Dick was caught out. He knew there was still contraband, but hadn't looked into its nature.

"Jewels, probably," he guessed. "And there's always spying."

Ernest considered the rings in the wall.

"I bet prisoners were chained here," he said, "until they turned to skelly-tones!"

"More likely people hold the rings while climbing the slippery stairs," suggested Violet, "especially if they're carrying heavy cases of . . . jewels and spy-letters."

Ernest was disappointed.

"But they *could* be used for prisoners."

Ernest cheered up.

"If I was a prisoner, I could 'scape", he said. He put his hand in a ring, which was much too big for him and for any grown-up too. Then he pulled and the ring came out of the wall.

Ernest tried to put it back.

Dick was tense, expecting tons of rock to fall on them.

No collapse happened.

"Be careful touching things," he warned his friends. "We were lucky that time, but there might be deadly traps."

He led the way up.

IV: DH *JTIFBSQQS*

The steps weren't steep, but went up a long way. The tunnel had been hewn out of rock. New timbers, already bowed and near-cracking, showed where the passage had been shored after falls.

"We must be under the Priory," he said.

They came to the top of the stairs, and a basement-looking room. Wooden crates were stacked.

"Cover your light," said Dick.

Ernest yelped as he burned his hand.

"Carefully," Dick added.

Ernest whimpered a bit.

"What do you suppose is in these?" asked Violet. "Contraband?"

"Instruments of evil?" prompted Ernest.

Dick held his candle close to a crate. The slats were spaced an inch or so apart. Inside were copies of *Omphalos Diabolicus.*

"Isn't the point of smuggling to bring in things people *want?*" asked Violet. "I can't imagine an illicit market for unreadable tracts."

"There could be coded spy messages in the books," Dick suggested hopefully.

"Even spies trained to resist torture in the dungeons of the Tsar wouldn't be able to read through these to get any message," said Violet. "My *deduction* is that these are here because Sellwood can't get anybody to buy his boring old book."

"Maybee he should change his name to Sellwords."

Dick had the tiniest spasm of impatience. Here they were, in the lair of an undoubted villain, having penetrated secret defenses, and all they could do was make dubiously sarky remarks about his name.

"We should scout further," he said. "Come on."

He opened a door and found a gloomy passageway. The lack of windows suggested they were still underground. The walls were paneled, wood warped and stained by persistent damp.

The next room along had no door and was full of rubble. Dick thought the ceiling had fallen in, but Violet saw at once that detritus was broken-up fossils.

"Ammonites," she said, "also brachiopods, nautiloids, crinoids, plagiostoma, coroniceras, gryphaea, *and* calcirhynchia."

She held up what looked like an ordinary stone.

"This could be the knee-bone of a *scelidosaurus*. One was discovered in Charmouth, in Liassic cliffs just like these. The first near-complete dinosaur fossil to come to light. This might have been another find as important. Sellwood is a vandal and a wrecker. He should be hit on the head with his own hammers."

Dick patted Violet on the back, hoping she would cheer up.

"It's only a knee," said Ernest. "Nothing interesting about knees."

"Some dinosaurs had *brains* in their knees. Extra brains to do the thinking for their legs. Imagine if you had brains in your knees."

Ernest was impressed.

"If *I'd* found this, I wouldn't have broken it," said Violet. "I would have *named* it. *Biolettosaurus,* Violet's Lizard."

"Let's try the next room," said Dick.

"There might still be useful fragments."

Reluctantly, Violet left the room of broken stone bones.

Next was a thick wooden door, with iron bands across it, and three heavy bolts. Though the bolts were oiled, it was a strain to pull them—Dick and Violet both struggled. The top and bottom bolts shifted, but the middle one wouldn't move.

"Let me try," said Ernest. "Please."

They did, and he didn't get anywhere.

Violet dipped back into the fossil room and returned with a chunk they used as a hammer. The third bolt shot open.

The banging and clanging sounded fearfully loud in the enclosed space.

They listened, but no one came. *Maybee,* Dick thought—recognizing the Ernestism—Sellwood was up in his Tower, scanning the horizon for spy-signals, and his Brethren were taking afternoon naps.

The children stepped through the doorway, and the door swung slowly and heavily shut behind them.

This room was different again.

The floor and walls were solid slabs which looked as if they'd been in place a long time. The atmosphere was dank, slightly moldy. A stone trough, like you see in stables, ran along one wall, fed by an old-fashioned pump. Dick cupped water in his hand and tasted it. There was a nasty, coppery sting, and he spat.

"It's a *dungeon,*" said Ernest.

Violet held up her candle.

A winch-apparatus, with handles like a threshing machine, was fixed to the floor at the far side of the room, thick chain wrapped around the drum.

"Careful," said Violet, gripping Dick's arm.

Dick looked at his feet. He stood on the edge of a circular hole, like a well. It was a dozen feet across, and uncovered.

"There should be a cap on this," announced Dick. "To prevent accidents."

"I doubt if Sellwood cares much about accidents befalling intruders."

"You're probably right, Vile. The man's a complete rotter."

Chains extended from the winch unto a solid iron ring in the ceiling and then down into the Hole.

"This is an *oubliette,*" said Violet. "It's from the French. You capture your *prisonnier* and *jeté* him into the Hole, then *oublié* them—forget them."

Ernest, nervously, kept well away from the edge. He had been warned about falling into wells once, which meant that ever since he was afraid of them.

Violet tossed her rock-chunk into the pool of dark, and counted. After three counts—thirty feet—there was a thump. Stone on stone.

"No splash," she said.

Up from the depths came another sound, a gurgling groan—something alive but unidentifiable. The noise lodged in Dick's heart like a fish-hook of ice. A chill played up his spine.

The cry had come from a throat, but hardly a human one.

Ernest dropped his candle, which rolled to the lip of the pit and fell in, flame guttering.

Round, green eyes shone up, fire dancing in the fish-flat pupils.

Something grey-green, weighted with old chains, writhed at the bottom of the Hole.

Ernest's candle went out.

Violet's grip on Dick's arm hurt now.

"What's *that?*" she gasped.

The groan took on an imploring, almost pathetic tone, tinged with cunning and bottomless wrath.

Dick shrugged off his shiver. He had a moment of pure joy, the *click* of sudden understanding that often occurs at the climax of a case, when clues fit in the mind like jig-saw pieces and the solution is plain and simple.

"That, my dear Vile, is your French spy!"

V: *OBDIJFBNTP MDMBQBGS*

"Someone's coming," said Ernest.

Footfalls in the passageway!

"Hide," said Dick.

The only place—aside from the Hole—was under the water-trough. Dick and Violet pinched out their candles and crammed in, pulling Ernest after them.

"They'll see the door's not bolted," said Ernest.

Violet clamped her hand over her cousin's mouth.

In the enclosed space, their breathing seemed horribly loud.

Dick worried. Ernest was right.

Maybee the people in the passage weren't coming to *this* room. *Maybee* they'd already walked past, on their way to smash fossils or get a copy of Sellwood's book.

The footsteps stopped outside the door.

Maybee this person didn't know it was usually bolted. *Maybee* this dungeon was so rarely visited they'd *oubliéd* whether it had been bolted shut after the last time.

Maybee . . .

"Fessel, Fose, Milder, Maulder," barked a voice.

The Reverend Mr. Daniel Sturdevant Sellwood, calling his brethren.

"And who's been opening *my* door," breathed Violet.

It took Dick long seconds to recognize the storybook quotation.

"Who was last here?" shouted Sellwood. "This is inexcusable. With the Devil, one does not take such risks."

"En cain't git ouwt of thic Hole," replied someone.

"Brother Milder, it has the wiles of an arch-fiend. That is why only *I* can be trusted to put it to the question. Who last brought the slops?"

There was some argument.

Maybee they'd be all right. Sellwood was so concerned with stopping an escape that he hadn't thought anyone might break *in*.

One of the Brethren tentatively spoke up, and received a clout round the ear.

Dick wondered why anyone would *want* to be in Sellwood's Church Militant.

"Stand guard," Sellwood ordered. "Let me see what disaster is so narrowly averted."

The door was pushed open. Sellwood set a lantern on a perch. The children pressed further back into shrinking shadow. Dick's ankle bent the wrong way. He bit down on the pain.

He saw Sellwood's shoes—with old-fashioned buckles and gaiters—walk past the trough, towards the Hole. He stopped, just by Dick's face.

There was a pumping, coughing sound.

Sellwood filled a beaker.

He poured the water into the Hole.

Violet counted silently, again. After three, the water splashed on the French spy. It cried out, with despair and yearning.

"Drink deep, spawn of Satan!"

The creature howled, then gargled again. Dick realized it wasn't making animal grunts but *speaking*. Unknown words that he suspected were not French.

The thing had been here for over a hundred years!

"Fose, Milder, in here, now. I will resume the inquisition."

Brethren clumped in. Dick saw heavy boots.

The two bruisers walked around the room, keeping well away from the Hole. Dick eased out a little to get a better view. He risked a more comfortable, convenient position. Sellwood had no reason to suspect he was spied upon.

Brother Fose and Brother Milder worked the winch.

The chains tightened over the Hole, then wound onto the winch-drum.

The thing in the *oubliette* cursed. Dick was sure *"f'tagn"* was a swear-word. As it was hauled upwards, the creature struggled, hissing and croaking.

Violet held Dick's hand, pulling, keeping him from showing himself.

A head showed over the mouth of the Hole, three times the size of a man's and with no neck, just a pulpy frill of puffed-up gill-slits. Saucer-sized fish-eyes held the light, pupils contracting. Dick was sure the creature, eyes at floor-level, saw past the boots of its captors straight into his face. It had a fixed maw, with enough jagged teeth to please Ernest.

"Up," ordered Sellwood. "Let's see all of the demon."

The Brethren winched again, and the thing hung like Captain Kidd on Execution Dock. It was man-like, but with a stub of fishtail protruding beneath two rows of dorsal spines. Its hands and feet were webbed, with nastily curved yellow nail-barbs. Where water had splashed, its skin was rainbow-scaled, beautiful even. Elsewhere, its hide was grey and taut, cracked, flaking or mossy, with rusty weals where the chains chafed.

Dick saw the thing was missing several finger-barbs. Its back and front were striped across with long-healed and new-made scars. It had been whipping boy in this house since the days when Boney was a warrior way-aye-aye.

He imagined Jacob Orris trying to get Napoleon's secrets out of the "spy". Had old Orris held up charts and asked the man-fish to tap a claw on hidden harbors where the invasion fleet was gathered?

Ernest was mumbling "sea-ghost" over and over, not frightened but awed. Violet hissed at him to hush.

Dick was sure they'd be caught, but Sellwood was fascinated by the creature. He poked his face close to his captive's, smiling smugly. A cheek muscle twitched around his fixed sneer. The man-fish looked as if it would like to spit in Sellwood's face but couldn't afford the water.

"So, *Diabolicus Maritime,* is it today that you confess? I have been patient. We merely seek a statement we all know to be true, which will end this sham once and for all."

The fish-eyes were glassy and flat, but moved to fix on Sellwood.

"You are a *deception,* my infernal guest, a lure, a living trick, a lie made flesh, a creature of the Prince of Liars. Own that Satan is your maker, imp! Confess your evil purpose!"

Sellwood touched fingertips to the creature's scarred chest, scraping dry flesh. Scales fluttered away, falling like dead moths. Dick saw Sellwood's fingers flex, the tips biting.

"The bones weren't enough, were they? Those so-called 'fossils', the buried lies that lead to blasphemy and disbelief. No, the Devil had a second deceit in reserve, to pile upon the Great Untruth of 'Pre-History'. No mere dead dragon, but a live specimen, one of those fabled 'missing links' in the fairy tale of 'evolution'. By your very existence, you bear false witness, testify that the world is older than it has been proved over and over again to be, preach against creation, tear down mankind, to drag us from the realm of the angels into the festering salt-depths of Hell. The City of the Damned lies under the Earth, but you prove to my satisfaction that it extends also under the sea!"

The man-fish had no ears, but Dick was certain it could hear Sellwood. Moreover, it *understood*, followed his argument.

"So, own up," snapped the Reverend. "One word, and the deception is at an end. You are not part of God's Creation, but a sea-serpent, an monstrous forgery!"

The creature's lipless mouth curved. It barked, through its mouth. Its gills rippled, showing scarlet inside.

Sellwood was furious.

Dick, strangely, was excited. The prisoner was *laughing* at its captor, the laughter of a patient, abiding being.

Why was it still alive? Could it be killed? Surely, Orris or Sellwood or some keeper in-between had tried to execute the monster?

In those eyes was a promise to the parson. *I will live when you are gone.*

"Drop it," snapped Sellwood.

Fose and Milder let go the winch, and—with a cry—the "French spy" was swallowed by its Hole.

Sellwood and his men left the room, taking the lantern.

Dick began breathing properly again. Violet let Ernest squirm a little, though she still held him under the trough.

Then came a truly terrifying sound, worse even than the laughter of the fish-demon.

Bolts being drawn. Three of them.

They were trapped!

VI: WSFF IMJTURQ-TK BH M'FYSR

Now was the time to keep calm.

Dick knew Violet would be all right, if only because she had to think about Ernest.

For obvious reasons, the children had not told anyone where they were going, but they would be missed at tea-time. Uncle Davey and Aunt Maeve could easily overlook a skipped meal—both of them were liable to get so interested in something that they wouldn't notice the house catching fire—but Cook kept track. And Mr. and Mrs. Borrodale were sticklers for being in by five o'clock with hands washed and presentable.

It must be past five now.

Of course, any search party wouldn't get around to the Priory for days, maybe weeks. They'd look on the beaches first, and in the woods.

Eventually, his uncle and aunt would find the folder marked *Trs Ndps ja qrs Dggjhbqs Dhhbrbfdqjm*. Aunt Maeve, good at puzzles, had taught him how to cipher in the first place. She would eventually break the code and read Dick's notes, and want to talk with Sellwood. By then, it would probably be too late.

They gave the Brethren time enough to get beyond earshot before creeping out from under the trough. They unbent with much creaking and muffled moaning. Violet lit her candle.

Dick paced around the cell, keeping away from the Hole.

"I'm thirsty," said Ernest.

"Easily treated," said Violet.

She found the beaker and pumped water into it. Ernest drank, made a face, and asked for more. Violet worked the pump again.

Water splashed over the brimful beaker, into the trough.

A noise came out of the Hole.

The children froze into mannequins. The noise came again.

"Wah wah . . . *wah wah* . . ."

There was a pleading tone to it.

"Wah wah . . ."

"'Water'," said Dick, snapping his fingers. "It's saying 'water'."

"Wah wah," agreed the creature. "Uh, wah wah."

"'Water. Yes, water.'"

"Gosh, Dick, you *are* clever," said Violet.

"Wat war," said the creature, insisting. "Gi' mee wat war, i' oo eese . . ."

"'Water'," said Dick, "'Give me—'"

"'—water, if you please'," completed Violet, who caught on swiftly. "Very polite for a sea-ghost. Well brought-up in Atlantis or Lyonesse or R'lyeh, I imagine."

"Where?" asked Dick.

"Sunken cities of old, where mer-people are supposed to live."

More left-overs from Violet's myths and legends craze. Interesting, but not very helpful.

Ernest had walked to the edge of the Hole.

"This isn't a soppy mer-person," said Ernest. "This is a Monster of the Deep!"

He emptied the beaker into the dark.

A sigh of undoubted gratitude rose from the depths.

"Wat war goo', tanks. Eese, gi' mee moh."

Ernest poured another beakerful. At this rate, they might as well be using an eye-dropper.

Dick saw the solution.

"Vile, help me shift the trough," he said.

They pulled one end away from the wall. It was heavy, but the bolts were old and rusted and the break came easily.

"Careful not to move the other end too much. We need it under the pump."

Violet saw where this was going. Angled down away from the wall, the

186

trough turned into a sluice. It didn't quite stretch all the way to the *oubliette,* but pulling up a loose stone put a notch into the rim which served as a spout.

"Wat war eese," said the creature, mildly.

Dick nodded to Violet. She worked the pump.

Water splashed into the trough and flowed down, streaming through the notch and pouring into the pit.

The creature gurgled with joy.

Only now did Dick wonder whether watering it was a good idea. It might not be a French spy or even a maritime demon, but it was definitely one of Granny Ball's sea-ghosts. If Dick had been treated as it had been, he would not be well disposed towards land-people.

But the water kept flowing.

Violet's arm got tired, and she let up for a moment.

"I' oo eese," insisted the creature, with a reproachful, nannyish tone. "Moh wat war."

Violet kept pumping.

Dick took the candle and walked to the edge of the Hole. Ernest sat there, legs dangling over the edge, fingers playing in the cool cascade.

The boys looked down.

Where water fell, the man-fish was changed—vivid greens and reds and purples and oranges glistened. Its spines and frills and gills and webs were sleek. Even its eyes shone more brightly.

It turned, mouth open under the spray, letting water wash around it, wrenching against its chains.

"Water makes the Monster strong," said Ernest.

The creature looked up at them. The edges of its mouth curved into something like a smile. There was cunning there, and a bottomless well of malice, but also an exultation. Dick understood: when it was wet, the thing felt as he did when he saw through a mystery.

It took a grip on one of its manacles and squeezed, cracking the old iron and casting it away.

"Can I stop now?" asked Violet. "My arm's out of puff."

"I think so."

The creature nodded, a human gesture awkward on the gilled, neckless being.

It stood up unshackled, and stretched as if waking after a long sleep in an awkward position. The chains dangled freely. A clear, thick, milky-veined fluid seeped from the weals on its chest. The man-fish carefully smoothed this secretion like an ointment.

There were pools of water around its feet. It got down on its knees—did it have spare brains in them?—and sucked the pools dry. Then it raised its head and let water dribble through its gills and down over its chest and back.

"Tanks," it said.

Now it wasn't parched, its speech was easier to understand.

It took hold of the dangling chains, and tugged, testing them.

Watering the thing in the Hole was all very well, but Dick wasn't sure how he'd feel if it were up here with them. If he were the creature, he would be very annoyed. He ought to be grateful to the children, but what did anyone know about the feelings of sea-ghosts? Violet had told them the legend of the genie in the bottle: at first, he swore to bestow untold riches upon the man who set him free, but after thousands of years burned to make his rescuer suffer horribly for waiting so long.

It was too late to think about that.

Slick and wet, the man-fish moved faster than anything its size should. No sooner had it grasped the chains than it had climbed them, deft as a sailor on the rigging, quick as a lizard on the flat or a salmon in the swim.

It held on, hanging just under the ring in the ceiling, head swiveling around, eyes taking in the room.

Dick and Ernest were backed against the door, taking Violet with them.

She was less spooked than the boys.

"Bonjour, Monsieur le Fantôme de la Mer," she said, slowly and clearly in the manner approved by her tutor, M. Duroc. *"Je m'appelle Violette Borrodale . . . permettez-moi de presente a vous mon petit cousin Ernest . . . et Rishard Riddle, le detective juvenile celebré."*

This seemed to puzzle the sea-ghost.

"Vile, I don't think it's really French," whispered Dick.

Violet shrugged.

The creature let go and leaped, landing frog-like, knees stuck out and shoulders hunched, inches away from them. This close, it stank of the sea.

Dick saw their reflections in its huge eyes.

Its mouth opened. He saw row upon row of shark-like teeth, all pointed and shining. It might not have had a proper meal in a century.

"Scuze mee," it said, extending a hand, folding its frill-connected fingers up but pointing with a single barb.

The wet thorn touched Richard's cheek.

Then it eased the children aside, and considered the bolted door.

"Huff . . . puff . . . blow," it said, hammering with fish-fists. The door came off its hinges and the bolts wrenched out of their sockets. The broken door crashed against the opposite wall of the passage.

"How do you know the 'Three Little Pigs'?" asked Violet.

"Gur' nam 'Ooth," it said, "ree' to mee . . ."

"A girl read to him," Dick explained.

So not all his captors had been tormentors. Who was 'Ooth? Ruth? Someone called Ruth fit into the story. The little girl lost with the *Sophy Briggs*. Sellwood's niece.

The sea-ghost looked at Violet. Dick deduced all little girls must look alike to it. If you've seen one pinafore, you've seen them all.

" 'Ooth," it said, with something like fondness. "'Ooth kin' to mee. Ree' mee story-boos. *Liss in Wonlan . . . Tripella Liplik Pik . . . Taes o Eh Ah Po . . .*"

"What happened to Ruth?" Violet asked.

"Sellwoo' ki' 'Ooth, an' hi' bro tah Joh-jee," said the creature, cold anger in its voice. "Tey wan let mee go sea, let mee go hom. Sellwoo' mak shi' wreck, tak ever ting, tak mee."

Dick understood. And was not surprised.

This was the nature of Sellwood's villainy. Charges of smuggling and espionage remained unproven, but he was guilty of the worst crime of all—murder!

People were coming now, alerted by the noise.

The sea-ghost stepped into the passage, holding up a hand—fingers spread and webs unfurled—to indicate that the children should stay behind.

They kept in the dark, where they couldn't see what was happening in the passage.

The man-fish leaped, and landed on someone.

Cries of terror and triumph! An unpleasant, wet crunching . . . followed by unmistakable chewing.

More people came on the scene.

"The craytur's out o' thic Hole," shrieked someone.

A very loud bang! A firework stink.

The man-fish staggered back past the doorway, red blossoming on its shoulder. It had more red stuff around its mouth, and scraps of cloth caught in its teeth.

It roared in rage and threw itself at whoever had shot it.

Something detached from something else and rolled past the doorway, leaving a trail of sticky splashes.

Violet kept her hand over Ernest's eyes, though he tried to pick at her fingers.

"Spawn of Satan, you show your true colors at last!"

It was Sellwood.

"Milder, Fessel, take him down."

The Brethren grunted. The doorway was filled with struggling bodies, driving the children back into the cell. They pressed flat against the wet cold walls.

Brother Milder and Brother Fessel held the creature's arms and wrestled it back, towards the Hole.

Sellwood appeared, hefting one of his fossil-breaking hammers.

He thumped the sea-ghost's breast-bone with all his might, and it fell, sprawling on the flagstones. Milder and Fessel shifted their weight to pin the creature down.

Still, no one noticed the children.

The creature's shoulder wound closed like a sea anemone. The bruise in the middle of its chest faded at once. It looked with hate up at the Reverend.

Sellwood stood over the wriggling man-fish. He weighed his hammer.

"You're devilish hard to kill, demon! But how would you like your skull pounded to paste? It might take a considerable while to recover, eh?"

He raised the hammer above his head.

"You there," said Violet, voice clear and shrill and loud, "stop!"

Sellwood swiveled to look.

"This is an important scientific discovery, and must not be harmed. Why, it is practically a living dinosaur."

Violet stood between Sellwood and the pinned man-fish. Dick was by her side, arm linked with hers. Ernest was in front of them, fists up like a pugilist.

"Don't you hurt my friend the Monster," said Ernest.

Sellwood's red rage showed.

"You see," he yelled, "how the foulness spreads! How the lies take hold! You see!"

Something snapped inside Milder. He rolled off the creature, limbs loose, neck flopping.

The sea-ghost stood up, a two-handed grip on the last of Sellwood's Brethren, Fessel.

"Help," he gasped. "Children, help . . ."

Dick had a pang of guilt.

Then Fessel was falling into the *oubliette*. He rattled against chains, and landed with a final-sounding crash.

The sea-ghost stepped around the children and took away Sellwood's hammer, which it threw across the room. It clanged against the far wall.

"I am not afraid of you," announced the Reverend.

The creature tucked Sellwood under its arm. The Reverend was too surprised to protest.

"Shouldn' a' ki' 'Ooth a' Joh-jee, Sellwoo'. Shouldn' a' ki'."

"How do you know?" Sellwood was indignant, but didn't deny the crime.

"Sea tol' mee, sea tel' mee all ting."

"I serve a greater purpose," shouted Sellwood.

The sea-ghost carried the Reverend out of the room. The children followed.

The man-fish strode down the passage, towards the book-room. Two dead men—Maulder and Fose—lay about.

"Their heads are gone," exclaimed Ernest, with a glee Dick found a little disturbing. At least Ernest wasn't picking up one of the heads for the office wall.

Sellwood thumped the creature's back. Its old whip-stripes and poker-brands were healing.

Dick, Violet, and Ernest followed the escapee and its former gaoler.

In the book-room, Sellwood looked with hurried regret at the crates of unsold volumes and struggled less. The sea-ghost found the steps leading down and seemed to contract its body to squeeze into the tunnel. Sellwood was dragged bloody against the rock ceiling.

"Come on, detectives," said Dick, "after them!"

VII: D*HQRMJKJP BNQRYJP IBJFFSQQD*

They came out under Ware Cleeve. Waves scraped shingle in an eternal rhythm. It was twilight, and chilly. Well past tea-time.

The man-fish, burden limp, tasted the sea in the air.

"Tanks," it said to the children, "tanks very mu'."

It walked into the waves. As sea soaked through his coat, Sellwood was shocked into consciousness and began to struggle again, shouting and cursing and praying.

The sea-ghost was waist-deep in its element.

It turned to wave at the children. Sellwood got free, madly striking *away* from the shore, not towards dry land. The creature leaped completely out of the water, dark rainbows rippling on its flanks, and landed heavily on Sellwood, claws hooking into meat, pressing the Reverend under the waves.

They saw the swimming shape, darting impossibly fast, zigzagging out into the bay. Finned feet showed above the water for an instant and the man-fish—the sea-ghost, the French spy, the living fossil, the snare of Satan, the Monster of the Deep—was gone for good, dragging the Reverend Mr. Daniel Sturdevant Sellwood with him.

". . . to Davey Jones's locker," said Ernest.

Dick realized Violet was holding his hand, and tactfully got his fingers free. Their shoes were covered with other people's blood.

"Anthropos Icthyos Biolletta," said Violet. "Violet's Man-Fish, a whole new *phylum.*"

"I pronounce this case closed," said Dick.

"Can I borrow your matches?" asked Violet. "I'll just nip back up the tunnel and set fire to Sellwood's books. If the Priory burns down, we won't have to answer questions about dead people."

Dick handed over the box.

He agreed with Violet. This was one of those stories for which the world was not yet ready. Writing it up, he would use a double cipher.

"Besides," said Violet, "some books deserve to be burned."

While Violet was gone, Dick and Ernest passed time skipping stones on the waves. Rooting for ammunition, they found an ammonite, not quite as big and nice as the one that was smashed, but sure to delight Violet and much easier to carry home.

IN THE PINES
KARL EDWARD WAGNER

Karl Edward Wagner died in 1994 at the young age of forty-eight. He is remembered at the insightful editor of fifteen volumes of The Year's Best Horror Stories *series from DAW Books (1980–94) and an author of superior horror and fantasy fiction.*

While still attending medical school, Wagner set about creating his own character, Kane, the Mystic Swordsman. After the first book in the series, Darkness Weaves with Many Shades, *was published in 1970 Wagner relinquished his chance to become a doctor and turned to writing full-time.* Death Angel's Shadow, *a collection of three original Kane novellas, was followed by the novels* Bloodstone *and* Dark Crusade *and the collections* Night Winds *and* The Book of Kane. *More recently, these books have been reissued in the omnibus volumes* Gods in Darkness *and* Midnight Sun *from Night Shade Books.*

Wagner's horror fiction appeared in a variety of magazines and anthologies, and was collected in In a Lonely Place, Why Not You and I?, Author's Choice Monthly Issue 2: Unthreatened by the Morning Light, *and the posthumous* Exorcisms and Ecstasies.

"'In the Pines' was written over a period of months in 1968," recalled the author. "The setting is based upon a vacation cabin once owned by my uncle in Sunshine, Tennessee. Description of the decaying resort area, the cabin and its furnishings is factual.

"Inspiration to use this setting for a story came from the song, 'In the Pines', which we had on an old Tennessee Ernie Ford album. It is an eerie song, especially when heard in the right setting. I later discovered that my friend, Manly Wade Wellman, had also been inspired by the song to write one of his John the Balladeer stories, 'Shiver in the Pines'—although Wellman knew the song from its folk roots."

A mountain cabin where the sun never shines harbors something seductive and long-dead. . . .

PROLOGUE

There is an atmosphere of inutterable loneliness that haunts any ruin—a feeling particularly evident in those places once given over to the lighter emotions. Wander over the littered grounds of an abandoned amusement park and feel the overwhelming presence of desolation. Flimsy booths with awnings tattered in the wind, rotting heaps of sun-bleached *papier-mache.* Crumbling timbers of a roller coaster thrust upward through the jungle of weeds and debris—like ribs of some titanic unburied skeleton. The wind blows colder there; the sun seems dimmer. Ghosts of laughter, lost strains of raucous music can almost be heard. Speak, and your voice sounds strangely loud—and yet curiously smothered.

Or tour a neglected formal garden, with its termite-riddled arbors and gazebo. The lily pond is drained, choked with weeds and refuse. Only a few flowers or shrubs poke miserably through the rank undergrowth. Dense clots of weeds and vines overrun the paths and statuary. Here and there a shrub or rambling rose has grown into a wild, misshapen tangle. The flowers offer anemic blooms, where no hand gathers, no eye admires. No birds sing in that uncanny hush.

Such places are lairs of inconsolable gloom. After the brighter spirits have departed, shadows of despair and oppression assume their place. The area has been drained of its ability to support any further light emotion, and now, like weeds on eroded soil, only the darker sentiments can take root and flourish. These places are best left to the loneliness of their grief. . . .

I

The road that climbed pine-hooded slopes was winding and narrow—treacherous with deep ruts and large stones. County work crews seldom came this far, and rains of many seasons had left the unpaved road with the contour of a dry stream bed.

In late afternoon sunlight the dusty Chevy bounced and rattled its cautious ascent of the pine-covered ridge. A rock outcropping struck its undercarriage and grated harshly. Janet caught her breath, but said nothing. Gerard Randall risked a quick glance from the wheel to note her tense fright. He scowled and concentrated on driving. Accustomed to wide, straight lanes of modern highway, Randall found this steep country road with its diabolical curves a nightmare. Rains had long since washed out whatever shoulder there was, and he watched in sick fascination as the road disappeared completely all too few inches from his jolting wheels.

"Can you see roads like this in Ohio?" he snorted, and wondered what would happen should two cars meet. With traffic almost nonexistent, that seemed unlikely. At any rate, he was barely crawling, as the light car wallowed over the rutted bed. Once again he felt a pang of regret for the Buick and its solid feel. But now life was strictly economy class.

The road made an impossible hairpin, so that Gerry had to stop the car to back and fill. He swore silently, keeping his anger to himself. What had this road been designed for, anyway—didn't these Tennessee hillbillies drive cars? The long drive from Columbus had been difficult. From wide interstate highway, the roads had steadily retrogressed down the evolutionary ladder—until now he followed a trail Davy Crockett would have scorned.

Their silence had been awkward, but conversation was a greater strain. Instead, he turned up the radio and pretended not to notice Janet's tight-faced nervousness. For miles now the radio had blared out twangy country music from the small-town stations along their route. When they left the paved road, it faded into static.

They were passing vacation cabins now, so he paid careful attention. "Help me find the place, Janet," he said levelly. "If we miss it, I'll never get turned around."

One of the last ones on the road, the agent in Maryville had told them when they stopped for the key. On the left, a good coat of green paint, with red fuel oil and water tanks in front. The sign over the door would read THE CROW'S NEST in red and white. Couldn't be missed.

"I hope it's . . . clean," Janet offered hesitantly. "Some of these look so run-down."

True enough, Gerry admitted. A few cabins were in good condition—fresh paint, aluminum screens, new car alongside. But most were half fallen apart—sagging wooden boxes perched on precarious stilts along the steep mountainside. A few had tumbled down the slope—pitiful heaps of crumpled and rotting timbers. Not encouraging. He voiced his annoyance: "So most of these places are fifty years old! What did you think seventy-five bucks a month would get you for a mountain cabin! In Gatlinburg we'd pay this much for a night!"

Her face drew tighter and her eyes looked damp. She was assuming her wounded-martyr expression. Gerry braced himself for the now familiar crisis. *Please God, not now, not here.*

"There it is!" He pointed suddenly. "Let's see if there's room to pull off the road." Cautiously, he edged the Chevy into a parking area beside the cabin.

Janet's face grew keen with interest. "It doesn't look too bad," she observed hopefully.

Gerry eyed the structure in quick appraisal. "No. No, it doesn't," he conceded. "At least, from the outside."

The Crow's Nest was a typical mountain cabin from the early twenties, days when this had been a major resort area. It clung to the steep slope with one end resting on the bank just below the road, while an arrangement of wooden posts supported the sections jutting out from the mountain. Its unlovely design was that of a stack of boxes anchored to the ridge. The top floor—on level with the road—was a large square; underneath was a rectangle about two-thirds the width of the first, and the bottom floor was an even narrower rectangle. Rusty screen enclosed porches running the length of each level on the side overlooking the valley.

"Well, we can't complain about the view," Gerry offered. "There's three porches to choose from. Hope it's not too drafty for you. Well, come on. You can explore while I unload stuff."

Getting out, he gratefully stretched his long body, then reached in. "Make it OK?" he inquired solicitously. She pulled herself erect unsteadily, tugging hard on his arm and gripping the door with the other hand. Gerry unloaded her walker, then went to unlock the cabin while Janet hobbled painfully across the pine-needle carpet to the door.

Inside she smiled. "Oh, Gerry! It looks so cozy! I know we'll be happy together here!"

"I hope so, darling!" He brightened.

The screen door slammed shut on squawling hinges.

Janet was exhausted and went to bed early. Gerry had not felt like sleep. The ordeal of driving had left his nerves on edge, and the strange surroundings made him restless. Instead he settled down in one of the huge rocking chairs, propped his feet on the edge of the porch screen and enjoyed the mountain night. Idly his fingers flicked the bottle caps nailed to the wide wooden armrests, while he thoughtfully nursed a Scotch and soda. He had brought several fifths down with him—the nearest liquor store would be Knoxville, and Tennessee liquor prices were terrible. He grimaced. Good Scotch was another luxury he could no longer afford.

The mountain breeze was cool and clean, and the night's silence astonished him. Dimly he could hear the whine, see the flicker of light as an occasional car passed along the highway in the valley far below. The house uttered soft groans and squeaks in the darkness, and the rocker answered with a rhythmic creak. From outside came the sounds of creatures of the forest night. Crickets, tree frogs, shrill insect calls. Mice, flying squirrels made soft rustlings in the quiet. An owl called from the distance, and a whippoorwill. Overlying all was the whisper of the pines. Gerry had often heard the expression, but until now he had never understood that pines actually do whisper. Soft, soothing whisper in the night. But a sound so cold, so lonely.

Even bad Scotch gets better with each drink. Maybe not Chivas Regal, but it does the job. Gerry rocked softly, sipped slowly, glass after glass. The night was soothing. Tension slipped from overstrung nerves.

Half in dream he brooded over the turn his life had taken. God, it had all seemed so secure, settled. His wife, their son. A rising position with the firm. Good car, good house, good neighborhood. Country club, the right friends. Bright young man already halfway up the ladder to the top.

Then a woman's inattention, a flaming crash. Only a split second to destroy everything. The funeral, weeks of visits to the hospital. The lawsuit and its cruel joke of an insurance executive whose own policy was inadequate.

All of it destroyed. A comfortable, well-ordered existence torn to twisted wreckage. He could never return to the old life. Despite the sincere best wishes of embarrassed friends, the concerned expressions of doctors who warned him about the emotional shock he had suffered.

Maybe it would have been best if he had been in the car, if he had died in the wreckage of his life.

No . . . that was a death wish. Part of the warnings of those concerned doctors after that scene in the hospital . . . Part of their reasons for urging this vacation upon him . . . "You both have scars that will have to heal . . ."

Gerry laughed softly at the memory of the psychiatrist's attempt to talk with him. In the stillness of the dark cabin his laughter was ghastly. He checked the bottle and noted it was almost empty. Drunk, by God. He supposed he should start bawling in his glass. Yes, Doctor, worry about me. Lose a little sleep in your $300,000 home. God knows how I've waited for the nights to end since then.

Time for bed. Try out that musty old mattress. He drew in a deep lungful of the mountain air. Curious fragrance he had not noticed before. Probably some mountain flower. Something that smelled like jasmine.

II

The cabin stairs were too treacherous for Janet, and so Gerry had to carry her—and then both nearly fell. But Janet insisted on exploring each drafty level of the old place as soon as the late breakfast was cleared. Hungover, Gerry reluctantly joined the game. Strange how frail she seemed in his arms—she had always been so solid. Maybe if she'd exercise her legs more, like the doctors had told her to do.

The cabin was in reasonable repair, but not much more. The floor sagged in places, and the roof showed signs of having leaked, but by and large everything seemed sound. Squirrels had slipped in and chewed up some of the furnishings. The furniture all was cheap, beat-up—caught in a limbo somewhere between antique and junk. None of it had captured the fancy of the countless prowlers who had broken in over the years. Disreputable iron-railed beds with collapsed springs and dirty mattresses, scarred tables and cheap dressers with many layers of paint, boxes and trunks of discarded items. A grimy bookshelf with several Edgar Wallace mysteries, a copy of Fox's *Trail of the Lonesome Pine,* a Bible, odd volumes of *Reader's Digest Condensed Books,* other nondescript items. Janet delightedly pawed through each new trove, and Gerry became interested despite himself. He joined her laughter when one drawer yielded a bedraggled two-piece man's swimming costume.

The first level included the kitchen with its ancient appliances, two bedrooms, a bathroom with an old chemical toilet, and a large open area for dining or sitting. Below were two more bedrooms and a narrower open space along the screened front. The lowermost level was a narrow porch with several army bunks and a room at one end that had once been a bar. The insubstantial posts that supported the cabin were a good twelve feet high at the far end, so that there was a large dry storage area underneath. This had been stuffed with boxes and piles of junk not worth the effort of hauling away.

Here Gerry returned after a light lunch; Janet was tired and wanted to lie down. The disorder was fantastic—a clutter of discarded trivia decades old. Gerry had an appreciation for the cash value of an antique, and with a treasure hunter's enthusiasm he rummaged through the tottering stacks of lost years.

More junk than any attic would attempt. Broken chairs, cracked dishes, boxes of Mason jars, heaps of newspapers, rusty tools, old tires, a wheel-less bicycle, fishing poles. Anything. Doggedly he worked his way from pile to pile, covered with a paste of sweat, red dust, and spider web. Once he found a scorpion under a wooden box, and remembered that black widow spiders, too, liked these places. Maybe there were snakes. But he paid no more attention to such misgivings than to the dirt—although a year ago he would not have braved either just to rifle through old junk.

It had been profitable so far. He had pulled out a tool chest, in case he felt up to making repairs. There was a stack of crumbling pulp magazines—*Argosy, Black Mask, Doc Savage, Weird Tales,* and others—that would provide a few laughs. A crockery jug—just like the moonshine jugs in the cartoons—would make a nice lamp. An old copper lantern might be a nice antique, along with the cane-bottomed chair. Some of these picture frames might be valuable. . . .

He stopped. Against one post leaned a stack of old pictures—mostly mountain scenes and calendar cutouts behind glass opaque with dirt. But as he shuffled through them, one picture suddenly caught his eye.

It was an original oil painting, he saw on closer examination, and did not look quite finished. For a moment he remembered stories of undiscovered masterpieces, but laughed the thought aside. Carefully he blew away loose dust. Sandwiched between several larger frames, the canvas was undamaged. Critically he held it to the yellow sunlight.

The picture caught him—drew his attention in a manner he had never experienced. Inexplicable. Art had never meant anything to him, aside from a few tasteful reproductions dutifully purchased to fill wall space.

A woman's portrait, nothing more. Curiously blurred, as if the oils were somewhat translucent. Was it unfinished—or was it an attempt at impressionism? She wore a simple green frock—a light summer outfit stylish in the '20s. Her auburn hair was cut in the short bob popular then. Almost in keeping with the latest styles, but for an indefinable air that proclaimed an older period.

It was a lonely picture. She stood against a background of dark pines, cold and lonely about her. There was a delicacy about her and, illogically, an impression of strength. The face was difficult, its mood seeming altered at each glance. Indefinable. Sensuous mouth—did it smile, or was there sorrow? Perhaps half open in anticipation of a kiss—or a cry? The eyes— soft blue, or did they glow? Did they express longing, pain? Or were they hungry eyes, eyes alight with triumph? Lonely eyes. Lonely face. A lonely picture. A song, long forgotten, came to his mind.

> *In the pines, in the pines,*
> *Where the sun never shines,*
> *And I shiver when the wind blows cold . . .*

He did shiver then. Sun falling, the mountain wind blew cold through the pines. How long had he been staring at the portrait?

Struck with a chill beyond that of the wind, Gerry cradled his find in cautious hands and started back up the dusty bank.

Janet was in a cheerful mood for a change. Not even a complaint about being ignored most of the afternoon. "Well, let's see what goodies you've brought up from the basement," she laughed, and glanced at the picture, "Oh, there's Twiggy! Gerry, how camp! Look—an original piece of nostalgia!"

He frowned, suddenly offended by her gaiety. In view of the profound impression the picture had made, laughter seemed irreverent. "I thought it was kind of nice myself. Thought I'd hang it up, maybe. Can't you just feel the loneliness of it?"

She gave him a hopeless look. "Oh, wow, you're serious. Hang that old thing up? Gerry, you're kidding. Look how silly she looks."

He glanced at her prefaded bell-bottoms and tank top. "Maybe that will look silly in a few years too."

"Hmmm? I thought you liked these?" She inspected herself in faint concern, wondering if she had gotten too thin. No, Gerry was just being pettish.

"Well, let me take a good look at your treasure." She studied the picture with a professional attitude. On Tuesday afternoons she had taken art lessons along with several of her friends. "The artist is really just too romantic. See—no expression, no depth to his subject. Pale girl against dark woods— it's corny. Too much background for a portrait, and that dress dates it too severely to be idealized—not even a good landscape. His greens are over-used and too obvious. His light is all wrong, and there's certainly no imagination with all those dark colors. Is it supposed to be night or day?"

Gerry bit his lip in annoyance. Snotty little dilettante. He wished he knew enough about art to tear apart her prattling criticism.

"This is pretty typical of the sort of maudlin trash they turned out in the '20s. Probably some amateur on vacation here did it of his girlfriend, and she had enough taste to leave it behind. Let's see—it's signed here on the corner, E. Pittman . . . 1951. 1951? That's funny . . ." she finished awkwardly.

Gerry's mustache twitched sarcastically. "And when did they make you valedictorian of your art class? That gossip session where bored housewives can splash on gobs of paint and call it a subtle interplay of neo-garbage."

That stung. "Oh, stop sulking. So I insulted your male ego because I don't care for your little Twiggy-of-the-woods."

"Because you're too damned insensitive to get into the mood of this painting!" Why had she gotten him so riled over an old picture? "Because you don't feel the . . ." *Damn!* How do art critics choose their phrases! "Because you're jealous over a portrait of a beautiful woman!" *What the hell sense did that make?*

"You're not hanging that piece of junk up here!" Now she was mad at him. Her lips made a white line across her blonde face.

"No! No, I'm not! Not where you can sneer at her! I'll hang her up downstairs!"

"Way downstairs, I hope!" she shouted after him, close to tears now. And things had been going so well . . .

Dinner had been awkward. Both sheepish but sulking, apologies meant but left unspoken, quarrels ignored but not forgotten. He left her fiddling with the portable TV afterward, making the excuse that he wanted to read without distraction.

Downstairs he had replenished the old bar. The portrait hung against the wall, watching him. In cleaning it, he had noticed the name "Renee" scrawled at the top. Maybe the artist's name—no, that was E. Pittman. Probably the title, then. Name suited her well. "Mind if I have a drink, Renee?" he murmured. "Wife says I have a few too many a bit too often. Cliche for the day: Bitter hero drowns his grief in booze." The eyes stared back at him. In pity? Loneliness? Hunger? How lost she looked!

Gerry flipped on a lopsided floor lamp and settled down to read some of the pulps he had resurrected. God, how ingenuous the stuff was! Were people ever so naive? He wondered how James Bond would appear to readers back then.

Bugs slipped through the rusty screen and swarmed to the light. Buzzed through his ears, plopped on the pages, fell in his drink. In vexation he finally clicked the lamp off.

His gaze was drawn back to the portrait, visible through the darkness by the glow of the bar light. He considered it with the careful patience four double shots of Scotch can bestow. Who was she, this Renee? She seemed too real to be only an artist's imagination, but it was curious that an artist of the '50s should paint a girl of the '20s. Had she once sat here on this porch and listened to this same wind? This cold, lonesome wind in the pines?

God. Getting sentimental from Scotch. Mellow over a painting that a few months back he'd have laughed at. He closed his eyes wearily and concentrated on the night, letting its ancient spell wash over him.

The cool, velvet-soft night. Pines whispering in the darkness. The sound of loneliness. And Gerry realized he had become a very lonely man. A lost soul—adrift in the darkness of the pines.

Again came the faint scent of jasmine, haunting perfume. Jasmine, antique like this cabin. Worn by enchantresses of another age. Fragrance lingering from dead years. Delicate floral scent worn when beauty was caressed by silken gowns, garlanded with pearls, glinted with lacquered nails. Gone now, vanquished by synthetics. Today a woman clothed, adorned, perfumed herself with coal tar and cellulose. No wonder femininity had declined.

He breathed the rare fragrance, the cool night, somewhere between waking and dreaming. Faintly he heard the rustle of silk behind him, a sound separate from the whisper of the pines. A cold breath on his neck, apart from the mountain breeze. Like the elusive scent of jasmine, sensations alien to the night, yet part of it. The wind brushed his dark hair, stroked his damp forehead, almost as if a cool, delicate hand soothed the lines of pain.

He sighed, almost a shudder. Tension softened, days of anguish lost their sting. A feeling of inexpressible contentment stole over him; anticipation of ecstasy came to him. He parted his lips in a smile of dreamy delight.

"Renee." The sigh escaped him unbidden. It seemed that another's lips hovered close to his own. Sleep came to him then.

III

The sign announced *PENNYBACKER'S GROCERY—DRINK COCA-COLA.* Maryville had modern supermarkets, and ordinarily Gerry would have driven the extra distance. But today the country grocery with its old-fashioned general store atmosphere appealed to him—and it *was* close-by.

The building was old. In front stood two battered gas pumps of some local brand. A long peaked roof overhung to form a sheltered enclosure between gas pumps and store front. Two wooden benches guarded the doorway. Their engraved invitation to *DRINK ROYAL CROWN COLA* was almost obliterated by countless carved initials and years of friction from overalls. The paint was starting to peel, and the windows were none too clean. Rusty advertising signs and a year's growth of posters made a faded patchwork of the exterior.

Inside was packed more merchandise than there seemed floor-space for. Strange brands abounded on the crowded shelves. Fresh produce from local farms stood in open baskets. Cuts of meat were displayed within a glass counter. Odd items of hardware, clothing, medicines, tackle augmented the fantastic clutter. Here was a true general store without the artificial quaintness of the counterfeit "country stores" of Gatlinburg's tourist traps.

Grocery buying was something of an adventure, and Gerry was glad Janet had not come along to quarrel over selections. A display of knives caught his eye as he waited for the proprietor to total his purchases on a clattering adding machine. Among the other pocket knives, he recognized the familiar shape of a Barlow knife.

"It that a real Barlow, or a Japanese copy?" he asked.

The storekeeper looked up sharply. "No, sir! Those knives are every one made in America. For your real quality knife you want your American one every time—though there's some likes the German. Take them Case knives there. Now you can't ask for a better knife. Lots of folks swear by a Case knife. Now that Barlow's a fine one too. It's a Camillus, and as fine a knife as any you could've bought fifty years ago. Cost you just four bucks. Want to see one?"

Gerry tossed the stubby knife in his palm and decided to buy it. He had never carried a penknife, and this one was too bulky for his pockets. Still, a good souvenir. The storekeeper was disposed to talk, and the knife led to a rambling conversation.

Lonzo Pennybacker had run this store since the Depression. His uncle had built the place about the time of the Great War, and the gas pumps were some of the first in the area. Lonzo was interested to learn that Gerry was from Columbus—two of his cousins had families up around there, although he supposed Gerry wouldn't know them. No, Gerry guessed he didn't.

Lonzo's expression was peculiar when Gerry mentioned he had rented The Crow's Nest. "So they've got somebody to stay in the old Reagan place again," he reflected.

"Oh?" Gerry's bushy eyebrows rose. "Why do you say that? Is the place haunted or something?"

Pennybacker scratched his pointed chin pensively. "Hants? No—don't think you can say that rightly. Far's I know, nobody's ever seen no hants around the old Reagan place. If it's hants now, you could've seen as many as you'd care in the old Griffin house. Everybody knew it was for sure hanted. Course it burned down in '61.

"No. Far's I know the Reagan place ain't hanted. It's just what they call unlucky."

"Unlucky? How do you mean that?" Gerry wondered if he should laugh.

Lonzo finished packing the groceries before answering. "Well sir, I was just through schoolin' back in '22 when David Reagan built The Crow's Nest. He was a mine owner out of Greenville and a wealthy man as we counted them in those days. Built the place as a honeymoon cabin for him and his wife. Fine handsome young lady, I can remember. She was maybe twenty years younger than David Reagan—he being in his forties and sort of stout. Renee, though, was a mighty prettysome girl."

"Renee?"

"Renee. That was her name. Quite a looker. Wore her hair bobbed and those short dresses and all. A real flapper. Women around here was scandalized with all her city ways and manners. Men though liked her well enough, I'll tell you. Red hair and the devil in her blue eyes. Used to draw a regular crowd down at the hotel swimming pool when she'd come down.

"Well, she liked it here in the mountains, so they spent the summers here. Back then this area was pretty lively. Tourists came from all over to spend their vacations here. Used to be some big fancy resort hotels and all the cottages, too. Yeah, this place was real busy back before they opened the park.

"Well, Renee was a little too much woman for David Reagan, they said. Anyway, summer of 1925 she took up with one of the tourists—good-looking fellow name of Sam Luttle, staying the summer at a resort hotel near here. Far as anyone can say, David Reagan must've found out about them—you know how gossip gets around. So one day Renee just plain vanished. And before anyone really noticed she was missing, David Reagan one night drove his Packard off the side of the mountain. Remember seeing that one. Threw him through the windshield, and his head was just about cut loose.

"When Renee didn't show up, they got to searching for her. But nothing ever did turn up of that girl. Disappeared without a trace. Since David Reagan was known to have a mean temper and a jealous streak besides, folks sort of figured he'd found out about his wife and Sam Luttle, and so he'd killed Renee and hid her body out somewhere in the mountains. All that pine forest—they never could find her.

"Some figured maybe she'd run off with Luttle, but he claimed he didn't know a thing. Anyway, he got chewed up by a bear out walking one night not long afterwards. So there wasn't nobody left who knew anything about the business. David Reagan had a brother who sold the cabin, and it's been passed around and rented ever since."

"And have there been stories since then of ghosts or something in connection with the place?" Somehow the idea did not seem as absurd as it should have.

"No, can't say there has," acknowledged Lonzo, his expression guarded. "Not much of anything unusual gone on at the Reagan place. Nobody's ever cared to keep the place for too long for one reason or another. Still, the only thing you might call mysterious was that artist fellow back in the early '50s."

"Artist? What about him?"

"Some New York fellow. Had some disease, I think. Kind of strange—crazy in the head, you could say, maybe. Anyway, he killed himself after living there a few weeks. Cut his throat with a razor, and didn't find him for a week. Had trouble renting the place for a while after that, you can guess. Fellow's name was—let's see. Enser Pittman."

IV

Janet seemed disgustingly solicitous during dinner, going out of her way to avoid mention of Gerry's long absence that afternoon. She had fixed Swiss steak—one of his favorites—and her eyes were reproachful when he gave curt, noncommittal answers to her attempts at conversation. If only she wouldn't be so overbearing in her attempts to please him, Gerry thought, then act like a whipped dog when he didn't respond effusively.

Dutifully he helped her clear away the dishes—even dried while she washed. Afterward she offered to play gin rummy but he knew she really didn't like the game, and declined. Conversation grew more dismal, and when Janet seemed disposed to get romantic, he turned on the TV. Presently he lamely mentioned paperwork, and left Janet protesting her loneliness. He thought she was crying again, and the familiar flash of anger returned as he descended the precipitous stairs. Anyway, she'd perk up for the Doris Day flick.

Drink in hand, Gerry once again studied the strange painting which had captured his imagination. E. Pittman—1951. Enser Pittman who had once stayed here. And committed suicide. Artists were never stable types.

But why had he painted a woman dressed in the fashion of a quarter century previous? *Renee*. Gerry felt certain that this Renee was the unfortunate Renee Reagan who had probably been murdered by her jealous husband in this cabin years before.

Of course! Pittman had discovered an old photograph. Certainly he would have learned of the cabin's tragic past, and the photograph of the murdered woman would have appealed to his artistic imagination. A mind on the brink of suicide would have found sick gratification in the portrayal of a murdered temptress from a decadent period like the '20s.

She *was* a beautiful creature. It was easy to see how much beauty could drive a man to adultery—or murder. Easy to understand why Pittman had been fascinated as an artist.

Moodily he stared at the painting. She was so vital. Pittman must have indeed been talented to incarnate such life within the oils. Strange how her eyes looked into your own. Her smile. If you looked long enough, you could imagine her lips moved, her eyes followed you. Amazing that he had painted it from only a photograph.

She would have been easy to love. Mysterious. Not a shallow housewife like Janet. Strange how things had changed. Once he had loved Janet because she was a perfect housewife and mother. A woman like Renee he would have considered dangerous, trivial—desirable, perhaps, like a film sex goddess, but not the type to love. So old values can change.

And Gerry realized he no longer loved his wife.

Bitterness flooded his mind. Guilt? Should he feel guilty for treating Janet so callously? Was it wrong to be unforgiving over an accident, a simple accident that . . .

"You killed my son!" he choked. Tears of rage, of pain, blinded his eyes. With a sob, Gerry whirled from the painting and flung his empty glass through the doorway of the bar.

He froze—never hearing his glass rip through the rusty veranda screen and shatter against a tree below.

Renee. She was standing in the doorway.

Only for a second did the image last. For an instant he clearly saw her standing before him, watching him from the darkness of the doorway. She was just like her picture: green summer frock, bobbed flame hair, eyes alight with longing, mouth half open in invitation.

Then as his heart stuttered at the vision, she vanished.

Gerry let out his breath with a long exclamation and sank onto a chair. Had he seen a ghost? Had they started bottling LSD with Scotch? He laughed shakily. An after-image, of course. He'd been staring at the painting for an hour. When he had abruptly looked away against the darkened doorway, the image of the painting had superimposed on his retina. Certainly! They'd done experiments like that in college science.

It had been unnerving for a second. So that was how haunted houses got their reputation. He glanced about him. The porch was deserted, of course. The wind still whispered its cold breath through the rhythmically swaying pines. Again came a faint scent of jasmine on the night wind. God! It was so peaceful here! So cold and lonely! He closed his eyes and shivered, unreasonably content for the moment. Like being alone with someone you love very much. Just the two of you and the night.

"Gerry! For God's sake, are you all right?"

He catapulted out of the rocker. "What! What? Of course I am! Damn it all, stop screaming! What's wrong with you?" Janet was at the top of the staircase. She called down half in relief, half in alarm. "Well, I heard a glass smash, and you didn't answer when I called you at first. I was afraid you'd fallen or something and were maybe hurt. I was about to start down these steps, if you hadn't answered."

Gerry groaned and said with ponderous patience, "Well, I'm all right, thank you. Just dropped a glass. Turn down the television next time, and maybe I'll hear you."

"The TV's off." (So that was why she took time to think of him.) "It's started acting crazy again like last night. Can you take a look at it now? It always seems to work OK in the daytime."

She paused and sniffed loudly. "Gerry, do you smell something?"

"Just mountain flowers. Why?"

"No, I mean do you smell something rotten? Can't you smell it? I've noticed it several times at night. It smells like something dead is in the cabin."

V

Gerry had been trying to move an old trunk when he found the diary. The rusty footlocker had been shoved into one of the closets upstairs, and Janet insisted that he lug the battered eyesore downstairs. Gerry grumbled while dragging the heavy locker to the stairs, but its lock was rusted tight, and he was not able to remove the junk inside first. So it was with grim amusement that he watched the trunk slip from his grasp and careen down the narrow stairs. At the bottom it burst open like a rotten melon and dumped its musty contents across the floor.

Clothes and books mostly. A squirrel had chewed entrance at one point and shredded most of it, while mildew had ruined the remainder. Gerry righted the broken trunk and carelessly tossed the scattered trash back inside. Let someone else decide what to do with it.

There was a leather-bound notebook. Its cover was thrown back, and he noted the title page: *Diary. Enser Pittman. June-December, 1951.* Gerry looked at the footlocker in alarm. Were these the possessions of that artist, left unclaimed after his suicide?

He set the diary aside until he had cleared away the rest of the debris. Then he succumbed to morbid curiosity and sat down to thumb through the artist's journal. Some of the pages had been chewed away, others were welded together with mould and crumbled as he tried to separate them. But he could read enough to fasten his attention to the tattered diary.

The first few entries were not especially interesting—mostly gloomy comments on the war in Korea and the witch hunts at home, the stupidity of his agent, and what a bitch Arlene was. On June 27, Pittman had arrived at The Crow's Nest for a rest and to try his hand at mountain-scapes. From that point, certain passages of the diary assumed a chilling fascination for Gerry.

June 28. Went out for a stroll through the woods today, surprisingly without getting lost or eaten by bears. Splendid pine forest! After N.Y.'s hollow sterile canyons, this is fantastic! God! How strange to be alone! I walked for hours without seeing a soul—or a human. And the carpet of pine needles—so unlike that interminable asphalt-concrete desert! Pure desolation! I feel reborn! Extraordinary those pines. Can't recall any sound so lonely as the wind whispering through their branches. Weird! After N.Y.'s incessant mind-rotting clamor. If I can only express this solitude, this unearthly loneliness on canvas! Fahler is an odious cretin! Landscapes are not trite—rather, the expression has cloyed. . . .

June 30. Haven't found those flowers yet. Guess the night breeze carries the scent a long way. Didn't know jasmine grew here. Weird. At nights it almost feels like a woman's perfume. . . .

July 2. The horns are growing. Several times at night now I've definitely sensed a woman's presence in the darkness. Strange how my imagination can almost give substance to shadow. I can almost make myself visualize her just at the corner of my vision. . . .

July 4. Wow! Too much wine of the gods, Enser! Last time I get patriotic! A little excess of Chianti to celebrate the glorious 4th, I drop off in my chair, and Jesus! Wake up to see a girl bending over me! Nice trick, too! Looked like something out of a Held illustration! Vanished about the time my eyes could focus. Wonder what Freud would say to that! . . .

July 7. Either this place is haunted, or I'm going to have to go looking for that proverbial farmer's daughter. Last night I woke up with the distinct impression that there was a woman in bed beside me. Scared? Christ! Like a childhood nightmare! I was actually afraid to reach over—even turn my head to look—and find out if someone was really there. When I finally did check—nothing, of course—I almost imagined I could see a depression on the mattress. The old grey matter is starting to short out. . . .

(The next several pages were too mutilated to decipher, and Gerry pieced together the rest only with extreme difficulty.)

. . . seems to know the whole story, tho it's hard to say how much the good reverend doth impart. Banner's a real character—strickly old-time evangelist. Mostly the same story as Pennybacker's and the other loafers—except Rev. Banner seems to have known Luttle somewhat. Renee was a "woman of Satan," but to him doubtless any "fancy city woman" would reek of sin and godlessness. Anyway his version is that she married Reagan for the bread, but planned to keep her hand in all the same. She seduced Sam Luttle and drove him from the path of righteousness into the morass of sinfulness and adultery. In Banner's opinion Renee only got . . . (half a page missing) . . . no trace of Renee's body was ever discovered. Still it was assumed Reagan had murdered her, since she never turned up again in Greenville or anywhere else—and Reagan seemed definitely to have been on the run when he drove off the mountain. Here Banner gets a bit vague, and it's hard to tell if he's just getting theatrical. Still he insists that when they found Reagan with his throat guillotined by the windshield, there wasn't a tenth as much blood spilled about the body as would be expected. Same regarding Luttle's death. Superficial scratches except the torn throat, and only a small pool of blood. Banner doesn't believe the bear explanation, but I don't get what . . .

(pages missing)

. . . know whether my mind is going or whether this cabin is actually haunted.

July 15. I saw her again last night. This time she was standing at the edge of the pines beyond the front door—seemed to be looking at me. The image lasted maybe 15–20 seconds this time, long enough to get a good look. She's a perfect likeness of the description of Renee. This is really getting bizarre! I'm not quite sure whether I should be frightened or fascinated. I wonder why there haven't been any other reports of this place being haunted. . . .

July 16. I've started to paint her. Wonder what Fahler will say to a portrait of a ghost. It's getting easier now to see her, and she stays visible longer too—maybe she's getting accustomed to me. God—I keep thinking of that old ghost story, The Beckoning Fair One! Hope this won't. . . .

July 17. I find I can concentrate on Renee at nights now, and she appears more readily—more substantial. Painting is progressing well. She seems interested. Think I'll try to talk with her next. Still unsure whether this is psychic phenomenon or paranoid hallucination. We'll see—meanwhile damned if Enser will let anyone else in on this. Tho aren't artists supposed to be mad?

July 18. Decided to use the pines for background. Took a long walk this afternoon. Strange to think that Renee probably lies in an unmarked grave somewhere under this carpet of pine needles. Lonely grave—no wonder she doesn't rest. She smiles when she comes to me. My little spirit remained all of 5–6 minutes last night. Tonight . . .

(pages missing)

. . . to no one other than myself, and I think I understand. This goes back to something Bok once talked about. Spirits inhabit a plane other than our own—another dimension, say. Most spirits and most mortals are firmly anchored to their separate worlds. Exceptions exist. Certain spirits retain some ties with this world. Renee presumably because of her violent death, secret grave—who knows? The artist also is less firmly linked to this humdrum mortal plane—his creativity, his imagination transcends the normal world. Then I am more sensitive to manifestations of another plane than others; Renee is more readily perceived than other spirits. Result: Our favorite insane artist sees ghosts where countless dullards slept soundly. By this line of reasoning anyone can become a bona fide jr. ghostwatcher, if something occurs to make him more susceptible to their manifestations. Madmen, psychic adepts, the dying, those close to the deceased, those who have been torn loose from their normal life pattern . . .

. . . for maybe half the night. I think I'm falling in love with her. Talk about the ultimate in necrophilia!

July 26. The painting is almost complete. Last night she stayed with me almost until dawn. She seems far more substantial now—too substantial for a ghost. Wonder if I'm just getting more adept at perceiving her, or whether Renee is growing more substantial with my belief in her. . . .

July 27. She wanted me to follow her last night. I walked maybe a mile through the dark pines before my nerve failed. Maybe she was taking me to her grave. It's auditory now: Last night I heard her footsteps. I'll swear she leaves tracks in the dust, leaves an impression on the cushions when she sits. She watches me, listens—only no words yet. Maybe tonight she'll speak. She smiles when I tell her I love her.

July 28. I swear I heard her speak! Renee said she loved me! She wants me to return her love! Only a few words—just before she disappeared into the pines. And she seemed as substantial as any living girl! Either I'm hopelessly

217

insane, or I'm on the verge of an unthinkable psychic discovery! Tonight I'm going to know for certain. Tonight I'm going to touch Renee. I'm going to hold her in my arms and not let her go until I know whether I'm mad, the victim of an incredible hoax, or a man in love with a ghost!

It was the last entry.

VI

Lonzo Pennybacker gave directions to the house of the elderly Baptist preacher. Eventually Gerry found the right dirt road and drove up to a well-kept house at the head of a mountain cove. Flowers bloomed in the yard, and dogs were having a melee with a pack of noisy children. The house presented a clean, honest front—a far cry from the squalor Gerry had expected in a mountain home.

Rev. Billy Banner sat in a porch rocker and rose to meet Gerry. He was an alert man in his seventies or better, lean and strong without a trace of weakness or senility. His eyes were clear, and his voice still carried the deep intonations that had rained hellfire and damnation on his congregation for decades.

After shaking hands, Banner motioned him to a chair, politely waited for his guest to come to business. This was difficult. Gerry was uncertain what questions to ask, what explanations to offer—or what he really wanted to find out. But Banner sensed his uneasiness and expertly drew from him the reason for his visit. Gerry explained he was staying at the old Reagan cabin, that he was interested in the artist Enser Pittman who had killed himself there.

"Enser Pittman?" The old man nodded. "Yes, I remember him well enough. He paid me a visit once, just like you today. Maybe for the same reason."

Plunging on, Gerry asked about the history of the cabin and was told little he had not already learned. Rev. Banner spoke with reluctance of the old tragedy, seemed to suspect more than he was willing to put into words.

"Do you have any idea what might have driven Pittman to suicide?" Gerry asked finally.

The preacher kept silent until Gerry wondered if he would ignore the question. "Suicide? That was the verdict, sure enough. They found him mother-naked in bed, his throat tore open and a razor beside him. Been dead a few days—likely it had been done the last of July. No sign of struggle, nothing gone, no enemies. Artists are kind of funny anyway. And some claimed he had cancer. So maybe it was suicide like the coroner said. Maybe not. Wasn't much blood on the sheets for a man to be cut like that, they tell me. All the same, I hope it was suicide, and not something worse."

"I thought suicide was the unforgivable sin."

"There's things worse." Banner looked at him shrewdly. "Maybe you know what I mean. The Bible talks about witches and ghosts and a lot of other things we think we're too wise to believe in today. That Renee Reagan was a daughter of Satan, sure as I'm sitting here remembering her. Well, I'm an old man, but no one's ever called me an old fool, so I'll just stop talking."

Feeling uncomfortable without knowing why, Gerry thanked the preacher and rose to go. Rev. Banner stood up to see him off, then laid a sinewy hand on his shoulder at the edge of the porch.

"I don't know just what sort of trouble you got that's bothering you, son," he began, fixing Gerry with his keen eyes. "But I do know there's something about the old Reagan place that gets to some kinds of people. If that's the way it is with you, then you better get back to where it is you come from. And if you do stay on here, then just remember that Evil can't harm a righteous man so long as he denies its power and holds to the way of Our Lord Jesus Christ and his Gospel. But once you accept Evil—once you let Evil into your life and permit its power to influence your soul—then it's got you body and soul, and you're only a plaything for all the devils of Hell!

"You've got that lost look about you, son. Maybe you can hear that Hellbound train a-calling to you. But don't you listen to its call. Son, don't you climb on board!"

VII

With a strange mixture of dread and anticipation, Gerry broke away from Janet's mawkish attempts to make conversation and retired to the lower veranda for the evening. All afternoon he had thought about returning to Columbus, forgetting this mystery. Yet he knew he could not. For one thing, he had to stay until he could be certain of his own sanity. Barring madness, this entire uncanny business must be either hoax or genuine. If it were an elaborate hoax, Gerry wanted to know who, how and why. And if the cabin were haunted . . . He *had* to know.

But it was deeper than the simple desire to explore an occult phenomenon. Renee—whoever, whatever she might be—held a profound fascination for him. Her image obsessed him. He thought of this passionate, exotic woman of another era; then there was Janet. Bitterness returned, and again the memory of the son and the ordered world her moronic carelessness had torn from him. Right now she was sitting like a mushroom, spellbound by that boob-tube, never a concern for her husband's misery.

His thoughts were of Renee when sleep overcame him. In dream he saw her drift through the screen door and greet him with red-lipped smile. She was so vivacious, so desirable! Pittman's painting had held only the shadow of her feline beauty.

Gracefully she poured two fingers of Gerry's Scotch and tossed it down neat, eyes wide with devilish challenge. Bringing the bottle with her, she took the chair beside his own. Her long fingers cozily touched his arm. "Nice of you to offer a lady a drink," she grinned impishly. "Good Scotch is so hard to get now. Been saving this stuff in your cellar since before Volstead—or is this just off the boat?"

"Oh, the Prohibition's been repealed for years now," Gerry heard himself say dully, as in a dream. It was a dream. Renee cast no reflection in the barroom mirror.

"Sure honey." She laughed teasingly. "Say, lover—you look all down in the dumps tonight. Care to tell a girl all about it?"

And Gerry began to tell Renee the story of his life. As the night grew deeper, he told her of his struggle to become successful in his work, his efforts to build a position for himself in society, his marriage to a woman who couldn't understand him, his son for whom he had hoped everything, Janet's accident and the death of all his aspirations. Quietly she listened to him, eyes intent with sympathy. God! Why couldn't Janet ever show such feeling, such interest! Always too busy feeling sorry for herself!

When he finished, mechanical sobs shook his angular frame. Renee expressed a wordless cry of concern and laid a white arm around his shoulder. "Hey, c'mon now, Gerry! Get it all out of your system! You've really had a tough break or two, but we can work it out now, can't we? Here now—think about this instead!"

She slithered onto his lap and captured his lips in a long kiss.

Somewhere in the kiss Gerry opened his eyes. With a gasp he started from his chair. No one was there, of course.

God! What a dream! His lips felt bruised, unnaturally cold—even her kiss had felt real. Got to go easy on the bottle. Still if this was DTs, it was pleasant enough. God! Had he ever carried on! That psychiatrist would have had a picnic. He reached for the Scotch. Empty. Had he had that much to drink? No wonder the dream.

Was it a dream? Gerry looked about him suspiciously. The chair beside him seemed maybe closer, although he really hadn't noticed it earlier. An empty glass on the floor—but maybe he'd left it there before. That peculiar scent of jasmine again—wonder what perfume Renee had worn? Absurd— it was mountain flowers.

He touched his lips and there was blood on his fingers.

VIII

"I'm going out for a walk," he told Janet after breakfast.

"Can't you stay around here today for a change?" she asked wistfully. "Or let's go someplace together. You've been off so much lately, I hardly get to see you. And it's so lonely here without anyone around."

"Without a phone to gossip with all the bitches in your bridge club," he snapped. "Well, I'm not sitting on my ass all afternoon watching television. If you want company, then walk along with me!"

"Gerry," she began shakily. "You know I can't . . ."

"No, I don't know! The doctors say you can walk whenever you want to! You're just so content playing the invalid, you won't even try to walk again!'"

Her eyes clouded. "Gerry! That was cruel!"

"The truth though, wasn't it!" he exploded. "Well, damn it, snap out of it! I'm getting disgusted with waiting on you hand and foot—tying myself down to someone who can't stop feeling sorry for herself long enough to . . ."

"Gerry!" Janet clenched her fists. "Stop it! What's happening to us! For the last several days you've been getting ever sharper with me! You shun me—avoid my company like you hated me! For God's sake, Gerry, what is the matter!"

He turned from her in wordless contempt and strode off into the pine forest. She called after him until he was beyond earshot.

The pines! How restful they were after her miserable whimpering! The dense shade, the deep carpet of fallen needles choked out undergrowth. The dark, straight trunks stabbed toward the sunlight above, leaving a rough shaft branchless for dozens of feet. It was so pleasant to walk among them. The needles were a resilient carpet that deadened all sound. The trunks were myriad pillars to support a vaulted ceiling of swaying green boughs.

It was eerie here in the pines. So unlike a hardwood forest, alive with crackling leaves and a wild variety of trees and underbrush. The pines were so awesome, so ancient, so desolate. The incredible loneliness of this twilight wilderness assailed Gerry—and strangely soothed the turmoil of his emotions.

The restless wind moved the branches above him in ceaseless song. Sighing, whispering pines. Here was the very sound of loneliness. Again Gerry recalled the old mountain folk tune:

> *The longest train I ever saw,*
> *Was a hundred coaches long,*
> *And the only girl I ever loved,*
> *Was on that train and gone.*
> *In the pines, in the pines,*
> *Where the sun never shines,*
> *And I shiver when the wind blows cold.*

What was happening to him? A year ago he would have laughed at the absurd idea of ghosts or haunted houses. Had he changed so much since then—since the accident?

No, this couldn't actually be happening to him. He must try to examine all the facts with the same clear, down-to-earth attitude he formerly would have taken. He had come here with his nerves in bad shape—on the verge of a breakdown, the doctors had implied. Then he'd found an unusual painting and read through the diary of a deranged artist. Nerves and too much Scotch had got the best of his disordered imagination, and he had assumed the same delusions as poor Pittman. Add to that the stories of the place he had gleaned from the locals, and his newborn romantic streak had run wild—to the point he was sharing Pittman's own mad hallucinations. Similarities were not surprising; the circumstances that induced the delusions were the same, and he had Pittman's notes to direct him.

Besides, if the Reagan place were haunted, why had no one else seen anything out of the ordinary? Pittman in his egotism had claimed his artistic soul made it possible for him to perceive what lesser minds had missed. But Gerry had no artistic pretensions or illusions of paranormal talents.

Pittman had suggested that someone might become susceptible to the spirit world, if he had somehow become alienated from his normal plane of existence. Gerry shrugged mentally. Perhaps then he had become receptive to the other world when the protection of his safe middle-class existence had collapsed about him. But now he was accepting the logic of a suicide.

He paused in bewilderment. The pine forest had suddenly assumed a sense of familiarity. Curiously Gerry studied his surroundings—then it occurred to him. Granted the passage of time, this section of the forest resembled the background in the painting of Renee. He had half assumed Pittman had done a stylized portrayal, rather than an actual landscape. How odd to happen upon the same grove of pines and then to recognize it from the painting.

Why had Pittman chosen this particular section of the pines? Probably he had simply wandered to this spot just as Gerry had done. Still, perhaps there was something that made this spot especially attractive to the artist.

Gerry stood in silence. Was it imagination again? Did the sun seem to shine less brightly here? Did the pines seem to loom darker, with a shadow of menace? Was the whisper of the pines louder here, and was there a note of depravity in the loneliness of the sound? Why were there no cries of birds, no sounds of life, other than the incessant murmur of the brooding pines? And why was there a bare circle of earth where not even the pines grew?

Gerry shivered. He hurried from the spot, no longer so certain of his logic.

IX

Janet was sulking when Gerry returned, and they studiously avoided each other for the remainder of the day. Monosyllables were exchanged when conversation was unavoidable, and whatever went through the mind of either was left to fester unexpressed. Mechanically Janet prepared dinner, although neither felt like eating.

"I can't take this!" Janet finally blurted. "I don't know what's happened to us since we got here, but we're tearing ourselves apart. This just hasn't worked for us, Gerry. Tomorrow I want to go home."

Gerry sighed ponderously. "Now look. We came here so you could rest. And now already you want to go back."

"Gerry, I can't stand it here! Every day I've felt you grow farther away from me! I don't know if it's just this place, or if it's us—but I do know we've got to leave!"

"We'll talk about it in the morning," he said wearily, and stood up.

Janet's lips were set. "Right! Now go on downstairs and drink yourself to sleep! That's the pattern, isn't it? You can't bear to be around me, so you get as far away as you can! And you stumble around all day either drunk or hungover! Always bleary-eyed, paunchy, and surly! Gerry, I can't take this any longer!"

He retreated stolidly. "Go to bed, Janet. We'll talk this over in the morning."

"Damn it, Gerry! I've tried to be patient. The doctors warned me you'd made an unhealthy adjustment to the accident—just because you came out no worse than hungover! But if this doesn't stop, I'm going to ask for a separation!"

Gerry halted, angry retorts poised on his tongue. No, let her yell. Ignore her. "Good night, Janet," he grated and fled downstairs.

Angrily he gulped down half a glass of straight Scotch. God! This Scotch was the only thing that held their marriage together—made this situation tolerable. And, he noticed, his stock of Scotch was just about gone.

Divorce! Well, why not! Let the leech live off alimony for the rest of her years. It was almost worth paying to be rid of her! Let her divorce him then! She'd made a ruin of everything else in his life—might as well finish the job right!

Once again he thought of Renee. There was a woman to love, to desire—a woman who could stand on her own two feet, who could return his love with full passion of her own! She and Janet shared their sex with no more in common than a leopardess and a cow. No wonder Pittman had fallen in love with his phantasy of Renee!

Damn Janet! Damn the doctors! Bitching him about his emotional stability. So he drank more than he used to! So he maybe threw a scene or two, maybe felt a little differently about things now! Well, it was a different world! A man was entitled to make adjustments. Maybe he needed a little more time. . . .

No! It wasn't *his* fault!

The glass slipped from his shaking fist, smashed on the floor. Gerry pawed at it clumsily, cursing the spilled liquor. He'd fix another and clear up tomorrow. Dully he noticed another broken glass. When had he . . . ?

It was late when Gerry finally drifted off to sleep, as had become his habit. Smiling, he welcomed Renee when she came to him. How strange to be dreaming, he mused, and yet know that it's a dream.

"Here again, darling?" There was secret humor in her grave smile. "And looking so sad again. What are we to do with you, Gerry? I so hate to see you all alone in a blue funk every night! The wife?"

"Janet. The bitch!" he mumbled thickly. "She wants me to leave you!"

Renee was dismayed. "Leave? When I'm just getting so fond of you? Hey, lover, that sounds pretty grim!"

Brokenly, Gerry blurted out his anger, his pain. Told her of the lies and insinuations. Told her how hard it was to get through each day, how only a stiff drink and the memory of her smile could calm his nerves each night.

Renee listened in silence, only nodding to show she understood, until he finished and sat quivering with anger. "It sounds to me like you've finally realized Janet has only been a nagging obstruction in your life," she observed. "Surely you've never loved her."

Gerry nodded vehemently. "I hate her!"

She smiled lazily and snuggled closer, her lips only inches from his own. "What about me, Gerry? Do you love your Renee?"

His Renee! "With all my soul!" he whispered huskily.

"Mmmmm. That's sweet." Renee held him with her glowing eyes. "So you love Renee more than Janet?"

"Yes! Of course I do!"

"And would you like to be rid of Janet so you could be with me?"

"God, how I wish that!"

Her smile burned more confident. "What if she died? Would you want Janet dead?"

Bitterness poisoned his spirit. "Janet dead? Yes! That would be perfect! I wish she were dead so we could be together!"

"Oh, sweetheart!" Renee squeezed him delightedly. "You really do love me, don't you! Let's kiss on our bargain!"

Somewhere in her kiss the dream dissolved to blackness.

From upstairs a shriek of black terror shattered the stillness of the night.

He started awake sometime later, groggily rubbed his head while trying to collect his thoughts. What had happened? The dream . . . He remembered. And suddenly he had the feeling that something was wrong, dreadfully *wrong*. Strangely frightened, he staggered up the stairs. "Janet?" he called, his voice unnatural.

Moonlight spilled through the rusty screen and highlighted the crumpled figure who lay in one corner of the room. A small patch of darkness glistened on the wood. Strange how small that pool of blood.

"Janet!" he groaned in disbelieving horror. "Oh, my God!"

Her eyes were wide and staring; her face set in a death grimace of utmost loathing, insane dread. Whatever had killed Janet had first driven her mad with terror.

It had not been an easy death. Her throat was a jagged gash—too ragged a tear for the knife that lay beside her. A Barlow knife. His.

"Janet!" he sobbed, grief slamming him like a sledge. "Who could have done this thing!"

"Don't you know, lover?"

Gerry whirled, cried out in fear. "Renee. You're alive!"

She laughed at him from the shadow, triumph alight in her eyes. She was just as he had seen her in the painting, in the dreams. Green silk frock, bobbed auburn hair, eyes that held dark secrets. Only now her lips were far more crimson, and scarlet trickled across her chin.

"Yes, Gerry. I'm alive and Janet is dead. Just the way you wished. Or have you forgotten?" Mockery was harsh in her voice.

"Impossible!" he moaned. "You've been dead for years! Ghosts can't exist! Not here! Not today!"

But Renee stepped forward, gripped his hand with fingers like frozen steel. Her nails stabbed his wrist. "You know better."

Gerry stared at her in revulsion. "I don't believe in you! You have no power over me!"

"But you *do* believe in me."

"God, help me! Help me!" he sobbed, mind reeling with nightmare.

Contempt lined her face. "Too late for that."

She pulled his arm, drew him to the door. "Come now, lover! We have a sealed bargain!"

He protested—willed himself not to follow. Struggled to awaken from the nightmare. In vain. Helplessly he followed the creature he himself had given substance.

Out into the pines Renee led him. The pines whose incessant whisper told of black knowledge and secret loneliness. Through the desolate pines they walked into the night. Past endless columns of dark sentinel trunks. Swaying, whispering an ancient rhythm with the night wind.

Until they came to a grove Gerard Randall now found familiar. Where the darkness was deeper. Where the whisper was louder and resonant with doom. Where the pines drew back about a circle of earth in which nothing grew.

Where tonight yawned a pit, and he knew where Renee's unhallowed grave lay hidden.

"Is this madness?" he asked with sudden hope.

"No. This is death."

And the illusion of beauty slipped from Renee, revealed the cavern-eyed lich in rotting silk, who pulled him down into the grave like a bride enticing a bashful groom. And in that final moment Gerard Randall understood the whispered litany of the merciless pines.

A GENTLEMAN
FROM MEXICO

MARK SAMUELS

Mark Samuels is the author of two collections, The White Hands and
Other Weird Tales *and* Black Altars, *as well as the novella* The Face of
Twilight. *His third collection of short stories is provisionally titled*
Glyphotech and Other Macabre Processes *and is scheduled to be pub-
lished by Midnight House.*

His stories have appeared in both The Mammoth Book of Best New
Horror *and* The Year's Best Fantasy and Horror *series. He has been
nominated twice for the British Fantasy Award.*

*"I spent the last few months of 2005 on holiday with my wife in
Mexico City," Samuels recalls, "where I was quite amazed to discover that
authors such as Lovecraft, Machen, and Blackwood were better known
there than I had ever anticipated.*

*"Nearly every bookshop I explored had imported copies of the
Valdemar editions from Barcelona. Even the bookstalls in the markets
and those in the metro system carried cheap editions of horror and ghost
story classics. It seemed to be the case that Latin America was keeping the
flame of classic weird fiction alive in the mass-market in a way that was
unmatched by the more negligent Anglophone countries.*

"'A Gentleman from Mexico' was the result of this insight."

As the title playfully indicates, the following story is also a tribute to the twentieth century's most influential writer of weird fiction. . . .

Barlow, I imagine, can tell you even more about the Old Ones.
　　　　　　　　　　　—Clark Ashton Smith to August Derleth,
　　　　　　　　　　　　　　　　　　　　　　　April 13, 1937

Víctor Armstrong was running late for his appointment and so had hailed a taxi rather than trusting to the metro. Bathed in cruel noon sunlight, the green-liveried Volkswagen beetle taxi cruised down Avenida Reforma. In the back of the vehicle, Armstrong rummaged around in his jacket pocket for the pack of Faros cigarettes he'd bought before setting off on his rendezvous.

"Es okay para mí a fumar en tu taxi?" Armstrong said, managing to cobble together the request in his iffy Spanish.

He saw the eyes of the driver reflected in the rear-view mirror, and they displayed total indifference. It was as if he'd made a request to fold his arms.

"Seguro." The driver replied, turning the wheel sharply, weaving his way across four lines of traffic. Armstrong was jolted over to the left and clutched at the leather handle hanging from the front passenger door. The right hand seat at the front had been removed, as was the case with all the green taxis, giving plenty of leg-room and an easy entrance and exit. Like most of the taxi drivers in Mexico City, this one handled his vehicle with savage intent, determined to get from A to B in the minimum possible time. In this almost permanently grid-locked megalopolis, the survival of the fastest was the rule.

Armstrong lit up one of his untipped cigarettes and gazed out the window. Brilliant sunshine illuminated in excruciating detail the chaos and decay of the urban rubbish dump that is the Ciudad de México, Distrito Federal, or "D.F." for short. A great melting pot of the criminal, the insane, the beautiful and the macho, twenty-five million people constantly living in a mire of institutionalized corruption, poverty and crime. But despite all this, Mexico City's soul seems untouched, defiant. No other great city of the world is so vividly alive, dwelling as it does always in the shadow of death. Another earthquake might be just around the corner, the Popocatépetl volcano might blow at any hour, and the brown haze of man-made pollution might finally suffocate the populace. Who knows? What is certain is that the D.F. would rise again, as filthy, crazed and glorious as before.

They were approaching La Condesa, a fashionable area to the north of the center that had attracted impoverished artists and writers ten years ago, but which had recently been overrun with pricey restaurants and cafés.

Armstrong had arranged to meet with an English-speaking acquaintance at the bookshop café El Torre on the corner of Avenida Nuevo León. This acquaintance, Juan San Isidro, was a so-called underground poet specializing in sinister verse written in the Náhuatl language and who, it was rumored, had links with the *narcosatánicos*. A notorious drunk, San Isidro had enjoyed a modicum of celebrity in his youth but had burnt out by his mid-twenties. Now a decade older, he was scarcely ever sober and looked twice his actual age. His bitterness and tendency to enter into the kind of vicious quarrels that seem endemic in Latin American literary circles had alienated him from most of his contemporaries.

Armstrong suspected that San Isidro had requested a meeting for one of two reasons; either to tap him for money or else to seek his assistance in recommending a translator for a re-issue of his poetical work in an English language edition in the United States. It was highly unlikely that San Isidro was going to offer him a work of fiction for one of his upcoming anthologies of short stories.

The taxi pulled up alongside the bookshop.

"*¿Cuánto es?*" Armstrong asked.

"*Veintiún pesos,*" the driver responded. Armstrong handed over some coins and exited the vehicle.

Standing on the corner outside the bookshop was a stall selling tortas, tacos and other fast-food. The smell of the sizzling meat and chicken, frying smokily on the hob, made Armstrong's mouth water. Despite the call of *"¡Pásele, señor!"* Armstrong passed by, knowing that, as a foreigner, his stomach wouldn't have lasted ten minutes against the native bacteria. Having experienced what they called "Montezuma's Revenge" on his first trip to D.F. a year ago, there was no question of him taking a chance like that again.

Across the street an argument was taking place between two drivers, who had got out of their battered and dirty cars to trade insults. Since their abandoned vehicles were holding up the traffic, the rather half-hearted battle (consisting entirely of feints and shouting) was accompanied by a cacophony of angry car-horns.

El Torre was something of a landmark in the area, its exterior covered with tiles, and windows with external ornate grilles. A three-storey building with a peaked roof, and erected in the colonial era, it had been a haunt for literati of all stripes, novelists, poets and assorted hangers-on, since the 1950s. During the period in which La Condesa had been gentrified some of El Torre's former seedy charm had diminished and, as well as selling books, it had diversified into stocking DVDs and compact discs upstairs.

Part of the ground floor had been converted into an expensive eatery, whilst the first floor now half occupied a café-bar from where drinkers could peer over the center of the storey down into the level below, watching diners pick at their food and browsers lingering over the books on shelves and on the display tables. As a consequence of these improvements, the space for poetry readings upstairs had been entirely done away with, and Juan San Isidro haunted its former confines as if in eternal protest at the loss of his own personal stage.

As Armstrong entered, he glanced up at the floor above and saw the poet already waiting for him, slumped over a table and tracing a circle on its surface with an empty bottle of Sol beer. His lank black hair hung down to his shoulders, obscuring his face, but even so his immense bulk made him unmistakable.

Armstrong's gaze roved around and sought out the stairway entrance. He caught sight of the only other customer in El Torre, besides himself and San Isidro. This other person was dressed in a dark grey linen suit, quite crumpled, with threadbare patches at the elbows and frayed cuffs. The necktie he wore was a plain navy blue and quite unremarkable. His shoes were badly scuffed and he must have repeatedly refused the services of the D.F.'s innumerable *boleros*. They keenly polished shoes on their portable foot-stands for anyone who had a mere dozen pesos to spare. The man had an olive complexion, was perfectly clean-shaven, and about forty years old. His short black hair was parted neatly on the left-hand side. He had the features of a *mestizo*, a typical Mexican of mingled European and Native Indian blood. There was something in the way that he carried himself that told of a gentleman down on his luck, perhaps even an impoverished scholar given his slight stoop, an attribute often acquired by those who pore over books or manuscripts year after year.

He was browsing through the books on display that were published by the likes of Ediciones Valdemar and Ediciones Siruela that had been specially imported from Spain. These were mostly supernatural fiction titles, for which many Mexican readers had a discerning fondness. Armstrong was glad, for his own anthologies invariably were comprised of tales depicting the weird and uncanny, a market that, at least in the Anglophone countries, seemed to have self-destructed after a glut of trashy horror paperbacks in the 1980s. But these were not junk, they were works by the recognized masters, and a quick glance over the classics available for sale here in mass-market form would have drawn the admiration of any English or American devotee.

Here were books by Arthur Machen, Algernon Blackwood, M.R. James and Ambrose Bierce, amongst dozens of others. Most striking however, was the vast range of collections available written by H.P. Lovecraft. The browsing man in the dark suit picked up one after the other, almost reluctant to return each to its proper place, although if his down-at-heel appearance were an indication, their price was surely beyond his limited means. New books in Mexico are scarcely ever cheap.

Armstrong looked away. He could not understand why this rather ordinary gentleman had stirred his imagination. He was, after all, merely typical of the sort of book-addict found anywhere and at any time. Meanwhile Juan San Isidro had noticed Victor's arrival and called down to him.

"¡Ay, Víctor, quiero más chela! Lo siento, pero no tengo dinero."

Armstrong sighed, and made his way up the stairs.

When they were eventually sitting opposite one another, Armstrong with a bottle of Indio and San Isidro with a fresh bottle of Sol, the Mexican switched from Spanish to English. He was always keen to take whatever opportunity he could to converse in the language. A huge bear of a man, he'd recently grown a shaggy goatee beard and the T-shirt he wore bore the logo of some outlandish band called Control Machete, whose music Armstrong did not know and did not want to know. Years ago Armstrong had foolishly mentioned San Isidro's literary efforts to the publisher of a small press imprint in California who was looking for cosmic or outré verse. The result had been a chapbook with a selection of San Isidro's Aztec-influenced work translated into English, and thereafter Armstrong had never been able to entirely shake off his "discovery".

"So," San Isidro said, "how are things with you? Still editing those antologías?"

"There's scarcely any money in them Juan," Armstrong replied, "unless I've managed to wrangle something original out of Steve King, the publishers want to nail my balls to the wall."

"You know him? King? Do you think he'd give me a loan? He's very rich, no? Help out a struggling brother artist?"

Armstrong tried not to smile inappropriately. He could only imagine how quickly San Isidro would piss away any handouts he'd receive on booze. No-one other than their agents, accountants, lawyers or publishers milks cash-cow authors.

"He's a busy man. I don't think he'd appreciate my . . ."

"You mean he's a *pinche cabrón.* Keeps his money up his *culo* where no one else can get at it. That's why *todos los gringos* walk around with their legs apart, like cowboys, no? All those dollar bills stuffed in there."

Armstrong was relieved to be British. Even liberal Americans who came south, seeking to atone for the recent sins of NAFTA and a long history of land grabbing, were objects of ridicule here. They might get away with such conscience posturing in the north, in cities like Monterrey that were closer to the border and which looked to rich U.S. States like Texas for inspiration, but in Mexico D.F. *gringos* are only ever *pinches gringos* and no amount of self-loathing or atonement on their part could ever erase the fact. The British, on the other hand, despite their Imperial past, were redeemed by virtue of having given the Beatles and association football to the world.

"Why did you want to see me, Juan?" Armstrong asked, taking out his packet of Faros and putting them on the table. His companion looked at the cheap brand with amused contempt. Nevertheless, this attitude did not stop him from smoking them.

"I want you to take a look at some *cuentos,"* San Isidro replied, puffing away on the cigarette he'd taken, "Read them and make me an offer. They're in your line of work."

He delved into a shoulder bag lying underneath the table and took out a pile of papers, individuated into sections by rubber bands, and handed them over.

"I thought you didn't write short stories." Armstrong said.

"I didn't write them. I'm acting as the exclusive agent. They're in English, as you see, and they're the type of horror stories you like. I handle all his stuff," San Isidro replied.

"Who's this author," Armstrong said, looking at the top sheet, "Felipe López? I can't say I've heard of him."

"*El señor López* has only been writing for a couple of years. He's my personal discovery, like you discovered me, no? *Es un autor auténtico,* not some hack. *Mira al cabellero* down there, the one who's looking through the books? That's *el señor López.* He doesn't want to meet you until you've read his stuff. I told him I knew you, and that you weren't the same as all those other *culeros* who'd rejected him."

So that man in the crumpled grey suit was San Isidro's first client, Armstrong thought. He hesitated for a moment but then relented. At least this man López had the appearance of being literate.

"Alright," Armstrong said, "I'll take them away with me and call you once I've read them. I can't promise anything though."

"Why not sit here and read them now, *compañero?* I tell you, these things are a gold mine. We can have a few more *chelas* while I wait for you to finish. He also does his own proof-reading, so you won't need to *trabajar mucho* yourself."

"Short stories," Armstrong riposted, "are fool's gold, Juan. I told you, there's no real money in them anymore. Have another on me if you like, but I've got to go. I'll be in touch."

With that closing remark Armstrong stood up, left a hundred pesos note on the table, and made his exit. He didn't notice whether or not *el Señor López* saw him leave.

Over the next few days Armstrong almost forgot about the stories by Felipe López. He hated being asked to read fiction by an unknown author that had been praised by one of his friends. All too often he had to prick their enthusiasm, usually fired by beer and comradeship rather than from an objective assessment of literary merit. And San Isidro had never acted as an agent for anybody before; he was far too consumed by his own literary ambitions. So it appeared obvious to Armstrong that San Isidro was paying back a favor of some sort. Though it seemed unlikely given the down-at-heel appearance of López, but perhaps it was a case of San Isidro owing him money.

Armstrong was staying close to Cuauhtémoc metro station in an apartment owned by Mexican friends of his. The couple, Enrique and María, were in London for a few weeks, staying in his flat there in an exchange holiday. It was something they did every other year to save on hotel bills. There were only three days left before they were due to cross each other high over the Atlantic in flights going in the opposite direction. Enrique and María were both involved in publishing themselves, and he'd struck up a friendship with them in 1995 whilst attending a fantasy and horror convention held in San Francisco.

Since he was staying in an apartment belonging to friends, Armstrong paid little attention to the telephone, as he knew he'd just be taking messages for his absent hosts. Anything desperately important that needed to be passed on to them would be left on the answerphone machine. When he got around to checking it, there were three messages, two for Enrique and María, and one for him. It was left by Juan San Isidro.

"Oye, ¿qué onda? Man, don't fuck me over. Have you read *los cuentos?* I think not. Otherwise you'd be chasing my ass like a *puto.* You don't leave Mexico until I hear from you, *¿te queda claro?"*

Despite his reluctance, Armstrong didn't see any alternative but to look the stories over. He took them out onto the little balcony overlooking the *privada* in which the apartment was situated. It was pleasantly warm outside in the evening, being October, and since the only traffic passing below consisted of pedestrians it was easy to concentrate. He sat down on the chair he'd moved out there, put the papers that he'd retrieved from his suitcase on his lap, and looked them over.

San Isidro had given him four stories, the longest of which was the third at around forty thousand words.

MARK SAMUELS

Armstrong had seen this type of story on dozens of occasions in the past, usually sent for his consideration by "fan authors" who were obsessed with the life and works of H.P. Lovecraft. Most of these pastiches contained long lists of clichéd forbidden books and names of unpronounceable entities to be incorporated into the so-called "Cthulhu Mythos". As he turned the pages of the first of López's tales though, he was surprised to discover that they did not also contain the other feature associated with Lovecraft fan pastiches—there were no obvious grammatical, spelling or common textual errors. The work had already been gone over by an author with a keen eye for copy-editing.

Additionally, it had to be the case that Felipe López was fluent in English to the degree of being able to pass completely for a native. The text contained no trace of any Spanish language idioms indicating his Mexican nationality. Indeed, López even favored the British spelling of certain words, rather than that used in the United States, in exactly the same fashion as Lovecraft himself had done.

Despite his disdain for pastiche, Armstrong kept reading. Eventually, to his surprise, he found that López's mimetic skills were so expert that he could almost believe that he was reading a previously undiscovered work written by Lovecraft himself. The story had the exact same sense of nightmarish authenticity as the best of the Providence author's tales. By the time he'd finished reading the first story, Armstrong was in a state of dazed wonder. Of course he realized, on a professional level, that the thing had no commercial potential. It smacked far too much of an in-joke, or a hoax, but it was nevertheless profoundly impressive in its own right.

He began to wonder what this López person might be able to achieve were he to wean himself from the Lovecraft influence and produce fiction utilizing a distinct authorial voice. It might result in another modern-day writer of the order of Thomas Ligotti.

Armstrong was dimly aware of the telephone ringing in the background.

He ignored the sound, allowing the answer-machine to deal with whoever it was. He supposed that he could be San Isidro again and that it might have been better to pick up, but he was too eager to discover whether the story he'd just read was a fluke or not. Since the mosquitoes were now busy in the night air, he took the manuscripts inside and carried on reading.

Whoever had left the weird message on Enrique and María's answer-machine was obviously some crank, thought Armstrong. He played it back again the morning after it was recorded.

There was click on the line and the sound of unintelligible voices conferring amongst themselves and then a jarring, discordant muttering in English. The voice had a Mexican accent but was unknown to Armstrong. It said, *"He belongs to us. His products belong to us. No-one will take him from us."*

That was all.

After listening to the message one more time, Armstrong wondered if it were not simply San Isidro playing a joke on him, pretending to be another rival party involved with the works of Felipe López. Perhaps he thought the idea of some competition might spur Armstrong to a quick decision. If so, it was an unnecessary ploy.

After having read the second of López's tales he was convinced that the author had unmatched imagination and ability, despite being almost ruinously handicapped by his slavish mimicry of Lovecraft's style and themes. However, there was more than enough pure genius in there to convince Armstrong to take the matter further. If he could meet with López in person, he was determined to press upon him the necessity of a last revision of the texts—one that removed entirely the Cthulhu Mythos elements and replaced the florid, adjective-ridden prose with a minimalist approach.

When he telephoned Juan San Isidro it was no surprise that the poet-turned-agent was deeply suspicious about Armstrong's insistence that he must meet López alone.

"You want to cut me out of the deal, ¡estás loco!. Forget it, man. Now you know *que es un maestro, lo quieres todo para ti.*"

"I only want to suggest a few changes to the texts, Juan. Nothing sinister in that, really. You'll get your commission, I'll not cheat you, believe me."

Their conversation went round in circles for ten minutes before Armstrong eventually convinced San Isidro that he had no underhand motive with regards to López's work. Even so, Armstrong realized that there was something more going on between the two of them than the usual protective relationship between an agent and his client. Nevertheless, he successfully elicited a promise from San Isidro that he would ensure López met with him alone in the Café la Habana on La Calle de Bucareli at 2:00 P.M. that same afternoon.

The Café la Habana was a haunt for distinguished old men who came to play chess, smoke their pipes or cigars and spend the better part of the afternoon dreaming over coffee or beer. It had a high ceiling and was decorated with framed photographs of Havana from the time before Castro's revolution. Many communist exiles from Batista Cuba came here, having fled persecution, and its fame dated from that period. The number of exiles had dwindled as the years passed, but it still had a reputation amongst all those who championed leftist defiance. The place had a long pedigree, having been a favorite meeting place, in even earlier decades, of those Spanish Republican refugees who'd settled in D.F. after escaping the wrath of General Franco's regime.

Armstrong sat in a corner, lingering over a glass of tequila with lime, when López walked in. He was half-an-hour late. His lean form was framed in the doorway by the brilliant sunshine outside. López cast his glance around the place before spotting Armstrong and making for the table at which he sat.

López had changed his dark grey suit for a cream-colored one, and this time he was wearing a matching Panama hat. He gave a nod of recognition towards Armstrong as he approached.

Before he sat down he shook Armstrong's hand and apologized in English. "I hope that you will excuse my tardiness Mr. Armstrong, but the truth is that I was distracted by a particularly fascinating example of 18th Century colonial architecture whilst making my way over here."

Armstrong did not reply at once. He was taken aback by López's accent. Unless he was mistaken, it was pure, authentic New England Yankee. There was not a trace of Mexican in it.

"No need to apologize," Armstrong finally said, "can I get you a drink; some beer or tequila perhaps?"

"Thank you but no. I never partake of alcoholic beverages, even for the purposes of refreshment. However, a cup of coffee, perhaps a double espresso, would be most welcome."

Armstrong ordered López's coffee and asked for another tequila with lime to be brought to their table.

"I liked your tales very much, it was quite an experience reading through them I can tell you. Of course they're overly derivative, but I imagine that you could easily tone down all the Lovecraftian elements . . ."

"I'm afraid, Mr. Armstrong," López said, with a chill tone entering his voice, "that alterations of any sort are completely out of the question. The stories must be printed as written, down to the last detail, otherwise this conversation is simply a waste of my time and your own."

The drinks arrived. López calmly began to shovel spoonful after spoonful of sugar into his cup, turning the coffee into treacly, caffeine-rich syrup. Armstrong looked at him incredulously. Now he understood what was going on. San Isidro was definitely having a joke at his expense. He must have coached this López character, telling him all about H.P. Lovecraft's mannerisms and . . . to what end?

"Why are you persisting with this absurd Lovecraft impersonation?"

Armstrong blurted out, "It's ridiculous. San Isidro put you up to it I suppose. But what I can't figure out is why, so let me in on the joke."

López looked up from his coffee and his eyes were deadly serious. And here it comes, boy and girls, thought Armstrong; here comes the line we've all been waiting for:

This is no joke Mr. Armstrong, far from it, for I am in reality Howard Phillips Lovecraft of Providence, Rhode Island.

"Surely the only rational answer has already suggested itself," López replied, very calmly and without any melodrama, "you are in fact sitting across the table from a certifiable lunatic."

Armstrong leaned back in his seat and very carefully considered the man opposite. His manner betrayed no sign of humor and he spoke as if what he'd suggested was an established truism.

"Then despite your behavior, you know that you're not really Lovecraft?" Armstrong said.

"Howard Phillips Lovecraft died in agony on the morning of Monday the 15th of March 1937 in Providence's Jane Brown Memorial Hospital. I cannot be him. However, since Tuesday the 15th of March 2003, I have been subject to a delusion whereby the identity of Lovecraft completely supplanted my own. I currently have no memories whatsoever of having once been Felipe López of Mexico City. His family and friends are complete strangers to me. Meanwhile everyone Lovecraft knew is dead. I have become an outsider in this country and in this time. Unless one accepts the existence of the supernatural, which I emphatically do not, then only the explanation I have advanced has any credence."

Armstrong was taken aback by these remarks. This was like no madman he'd heard of—one who was not only able to recognize his derangement, but who also was totally a slave to it. It was more like some bizarre variant of a multiple personality disorder.

"What did the doctors here have to say?" Armstrong asked.

"They did their best, but with no appreciable effect, let alone any amelioration, upon my malady. They tended to agree with my analysis of the situation." López said, after taking a sip of his coffee.

"What about López before this happened? Did he have any interest in Lovecraft prior to your—umm—alteration? I can't believe something like that would come out of nowhere."

It was annoying, but Armstrong found himself questioning López as if he were actually addressing Lovecraft inhabiting another body.

"Quite so. I have discovered that López was a fanatical devotee of Lovecraft's life and work. Moreover, he was one of that rather contemptible breed of freaks who adhere to the outlandish belief that, rather than writing fiction, Lovecraft had unconscious access to ultra-mundane dimensions. The group to which he belonged, who styled themselves "The Sodality of the Black Sun", advocated the piteous theory that Lovecraft was an occult prophet instead of a mere scribbler. This indicates to me a brain already on the brink of a potential collapse into total chaos. You see before you the inevitable consequence."

There are a lot of sad crazies out there, thought Armstrong, who believe in nothing except the power of their own imaginations to create whatever they want to create from a supposedly malleable reality. A whole bunch of them had doubtless fastened upon Lovecraft's mythos for inspiration, but he doubted that any others had wound up like Felipe López.

"Well," Armstrong said, "I don't know what to make of all this. But surely one consideration has occurred to you already? If you really were Lovecraft, you'd know certain things that only he could possibly have known."

"An ingenious point," said López, "but with all his contemporaries in the grave, how then to verify that information? Mr. Armstrong, I must remind you that the idea of Lovecraft's consciousness not only surviving the death of his physical form, but also transferring itself to another body, is patently ridiculous. I make no such claim."

López stared at him wordlessly and then, having finished the dregs of his coffee, got up and left.

When Armstrong arrived back at Enrique and María's apartment, he found the door already ajar. Someone had broken in, forcing their entrance with a crowbar or similar tool judging by the splintered wound in the side of the door's frame. He was relieved to find that the intruders had not torn the place apart and seemed to have scarcely disturbed anything. When he examined his own room however, he noted at once that the López manuscripts were missing. He unmistakably remembered having left them on his bedside table. However, in their place, was a note left behind by whoever had stolen them. It read:

DO NOT MEDDLE IN OUR AFFAIRS AGAIN, LEST THE DARKNESS SEEK YOU OUT.

Obviously, this was a targeted burglary by the people who'd left that answerphone message warning him off having dealings with López. They must have wanted to get hold of the López stories extremely badly. Whoever they were, they must have also known that San Isidro had passed them to him, as well as knowing that Armstrong had an appointment with López, thus giving them the perfect moment to strike while he was out.

It was difficult to figure out what to do next. Everyone in Mexico City realizes that to call the police regarding a burglary has two possible outcomes. The first is that they will turn up, treat it as a waste of their time and do nothing. The second is that things will turn surreal very quickly, because they will casually mention how poorly paid police officers are, and, in return for a "donation", they are able to arrange for the swift return of your goods with no questions asked. Given that the burglary was not the work of organized crime but some nutty underground cult, Armstrong thought better of involving the police.

Great, thought Armstrong, now I'm in trouble not only with the local branch of occult loonies, but with San Isidro and López for having lost the manuscripts. The first thing to do was give San Isidro the bad news. Since a matter of this delicate nature was best dealt with face-to-face Armstrong decided to make his way over to the poet's apartment, after he'd arranged for someone to come over and fix the door.

A cardinal, though unspoken, rule of travelling by metro in Mexico City is not to carry anything of value. If you're a tourist, look like a tourist with little money. The security guards that hover around the ticket barriers are not there just for show. They carry guns for a reason. D.F. is the kidnapping capital of the world. Armstrong had always followed the dress-down rule and, although he stood out anyway because he was a pale-skinned *güerito,* he'd encountered no problems on his travels.

The stations themselves were grimy, functionalist and depressing. Architecturally they resembled prison camps, but located underground. Nevertheless Armstrong enjoyed travelling by metro; it was unbelievably cheap, the gap between trains was less than a minute, and it was like being on a mobile market place. Passengers selling homemade CDs would wander up and down the carriages, with samples of music playing on ghetto blasters slung over their shoulders. Others sold tonics for afflictions from back pain to impotence. Whether these worked or not there was certainly a market for them, as the sellers did a brisk trade.

One of the carriages on the train that Armstrong took must have been defective. All its lights were out and, curiously, he noticed that when anyone thought to board it anyway changed their minds at once and preferred to either remain on the platform or else rush over into one of the adjacent carriages instead.

Armstrong alighted at Chapultepec station, found his way through the convoluted tunnels up to the surface and turned left alongside the eight-lane road outside. The noise of the traffic blocked out most other sounds, and the vehicle fumes were like a low-level grey nebula held down by the force of the brilliant afternoon sunshine. People scurried to and fro along the pavement, their gazes fixed straight ahead, particularly those of any lone women for whom eye-contact with a *chilango* carried the risk of inviting a lewd suggestion.

A long footbridge flanked the motorway, and was the only means of crossing for pedestrians for a couple of miles or so. At night it was a notorious crime spot and only the foolhardy would cross it unaccompanied. However, at this time of the day everyone safely used it and a constant stream of people went back and forth.

Juan San Isidro's apartment was only a five-minute walk from the bridge, and was housed in a decaying brownstone building just on the fringes of La Condesa. Sometimes Armstrong wondered whether the poet was the structure's only occupant, for the windows of all the other apartments were either blackened by soot or else broken and hanging open day and night to the elements.

He pushed the intercom button for San Isidro, and, after a minute, heard a half-awake voice say, *"¿Quién es?"*

"It's me, Victor, come down and let me in, will you?" Armstrong replied, holding his mouth close to the intercom.

"Stand in front where I can see you," the voice said, "and I'll give you *mis llaves.*"

Armstrong left the porch, went onto the pavement and looked up. San Isidro leaned out of one of the third floor windows, his lank black hair making a cowl over his face. He tossed a plastic bag containing the keys over the ledge, and Armstrong retrieved it after it hit the ground.

The building had grown even worse since the last time he'd paid a visit. If it was run-down before, now it was positively unfit for human habitation and should have been condemned. The lobby was filled with debris, half the tiles had fallen from the walls and a dripping water pipe was poking out from a huge hole in the ceiling. Vermin scurried around back in the shadows. The building's staircase was practically a deathtrap, for if a step had not already collapsed, those that remained seemed likely to do so in the near future.

As Armstrong climbed he clutched at the shaky banister with both hands, his knuckles white with the fierce grip, advancing up sideways like a crab.

San Isidro was standing in the doorway to his apartment, smoking a fat joint with one hand and swigging from a half-bottle of Cuervo with the other. The smell of marijuana greeted Armstrong as he finally made it to the third floor. Being continually stoned, he thought, was about the only way to make the surroundings bearable.

"*Hola, compañero,* good to see you, come on inside."

His half-glazed eyes, wide fixed smile and unsteady gait indicated that he'd been going at the weed and tequila already for most of the day.

"This is a celebration, no? You've come to bring me *mucho dinero,* I hope. I'm honored that you come here to see me. *Siéntate, por favor.*"

San Isidro cleared a space on the sofa that was littered with porno magazines and empty packets of Delicados cigarettes. Armstrong then sat down while San Isidro picked up an empty glass from the floor, poured some tequila in it and put it in his hand.

"*Salud,*" he said "to our friend and savior Felipe López, *el mejor escritor de cuentos macabros del mundo, ahora y siempre.*"

"I want you to tell me, Juan, as a friend and in confidence, what happened to López and how he came to think and act exactly like H.P. Lovecraft. And I want to know about the people that are after him. Were they people he knew before his—um—breakdown?" Armstrong said, looking at the glass and trying to find a clean part of the rim from which to drink. At this stage he was reluctant to reveal that the López manuscripts had been stolen. San Isidro was volatile, and Armstrong wasn't sure at this stage how he might react to the news.

San Isidro appeared to start momentarily at the mention of "H.P. Love-craft", but whether it was the effect of the name or the cumulative effect of the booze and weed, it was difficult to tell.

"So he told you, eh? Well, not all of it. *No recuerda nada de antes,* when he was just Felipe López. *No importa qué pasó antes,* sure, there was some heavy shit back then. *Si quieres los cuentos, primero quiero mucho dinero.* Then maybe I'll tell you about it, eh?"

"I'll pay you Juan, and pay you well. But I need to understand the truth." Armstrong replied.

What San Isidro told Armstrong over the next half-hour consisted of a meandering monologue, mostly in Spanish, of a brilliant young *gringo* who had come to Mexico in the 1940s to study Mesoamerican anthropology. This man, Robert Hayward Barlow, had been Lovecraft's literary executor. Armstrong had heard the name before, but what little he knew did not prepare him for San Isidro's increasingly bizarre account of events.

He began plausibly enough. Barlow, he said, had taken possession of Lovecraft's papers after the writer's death in 1937. He had gone through them thereafter and donated the bulk to the John Hay Library in Providence, in order to establish a permanent archival resource. However, he was ostracized by the Lovecraft circle, a campaign driven by Donald Wandrei and August Derleth, on the basis that he had supposedly stolen the materials in the first place from under the nose of the Providence author's surviving aunt.

However, what was not known then, San Isidro claimed, was that Barlow had kept some items back, the most important of which was the *Dream Diary of the Arkham Cycle,* a notebook in long-hand of approximately thirty or so pages and akin to Lovecraft's commonplace book.

It contained, so San Isidro alleged, dozens of entries from 1923 to 1936 that appeared to contradict the assertion that Lovecraft's mythos was solely a fictional construct. These entries were not suggestive by and of themselves *at the time they were supposedly written,* for the content was confined to the description of dreams in which elements from his myth-cycle had manifested themselves. These could be accepted as having no basis in reality had it not been for their supposedly *prophetic* nature. One such entry San Isidro quoted from memory. By this stage his voice was thick and the marijuana he'd been smoking made him giggle in a disquieting, paranoid fashion.

"A dream of the bony fingers of Azathoth reaching down to touch two cities in Imperial Japan, and laying them waste. Mushroom clouds portending the arrival of the Fungi from Yuggoth."

To Armstrong, this drivel seemed only a poor attempt to turn Lovecraft into some latter-day Nostradamus, but San Isidro clearly thought otherwise. Armstrong wondered what López had to do with all of this, and whether he would repudiate the so-called "prophecies" by sharing Lovecraft's trust in indefatigable rationalism. That would be ironic.

"How does all this tie in with López?" Armstrong asked.

"In 1948," San Isidro slurred, "there were *unos brujos, se llamaban La Sociedad del Sol Oscuro,* cheap *gringo* paperbacks of Lovecraft were their inspiration. They were interested in revival of worship for the old Aztec gods before they incorporated Cthulhu mythology. The gods of the two are much alike, no? *Sangre, muerte y la onda cósmica.* They tormented Barlow, suspected that's why he came to Mexico, because of the connection. Barlow was a *puto,* he loved to give it to boys, and soon they found out about the dream-diary. That was the end. Blackmail. He killed himself in 1951, took a whole bottle of seconal."

"But what about López?"

"They had to wait *cincuenta años para que se alinearan las estrellas.* Blood sacrifices, so much blood, the police paid-off over decades. But it was prophesized in his own dream-diary: *El espléndido regreso.* Even the exact date was written in there. López was the chosen vessel."

"How do you know all this, Juan?"

"I chose him from amongst us, but I betrayed them, the secret was passed down to me, and now I need to get out of this *pinche* country *rápido,* before *mis hermanos* come for me. López, he wants to go back to Providence, one last time," San Isidro giggled again at this point, "though I reckon it's changed a lot, since he last saw it, eh? But, me, I don't care."

He's as insane as López, Armstrong thought. This is just an elaborate scheme cooked up by the two of them to get money out of someone they think of as simply another stupid, rich foreigner. After all, what evidence was there that any of this nonsense had a grain of truth in it? Like most occultists, they'd cobbled together a mass of pseudo-facts and assertions and dressed it up as secret knowledge known only to the "initiated". Christ, he wouldn't have been surprised if, at this point, San Isidro produced a *Dream Diary of the Arkham Cycle,* some artificially-aged notebook written in the 1960s by a drugged-up kook who'd forged Lovecraft's handwriting and stuffed it full of allusions to events after his death in 1937. They'd managed to pull off a pretty fair imitation of his stories between themselves and whoever else was involved in the scam. The results were certainly no worse than August Derleth's galling attempts at "posthumous collaboration" with Lovecraft.

At last, as if San Isidro had reached a stage where he had drunk and smoked himself back to relative sobriety, he lurched up from the easy chair in which he'd been sitting. He ran his fingers through his beard, stared hard at Armstrong and said, "We need to talk business, how much are you going to give me?"

"I'll give you enough to get out of Mexico, for the sake of our friendship," Armstrong replied, "but I can't pay for the stories, Juan. Anyway, someone has stolen them."

Probably you or López, he thought cynically.

The only reaction from San Isidro was that he raised his eyebrows a fraction. Without saying a word he went into the kitchen next door and Armstrong could hear him rattling around in some drawers.

"If you're going to try to fleece me," Armstrong said, raising his voice so that he could be heard in the adjacent room, "then you and López will have to do better than all this Barlow and the 'Sodality of the Black Sun' crap."

When San Isidro came back into the room, his teeth were bared like those of a hungry wolf. In his right hand he was clutching a small caliber pistol, which he raised and aimed directly at Armstrong's head.

"Cabrón, hijo de puta, di tus últimas oraciones, porque te voy a matar."

Sweat broke out on Armstrong's forehead. His thoughts raced. Was the gun loaded or was this only bravado? Another means of extorting money from him? Could he take the chance?

Just as Armstrong was about to cry out, everything went black. Despite the fact that it was the middle of the afternoon, with brilliant sunshine outside, the room was immediately swallowed up by total darkness. Armstrong could not believe what was happening. He thought, at first, that he had gone blind. Only when he stumbled around in the inky void and came right up against the window did he see the sunlight still outside, but not penetrating at all beyond the glass and into the room.

Outside, the world went on as normal. Armstrong turned back away from the window and was aware of a presence moving within the dark. Whatever it was emitted a high-pitched and unearthly whistle that seemed to bore directly into his brain. God, he thought, his train of reasoning in a fit of hysterical chaos, something from Lovecraft's imagination had clawed its way into reality, fully seventy years after the man's death.

Something that might drive a man absolutely insane, if it was seen in the light.

Armstrong thought of the hundreds of hackneyed Cthulhu Mythos stories that he'd been forced to read down the years and over which he'd chortled. He recalled the endless ranks of clichéd yet supposedly infinitely horrible monstrosities, all with unpronounceable names. But he couldn't laugh now, because the joke wasn't so funny anymore. So he screamed instead—

"Juan! Juan!"

Armstrong bumped into the sofa in a panic, before he finally located the exit. From behind him came the sound of six shots, fired one after the other, deafeningly loud, and then nothing but dead, gaunt silence. He staggered into the hallway and reached the light outside, turned back once to look at the impenetrable darkness behind him, before then hurtling down the stairs. He now gave no thought, as he had done when coming up, as to how precarious they were. He did, however, even in the grip of terror, recall that the building was deserted and that no one could swear to his having been there.

After what had happened to him, Armstrong expected to feel a sense of catastrophic psychological disorientation. Whatever had attacked San Isidro, he thought, carrying darkness along with it so as to hide its deeds, was proof of something, even if it did not prove that everything San Isidro had claimed was in fact true.

At the very least it meant that The Sodality of the Black Sun had somehow called a psychic force into existence through their half-century of meddling with rituals and sacrifices. Armstrong had no choice but to discount the alternative rational explanation.

At the time when day had become night in San Isidro's apartment he had been afraid, but nothing more, otherwise he was clear-headed and not prone to any type of hysterical interlude or hallucinatory fugue. Rather than feeling that his worldview had been turned upside-down however, he instead felt a sense of profound loneliness. What had happened had really happened, but he knew that if he tried to tell anyone about it, they would scoff or worse, pity him, as he himself would have done, were he in their position.

Enrique and María returned to their apartment on schedule and Armstrong told them of his intention to remain in Mexico City a while longer. They noticed the curious melancholy in him, but did not question him about it in any detail. Nor would he have told them, even if prompted.

Armstrong moved out the next day, transferring his meager belongings to a room in a seedy hotel overlooking La Calle de Bucareli. From there he was able to gaze out of a fifth-floor window in his *cuartito* and keep watch on the Café la Habana opposite. His remaining connection to the affair was with Felipe López, the man who had the mind of Lovecraft, and he could not leave without seeing him one last time.

He had no idea whether San Isidro were alive or dead. What was certain was that it was inconceivable that he attempted to make contact with him. Were San Isidro dead, it would arouse suspicion that Armstrong had been connected with his demise, and were he alive, then Armstrong had little doubt that he'd want to exact revenge.

Days passed, and Armstrong's vigil yielded no results. There was no sign of López and he had no way of contacting him directly, no phone number, and no address. He was fearful that the Mexican police might call upon him at any instant, and scanned the newspapers daily in order to see if there were any reports mentioning San Isidro. He found nothing at all relating to him and recalled what he'd been told about the authorities having been paid-off with blood money over decades.

When Armstrong left his room it was only to visit the local Oxxo convenience store in order to stock up on *tortas de jamón y queso, Faros, y tequila barato*. The last of these items was most important to him. He spent most of the time pouring the tequila into a tumbler and knocking it back, while sitting at his pigeon-shit stained window, hoping to see López finally enter the Café la Habana in search of him. All he saw was the endless mass of frenzied traffic, drivers going from nowhere to anywhere and back in a hurry, oblivious to the revelation that separated him from such commonplace concerns, and which had taken him out of the predictable track of everyday existence.

And then, twelve days after he'd rented the room in the hotel, he finally saw a slightly stooped figure in a grey suit making his way towards the Café la Habana. It was López; there could be no doubt about it.

• • •

López was seated in a table in the corner of the Café, reading a paperback book and sipping at a cup of coffee. As Armstrong approached he saw that the book was a grubby second-hand copy of *Los Mitos de Cthulhu por H.P. Lovecraft y Otros.* The edition had a strange green photographic cover, depicting, it appeared, a close-up of a fossil. López immediately put down the volume once he caught sight of Armstrong.

"San Isidro seems to have disappeared off the face of the earth," he said, "I've been endeavoring to contact him for the last two weeks, but all to no avail. I admit to feeling not a little concern in the matter. Have you crossed paths with him of late?"

Armstrong could not take his eyes off the man. Could The Sodality of the Black Sun have succeeded? Was the creature that conversed with him now actually the mind of Lovecraft housed in the body of some Mexican occultist called López? God, what a disappointment it must have been for them, he thought. What irony! To go to all that trouble to reincarnate the consciousness of the great H.P. Lovecraft, only to find that after his return he denied his own posthumous existence! But why keep such a survival alive, why allow the existence of the last word on the subject if it contradicted their aims? It made no sense.

"I'm afraid," said Armstrong, "that San Isidro has vanished."

"I don't see . . ." said López.

"Not all of Lovecraft came back did it? I don't think they salvaged the essence, only a fragment. A thing with his memories, but not the actual man himself. Some sort of failed experiment. You're the one who's been leaving me those warning notes, aren't you?" Armstrong said, interrupting.

"You presume too much, Mr. Armstrong," replied López, "and forget that I have not, at any stage, asserted that I believe myself to be anything other than the misguided individual called Felipe López."

"That's just part of the deception!" Armstrong said, getting to his feet and jabbing his finger at López, "that's what you *know* Lovecraft would have said himself."

"How on earth could I be of benefit to the designs of an occult organization such as The Sodality of the Black Sun if I deny the very existence of supernatural phenomena? You make no sense, sir."

López's lips had narrowed to a thin cruel line upon his face and he was pale with indignation. His voice had dropped to a threatening whisper.

Everyone in the Café la Habana had turned around to stare, stopped dreaming over their pipes, newspapers and games of chess, and paused, their attention drawn by the confrontation being played out in English before them.

"The Old Ones are only now being born, emerging from your fiction into our world," Armstrong said. "The black magicians of The Sodality of the Black Sun want to literally become them. Once they do, the Old Ones will finally exist, independent of their creator, with the power to turn back time, recreating history to their own design as they go along."

"You, sir," said López, "are clearly more deranged than am I."

"Tell me about the notebook, Lovecraft, tell me about your *Dream-Diary of the Arkham Cycle,*" Armstrong shouted.

"There is no record of such a thing," López replied, "there are no indications that such an item ever existed amongst Lovecraft's papers, no mention of anything like it in his letters or other writings, no evidence for . . ."

"Tell me whether history is already beginning to change, whether the first of the Old Ones has begun manipulating the events of the past?"

As Armstrong finished asking his question he saw a shocking change come over López's features. Two forces seemed to war within the Mexican's body and a flash of pain distorted his face. At that moment the whites of his eyes vanished, as if the darkness of night looked out through them. But then he blinked heavily, shook his head from side to side, and finally regained his composure. As he did so, his usual aspect returned. The change and its reversal had been so sudden that, despite how vivid it had been, Armstrong could have just imagined it. After all, his nerves were already shredded, and he jumped at shadows.

"I can tell you nothing. What you are suggesting is madness," López said, getting to his feet and picking up the copy of the book he'd left on the table. He left without looking back.

Armstrong did not return to London. He acquired a certain notoriety over the years as the irredeemably drunk English derelict who could be found hanging around in the Café la Habana, talking to anyone who would listen to his broken Spanish.

However, he was never to be found there after nightfall or during an overcast and dark afternoon. At chess, he insisted on playing white, and could not bear to handle the black pieces, asking his opponent to remove them from the board on his behalf.

THE CITY OF LOVE
JOEL LANE

Joel Lane is the author of two collections of supernatural horror stories,
The Earth Wire *(Egerton Press) and* The Lost District and Other Stories *(Night Shade Books), as well as two novels,* From Blue to Black *and*
The Blue Mask *(both Serpent's Tail). Also the author of two collections
of poems,* The Edge of the Screen *and* Trouble in the Heartland, *he is
currently working on a third novel,* Midnight Blue.

*"'The City of Love' was inspired by a weekend in Paris in 1991,"
remembers the author, "during which my partner (who was not a film-
maker) and I visited the Catacombs.*

*"I became preoccupied with the idea of a second Paris underneath the
visible one, and the human metaphors that image suggested."*

*For one aspiring film actress, it is a journey into the dark heart of an
ancient metropolis. . . .*

The aeroplane lurched like an ice dancer with food poisoning.
Through the eyeholes in her mask, Belinda saw the stiff grey
tissue of cloud tilt upwards and back again. She tried to turn her
head and couldn't.

The unfamiliar crust on her face was light, but hard; it smelt like chalk. She lifted both hands at once, and touched it. The mask was as thin as paper, and fitted her face perfectly. Its lower edge traced her jaw line. She couldn't lift it off; there was no space underneath.

For a moment, Belinda considered leaving it in place. Then she thought *Fuck this,* and punched herself in the cheek. The shell fractured; some pieces fell in her lap. Others stuck to her face and had to be picked off. Within minutes, the whitish crust had disintegrated and blown away, becoming cigarette smoke.

Simon coughed and woke up as the plane was landing. It was still early morning; they'd had little sleep. Belinda smiled at him, though her face was still raw. He stared at her with the photographer's appraising gaze that she'd got used to (and by). "You don't look so good," he muttered.

"I feel okay," Belinda said.

"That's not what I meant." He turned away to catch the air hostess' oddly formalised welcome in three languages. "Like a Cindy doll, isn't she? Only less well developed." The plane taxied through several miles of runway. Pale buildings shivered as the morning light picked them out from a faint mist. The flight had taken less than an hour. Subdued by the cold outside the aircraft, Simon and Belinda walked across the gravel to the vast Gare du Nord concourse.

They were only here for the weekend. It was business, not pleasure; or rather, Belinda thought suddenly, it was business for him and work for her. She was here with him; that was all. Today they would act like a couple. Tomorrow, as themselves, they would make a film.

The Paris Metro was better decorated than the London underground, and less crowded. There were fewer homeless people—though you could still see them, crouching behind staircases or curled up on wooden benches, clutching plastic bags or silent children. Between two stations, a group of

Arab youths played a faithful rendition of 'Water of Love' to the indifferent passengers, then walked through the carriage with open purses in their hands, collecting nothing.

Their hotel was near the Tour de Montparnasse. Simon handed their passports to the receptionist, who greeted them in English. A tired-looking maid led them up the spiral staircase to the fifth floor. Their room was sparely furnished, immaculate and surprisingly warm. Belinda felt out of breath; she unfastened the windows and pulled them open. The room faced inwards: a hexagonal courtyard, paved with concrete and enclosed on all sides. She could see into a dozen or more rooms, all empty. It was like looking at the window of a TV shop.

Simon hung up his jacket and sprawled on the double bed. Belinda stretched out beside him, tender with fatigue. She liked him more when his eyes were closed. They kissed briefly; normally Simon pulled away to look at her, but this time he fell asleep in her arms. The bedclothes smelt of lemon and some very faint detergent. Belinda drifted into a fantasy about hidden passions, betrayal and an unshaven demon-lover with a face like a passport photograph; but when she fell asleep, she dreamed of nothing at all.

They woke up near midday. The first thing Simon wanted to do was go shopping for clothes. He outdid her in that as in everything, having more money and more vanity. "Paris clothes are months ahead of London," he said. "Every new image gets tried out here . . . it's like going home with the butterfly while everyone else is still feeding caterpillars." After three hours of hunting, rejecting, trying on and arguing with mirrors, he had two complete outfits, mostly by Gaultier. Belinda had an embroidered shirt, some impressive underwear and a pair of ankle-length calf leather boots; and a nervous headache induced by trying to think about money in English while making purchases in French.

Late in the afternoon, they went to visit the Catacombs, not far from the hotel. They walked through the Cimitière de Montparnasse, where the tombs were like small chapels—through their barred windows you could see photographs, icons, candles. Two stone angels were lifting a vault above the ground. One new headstone contained the perfect spiral of a fossil ammonite. Belinda thought of Egyptian burial places, ideal homes for the dead.

The entrance to the Catacombs was in a small grey building surrounded by traffic. They walked a long way down a pale spiral staircase, and along a series of tunnels underneath the Metro. It was warmer here than at the surface; the air was still, so there were no echoes. Belinda didn't think she had ever been in such a silent place. The walls were lined with ancient-looking grey slabs. Moisture formed beads on the stone.

They had been walking for about a mile when they reached a black stone archway, beyond which the burial vaults started. Human bones were stacked against the walls, all horizontal, the ends outwards. Layers of skulls formed lines across each stack. The bones were grey or yellow, and perfectly clean. Belinda noticed one skull with a round hole in its forehead. Around the next corner, the tunnel was also lined with bones; and the one after that, and so on for a long time. They were piled six feet deep, and at least three feet thick.

In one closed-off tunnel, a stack had collapsed and covered the floor. There had to be millions of human skeletons here—all removed from the cemeteries, to make space for new burials. Belinda walked along in a nervous silence, unable to believe that she wasn't just seeing the same few skulls over and over again.

Simon paused, examining one of the relics. Carefully, he pulled a skull free and held it up. Belinda's throat tightened. She wanted to tell him to stop being a prick and put it down; but she couldn't breathe. Her face was coated with a film of sweat. Looking bored, Simon tossed the skull back onto the wall of bones. She heard a dull crack. They walked on, soon reaching the foot of the spiral staircase that brought them back to street level.

Belinda tried to thaw out over dinner, but couldn't. The problem wasn't Simon; she didn't care enough to stay angry with him. They ate in a large, crowded restaurant where they shared a table with two men—one middle-aged and taciturn, the other young and camp. Perhaps they were a couple; if so, they weren't getting on very well. The younger man tore up bread and dissected chicken with a kind of subtle violence. Waiters shot from table to table with armloads of plates and menus. Belinda drank several glasses of water, though she wasn't conscious of thirst.

On the Metro, a small girl stood alone in the middle of their carriage and recited a scarcely audible plea for money. No-one took any notice.

Later, they passed the fairground at one end of the Rue des Champs-Elysées. The big wheel was lit up like a delicate revolving crystal, lifting its passengers high above the treetops and the buildings. Simon put his arm around Belinda's waist, steadying them both. Lights were always brighter and more fluid when you were drunk.

They watched some teenagers on a spinning platform, falling together and scrambling for their seats; laughter drifted from their mouths like vapour. Belinda squeezed Simon's hand, which felt cold. "Come on. Let's have a ride."

Simon smiled to himself. "You go. I'll watch."

"Why have you always got to be in control?"

"I'd rather see you do it. That's why you're here." Belinda felt something hard in her chest, like a swallowed bone.

They walked on to the Metro station in silence. She tried to light a cigarette, but her hand was shivering with cold. Simon didn't offer to help. On the underground platform, he said: "I want to call the film *Foreign Bodies.*"

Their hotel room was uncomfortably warm after the chill of the street.

That and the delayed effect of drinking made Belinda feel displaced. She fell asleep quickly, hiding from Simon and herself.

The dark corridor seemed to go on forever. Through arched doorways, she could see white figures stretched out on the frames of beds. People were crying, but the sound didn't carry for any distance. One door had black paper stuck over the glass. Behind it, an audience was sitting around a small operating table where three doctors were removing a child's face. The only sound was the drip of water from the stone ceiling. Belinda closed the door and walked on, looking for the exit.

The waiting room was a huge vault like a railway station. People were huddled on seats and behind pillars, wrapped in sheets to keep out the cold. At the far end of the room was a full-length mirror. Belinda stared at herself: the thin naked body, the bleached hair that looked colourless in light as bad as this. There was something like chalk on her face. Before she could wipe it off, her reflection broke free of the glass and floated upwards. She saw it break the surface and pass easily into a white marble vault, with stained-glass windows and carvings of angels, where the rest of her family was waiting for it.

She looked back at the mirror, and saw only an empty frame leading into a tunnel filled with broken-up skeletons. As she stepped through the doorway, she felt herself come apart. The clean bones of others, without sex or identity, locked into place between her own.

It was still dark, and the strangeness of the hotel room made Belinda feel she was still asleep. She got out of bed, showered and dressed. Simon hadn't moved. The smell of alcohol and tobacco lingered in the overheated air. She drew back the curtains, opened the window and took several deep breaths. The courtyard below was unlit, but there were lights in a few of the windows. The early morning chill made her face stiffen.

It was an effort to breathe. Her ribs and stomach were bruised, and the scratches on her back were still raw. Her vagina ached like a throat dry from shouting. It was late evening, but she didn't remember having gone through the day. She knew, as if someone had told her, what had happened. They'd caught a train to someone's house outside Paris, and spent five hours making a forty-minute film. Why couldn't she remember being there, or what it had been like?

Simon was standing just behind her. He was fully dressed. "Help me," she said to him. "Please help me." He stepped closer, almost touching. "I can't remember today. We made the film. I can't remember it."

"That's because it's still going on," he said calmly. "It hasn't happened till it's over. We're the camera, the lovers."

Belinda couldn't turn round to face him. "So what happens now?" The cold felt like a screen against her.

"Only the wrap-up," he said. "And the flight home." His hands pressed hard into her back. She twisted in falling, trying to right herself. Simon looked down.

By midnight, he was on the plane back to London. The air hostess brought round a selection of newspapers with the coffee and food on plastic trays. Simon glanced at the front page, then looked out the window at the perfect sheet of cloud that held every word or image he'd ever wanted.

It was early morning before the woman in the courtyard was discovered. Both her knees had been shattered by the fall. The hotel staff found no trace of her luggage or passport, and no-one remembered having seen her.

Even when she regained consciousness, the hospital was unable to identify her. She didn't speak a word of French, nor of any other language. She sat in a wheelchair and watched everything without reacting—as though day and night meant nothing more to her than the opening and closing of a shutter.

THE CHARNEL HOUSE

D. LYNN SMITH

D. Lynn Smith has spent most of her career writing for and producing such television shows as Touched by an Angel, Dr. Quinn Medicine Woman, and Murder She Wrote.

In addition to her TV credits, she has published non-fiction articles in the Dark Shadows Almanac and Fangoria, while her short fiction can also be found in the anthologies Dark Delicacies and the forthcoming Hot Blood 13.

As she recalls: "While in Egypt and visiting Djoser's step pyramid at Saqqara, I was walking through an ancient hall behind two American tourists. The couple stopped between each set of lotus-topped pillars that lined the hall, raised their hands, palms facing outward and tried to 'feel' the energy. I wondered what would happen if one of the less-than-benign Egyptian deities stepped out and confronted them.

"I later visited St. Catherine's Monastery and its rather morbid charnel house. When I read the brief for this anthology, the two experiences came together and this story was born."

For one unwary tourist, the gods of Ancient Egypt are not quite as dead as she may have believed. . . .

"**A** left, another left, a right and then a left," Leah recited softly as she threaded her way through the narrow alleyways of Cairo's great Khan el-Khalili marketplace. She was sure she had correctly followed the concierge's directions to the elusive spice market. And yet here she was lost in a maze of shops and people and shadowy streets. She'd retraced her steps once already and was too hot and tired to do it again. So she gave up on the idea of buying fresh saffron at cheap prices and settled for browsing the shops she'd glimpsed along the way.

The buildings of the Khan el-Khalili pressed heavily at the narrow slice of sky above her. Generations of small rooms and balconies had accreted to the upper floors like a great wound that in its healing would eventually shut out that thin slice of blue. At street level, however, the alleyways were still wide enough for two loaded camels to pass one another as required by ancient law. The air within this maze was hot and stale, filled with the overpowering odors of unwashed bodies, sweet perfumes and exotic foods. A feeling of claustrophobia stole over Leah, one she stubbornly pushed aside, though it didn't completely recede.

The shops themselves were as claustrophobic and full of shadows as the streets. Nonetheless, Leah couldn't resist the lure of shiny brass plates embossed with lotus and papyrus flowers or the china vases that bore the images of Tutankhamun. She loved trying on the denim lapis or jasper necklaces with their small round beads that felt so cool against the heat of her skin.

More easily resisted were the shops crammed with hookahs, cheap belly dancing costumes, gaudy museum replicas and oil-based fragrances cut with water.

As Leah wound her way through the marketplace the shopkeepers she passed called out, offering her "delicious" hibiscus tea and "very good bargains". Her guidebook had assured her that she wasn't insulting or offending them when she didn't buy their goods for it was, after all, her money. However, she was sure the book's author hadn't been a woman on her own in Cairo. It was intimidating walking past the groups of dark handsome men calling for her to come inside and who, when she passed them by, clutched their chests and cried, "Why are you breaking my heart? Please come inside."

Leah swiped at the sweat collecting on her upper lip. She was beginning to feel a bit light-headed when she saw the man standing at the door to his shop. He was watching her with kind, keen eyes and smiled when she approached.

"My shop is cool inside," he said, his voice soft and gentle. "And my wife has made a cool drink that is sweet. It will help you fight this heat."

Leah liked the man's voice. He wasn't loud or boisterous like the other shopkeepers, and he was the only one to mention a wife. Plus, she really did need to cool off. So she smiled at him in way of accepting his invitation and stepped through the doorway.

Cool somewhat musty air caressed her face and she closed her eyes to savor the feeling. When she opened them again an Egyptian woman offered her a customary glass filled with a reddish liquid indicative of hibiscus tea. Usually she would refuse this act of hospitality, not wanting to be obligated to buy. But this tea also contained a couple of ice cubes, highly unusual in this part of the world. So she accepted the drink and took a cool sip. It had a light but cloying sweetness to it and after a second eager draught, she felt her head begin to clear.

"It is very good, just as your husband promised," Leah said to the woman. "Shokran." Leah knew that her pronunciation of the Arabic word was not the best. Still the woman smiled in surprise, pleased that this American woman had made the effort to thank her in her own language.

Leah took another sip and began to browse around the store. It was somewhat different than the others, not as overcrowded or filled with garish museum replicas. Instead there were old wooden display cases full of small stone and faience Ushabti figurines, amulets, pots, jars and miniature ceramic statuary. One whole case against the wall was dedicated to intricately carved scarabs.

Wandering towards the back, she found a section displaying hand-appliquéd quilts with the complicated lotus blossom and papyrus flower designs of Upper and Lower Egypt. Each quilt was made of fine Egyptian cotton, the stitch work almost invisible.

Papyrus scrolls with colorful images of the gods and goddesses of ancient Egypt decorated the walls. Leah recognized the goddess Nut in her role as "Coverer of the Sky" as well as some of the scenes from the *Egyptian Book of the Dead*. In the corner she saw Akhenaten worshiping his "One God" Aten.

In a small corner of the shop were the requisite museum replicas. Leah was about to turn back to the quilts when she saw a statue that was different from all the rest. It was made of some kind of white material with a black wash over the top. The goddess's feet were bare, her arms spread in a welcoming gesture. Her face bore distinctly African features and there was a scorpion perched on her head.

Reaching for her, Leah jumped as the shop owner came up on her unawares and said, "That is Selket, the scorpion goddess of the dead and of retribution. Her names means: 'She Who Lets Throats Breathe'."

"I think I've seen her before," said Leah, struggling to remember where.

"She is one of four goddesses that protect the canopic jars of King Tutankhamun."

Of course. She'd seen her at the Egyptian Museum.

"This statue is very rare," continued the man.

Leah looked up at him. He watched her with gentle black eyes that made her not want to offend him, and yet she couldn't let this pass.

"It looks like it's made of limestone."

"But the image is rare. Not like all the others you will find. It does more honor to the goddess."

She had to agree with that. No gold and blue paint. No MADE IN CHINA stamped on the bottom. She had never heard of Selket before and yet there was something very compelling about her.

So after some minor haggling, she thanked the shopkeeper and his wife for their hospitality and walked out of their shop, the statue wrapped in bubble-wrap and tucked away in her purse.

The heat was palpable, striking her the moment she stepped from the shop. It was time to find a taxi and go back to the hotel. She turned into the crowd and tried to take the straightest line through the marketplace, hoping to find her way out. But the Khan el-Khalili's dark, twisting passageways were too much for her directionally challenged mind and she lost her way.

She turned from the gloom of one passage into the light of another. Shopkeepers called out but she kept her head down, her eyes averted. Wings of panic thumped inside her chest as she become more and more disoriented.

She made another turn, this time onto a dark, cool street, and was stopped in her tracks by the intense odors that made her sneeze several times.

When the fit passed and her eyes became accustomed to the twilight atmosphere, she realized she'd found the spice vendors and her panic began to abate in the face of delight and wonder. Somehow, she'd stumbled across her original destination.

The small side street was crowded with vendors whose storefronts were lined with orderly barrels and burlap sacks, all filled to their brims with spices. She felt like she was standing at the edge of an experiment in color: a kaleidoscope of yellows, reds, blues, blacks and browns. The wash of color and scents extended into the air as the spices, sharp odors collided into a nose-tickling blend and steep shafts of sunlight cut though the canvas-covered street to brighten the exotic dust that filled the air.

Leah walked down the street in a state of sensual overload until one man came and took her arm, guiding her to his booth.

"My name is Abdul and I speak very good English," he said with a huge grin on his face. "This is my family's business. We have good spices. You want curry. We have all different kinds. You want saffron, we have the best."

Abdul showed her jars of white, green, red and black peppercorns and barrels of different kinds of curries and teas. Leah chose some saffron and dried hibiscus blooms for tea, but Abdul wasn't satisfied.

"You must have this. It is a special blend of forty-two spices with a touch of cinnamon, very good for the kebabs. You can't leave without some of this." He began spooning some out of a large jar.

"No," said Leah. "Just the saffron and tea."

The look he shot her was hard and threatening and Leah felt her panic return. She took a step backward, and he turned back into the affable shop-keeper he'd been before.

"Then some green pepper. You don't have green pepper in America. You must take some for your friends and family."

Leah didn't know what to say. She didn't want any pepper. She looked around and saw the other shopkeepers watching. There were a few tourists, but no one who would come to her rescue.

"I don't really need pepper . . ."

But Abdul kept measuring out the hard green peppercorns as if he didn't hear her.

A woman appeared beside Leah. She was tall and swathed in white linen that showed off her smooth, brown skin. A pocket of calm enveloped Leah and the woman's cool, clean odor seemed to hold all the spice smells at bay.

"Abdul," said the woman, her voice softly accented. Abdul looked up from measuring out the green pepper, his face going pale at the sight of her.

"Just the saffron and the hibiscus," said the woman.

Abdul dropped the pepper as if he had found a scorpion hiding in the jar. Leah noticed that his hands shook slightly as he took the money they'd agreed upon and wrapped up the spices. He threw in a box of lavender incense.

"Free," he said. "A gift."

Leah turned to the woman, feeling shy and totally inadequate. "Thank you," she said.

The woman smiled. "Come."

Leah followed as the woman led her through the maze of streets to Fishawi's café, where she ordered them some lamb kebabs with pita bread and diet cokes.

"It is difficult for a foreign woman to visit the Kahn el-Khalili alone," said the woman once the waiter had gone. "Too many people like to take advantage."

"I realize that now."

"Are you otherwise enjoying your trip to my country?" she asked, her dark eyes staring into Leah's.

"Yes. Very much."

"But . . ."

Leah looked up surprised. She was sure she had answered enthusiastically with no trace of a "but", even though there was one.

The woman smiled at her and Leah felt herself relax. "I was expecting more," Leah heard herself saying.

"Spiritual revelation."

Suddenly all Leah's frustration and disappointment with this trip overwhelmed her. "Yes. I thought when I visited the pyramids I'd, you know, feel something. Some inkling of power. But they just felt dead to me. Even when I went inside the Great Pyramid, all I felt was claustrophobic and I couldn't wait to get outside again."

The woman sipped her diet coke, waiting.

"I sort of felt something at Saqqara, in that long pillared hall at the entrance to the temple. And maybe there was something inside Djoser's step pyramid, but they wouldn't let us go down the really interesting passages. Maybe if they had . . . I don't know." She felt like a child disappointed with the pony she'd gotten for Christmas. "You must think I'm a nutty New Ager."

"Not at all," said the woman. "I think the people who come to the pyramids and hold their ceremonies and say they've had some great spiritual experience are crazy New Agers."

Leah felt relief wash over her. "You don't believe in the power of the pyramids?"

"A pyramid is a human construct; built by men simply to celebrate a Pharaoh's greatness. They do not honor the Gods or the power of this land."

"I thought Egyptians held them in great reverence."

The woman shrugged, dismissing this. "If you really want to feel the power of Egypt you should visit St. Catherine's Monastery."

Leah's heart dropped. A Christian. No wonder she didn't believe in the power of the pyramids. "I really want to experience something . . . Egyptian," said Leah, choosing her words carefully so as not to offend her rescuer.

"You know, don't you, that St. Catherine's is in the shadow of Mount Sinai."

"Where Moses received the Ten Commandments."

The woman nodded. "Would it surprise you to know that many scholars theorize that Spell Number One-Twenty-five in the *Egyptian Book of the Dead* was the basis for the Ten Commandments?"

"So you're saying that God's commandments are really the commandments of the Egyptian gods?"

The woman raised an eyebrow but said nothing.

Leah had never heard this before and to say it piqued her interest was an understatement. "I've never read the *Book of the Dead*. I suppose I should."

"Don't bother," the woman replied. "It's all rather boring . . . unless it's happening to you."

Leah wondered what she meant by that, but didn't have the chance to ask as the woman continued.

"This has led other scholars to posit that Moses and Akhenaten were one and the same."

Leah knew that Akhenaten, along with his wife Nefertiti, had tried to introduce the worship of just one god to Egypt. And that Moses had been raised as a pharaoh's son. It made sense that after he freed his people from the Pharaoh Ramses, and after his experience with the burning bush and the Ten Commandments, that he would return to claim his birthright and bring the concept of the "One God" to Egypt. Especially since he hadn't been allowed to enter the Promised Land.

Her thoughts were interrupted when a commotion started up at another table. "This isn't even edible," groused a man, obviously American. "Why can't you people serve normal food like a hamburger or spare ribs?"

Listening to the man as he continued to curse the wait staff, Leah wanted to crawl under the table. It was tourists like him that gave American's a bad name.

The woman's eyes flickered to him, than back to Leah. She handed Leah a card. "This is the name of a very reliable driver. Visit St. Catherine's. You'll find the Charnel House there; it's a personal favorite of mine."

She signaled the waiter. He bowed and waved away the money the woman offered. She rose.

"Visit St. Catherine's," she said. "I believe you'll find what you're looking for there."

It wasn't until she had walked away that Leah realized she did know the woman's name.

The last leg of Leah's visit to Egypt was Sharm el-Sheikh, the Sinai's premier resort area at the southern tip of the Sinai. There the desert sands spilled over the coast and into the Red Sea. It was as different from Cairo as Los

Angeles was from Maui. Here she could snorkel, sun on the pristine white sand beaches, and shop in modern-looking malls, though these malls carried much the same items as the Khan el-Khalili. At higher cost, of course.

But her thoughts often turned to her encounter with that woman in Cairo and their peculiar conversation. So she bought a small guidebook that informed her that St. Catherine's monastery was just a two-hour drive from Sharm el-Sheikh.

In its thumbnail history of the place, the guide stated that the monastery had stood in the heart of the Sinai Desert for at least 1400 years. Characters as diverse as Mohammed, Arab caliphs, Turkish sultans and even Napoleon had all put the Monastery under their protection at one time or another, thereby protecting it from the pillage and destruction that had swept through the region so many times. In all of its long history it had never felt the heavy hands of a conqueror, had never been looted.

How odd, Leah thought. When so many Christian monasteries had been destroyed by these very same people, why had St. Catherine's been spared, and even protected?

Then Leah learned that the monastery was home to the burning bush, the bush out of which God spoke to Moses. The bush was no longer on fire, of course, but it was still alive and putting forth new shoots. It couldn't really be the actual burning bush from the Bible, reasoned Leah, but the guidebook asserted the plant had been dated back to the time of Moses.

So she dug out the card the woman had given her and hunted down the hotel's concierge. She wasn't sure the number would be good from Sharm, but the next morning a driver was waiting for her in the lobby.

He was a small man with a somber face. He spoke just enough English to identify himself and, with the translating help of the concierge, Leah learned that an unknown benefactor had already paid for both car and driver. She suspected it was the woman from the Kahn el-Khalili and sent a silent "shokran" her way.

Once she was settled in the backseat of the car, she looked up to find the driver watching her in the rearview mirror. She smiled. "Yalla beena," she said, using a little more of the Arabic she'd learned to say, "let's go." The man cracked an appreciative smile. "Yalla beena," he repeated. And off they went.

The first half hour of the drive Leah found rather boring. After an aborted attempt to ask the driver questions he didn't understand, she let the rocky desert scenery and the motion of the car send her into a fitful sleep.

She woke with a start as the car bumped and rumbled across a section of rough road where it crossed a wadi. Looking at her watch, she saw they were an hour into the drive and things had changed. Mountains jutted up in a moonscape of granite crags scarred by jagged veins of blue and green rock. Leah could feel the power flowing down the slopes, the power she'd expected to feel at the pyramids.

She stared out the window, fascination replacing boredom. She saw natural rock formations that looked just like pyramids, complete with rock spires standing sentinel in front of them.

These are the true pyramids, she thought, smiling at this sudden insight.

Leah glanced up and saw the driver watching her in the mirror. It was as if he could read her thoughts. Then his eyes went back to the road.

"Bedouin," he said as he pointed off to their left.

Leah looked and saw three men swathed in black riding through the magnificent scenery on the backs of their camels. Off in the distance was a loose collection of huts and tents.

As their car drew closer to the settlement, Leah watched two young boys attempt to impose their will on a small heard of goats and sheep that grazed by the camp. She had to laugh; the animals seemed less than impressed by their antics.

At the side of the road, busses and cars full of sightseers had stopped at the tables set up by the Bedouin in their effort to separate tourists from some of their euros. The driver took her past the site and on deeper into the desert, past mountains that looked like a herd of dragons had lain down to sleep the sleep of the ages. They drove on; past the wadis, the channels where water flowed on the rare occasions when there was surface water, and on past the dunes of desert sand so white and pure the reflection of the sun off the crystalline surface stung Leah's eyes.

When they arrived at St. Catherine's, she could feel the power of the land pulsing like a heartbeat. She was eager to get up the hill and into the monastery, but the driver pulled a small envelope from his jacket and handed it to her. Inside was a note written in English.

Save the Charnel House for late in the day as the Sun descends behind the mountains.

Leah looked up at the driver in surprise. Was the note from that strange woman? The handwriting looked feminine. But the driver either didn't understand her questions, or pretended not to understand. So Leah put the note into her purse and started up the lane toward the fortified walls that surrounded the monastery.

Of course the woman had been right. Leah had come to Egypt looking for a spiritual experience. Organized religion had failed her and paganism, with its rituals and spells, left her feeling rather silly. But here at St. Catherine's there was real power; she could sense it deep in her bones. Here, perhaps, she could find something that would make her believe there was more to life than the miscellany she'd been able to piece together over the years.

Her first stop was the church proper, with its chandeliers and wall sconces that depicted dragons looking very much like the mountains through which she had just driven. They were interesting enough, but the revelation she sought was not to be found among the busy mosaics, icons and pushy crowds of noisome tourists.

The "burning" bush was certainly like nothing she'd ever seen before, but she felt only dismay at the way herds of tourist plucked at the sweeping crown of woody fronds with their delicate leaves and tiny thorns. The bush looked as if camels had been grazing beneath it.

Standing at the well where Moses had met his wife was similarly disappointing. After all, it was only a well, albeit a really old well.

She attempted to enter St. Catherine's library to see the collection of ancient sacred texts, a collection second only to the Vatican's. But it was closed to tourists. Only those who had made special arrangements through religious or academic channels were allowed to enter.

When she exited the church compound, she was drained and hot and tired of being elbowed by discourteous tourists. So when a bevy of small boys swarmed her trying to sell their fist-sized geodes and polished alabaster eggs, all she could do was yell "La, la, la," which translates as "No, no, no".

The boys scattered laughing and immediately pounced on their next victim. With some bemusement, Leah saw it was the American man who had been so obnoxious at the café in Cairo. Odd that he had chosen this day to visit St. Catherine's as well, Leah thought.

"Leave me alone you thieving bastards," he yelled at the boys. One boy shot a look at Leah, then pointed a finger to his temple and made it go around. Leah got the message. Crazy American. She ended up buying a geode from the boy for five dollars American.

The sun was sinking below the mount and Leah had one place left to visit. The Charnel House. It was the repository of the bones of all the monks who had ever lived and died at St. Catherine's. But when Leah finally made it to the entrance there was a sign notifying her that it had closed for the day only thirty minutes earlier.

Perfect, thought Leah. Just perfect. She sat down on a low rock wall, the energy draining out of her as if some plug had been pulled. The monastery must have changed the visiting hours. Otherwise why would she have been directed to wait until sunset before she visited?

In the midst of her commiserating, a small lizard ran out from beneath a rock and raced past her. She tracked it through the gathering gloom until it disappeared through a door that had been left slightly ajar. A door that looked like it led into the Charnel House.

Leah glanced around her. For the moment, she was alone. And before she could talk herself out of it, she was up and slipping through the unlocked door.

Just a peek, thought Leah, then I'll go.

All the bustle of sound created by the tourists and their guides receded as Leah descended a set of stairs into the cool depths of the house of bones.

A chill ran over Leah's skin as cool air hit her perspiration-dampened body, raising a legion of goosebumps up and down her arms. As she had suspected, the short hall led her right into the Charnel House where she stepped into a room piled high with skulls. Here she stopped, staring at the heads of St. Catherine's dead monks while their blank, empty eye sockets gazed back. Slowly she turned around to take in the entire room. Skulls on one wall, bones of limbs on another; everything neatly sorted in piles of tibias and ulnas and flanges.

She'd read in the guidebook that digging graves in the stony ground around the monastery was too difficult and what did get buried in the loose sand didn't stay put. So deceased monks were first buried and then disinterred; their bones cleaned and deposited in the skull house, where she now stood. Earlier she'd overheard a guide telling his group that two of the monastery's monks had recently died and been buried in the small graveyard. They were due to be disinterred any day now. The thought sent a chill up Leah's spine.

All the skeletons had been disassembled except for one, which was dressed in the black vestments of a monk and sitting upright. Leah had read this skeleton was that of a hermit named Stephanos, a 6th Century monk who had been but one of the many hermits living a life of monasticism on the flanks of the holy mountain.

Leah went over to take a closer look, and noticed that behind the macabre statue was a section of stone wall that was slightly agape. She put out her hand and pushed, her heart racing as a secret door swung open.

Beyond the opening a stairway carved into the granite bedrock led down into a pool of darkness. A cool breeze wafted up the stairs, bringing with it the sharp smell of incense and the indistinct sound of voices somewhere down below.

A ceremony, thought Leah. Someone must be down there performing a ceremony.

Leah stepped through the doorway to the top of the stairs. The bottom of the stairs was lost in shadow.

The darkness seemed to exhale softly through the constricted throat that was the doorway. Leah inhaled, filling her lungs with the scent she'd come to associate with New Age shops, and started down the stairs.

Her heart pounded harder and harder as she sneaked down the dusty flight of steps. While part of her mind screamed in terror, another part wondered, in a detached way, why she was doing this. Why was she descending into such a frightening place? Yet another part was laughing in manic delight at the thought that she was going somewhere other tourists never got to see.

She stumbled when she reached the end of the stairway, her left foot having reached downward for a next nonexistent step. She caught herself against a segmented wall, the rock cool and rough and reminding her of the claustrophobic passage into the depths of the Great Pyramid.

She stood there, her breath coming in rapid gasps, straining her ears and eyes for anything that would help determine where she was.

Once again that tantalizing whiff of incense and, accompanying it, the distant sound of chanting. She turned in a tight circle, trying to determine the direction of the sound. As her eyes adjusted somewhat to the darkness, she spotted a dull glow of orange light about fifty feet in front of her. From what little illumination it afforded, she could see the floor of the chamber was covered with stacks of bones, but there was a passage through the rubble just off to her right, along the wall.

She let her fingers trail along the cool rock as she made her way through the passage—the light, the chanting, and the incense drawing her inexplicably forward.

A barely heard sound of scuttling made Leah jump and stop with her back pressed against the wall. This is stupid, she thought. Just turn around and go back up. Your driver is waiting for you. If you don't go now, he'll leave without you.

She closed her eyes and listened. There were no more strange noises. She took a few deep breaths and, when her heart calmed down a bit, opened her eyes. She pushed away the insistent voice commanding her back up the stairs and continued forward.

A few steps later Leah came to a doorway that opened into a small room. Two torches were on the wall illuminating a beautifully wrought painting of the goddess Nut, her body stretched up one wall, across the ceiling and down the opposite wall. When Leah entered the room the image arched over her, toes touching the floor on one side and fingertips touching the floor on the other. On the wall opposite the door was an image of Selket looking very much like the statue she had purchased; with arms held wide and a scorpion perched on her head. Three wooden steps led up to a small opening placed just where her womb would be.

Leah stumbled a bit as she walked across the room, the clouds of incense beginning to make her head swim.

She reached the opening and leaned through just enough to see what was happening on the other side. Another set of granite stairs hugged the wall to her left, leading to a chamber far below. There was no railing and the drop from the open side of the stairs was dizzying.

In the room below, people were dressed in what looked like ancient Egyptian costumes and were engaged in a ceremony of some sort.

Leah really wanted to get a closer look. The stairway was deep in shadow, so she decided she could descend partway and watch with little risk of being spotted. With her back pressed against the wall, she took the steps sideways, eyes straining to make out the ritual that was taking place far below.

Her calves began to ache, threatening to cramp as she crept down the staircase. Her foot had just reached a small landing near the midway point when she felt a sharp sting and looked down to see a scorpion scuttling off her left foot. She yelped as there was another sting, this time on her right foot.

Leah's mind struggled to grasp what was happening to her as the intense pain in her feet spread quickly up her body, paralyzing her. She had just enough time to remember that the stings of North African scorpions were often fatal. Then all went black.

Leah's first sensation was that of cold. Then an awareness that she laid upon a rough, hard surface. She tried to move, but was drawn up short.

As her consciousness struggled towards the light, the odor of incense brought back her memories in quick succession: Egypt, the woman, Charnel House, the scorpions.

Leah's eyes flew open, but it took her a moment to realize that she wasn't lying on the floor, but standing against the rough-hewn wall of the lower chamber, her arms and legs in shackles.

The rush of adrenaline that accompanied this realization cleared away the last of the shadows clouding her mind and she was wide-awake. This awareness also disabled whatever autonomic reflex that had kept her body upright, and her knees buckled, the shackles jerking at her arms as she sagged.

Pain shot through Leah's wrists, shoulders and ankles and tears sprang to her eyes. Beneath the sharp odor of incense she could smell the sickly sweet odor of decay. Panic crashed over her, her heart threatening to burst through her chest.

But it was nothing like the panic she felt when she looked up and saw whose captive she was.

What she saw was impossible. Her mind must not be working. It was a terrible nightmare, a scorpion induced hallucination.

For there, standing in front of her, was Anubis, the jackal-headed Egyptian god of the underworld; judge of the dead.

It must be a mask, she thought. It must be.

And yet she could see the individual hairs of the fur covering his black head, and when the jaws parted, the white, pointed canine teeth that lined them.

Leah frantically tore her gaze away from the figure and it came to rest on a woman dressed in a robe that hugged her womanly curves.

When she turned, Leah's shock deepened. It was the woman from the Khan el-Khalili, the woman who had told her to visit St. Catherine's, the woman who'd directed her to wait until sunset to visit the Charnel House.

Her robe shimmered with gold as she moved in the torchlight, and Leah saw that what she had at first taken as the golden coins typical of Bedouin dress, were actually dozens and dozens of scorpions clinging to the woman's gown.

Selket. Leah's mind struggled against the knowledge. The woman in the market had been Selket and she had lured Leah here.

Leah tried to speak, but her throat was closed with panic. Tears of fear and pain streamed down her face.

Through the blurry curtain she saw another figure, a man arranging bones on an altar. A strangled sob escaped her as she realized it was her driver and that he was meticulously assembling a skeleton. On another altar, a second skeleton was already complete and in place.

Meanwhile, the Anubis creature was placing four canopic jars at the end of each altar. When he was finished, he turned toward Leah. Her heart stopped as his gaze found her and her bladder let go. She pulled against her chains, the cold steel biting into her wrists and feet.

Then Anubis' gaze moved on and for the first time Leah realized she was not alone, not the only one in chains. The insufferable American was chained to the wall on her left. His expression was blank and a bit of drool ran from his mouth and was soaking a spot on his shirt. When Anubis approached him, he began to make a chirping sound so full of terror that Leah's knees collapsed again, leaving her hanging by her wrists.

She sensed that something was about to happen, something she knew she couldn't watch. Yet neither could she look away.

Anubis reached out and pushed his hand into the man's chest. The man continued to squeak and twitter even as Anubis pulled out his still-beating heart.

The man looked stunned, but surprisingly, not dead.

Anubis took the man's heart to a podium that bore what Leah recognized as the scales of justice. Selket approached the scales and on one side put a feather. On the other Anubis placed the heart. The side with the heart dropped abruptly.

As if on cue, scorpions began to emerge from every crack and crevice in the wall to which Leah and the man were chained. They swarmed over him. The man found his voice and began to scream as the massive horde of scorpions attacked his flesh.

Anubis left the podium and approached the writhing mass that had been her fellow traveler. The scorpions scuttled away. The man's head lolled toward Leah, his eyes fixing her with their dead stare.

Anubis removed three more organs from the man's body and placed them in the waiting canopic jars. The heart went into the final jar.

Selket reached out and touched the skeleton's throat. The scorpions clinging to her gown scuttled off her and onto the bones, stinging as they went. And the bones began to change. Tendons, ligaments, muscle, blood vessels and organs sprang into being. Skin crawled and spread across the body. Leah watched in horrified fascination until the body was whole and the scorpions returned to Selket's dress.

Then Selket touched the man's throat again and it began to breathe.

Light flowed from the ceiling and Leah saw that an image of Nut stretched across this great chamber as well. But it was more than an image, for Nut reached down with one hand and touched the man's chest.

And the man rose.

Leah tried to scream but her throat was closed to all but the same panicked chirping she'd heard from the dead American.

Her driver clad the newly risen man in the robe of a monk and comprehension forced itself into Leah's mind. The bones in the skull house were not those of the monks. They were the bones of those who had been sacrificed to bring the monks back from the dead.

Then Leah remembered: There was one more monk awaiting resurrection.

Anubis approached and stood in front of her. Accepting the inevitable, Leah didn't struggle. She knew that it was useless.

"Is this Egyptian enough for you?" It was the voice of the woman in the market. Leah looked up and over Anubis' shoulder, and met Selket's black, soulless eyes.

"You came looking for spiritual revelation. I shall give it to you."

Anubis' hand entered Leah's chest. She felt the removal of her heart, but there was no pain, no feeling at all.

Anubis took her heart to the podium.

"If your heart is filled with the lightness of a virtuous life, with goodness and mercy," said Selket, "We'll find that a balance has been achieved and your heart will not displace the scales of justice when weighed against this feather." With great ceremony, Selket placed the feather on one side of the scale.

"If it is dense with deeds of evil, contempt and deceit, it will show in the balance and your body will be forfeit."

Anubis raised Leah's heart above the scales.

Struggling, Leah managed to open her throat just enough to whisper.

"Selket," she said. "Protect me and I will praise your name. Protect me and foreign lands will come to know your power through my praise."

Anubis placed Leah's heart upon the scale.

She never saw what happened next for the scorpions flooded out of the walls and swarmed over her body. Their legs spidered over her skin, pinching and scratching. She felt a sting on her thigh, her hand, her stomach, and her face as they attacked her *en masse*. Her lips parted to release a scream and scorpions streamed into her mouth and down her throat, stinging as they went.

Darkness consumed her.

Leah awoke in a hospital room in Sharm el-Sheikh.

"You were on some old stairs in the basement of the Charnel House," the doctor was saying. "You were stung by a scorpion. He pointed to her bandaged foot, which was still swollen and red. "The place was closed off for a reason. You shouldn't have gone there.

"Only one sting?" asked Leah.

The doctor's eyes glittered. "It only takes one. You are very lucky to still be with us."

"I thought . . . I thought I'd been stung more."

"Hallucinations. It happens sometimes."

But Leah still remembered the feel of all those scorpions scuttling across her body and the frightening intensity of their strikes.

She was released from the hospital two days later and spent the rest of her holiday sitting on the beach at Nama Bay, thinking about nothing. And when a screaming child on the beach would bring that poor man's screams to mind, she'd push those thoughts, those memories into a small compartment deep in her mind to be locked away, hopefully forever.

The swelling on her foot finally receded, but it had left a wine-colored scar in the shape of a crudely sketched scorpion.

When she'd returned to the States, Leah set up an altar in her home. She placed the statue of Selket upon it and burned the lavender incense that Abdul had given her. She didn't know if her heart had balanced against the feather; didn't know if Selket saved her because of her promise; didn't know if it had all been a hallucination as the doctor had implied. But she lit the incense every day and thanked the goddess for her life.

Leah's friends were abuzz with the news that two tourists had gone missing in the Sinai desert while Leah was there.

"We were so frightened," Leah's friends had said. "Thank god it wasn't you."

To which Leah could only reply, "No, thank the Goddess."

If the reply seemed strange to them, they didn't say. They were too full of the news that one of the missing was an American man visiting St. Catherine's and who, authorities believed, ignored all warnings and advice and went out into the desert in the heat of the day alone and without supplies. The other tourist disappeared from St. Catherine's late the same day and there was speculation that perhaps terrorists or brigands of some sort were operating in the region. After a week or two, Egyptian officials had given up on their investigation and were no longer searching for their remains.

But if investigators were to question her, Leah could tell them where to find the remains of the two missing tourists. They were buried in shallow, rocky graves. And once their flesh had finally melted away, their bones would be disinterred and deposited in the Charnel House, the not so final resting place of the monks of St. Catherine's Monastery.

MILLWELL

GLEN HIRSHBERG

*Glen Hirshberg lives in the Los Angeles area with his wife and children.
His most recent collection,* American Morons, *was published by Earthling Press.* The Two Sams, *his first collection, won the International
Horror Guild Award, and was selected by* Publishers Weekly *and* Locus
as one of the Best Books of 2003. Hirshberg is also the author of the novels
The Snowman's Children *and the forthcoming* Sisters of Baikal.

*His fiction has appeared in numerous magazines and anthologies,
including multiple appearances in* The Mammoth Book of Best New
Horror *and* The Year's Best Fantasy and Horror, Dark Terrors 6, The
Dark, Inferno, Trampoline, *and* Cemetery Dance.

*With Dennis Etchison and Peter Atkins, he co-founded The Rolling
Darkness Revue, a traveling ghost story performance troupe that tours the
West Coast of the United States each October.*

*As Hirshberg explains, "The first sentences of 'Millwell' were scribbled
in a parking lot outside the World Midsummer Curling Bonspiel in
Nelson, British Columbia, during a sweltering heat-wave (we weren't,
sadly, entered in the tournament).*

*"However, the story has its origins in a sleet storm that ambushed my
wife and I on the Columbia Glacier just south of Jasper during a summer
trip in the late 1990s, and also in the ten o'clock twilight of an endless*

July day in 1990 when my friend Russ and I slid down the ice fields above Logan Pass in Glacier National Park on garbage bags, pursued by mountain goats. The goats, alas, did not make the final cut."

In the following story, something monstrous exists deep beneath a Canadian glacier. . . .

"We stumbled upon the skeleton of a chamois, which had probably met its death by falling into a chasm, and had been disgorged lower down. But a thousand chamois between these cavernous jaws would not make a mouthful."

—*John Tyndall,* A Day Among the
Seracs of the Glacier du Geant

So the first thing you're going to ask is what we were doing up there, right? It's a stupid question, because you already know, but you want to hear me say it. Alright, I'll say it. We were looking for him.

See? Not even worth an eye-roll, is it? So come on, Mr. Sgt. Preston Mountie, what else you want to know? Wait, let's see if I can guess.

Were we stoned, want to know that? No we weren't, at least I wasn't, and even if the Indian was, by the time we came down . . . by the time I came down . . .

Just . . . hold on. Okay? Go feed King or something. Just hold on.

Aren't you hot in that? *No,* Jesus, I don't want another blanket, I don't even want this one. You look hot in that uniform. And no, I don't mean you look *hot.* Although the way you're staring, you seem to think I do. Come on, all these years patrolling the foot of the ice fall, you're telling me I'm the *first* teen you've seen stupid enough to climb the glacier in a miniskirt? People do it all the time, half the summer tourists who go up there do it with their shirts off. Course, I'm not exactly a summer tourist, I mean not like that, and yes, I've heard the warnings, and . . .

Godgodgodgoddammnit. Okay. Okay. Wait. Okay.

From the top, yeah?

First of all, right, I know better. Even though I'm American. My family's been coming here every summer since I was seven. I've been on the glacier half a hundred times. I was here the year that kid—what was he, German?—walked five feet out onto the toe, in full view of the parking lot, and dropped down that crevasse. Remember? Remember just standing there and listening to him scream until he froze to death, because he was so far down you guys couldn't even find him, let alone figure how to get him out in time? Were you here then? God, I've never forgotten. At the end he didn't even sound like a kid anymore, remember? That growl? Like a bear in a trap.

Okay, fine, stare some more. When did everybody get so stare-y around here?

Like I said. We've been coming for years, and I've got lots of friends here, including the Indian. You know the Indian? Yeah, I thought you might. But tonight . . . let's just say I've never seen him like that.

You actually met the Indian? Well, whatever they've told you, they're wrong. He's really smart. And he's like the world's happiest kid. When the Eskimo was around, the two of them used to play warring tribes. Have canoe races on land, stupid stuff. The whole idea of having "enemies" just cracks him up. Everything does. That's such a dumb philosophy? I don't think so.

But he wasn't laughing tonight. None of them were. They were just sitting around the fire-circle pounding Molsons and staring at the trees. And no, by the way, we didn't have the fire lit, 'cause when you guys say there's fire danger we pay attention, even though you think we don't, and also, it's blazing outside, who needs one? More like the Okanagan than North Jasper.

Those kids . . . we used to have a lot more fun. Land canoes and ice-blocking. Hi-ball, back before they took it away, jumping in lakes from trees and rafts we made, playing tag in the abandoned railway tunnels.

God, I used to love how *not* uptight you all were. Remember? When cops were for criminals and insurance companies were for car crashes and everything else was for playing on?

Before the Eskimo disappeared. Now the rest of them pretty much do what you want us to. Sit around. Except for the drinking part. It's true, they drink. A *lot*. They do. They don't even mack on each other.

Don't check your fancy Mountie watch on me, alright? Amazingly enough, I don't actually *want* to think about it yet, I know that must just seem astonishing to you. I still don't even understand . . . Can you at least pass the Kleenex? Thanks.

Like I said. The Indian was like my last holdout. Last summer he took me owling all the time. Just prowling around the woods, going, *hoohoo-hoooo.* He was damn good at it. We saw owls like half the time. Barn owls. Snowy owls. The rest of the time we'd just go way the hell deep in the trees. So weird. I mean, it's not like the ocean or the desert or even the glacier, is it? Everyone talks about all the bird cries and the insects and all that. Must be some other woods. Yours are dead flat silent.

So here we are, first party of summer, and it's a hundred-five degrees—in *Canada*—and I want to float the river or owl the woods or whatever. And even the Indian's just sitting on a rock, glugging a Molson. Chucking stones in the water, not even skipping them. I'm about to leave, and the Indian catches my eye and mouths, "Wait."

And I know right away he's faking, making fun of everyone else's mood and they don't even realize it. There's this twitch around his mouth. It's really sexy and it always means . . . meant . . . anyway, right then, he just dropped his beer in the dirt and bellowed, *"Bear!"*

Well, they turned around. Most of them. No one got up or anything. I think somebody probably said, "Good one, Indian" on the way to sticking a bottle back in his mouth.

Then he and I got out of there.

First thing he said when we got back to the road was, "Let's go to town. Let's go jump up and down in front of the gas station where the hi-ball used to be until they bring the hi-ball back. Why'd they take it, anyway?"

"Uh, because half the people who played wound up breaking their ankles or falling off the edge of the trampoline?"

"Yeah, but the other half went *really high*." Then, all of a sudden, he says, "To the woods." And he grabs my arm and we go running through the trees. He was in full Indian mode now, talking to the forest and yanking me behind him and not slowing for anything. Saying stuff like, "Ho-ho, elk. Surprised you, didn't I? Indian and Barrett, coming through. Hello, timber-wolf, long time no see. Meet Barrett. She's a hottie, eh?"

Then he stopped in his tracks and grabbed me and mashed his mouth against mine.

He was crazed. Hopping everywhere, all that shine to him. Like a firefly in a jar. I didn't mind him kissing me, I just couldn't get him to stand still. I couldn't figure out his mood. Then he says, "My uncle's dying," and then, "I *really* miss the Eskimo." And he just sits down in the dirt.

Honestly, I was kind of stunned, at first. Mostly because he went so still. Just sitting there. I crouched down, and I guess my sucky insect repellent was wearing off, because there were bugs crawling up my legs. "What made you think of the Eskimo?" I asked.

He slapped a mosquito dead on my neck. "I always think of the Eskimo. Especially lately. He was the only one who . . . He was my best friend. And he *never* went up there unprepared. He was always careful, he knew the ice, it's been three years and I still don't understand it."

"You know understanding doesn't mean anything on the glacier. You taught me that, remem—"

He stood up and yanked me to my feet, and I mean *hard*. And there was this look on him. No twitching mouth, now. He looked like he was going to punch me.

"Let's go back," he said.

Well, I was pretty bewildered by now. And hot, and sweaty. And the whole night just . . . I let him pull me along. I tried one *hoo-hoo-hooo.* No owls came, and the Indian didn't even turn around. We were halfway back to the others when I grabbed his hand and made him stop.

"If that's how you feel," I said, "let's go find him."

The Indian stared at me. When he spoke, he was mostly talking to himself. "I haven't been up there since . . . *why haven't I?*"

Why hadn't any of us? We'd loved it up there. Even after the Eskimo, that first year. That's when the game started. The looking-for-him game. It was our excuse. Plus we really *were* looking for him. I think the Indian even thought we'd find him. For a while.

Twenty minutes later, we were standing at the edge of the tourist center parking lot, a soft stone's throw from the toe of the glacier.

She doesn't look so good, you know. Your glacier. I mean, she was never exactly the most *picturesque* twenty thousand year-old ice floe, was she, always reminded me of a giant, bumpy, white tongue. Only now it's not so white anymore, and it's a *lot* more bumpy. A giant, twenty thousand year-old *diseased* tongue.

It's also quieter than it used to be. At least before you're on it. God, I remember standing in that parking lot when I was a kid, and it freaked me so badly. That rushing sound, with absolutely nothing moving. Like breathing, but in no rhythm. Plus all the snorting and smacking.

"It looks sleepy," I told the Indian. "Or dead."

"It's not daytime," he murmured, and started hunting around at his feet. "Help me find a stick."

We were looking for something long and thick, you know, to poke for crevasses. I told you, he wasn't stupid, not even reckless. Unless you count being up there at all, which I guess you probably do.

Oh, *shit.* Oh, Indian.

Go ahead, stare, I don't care.

Nnnnnnhhh . . .

I'd never been up it at night before. Never even at dusk. And when the Indian found a stick he thought was long enough, and shot me his new, tough-guy face, and I realized we really were about to head up the moraine . . . hell yeah, I was scared.

But it was a hundred degrees. At eleven o'clock at night. And it was my idea, remember. I wasn't pulling back now.

Before we even hit the ice, the Indian turned his ankle all the way around on some loose rock, and he swore and hopped all over the place. When he managed to put both feet down again, there were tears on his cheeks.

"Maybe this is a bad plan," I said.

"It's the only plan," he told me, and the moon just *appeared* over the peaks, like someone stuck a knife through the sky and slit it. We got a single shiver of wind, too. One deliciously chilly breath. That was our warning.

"Wait here," the Indian told me, and stumbled back to the parking lot.

I thought he was headed to improvise a wrap for his ankle. I stared a while at that moon-slit cat-eye hole in the sky for a while. But when I turned around, the Indian had the lid off one of those park service trash cans, and the bag already out. Then he leaned over and tipped himself halfway upside down inside the can.

"Indian, what the . . ." I shouted, and he popped back up with a couple black plastic squares in his hands. He waved them at me, and I realized they were garbage bags. He dropped the one with garbage in it back in the can, replaced the lid, and limped back to me.

And by the way, no, they weren't for body bags. It's like I keep telling you, not that you seem to hear a single word. *We didn't know.* Understand?

"Might need these, if we can find a long enough icy patch," the Indian said.

"How'd you know they were stored there?"

"What, you didn't?" When I shrugged, he did, too. "Ancient First

Nations lore, I guess. Where mysterious white man park service hide-um spare bags."

He stuck his stick in the first scrap of snow at the toe of the ice floe, and it went right through, but not far. Two inches, maybe, then *clunk*. Rock. More like a melting mini-drift from some freak summer storm than the bottom of that glacier. Up we went.

The Indian kept poking around just to be extra safe, even though he could barely find enough snow to get the stick tip wet, let alone hide a crevasse. But the night got brighter. And bluer. It was like the moraine still had a shine on it, or a frost. Also, we could at least hear sounds, now. That rushing, way down underneath us. Which doesn't make sense, does it, I mean, it can't be colder *inside* the planet, right? Also there were these weird *shushes*. I couldn't even tell you where those were coming from.

The point is, we were watching the ground. Listening to the ground. I'd started to get this tickling in my feet and the backs of my knees. Like when you're standing at one of those summit viewpoints with no railing? We'd finally gotten to where there's still more ice than rock—maybe a hundred feet from the lot?—and I don't know why, I just *looked up*.

I'm not the screaming kind. But I'll admit it, I made a noise, and that's why the Indian jumped straight ahead and landed on what looked like a little white smear of dust and then *dropped* all the way to his thighs in ice. Just *bang*.

The funniest part—I mean, it wasn't funny, *believe* me, it so already wasn't funny—was that *he* didn't even react until like five seconds later. He just stood in the hole, gaping like a ground squirrel, and then he started barking, "Crap, crap, crap, crap, crap," scrabbling with his hands and scattering rock and ice clods all over the place, and I kind of panicked, it was like watching a movie of someone in quicksand. I dropped down and crawled forward and grabbed his wrist and helped draw him out.

As soon as he was lying beside me, he rolled over and stared in my face with that punch-something look again. And the ground . . . I've felt it before, but it's the weirdest sensation. That surface-layer of heat from being in the sun, but you know it's fake. Or, fragile. A warm that won't last, a cold you *know* is under there. Like fried ice cream. Or something that was living five seconds ago.

"Why did you *do* that?" the Indian shouted.

I waved my hands, trying to quiet him, then pointed up. There were actually tears in my eyes, I have no idea why. "I saw that," I said. "For this retarded second I thought it was a grizzly bear."

He looked where I'd indicated. His face didn't change, exactly. But his tone did.

"One of those rare *yellow* Grizzlies?" he said quietly.

"With really big tires. Yeah."

Neither one of us exactly smiled. But he let me pull him up.

When did they start parking those crazy buses up there, anyway? I guess the tour company's not as nervous about the glacier anymore either, huh? God, the first time I went down on the ice was in one of those. I was maybe eight, and it scared me so bad. Driving halfway up the mountain along the side of the glacier, first of all. The way the guide was talking, and the way they drove—maybe two miles an hour, I could have handwalked faster—made it seem like we were skirting something, alright. Then the turn, and those *huge* tires just grabbing the land. Like they didn't want to go. And the inching down. Inching. Inching. So, so slow. I think they said it was the steepest incline traversed by a four-wheel vehicle in the whole hemisphere, is that right? And they did it that way because it was the only place they were sure the glacier wouldn't open up and swallow them.

By now, the Indian had the garbage bags shaken out, and he was cutting head-sized holes in them with his pocketknife. This is probably offensive to say, but he did it so skillfully. It really was like watching someone skin a buffalo. He didn't tell me what he was doing, and I didn't ask, and a few minutes later he re-folded the bags, started poking again with the stick, and we went up again.

The rocks disappeared. And even though you could barely hear that whooshing sound, it was there. And this . . .*breeze* isn't really the word . . . *chill,* I guess, started rising around our ankles. It was like wading way out to the ocean. And back ten thousand years.

Anyway. We were moving slow, now, inching just like those buses. Putting our feet down extra-light, as if that would help if we happened to hit a spot with no ground. I kept glancing up at the peaks above and the black cliffs to the sides. All that dead, hot rock. Once I turned around, and it was kind of amazing. We hadn't gone very far. The parking lot was maybe a hundred yards away. And yet on a whole other planet. It was like looking at the earth from space.

I kept almost tripping, because I kept forgetting the glacier isn't flat. It humps up, drops down, smacks up against itself in little ridges.

Where are all your birds, by the way? Didn't there used to be eagles?

The Indian hadn't said a word in quite a while. Way, way below, I heard a truck pass. The loudest sound in half an hour. I was keeping my eyes on the ice, now, and even so, I couldn't have said when we hit the weeping.

I realize that's not a scientific term. It's what I've always called it, though. You know what I'm talking about? How all of a sudden there's runoff just *pouring* down the ice? Streaks here, gushes there, not a continuous flow, more like a hundred thousand transparent little ant colonies racing all over the place. Channeling through grooves they've made themselves, diving a thousand feet down holes they've drilled in the ice, what do they call those, millwells? The flow is silent, all the glacier sounds are coming from underneath, but the *movement.* And the color. Even in the dark, in almost no moon. That *blue,* like the blood in your veins you can't ever see because it turns red in the air. You ever think about being blue inside?

Finally, it occurred to me that even at the pace we were going, we'd climbed a long way. Not only that, but we'd consistently angled to the right. As if the Indian had a destination in mind after all. And he did, it turns out, just not the one you're thinking.

"Hey, Indian," I called, and was startled to see him fifteen feet ahead, climbing faster and faster. Stepping over rises. Still limping. "Wait up."

Instead of slowing, he pointed. At least now I knew what the bags were for.

"No way," I told him.

He turned around, and there was his Indian grin, in all its glory. "Way," he said.

He was pointing at this long, flat plain of ice that dropped at a steeper angle than the slope we'd climbed. It skimmed halfway back down to the parking lot and emptied into a jumble of piled moraine. The Indian flipped me a garbage bag. "Put this on."

"But . . . how do you know it's safe? How do you know there's not some gaping hole under there that's going to eat us when we slide by?"

"Look at the flags."

I looked. All the way down the pitch, the park service had planted little green flags.

"How do you know those aren't the *Keep Off: Ten Thousand Foot Plunge* flags?"

"'Cause those ones aren't green," the Indian said, and grinned even wider.

Before I could think what else to say, he was on his ass, sliding back and forth on the ice. Testing out the bag. Like he was getting ready to luge, you know? Bending at the waist, bending back. I knew he was right; I remembered the flags from my bus trip. They meant that the rangers had checked this stretch within the last forty-eight hours, so the buses could let tourists off to walk there.

One more time, I looked up, and this is almost funny, now, but I was kind of disappointed. We'd gotten, I don't know, maybe a fifth of the way to the top? I figured it might take us eight seconds to slide down the Indian's ice patch, then another five minutes of moraine-stomping to return to ordinary old paved land. It seemed like we'd gone farther. Talking to you now, I'd have to say yes, it was blacker than it had been a few moments before. A lot blacker. That moon-slit in the sky had sealed up, for one thing. And yes, I think I even caught the first real gust in my teeth. But I just thought it was the glacier. Or I didn't think about it at all. I glanced down and saw the Indian knifing away from me across the ice, howling like a timberwolf.

"You bastard," I called after him, dropped on my own ass, and kicked off.

The ice bumped underneath me, because of course it wasn't anywhere close to flat, and also, it was *wet*. Even through the bag I could feel it. I started to spin sideways, like I was on one of those flying saucers, so I decided I'd be better off the Indian's way and started to lie back, and then the Indian said, "Oops."

That was it. *Oops.*

Obviously, I tried to stop right away, flipped over on my stomach and grabbed the ice, and a whole clod of it came up in my fingers, like I'd raked its face. My own face bobbed up and down with the jouncing I was getting, and I must have hit my forehead at least once, which is how I got the shiner you still haven't bothered getting me anything for. But I was too panicked to notice. It took forever—as in, probably two seconds, but it felt like forever—to claw myself still.

When I did, I shook my head to clear it. I was blinking furiously, too, trying to see through the wetness all over my eyes, some of which was tears and some glacier melt.

All around me, I saw dirty, lumpy blue ice. No Indian.

By now, my fingers had figured out they were joint-deep in really serious cold, because they started aching so bad that I jerked them out of the ground. That set me skidding again, so I jammed my feet down and pushed hard and stood up.

"Ind . . ." I started to yell. But I'd seen him by then.

Somehow, he'd plummeted down an ice-waterfall that hadn't been there when we'd started. At least, it hadn't been visible. A big one, like twelve feet. He was lying on his stomach, completely still, with his head mashed down in the blue wet.

I thought he'd broken his neck. I think I was chanting, "Shit, oh shit," as I scrambled sideways toward him. His head came up, and his *skin,* God, the glacier had already turned it white, white and blue, and there was ice-water just *streaming* down it.

"Hold on—" I started to call.

Then the idiot jammed his face *back down.* And I realized he wasn't moving like anyone hurt. He looked like a goddamn snorkeler.

"Indian . . ." I murmured, and skidded the rest of the way.

Without lifting his head or turning toward me, the Indian slapped the ice beside him. Slapped it again. On the third slap, I saw it.

I know what you're going to say. I also know it's true, okay? The glacier *moves,* I get it. Constantly, all the time. Not just up or down, but side to side, in and out. That's how mammoths roll out of the earth ten thousand years after they've vanished. And why whole skeletons aren't ever found, even of people who died just a few days or months ago. The glacier rips them to pieces.

But I'm telling you . . . this was *planted there.* And it was whole. And on purpose. The most perfect little *inukshuk* I've ever seen in my life.

"You know what that means," the Indian snarled, still without lifting his head. His voice came out hissy and echoey, as though one of those little rivulets had drilled into his throat.

Ripping the garbage bag off my head, and also aware, finally, of the ache and swelling over my right eye, I dropped to my knees. That little thing. So . . . *pitiful,* somehow. Like an abandoned kitten. I almost scooped it up.

Except I didn't quite want to touch it, either.

It wasn't only the way the stones fit together. Those things always seem so perfectly balanced, you know? As if the top of the earth really were a broken whole, not a bunch of randomly spewed or churned up crusty bits. But this one . . . the rocks looked almost locked in place, and they formed this totally human shape. Little round legs, little round chest, littler, pinker round head. And two twiggy sticks drooping out of the sides, like miniature snowman arms.

I just stared at it. It didn't stare back or anything. It just sat in the ice in its little hole. Ever seen the picture of those English guys that lost the race to the South Pole? After they were dead? That photo with the flags just barely sticking out of the snow? That's what this thing looked like.

"It's so . . ." I murmured, dazed. And cold. Which I still thought was because I was kneeling on a glacier.

"It marks places of death," the Indian said. Without looking at me, he wriggled around and jammed one of his eyes even deeper into the ice.

"What the hell are you *doing?*" I asked.

"It also marks places you shouldn't try to cross."

"So it's either a warning or a tombstone."

"Which means that either way," the Indian said quietly, "he's here."

I was still gaping at him when the sleet hit us.

I know the glacier makes its own weather. I know the time of year and the temperature on the rocks right beside it in the regular world has nothing to do with what happens on the ice. But we didn't even hear this storm coming. It's like it was hiding up top, peeking over the ridge to see when we had our backs turned. Then it flung itself over.

Sleet. Hail. Whatever was in that wind banged so hard off my skull that I swear it set off echoes inside me. I ducked, cussing all over the place, and the Indian twitched where he was lying and started to curl into a ball, but he didn't get up. The wind crashed down next, this gurgling, thrashing wave that boiled over us like whitewater but didn't suck back. I tried getting a look at the top of the glacier, but I couldn't even see the rocks fifteen feet to our right anymore. Shivering and swearing, I started to stand, my foot accidentally kicking the *inukshuk,* which tipped over and vanished, and just as I started straightening out of my crouch, the Indian grabbed my wrist and yanked me face first into the ice beside him.

"Hey!" I screamed *"Get off!"*

Instead, he popped up on his knees and grabbed the back of my head with both hands.

"What are you . . ." I started, and he mashed me into the snow.

"Look," he snarled.

I was squirming, flinging one pathetic fist into his ribs, half-thinking he was going to murder me right there. But his tone stopped me. He wasn't angry, or murderous. He was panicking.

"Barrett, please. Holy shit."

And he pulled me, by my hair, to the lip of the millwell he'd been staring into. It couldn't have been more than three inches in diameter, but all that water hurtling across the surface of the glacier was plunging into it. So much water. As though the ice were trying to sweep us into itself through that little hole, and not just us. The mountains all around, the lakes at the bottom. The whole world it had carved and made.

The sleet was driving needles into my back, and the shivers sweeping up my spine were smashing my jaws together. I could feel my bare legs and my ears and my fingers and the tip of my nose screaming. But I hardly noticed. I was too busy jamming my eyes shut, because no matter what, I *did not want to look where the Indian was forcing me.*

"Indian," I whimpered, and he positioned my face directly over the millwell and shoved down, and the shock of it rattled my eyes open. Then I went slack. Staring.

"Tell me what you see," he hissed.

But I couldn't see anything. Just blue, gushing water. My lids started blinking frantically—can eyes drown?—and I tried lifting my head and

303

the Indian just shoved down harder, and then I saw it. Thought I did. Thought I saw . . .

"I see its eye," I babbled. I can't even tell you what I meant. I was staring down a thousand year-old channel into the ten-thousand year-old ice that made the world. And seeing an eye. All pupil, totally black. And blinking. The Eskimo's eye? The *glacier's?*

Rearing back, screaming, I broke free and scrambled away, not even thinking about the flags, the sleet, anything except that blinking *whatever* below. And the thing is . . . you'll say I dreamed it, and maybe I did . . . but I could feel movement underneath. Not just the streaming water. Something heavy. I shoved off my hands and knees and staggered to my feet and finally, finally whirled around.

No Indian. No anything, except sheeting, frozen rain, streaming ice, empty space.

"Fucker!" I shrieked, and the wind ate my voice, and nothing answered. I started looking around frantically, trying to figure out where the flags were, which way I was facing. And then I just lit out, straight down. I knew I could drop through at any second. I knew how dumb it was. I knew I should have stayed right there at least a little longer. Until the Indian found me, or I could see.

But I'm telling you, I could still feel it. And when I moved, it moved, too. Just gliding along under there. You ever seen a killer whale stalk a seal from under an ice cap? Also, the glacier was deafening. Even over the wind, I could hear it *shushing*, gnashing away at itself. Twice I went down flat on my face, which is how I got the rest of the bruises you still haven't bothered bringing me anything for. Every time I went down, I kept expecting the ice to open up, or something to explode through it. I have no memory whatsoever of the moment I hit moraine. All I do remember is this weird, beady feeling on my arms—like I was falling through a curtain—and just like that, it was a hundred degrees again. And absolutely silent.

It was a long time before I could make myself turn around. When I did, I saw the storm still raging up there, whirling around on itself. After a few minutes, it just kind of *collapsed,* like an imploding building. Clouds and sleet and wind and all. And it was just the rocks, the pathetic scrap of glacier. The parked bus. And no one and nothing else.

And that is exactly as much as I can tell you about what happened to the Indian, and how the Eskimo wandered into the glacier parking lot and right into the arms of your boys in the cruiser.

As for why he's just sitting in that chair in the lobby like that, how the hell should I know? Maybe that's what happens when you're frozen alive, or swallowed by a dying glacier, or whatever the hell happened to him. As far as I'm concerned, he fits right in, looks pretty much like everyone else around here these days. It's like when the glacier melted, and all that white, wonderful wildness went out of the world, all that *cold* had to go somewhere, so it just poured off the rocks into town . . .

Into everyone around here and . . .

Wait . . .

Oh.

Man, that really *sucks* . . .

THE BOHEMIAN OF THE ARBAT

SARAH PINBOROUGH

Sarah Pinborough lives in Milton Keynes, England, and is the author of four horror novels published by Leisure: The Hidden, The Reckoning, Breeding Ground, *and* The Taken. *She is currently working on two new novels and a screenplay.*

"Towards the end of the Cold War," she reveals, "from 1984 to 1988, my father was posted to Moscow with the British Foreign Office. Although at boarding school, I spent all the school holidays there, in what was at the time considered by Westerners to be the heart of the evil empire. Funny how a quarter of a century can change our perceptions.

"I think maybe I knew much more about Russia when I left than my parents ever learned from behind the high Embassy gates. I loved the city and my time there, and once we'd left and the world changed I realized how privileged I'd been to really see a country that others never would— Communist Russia behind the Iron Curtain. Where Santa Claus was Father Frost who came on New Year's Eve with presents. Where all the shops looked the same. And yes, where people sometimes just disappeared in the night. Where anyone different was forced outside, and where human passions and individuality bubbled away somewhere just below the surface.

"I've always intended to write something about that lost forever city,

and now I have. I hope it captures a little of the darkness and beauty of the place."

In the story that follows, a woman's secret assignation leads to a terrible transformation. . . .

Staring out of the hotel window, Anna could still feel his damp sweat clutching at her naked skin and her left palm throbbed slightly. Her nails had dug in a little too tightly as she'd gripped the mattress beneath them, the springs creaking rhythmically as she and Bob had gone through the motions of making love. It had been a relief when he'd rolled away, panting, satisfied and unaware of how untouched she was. It seemed to be that way too many times recently but once again she chose not to dwell on it. *If you marry for money, honey, then trust me, you'll earn every penny.* She pushed the memory of Jane's words away, just as she'd pushed Jane away when she'd strode out of their tatty London flat and into the glamour of Bob's world a year and a lifetime ago.

"Jesus, Anna. It just gets better and better between us, doesn't it?" From the bed she could hear her husband's breathing returning to normal and she fought the small trickle of revulsion that slid down her spine, peering instead through the old glass pane of the imposing Urkraine hotel. Down below, the sun danced on the surface of the wide river and alongside it, under the shadow of a resolute bronze statue, a young man in a gray military uniform removed his peaked cap as a plain, stocky young woman ran to greet him. Anna watched them as they walked away, for a moment fascinated by their blandness and their happiness with each other's bleak appearance.

"Are you okay?" Her silence obviously bothered him, his need for her approval almost cloying, but she paused for a second before answering.

"I didn't expect it to be so hot. Last night it was so warm I couldn't breathe." She watched her reflection shaping the words, taking comfort from the sensual smoothness of her lips and face and teeth.

He laughed, amused by her, and patted the bed sheets. "Even Russia has a summer. Although Perestroika or not, they've still got a bit of a way to go with air-conditioning."

Turning away from the window, she moved back to the bed, pretending not to see the way his eyes ran over her body, assessing her, evaluating her, just as he had all those nights that he'd visited her in the club. Although then it had been different. Then she'd felt her power over him as she'd danced, her movements provocative, lost in the music until her own sweat covered her naked body and his eyes were so glazed that she was sure he couldn't see her properly, and then she would smile triumphantly and lean forward, brushing his face with her long sandy hair as she took his money and a small part of his soul, watching him tremble with the contact that hinted at so much more. She'd worked hard at him, that much was for sure, and each little victory, each affirmation of her allure, had been an aphrodisiac. Knowing how much he wanted her, what hoops he would jump through for her, made her want him.

Now that they were married things were different. She didn't dance anymore. He didn't want her to. *You've left all that behind you now.* She didn't like his eyes on her anymore. Things had changed. She *had* more. She *was* less.

Avoiding looking at his body, she looked into his eyes and smiled. It seemed to please him. "You are so beautiful." His words were as soft as his plump hand as it ran along the smooth curves of her skin, leaving a wake of goosebumps that perhaps he took as shivers of pleasure. "And I don't mean just on the outside. It wasn't your body that made me want to take you away from that life and marry you. It was the inside." He touched her face. "That clever, witty brain is what won me over, Mrs Jackson."

He'd said this many times, so many times that she figured he'd convinced himself that it wasn't his desire that had made him chase her, that it wasn't her power over him that he'd wanted to tame, that it wasn't the need to reduce her by ownership that had driven him to risk shame and ridicule by marrying an *exotic dancer.* Not that many of the men that had seen her dance or strip or something in between would mock him for that. She was different from the rest; her abilities as a dancer matched by her sensuous beauty, and despite their jealousy she knew the other girls were as pleased as her customers were devastated when she dragged herself from the neon depths of the basement strip club and stepped out into the sunlight.

Still, she thought, as she folded up the empty place inside her, Robert Jackson was a very wealthy man and if he wanted to think there was more to her than beauty—that there was more to anything than beauty—then she would let him believe it. He thought his intelligence and his money were powerful, but it was her beauty that had brought him to his knees, although she was clever enough never to remind him of it.

"That's why I wanted to bring you here. To show you Moscow. It took a long time to get that visa for you. Not many businessmen's wives get to see behind the Iron Curtain." He smiled, pushing back the sheet and grabbing a towel, wrapping it across his thick, pale waist. "I could have taken you to Paris or New York. But this place . . ." he gestured around the grandly old-fashioned hotel room with the slightly threadbare ornate carpet, "this city is something not many people from the west get a chance to experience. And once the reforms are fully in place, it'll be changed for good and this way of life will be gone." Heading towards the bathroom, he paused to kiss her. "You're getting to see history, Anna."

He could have taken me to Paris or New York. She returned his kiss mechanically. "But it's so ugly. Everything's so dull." The words were out before she could stop herself, and for a few moments he paused, his hand against her cheek, looking at her and into her. "Beauty isn't always obvious. Sometimes you have to look past the surface." He grinned. "Anyway, today you're going to see lots of beautiful things. I've arranged for you to visit the Armoury of the Kremlin. It's amazing in there. A museum of national treasures. I've got meetings all day but a driver'll pick you up at ten and wait while you have the tour. Make sure you get to Red Square too."

She frowned slightly, her brow furrowing. "Why do I need the driver? Surely I can make my own way there." She'd fought hard to shake off her gritty roots but the independent desire that had made her leave home at fifteen still occasionally roared inside. Sometimes it was only when she was alone and anonymous, surrounded by streets full of strangers, that she felt she could breathe and be herself, whoever that was. The Anna that she had left behind or the Anna that she had become. She didn't know if either really existed, but both were beautiful enough to make men and women stare as she passed by, and that was really all that mattered. That was enough to make her feel whole.

She watched her husband as he walked to the bathroom. Being owned was trapping her; something she hadn't banked on when she'd taken the gold band and the gold credit card and everything else that went along with it. She missed the admiration she'd received when she was single. *Available.* Full of potential promise. She was still admired, but now it was as Robert's appendage, as the cool and sophisticated wife of a prominent businessmen. It was tamed admiration. She reeked of aloof unavailability.

He turned the shower on and left the door open as he peed. "This is still communist Russia, sweetheart. A driver is best. I don't like the idea of you getting lost in the city on your own."

"I thought you said there was no crime here. I thought everyone was too scared to hurt Westerners," she muttered, moving back to the window, away from the sights of the bathroom. There was no sign of the couple she'd seen earlier, but an old woman dressed in black apart from her colourful headscarf, waddled along the path clutching a plain bag, a few grocery items making jagged shapes in its sides where back in England a supermarket logo would have been. As they'd driven through the city from the airport, Bob had pointed out the lifeless shop fronts. Here there was no Sainsbury's or Waitrose screaming for customer attention, just the universal *gastronom,* literally translated as food shop, with no branding, no competition, no need to lure anyone in. It didn't matter which food shop was used. This one or that. The state owned everything. All the products were the same. All the prices were the same. Individuality was dead. The different culture seemed to fascinate her husband but it frightened Anna slightly that everyone was supposed to be equal; exactly the same as everyone else.

"Well that's true," he called out to her. "But a couple of months ago the wife of an American diplomat went missing and was never found. She was quite a stunner, by all accounts. They'd only been here a few weeks." He poked his head round the paint-chipped doorway. "I would hate to think what I would do if anything happened to you."

She felt his love tighten like a noose around her neck, and glanced into the mirror on the other side of their tarnished suite, soothing herself with her reflection as she waited for him to go to work and leave her in peace.

Once he had gone, full of promises to return early to have some time with her before they met his government contacts for dinner and an evening at the Bolshoi ballet, she leisurely dressed herself, picking out a pale pink silk shirt dress, that pulled in tight around her slim waist. If Bob was with her, she would have worn a full length slip demurely under it, but she left it off, knowing that without it the sun would shine through, outlining the toned curves underneath. She pulled her hair back into an easy chignon, a few strands casually loose, as if blown free rather than carefully arranged, and then slipped her feet into the soft leather matching high-heeled sandals. Looking into the mirror, she could see that she oozed Western affluence, beauty and style in equal measures, and as she left Stalin's gothic skyscraper hotel, all eyes following her, she felt happy for the first time since she'd stepped down from the plane.

Even without any modern air-conditioning, the inside of the armoury was deliciously cool on her bare arms as she followed the small group of quietly whispering tourists through the open wooden doors, and despite herself her eyes widened. The hall yawned wide ahead of them, the polished ebony-inlaid parquet floor covering at least a hundred yards before the next set of doors, beyond which, no doubt, another hall lay. The bloody crimson of the walls oozed down from stripes in the high white domes of the ceilings as if the bodies of those murdered throughout Russian history were piled high and leaking somewhere above. Opulent golden chandeliers sparkled light onto the huge glass cabinets militarily lined in three columns leading down to the far exit, each shelf within ruby velvet coated, soft for their delicate contents.

The guide smiled, pleased with her small crowd's response, and Anna watched her as she spoke, first in Russian and then in English, her accent thick and monotone. *"The Kremlin armoury is a unique treasure store of decorative and applied art. The museum's foundation dates back to the beginning of the nineteenth century and its oldest exhibit is the helmet of Prince Yaroslav which dates back to the early thirteenth century. Our tour today should last approximately two hours."* Above the obligatory gray military uniform, fitted to show the woman's shape but deny her sexuality, the guide's hair was over-bleached and her lips just a little too red against her pancaked face. It was a look Anna had seen on several Muscovite women who seemed to grab at an ideal of glamour borne out of movies from the forties, a look that was forever to be out of their reach in this equal society. The woman didn't fit into these surroundings that leaked whispers of a decadent past. She was too coarse. Too obvious.

The first hall was filled with ancient firearms and weaponry, none of which really held her interest, but Anna moved dutifully from cabinet to cabinet, glancing at the exhibits and letting her eyes drift across the small information cards next to each. Her companions on the tour seemed to mainly comprise of about fifteen middle-aged Russian men and women that had been climbing down from a bland Intourist coach as her car had dropped her off. One man however, seemed different, his suit tailored and sophisticated on his tall frame as he kept himself apart from the rest. Anna had noticed the guide giving the man a small smile and nod when she saw him, and for a moment had wondered if perhaps there was romance between them, but then dismissed the idea. Anna knew men and a man like that would not look twice at a woman like the guide in her sensible uniform.

Bored with the exhibits, she moved around to the other side of the cabinet and studied him through the glass. For a moment or two she feigned interest in a pair of ornate pistols and then let her eyes slide to the left, through to where he stood. How old was he? Maybe forty? Perhaps slightly older? Not a bad age for a man, she concluded. His dark hair shone slightly in the light where it had been combed backwards above the worn skin of his face. His eyes flicked up and met hers, twinkling slightly as if he had known she was watching him, and they were a brighter blue than any she had ever seen. Her insides warmed as she looked away. The day seemed at once more interesting and, as she followed the guide into the next hall, she could feel the stranger's gaze still on her, rising and falling with her walk. As she allowed herself a tiny secret smile, she wondered if the light was shining through her dress.

For the next forty minutes they carried on their secret dance, pretending ignorance of the other's presence as the guide led the group through collections of carved gilt carriages, breath-taking sleighs and an array of heavily jewelled gowns owned by Catherine the Great and some less famous Russian Tsarinas, whole surfaces of faded fabric covered with priceless rubies, diamonds and emeralds.

Staring up at them, Anna wondered how a nation had given this elegance up, opting instead to become the mediocrity of the masses, and for a moment the dark stranger on the other side of the room was forgotten. How she would have loved to have lived in the grandeur of these palaces, fires roaring in the grates as winter turned the gardens outside into a frozen sculpted wasteland, inside a constant swirl of parties and witty flirtations to keep out the cold. She would have been queen of them all, and if not in title then in beauty. She always was. Those days wouldn't have been any different.

It was the final hall that held the Armoury's greatest treasures though, the delicately painted and gold inlaid icon frames, pocket watches, and the pinnacle of the exhibition, the world famous Faberge eggs. Moving from cabinet to cabinet, each display seemed more enchanting than the last. It was when she was gazing at one of the eggs, its intricate ebony and silver lid open revealing a perfectly detailed replica of the winter palace, tiny windows with lights inside hinting at a miniature world within still enjoying the glamour of the old regime, that the man came alongside her, his reflection filling the range of her vision on the glass like a ghost.

"They are beautiful, are they not?" His voice was low, speaking only for her, and although coated in the guttural Russian tones, his words were melodic and smooth.

"Yes. Yes they are. Exquisite."

He turned to her and smiled. "As, if I may say, are you." He held out his hand. "Gregori Ivanovitch. A pleasure to meet you."

"Thank you." Her lips hesitated over her married name unable to let it out. "Anna."

He raised a dark eyebrow. "Anya. A Russian name."

She didn't correct his pronunciation, taking pleasure in the exotic sound of it.

"Are you enjoying looking into our past?" He said.

"Yes. Yes I am." She met his confident gaze with one of her own, before taking a few steps to the side and looking back into the cabinet, knowing that he would follow her. "Are you with the group?"

He laughed, amused, the loud noise echoing slightly in the hush, as if he, like her, were born to fill this room. "No." He looked over to the huddled group on the other side of the hall. "No, I'm not with them. They are factory workers from Kiev on their first visit to our great capital." He leaned in to whisper to her. "If you stand close enough to them you can smell their awe and their fear." He chuckled. "As well as the stench of boiled cabbage."

From the heat of his skin she could smell a hint of cologne. Not one she recognised, but warm and musky. She kept herself close knowing that he too would be drinking her scent in. "Why would they be afraid?"

"I think maybe you understand very little about this country of mine." He looked across the room again and then back at her. "Sometimes invisibility is not such a terrible thing."

Her finger, elegant and manicured, traced the outline of one of the exhibits while inside she brushed away his words. There was nothing worse than invisibility.

"So, is this your first time to the Armoury too, Gregori Ivanovich?" Her tone was light and playful. It would draw him in, she was sure, this routine being a game she had played out many times with many men. Where this particular version of the game would lead, she didn't know and she didn't care. Robert and the chill of her life with him were back at the hotel. In the here and now she was herself, or maybe not herself. She was *Anya,* something new, something *more.* She could feel the power tingling in her fingertips.

"No," He shook his head. "I come here often to look at the pieces in this hall. I like to look at things of beauty to inspire me in my work." He looked down at her, those blue eyes twinkling. "I have, what I think in your country would translate as, a free pass."

"What is it that you do? Are you an artist?" She looked once again at the fine wool of his suit. There was no smell of the death of the individual clinging to this man who she thought would be as at home strolling down Bond Street as he was here. He stood out against the backdrop of this modern Moscow as much as she did.

He pointed into the cabinet of priceless decorated eggs. "My great-great Uncle was Fabergé's assistant. He worked on many of the internal decorations for these creations. In fact, I think the miniature Winter Palace that you were looking at is one of his pieces." His voice dropped to a murmur as he stared through the glass into the past. "But, as there would always be with two great craftsmen, they had a falling out, and my great-great Uncle left Faberge and St Petersburg and came to Moscow to make treasures of his own. Come. I'll show you."

He led her to a smaller cabinet, less well-lit, pressed against a crimson wall. Anna peered inside and gasped. "They're dancers!" There were six female figurines within, each on an ivory pedestal, and gazing at them, Anna was intrigued by their detail and life-like qualities. One woman, her brunette hair piled high, twisted in a loose pirouette on the stand, the shape of the movement unconventional but natural as if she were dancing for no-one but herself. Pressing her face closer to the glass, it seemed to Anna as if there were a bead of sweat trickling down the dancer's flushed face. Each of the others was equally detailed, but unique, as if they were photographs rather than china.

"They're magnificent." She breathed eventually. "The colours are so real. They don't even look like china."

"They're not. They're made from a clay compound, a secret mixture that my Great Uncle developed."

"Why are there so few? And why are they over here rather than with the main exhibits? They're far more beautiful than most of those things."

"His career was ended rather abruptly by death. He was murdered. I don't know the exact story, so much of our history has been re-written or lost, but I know that the husband of one of his aristocratic models was executed for the murder, not long after the sixth doll was completed. He was rambling like a madman about magic and the Devil all the way to the executioner's block. His wife went to a nunnery where she remained in seclusion until she died." He smiled slightly. "How lucky that we have killed God now, eh? No nunneries, no Devil. No magic. Not in Mother Russia."

Anna looked at the dolls again and shivered pleasantly thinking about the story. There had been passion in Russia once at least, even if it seemed dead now.

Looking up at him, she raised a curved eyebrow. "You still haven't answered my question. Are you an artist?"

"Of sorts. I am a doll-maker like my Great Uncle. I have a small showroom and studio on the old Arbat. I don't pretend at his talent, but I have my own successes. Most of my clients come from the new aristocracy, the polit-buro and the KGB. These things allow me certain freedoms that perhaps aren't extended to most of my comrades. Even in these times, people still appreciate things of beauty."

The guide was ushering them out, and Anna and her companion walked in silence until they were back in the sticky heat of midday Moscow. As the tourists from Kiev were herded back onto their coach, she looked at her waiting driver with dismay, the shackles of her life closing around her.

"Is he waiting for you?" His breath tickled her ear, and she resisted the urge to tilt her neck and feel his lips there.

"Yes. I'm staying at the Ukraine Hotel. I was going to get him to take me to Red Square before returning though."

"I could show you Red Square, if you like. We can walk from here along the river and he can pick you up at the bridge later. Would you like me to speak to him?"

She smiled up at him. "I would like that very much."

The driver stood tall as Gregori approached, and watching them talking, it wasn't long before Anna saw some folded notes exchanging hands. Always money, she thought. She would always be able to value herself on the money men spent to be with her. But maybe with this man it was different. He wasn't as needy as the men in the club, *as Robert*, and that set her pulse racing. Not because of love or passion, but because of the thrill of the challenge. The need to subdue him. The driver got in the car and pulled out of the Armoury gates, and smiling as she took the Russian man's arm, Anna felt free.

Red Square was not what she had expected. She had thought to find something like the famous squares in London, with one central statue or feature and perhaps some gardens, but as with everything else in this city, she found it strange. The vast uneven area to the right of the walls of the Kremlin was paved with huge slabs of gray, like cobbles for a giant, one corner taken up by an imposing non-descript building that her new and more charming guide told her was GUM, the city's largest department store. When she had asked to see inside, he had smiled and said that there was nothing to interest her within its walls, and after only a few minutes she knew he was right. It was more like a bland indoor market than a store, full of necessities rather than luxuries, and it reeked of the stale sweat of those that worked too hard for a living. He must have seen the displeasure rippling on her face, because they were swiftly outside again.

Passing Lenin's tomb, and the long shambling queue outside it, they strolled towards the bridge.

"And this," Gregori said, gesturing to his left as he brought them to a halt. "Is St. Basil's cathedral; one of the most famous pieces of architecture in the city. It was built nearly five hundred years ago, and took five years to complete, the workers out in all weathers, several dying during their labour. Imagine spending so long on one project. How much dedication would that take? But it was worth it don't you think? All art requires sacrifice."

Anna stared up at the church that looked like nothing she had ever seen before. To her it was a garish mass of colour, too many domes for its small size, and each one and the area below it decorated in a different design with a different bright shade. There were candy-stripes and zig-zags, gold and red, too much for the eye to take in. To Anna it was like the Armoury guide's make-up and hair; ugly from trying to hard.

"You don't like it, do you?" He asked, and she shook her head, honestly.

"I think it's too much. It all jars on the eye." She paused. "It stands out in all the wrong ways."

319

Gregori didn't seem to take offence at her comments, but laughed gently. "That is because you are not Russian. In the west you can only see what is obvious. You look for obvious beauty and never test your vision by looking closely. It is all too easy for you." He raised his hand, pointing at the shapes and colours of the church. "To me, this is a glorious symbol of all that is mysterious and misleading about Russia, in the old days and now. Its symmetry is not easy to detect, nor it glory immediately apparent. Because you are a foreigner, you cannot see past its mixture of dissonant shapes and colours but if you could you would be able to discern the intrinsic harmony, the clever design, and the beauty of the streamlined contrasting contours and the cathedral would leave you as breathless as Faberge's eggs did."

She smiled at him, almost absently. Why did all men want to teach her? Improve her. Imprint their mind on hers as if she were a blank canvas to paint on and own. *Because it's part of the game, that's why. The power struggle. What will win, brain or beauty?* She already knew the answer to that; it was the men that didn't.

"Tell me, Anya," his voice was thoughtful, "what do you see when you look at Moscow and her people?"

For a moment, she let her eyes wander around the square, at the soldiers and the queues to see the corpse of the long dead leader that had brought them to this stale existence, and the others that scurried from work to home or back again, all dark overcoats and hunched shoulders. "I see equality of the lowest level." She couldn't keep the disdain out of her voice and he smiled.

"Very good." He stood behind her, his hands on her shoulders, the silk thin between them and her naked skin. "Now tell me what you don't see. Tell me *who* you don't see."

"I don't understand." She could feel his chest against her back, and she wondered if touching her was sending the same electric tingle through him that it was through her.

"Look again. Is this what the capital city in your England would look like? This mixture of people?"

She stared, lost for a few seconds, and then his meaning dawned on her and she sucked in the hot, muggy air. "Oh, I see. I think I see . . ." She turned to him. "There are no black people. No ethnic people at all."

"Who else?"

She could feel herself flushing, as her mind scanned back through her memories of her experiences here. "There are no disabled people. None." She turned to look at him, confused. "How can that be?"

He smiled. "Equality comes at a price, Anya. The weak and those considered inferior aren't allowed in the city. Not in the greatest city of the Soviet Union. Maybe in Kiev or Siberia. But not Leningrad or Moskva." He drawled the last syllable of the Russian word, and despite herself Anna was fascinated. She stared out at the moving people, for a moment her overwhelming sense of self forgotten.

"So what happens to all the disabled people that come from here? Born deaf or blind or with something like cystic fibrosis? Surely there must be some native to the city. I can't imagine parents banishing their children so easily."

Gregori smiled again, his teeth straight and white against his weathered skin. "Ahh, so you have a sharp mind under that beautiful face." He moved away and started leading her slowly to the bridge where her car would soon be waiting. "Now you just have to learn to see my city properly." He put his arm around her shoulder as if she belonged to him. "You look around and you say you see equality. But you know as well as I that true equality cannot be. It is a veneer, a pretence. Perhaps not for everyone. Maybe for those poor, exhausted workers that we saw back in the Armoury the dreams of Lenin are reality. But existence for the rest of Russia? For the passionate artists that litter our history and still must exist today? To see *their* lives you need to look for the things that move in the corner of your eyes. The blackmarketeers. The whores and the pimps. The

321

whole communities that live beneath Stalin's great Metro network. Those are the truly alive Moscovites."

She frowned slightly, a wisp of hair blowing against her face. "It all sounds a little ugly to me. I don't think those are my kind of people."

"Oh Anya." He whispered. "You'd be surprised. One day you will learn that there are so many more interesting things than beauty and that beauty and ugliness are sometimes so close they are indistinguishable."

This time it was she that laughed; a flirtatious throaty sound. "Ah, but then there will hopefully be an obliging plastic surgeon ready to fall in love with me and literally save face."

He raised an eyebrow, his own smile soft. "Perhaps. Perhaps not. I wonder how you would live without your beauty."

"I don't intend to find out." She paused. "What do you mean there are whole communities under the Metro?" Ahead a black Zil pulled to the curb of the road and her driver stepped out.

Gregori kept his voice low, as if even he, with all his elusive debonair charm and Polit-Buro privileges, was still a little afraid of the power of the system, the big brother of the KGB. "Where do you think all the people who refuse to be equal live? Those that don't want to be, or can't be, worker ants of the state?" He pointed downwards. "They're under our feet, pretty Anya. The gypsies, the hermits, the political refugees, and the eccentric artists that seem to like to be free, all tucked away in the old tunnels and boiler rooms and bomb shelters, living in tribes. Scurrying like rats in and out through the ventilation shafts at dusk and dawn. Invisible and yet alive. Fascinating, isn't it?"

Watching the dark humour in his eyes, Anna wasn't sure how seriously to take him, but there was something romantic about the idea of a whole second civilisation beneath her feet. It made her think of the strip club and her Soho friends that only ever came out at night, as if drawn into town by the rhythm of promised music and laughter and the buzz of neon as the sun went down.

They were only a few feet away from her car and the driver opened the rear door, the gloom within uninviting, and Anna sighed. Her little day-time adventure was over. In the distance she could see the peaked towers of the Ukraine reaching dauntingly into the hazy sky, waiting to suck her back into Robert's world. *Her world now. Whether she liked it or not.* She bit the inside of her mouth. She would like it. She *did* like it. It was an easy life.

She tilted her chin upwards. "It seems that it's time for us to say good-bye. Thank you so much for your very charming company, Gregori Ivanovich. If the art doesn't work out, I will be more than happy to give you a reference as a tour guide." For a fleeting moment she saw his eyes linger on her lips and felt once again the *frisson* of the unspoken attraction, the whirs and clicks of the game playing out.

"Perhaps it doesn't have to be good-bye." He pulled a small notebook and pencil from his pocket and scribbled on a sheet before ripping it out and handing it to her. *Arbatskaya.* And then the word written again in the strange shapes of the Cyrillic script. "I would very much like to use you as a model for one of my dolls. I think you would make one of my best works, and I don't yet feel ready to say farewell to you." He smiled. "If you find that you are free this evening, then take the Metro from the Kievskaya station outside the hotel four stops to the Arbat. When you leave the station, the old Arbat is on your right, a long pedestrian road. You won't miss it," He flashed his dangerous white teeth. "It is a place that comes alive at night. That's why I like to work there. By day, the shops selling the memorabilia of the revolution rule, touting the posters and badges that we all must wear to prove ourselves. But by night?"

He leaned in, brushing his lips against her cheek with his whisper. "By night the Arbat belongs to the vodka drinking Bohemians."

"I'm not sure that I'll be able to . . ."

He shrugged, cutting her off. "If you come, you come and I shall immortalise you in art. If not, then it has been a pleasure, if only a brief one, to know you my Anya." He winked. "As we say in Russia, *dos vidanya*." He kissed her hand before turning and walking away.

Anna watched until he had disappeared into the milieu of Red Square. He didn't look back and that made her smile. Maybe he was going to be as good at this game as she was.

The room was stifling when she returned, the old windows refusing to open, as if not even air was allowed freedom to move without the state's permission, and drawing the heavy curtains Anna peeled away the clingy skin of her dress and lay on the bed. Beneath her the sheets were pulled tight into regimented hospital corners, their tension palpable even with the bedspread over them. She stared up at the ceiling and at nothing as her mind drifted contentedly through the memories of the morning. Her new admirer was interesting, that was for sure, and she wondered how he would react if she danced for him. Not like Robert had done certainly, all wide-eyes and open lust, and for a moment she imagined herself back in the club, but this time it was Gregori Ivanovich watching her dance, his dark eyes following her twists and turns, watching her as if she was a beautiful object rather than an object of lust. But still, she thought, closing her eyes and savouring her private darkness, how they viewed her was almost irrelevant. It was always with desire of some kind. *I would like to use you as a model for one of my dolls.*

Sleep crept in at the corner of her eyes and she let it take her into vague dreams of haggard strangers that she could almost see hiding in dark corners, their faces twisted, all of them staring at her as she danced.

It hadn't taken much to convince Robert that she had a headache, given that she was fast asleep when he'd returned back. His disappointment at what she would be missing out on almost made her smile as she slid under the covers and allowed him to fetch her some aspirin and bottled water. The Bolshoi held no interest for her, ballet too technical and anodyne to truly enjoy, all about the story and classical music instead of the freedom of movement that she loved. And having sampled a Russian dinner for the past two nights, the idea of more vegetables in aspic and home-grown too-sweet champagne in the company of fat men and their dour wives held no appeal for her.

"I probably won't be home 'til after one, sweetheart." He said, gently kissing her on the forehead. "I'll try not to make too much noise."

Her heart thumping, she waited in bed for twenty minutes after he left, just in case he popped back, and then when she was sure he had definitely gone for the night, she leapt up and into the shower. It was seven o'clock, which gave her a safe five hours until Robert got back, and, she reasoned as the water ran steaming through her hair, even if he came home before her she could always say that she'd just gone out for some fresh air. He wouldn't question her. He never did.

Wanting a different look, something that she could feel good dancing in, she left her hair loose and pulled on some ripped jeans that sat suggestively on her hip bones, and a tight-fitting black vest top. Jane had liked her in this outfit best, in the days when they used to disappear into the London nights and taken them by storm. It made her look wild and sexy, and tonight that was exactly how she wanted to feel.

Checking her handbag to make sure she had her passport and money, she tugged on her boots and headed out into the night.

It was eight o'clock when she took the stairs down into the opulent marble of the Kievskaya Metro station and although there were still a few people milling about, mainly young people wishing there was somewhere to go, rush hour was over for the day and she was alone as she pushed her five kopeks into the turnstile slot and passed through to the long escalator leading down to the trains. The walls were mosaic with glorious images of Stalin and Lenin and the people of the Revolution, and Anna was surprised at how superior the décor was to that of the grimy London equivalent.

The platform was clean, with a huge open space between it and its counterpart for trains going the other way that was filled with a huge bronze statue of Lenin, one arm raised with a flag lifted high, and around it were circular seating areas. Looking at the map against the wall, Anna checked that she was on the right side and then waited, peering into the dark gaping tunnel. Behind her legs she felt a blast of warm air and, looking down, saw a large square vent.

No one else being on the platform with her, she crouched and peered into it thoughtfully, her conversation of earlier with Gregori still fresh in her mind. Surely there weren't whole communities of people living down there in the dark and gloom? That couldn't be. She waited, peering through the grate until a train rumbled by somewhere else in the system and another stream of air rushed past her face. She wasn't certain if it was her imagination, but she was sure it carried the warm sweet but sickly scent of birth and death and everything in-between.

A little disgusted, she stood up and was pleased to hear a train approaching on her platform. She turned in time to see a small, huddled figure in a black, hooded coat, pressed against the far wall by the mouth of the tunnel. Anna's brow furrowed. Where had she come from? The stairs from the turnstiles and escalators above led into the mid-point of both platforms. She was standing only a few feet away from them so surely she'd have heard or seen someone else arriving. How odd. Something about the way the figure seemed to be staring unsettled her, and she was glad that the train was slowing to a halt.

From speakers above her head a female voice blasted out foreign words, but Anna was sure she heard Arbatskaya amongst them. She took one more look at the strange figure in black as the doors of the train opened, and thought about the smell of the air coming from the vent. *The only place the woman could have come from was the tunnel.* It was the only logical answer. Shivering slightly, she was pleased when the doors closed behind her and the train moved away, letting her mind look forward to the pleasures of the evening ahead and Gregori Ivanovich.

Her excitement was strangled somewhat when she stepped out of the train and on to the escalator and realised that the strange black figure was following her, a few steps behind, her reflection clear in the brushed steel of the parallel stairs. There was something repellent about the cowled woman, and although Anna wasn't afraid, she did feel unsettled. Still, eager to leave the ugliness behind, she started to walk up the moving stairs rather than letting them carry her. The woman behind did the same, even though she seemed slightly crippled, her back hunched over a little too far, and it must have taken some effort to keep up a matching pace.

Irritation washed over Anna. What did the woman want? Money? If she was a beggar then why didn't she come straight out with it and ask for something? She peered cautiously over one shoulder. The woman's face was down, but from beneath the hood Anna could see that her skin was covered in lumps or boils or symptoms of some kind of disease. One thing she was certain of was that she didn't want the hag any closer to her. The idea of being touched by such a creature made her feel slightly nauseous.

Gratefully exiting the station, Anna immediately saw the long cobbled street to her left, the strains of a Beatles track wafting out of it, old-fashioned lantern-style streetlamps spread out evenly in the centre shedding a pale yellow light. It was the Arbat, immediately recognisable from Gregori's description. As she hurried down it, she was aware of the woman, *the thing*, that was following her, now trying to catch up rather than just keep up.

Moving quickly across the cobbles, well trained in managing the high-heels of her boots, Anna passed a small bar that was the source of the music. One neon light hung above it, the tiny dark space seemingly filled with young men and women talking earnestly and sucking hard on cheap Russian cigarettes. No-one was dancing.

From another establishment a little further up, a group of men had taken a table and some chairs out into the muggy air of the street and were drinking shots of Vodka and laughing loudly, their easels and paints leaning up against the wall behind. Anna was pleased to see them, and at least if the woman tried to grab her there would be someone to help. Always aware of the disfigured creature's silent approach behind, Anna searched for Gregori's shop, and as she passed the group of men they wolf-whistled and called out to her, the words unfamiliar, but the language universal. She smiled at them, enjoying the way the calls increased as she sashayed away from them. Gregori must have heard them too, because he appeared from a darkened doorway, stepping out into the street so suddenly that it made her jump.

"So you came, Anya." Although dressed in the same outfit as earlier, the suit jacket was gone, his shirt now untucked and loose at the neck.

"Yes, yes," she looked behind her, to see that the figure had stopped a few feet away and now hesitated. "But someone was following me from the train . . . that woman."

Gregori looked up and his face hardened. "Wait here."

He ran over to the woman who had turned to go, and Anna watched as he spoke angrily to her, visibly terrifying her. After a moment he calmed down, and after talking quietly, Anna saw him reach into his pocket and hand her some roubles. She scurried away and he returned to Anna, his smooth smile back. "Just a beggar woman. She shouldn't have frightened you."

Anna watched as the figure ducked into a side street. "You were very angry with her. For a moment I thought you maybe knew her."

He laughed. "Thank you, but I prefer my women beautiful. I just did not want her upsetting you. Or waiting for when you returned." He stroked her face. "Now come inside and drink some vodka, and let me immortalise you."

The interior of the small shop was lit only from the cabinet lights, and she peered into them as he led her towards the door at the back. The mahogany cases were divided into individual show spaces and within each were one or two dolls, all female and engaged in some daily activity, their positions natural. Looking through the first few displays, the high prices marked on small hand written cards, Anna could see that he was a talented craftsmen, but it was only when she reached the silver cases along the back wall that she gasped. There were no price tags on these dolls, and Anna knew why. They were priceless. As good as his great-great uncle's or maybe even better.

She stared at the one closest to her, the figure of a blonde woman in an expensive dress, one hand on her hip, her head thrown back as she laughed, hair falling loosely over her face and shoulders. She was stunning. The doll was stunning, and for a second Anna was glad that she would never know the woman who modelled for this, a small hint of green envy digging at her.

Gregori came alongside carrying two small glasses with thick brown liquid in them. "Do you like my work?"

She nodded, still staring at the doll. "Those other ones are good, but these, these are . . ." she hunted for the right word, "these are magnificent." The laughing blonde doll seemed to be taunting her, challenging her, and she turned to her host. "Tell me. Are you going to make one of me like this one, or like those others?"

He smiled and handed her the shot glass. "One of these of course, beautiful Anya. I think you could be my best doll yet."

The answer pleased her. "Will you make one of me dancing?"

He nodded. "A dancing doll. Like one of my great-great Uncle's, but better."

Anna grinned victoriously and knocked back her drink, the unexpected heat of it making her lose her breath and then giggle. "What is this? I've drunk some vodka shots in my time, but this is something else."

"Pepper vodka. Vodka Russian style, thick and passionate. The opium of the masses." He took her hand and she let him. "Now come. Let's go to the workshop, drink some more and find some music for dancing!" He laughed, and her face glowing from the heat of alcohol and freedom, she laughed with him, high on his promise to immortalise her beauty.

The vodka was strong, that much was for sure, and as she poured and drank her fourth, time became as thick as the liquid, moving slowly around her, viscous to her mind's invisible touch. The small studio was lit only by one strong white spotlight above a slightly raised dais in the centre of the room, clean against the dusty floor. A few feet in front of the platform stood a workbench with a small pottery wheel. Next to it was a table with a bowl of dirty water, a cloth and a container that Anna presumed held the clay or whatever substance it was that Gregori's great-great Uncle had invented to make his beautiful dolls.

Even with her head giddy, the equipment seemed too crude to fashion the detailed work that filled the cabinets in the shop, and she wondered how talented his hands must be to work such magic. She swayed to the disco music that was playing from the tape recorder on the floor, the vodka evaporating any few inhibitions she may have had. The tune wasn't one she knew, the words foreign, but it had a good beat and it pumped through the soles of her boots. For a moment she felt as if she'd been transported back to her old life, and in her hazy mind she was surprised at how happy that made her feel. The predator in her was alive again.

Hair falling seductively over her face, she grinned at Gregori who lay on the mattress in the corner, resting up on one elbow, watching her from the gloom. Maybe she would sleep with him after dancing for him, maybe not. But one thing she was sure of was that he would *want* to. And maybe that would be enough.

She stepped up onto the dais, enjoying the heat of the light on her. "Are you ready to immortalise me, then?" She turned in a mock pirouette, and laughing, Gregori pulled himself to his feet and peeled off his shirt. From under the work bench he pulled a different bottle, this time of flame-red liquid. He filled his own glass and then one for her. "Let's make magic."

His pale chest glowed in the light and for a second Anna wanted to lean forward and run her tongue along the muscles there, but it could wait. She lifted her glass to his and then drained the drink in one, in harmony with him. Expecting the harsh burn of vodka, she was surprised by the sweet warmth that slid down her throat, filling her chest and stomach and then exploding outwards through her nerves and capillaries, her entire body tingling.

Somewhere in the depths of her mind a small part of her thought she should be concerned. However, the heat was too good to ignore and, abandoning the voice inside that clamoured of drugs, she lost herself in the sensations. Seated at his workbench, she saw Gregori reach into the container and scoop out a lump of shiny, pink clay, the wheel starting to turn, and his hands shaping it while never taking his eyes from her. Watching the spinning wheel, she had the strangest feeling that something inside her was spinning too, but her mind was too numb to think about it, and she was sure it couldn't be important. Nothing seemed particularly important apart from her urge to dance. Vaguely she realised that the music was louder, and rolling her head backwards she started to move, lost in the light and the rhythm, the pink liquid and the spinning wheel.

Time passed in a kaleidoscopic blur and despite the alcoholic haze, somewhere deep inside, Anna was sure that she was dancing better than she had in her whole life. Her limbs and joints were fluid as she bent and stretched, hips twisting expertly, her hair slick with sweat down her back.

At some point, she dimly became aware that her heels and toes were blistering, *or maybe bleeding, inside her boots her feet felt wet,* and her knees were starting to ache, but she couldn't stop herself moving as if she and the wheel and the music were all tied in together. The foot pedal that was driving Gregori's pottery wheel was also driving her body, the control over it no longer hers. Cramp shot up through her right calf and she tried to cry out, but her voice didn't seem to work anymore. Panic and exhaustion fought for supremacy in her synapses and the bright light above filled her head, her movements so fast that it seemed like a strobe. Somewhere behind her eyes, tears formed, tears of confusion and fear, and her last thought before she passed out was of Robert and the realisation of how much he loved her.

She knew something was wrong as soon as she opened her eyes. Her cheek was pressed into the dais, her body curled up in the foetal position, skin trembling and numb. Somewhere across the room, a woman laughed but from her place on the floor the sound seemed like an eternity away and she didn't yet have the energy to focus her eyes. What had happened to her? What was in that red drink? For a minute or two she didn't move, her head throbbing as she became aware of pins and needles tingling in her fingers. Eventually, slowly accepting that this wasn't a dream, she lifted herself up slightly, pain in her joints flaring into life, deep in the core of her bones. Anna's heart trembled. This wasn't just stiffness, this was more than that. As if at some point during her dance she'd developed crippling arthritis.

Pulling herself into a sitting position, she moaned as she looked down at her hands. This couldn't be right, this couldn't be right at all. What was happening to her? What had he *done* to her? Where her skin had been pale and elegant, the fingers long and manicured, she was now covered in unsightly red and brown blotches and her left hand curled up like a claw. Trying to stretch it, she cried out in pain, dispelling any last shred of hope that this was merely a nightmare brought about by an excess of vodka.

Raising her head, she looked at the workbench. Frozen in a moment of sensuous movement, there stood a perfect replica of her, exotic against the rough wood. She stared at it. It wasn't just a copy of her; it was as if the model was imbibed with her beauty and sex, the tiny figure mesmerising. Looking down, her jeans seemed too baggy, as if she were just skin and bone underneath. Painfully she dragged herself to her feet, the crookedness in her back not allowing her to straighten fully. Tears prickled at the back of her eyes as she stepped down from the dais and shuffled towards the two figures on the tatty mattress.

Gregori had his arm around a peroxide blonde in a tight-fitting T-shirt dress who was laughing and speaking to him in Russian as she went through Anna's bag, removing her passport. Looking up, she smiled and threw the roubles from Anna's Gucci bag at her feet. Ignoring the money, not sure that if she bent down she would be able to get up again, Anna watched as Gregori kissed the woman with all that Russian passion. It was the guide from her tour of the armoury, and with sudden clarity Anna saw how beautiful the woman was without the overdone make-up and set hair. Sitting by Gregori, she was fresh-faced, her hair hanging loose, the bob chopped and edgy, free from the strict confines of the day. The woman looked at her with disdain, and then whispered something to the still bare-chested man beside her. Gregori stood up and walked to the work bench, picking up the doll. Anna stood silent, unable to move, unable accept his duplicity. Unable to accept her own arrogant foolishness.

"So what do you think of my art, Anya?" He held the figurine up close to her face and seeing all of herself within it, the tears fell free.

"What have you done to me?" Even her voice didn't sound like her own, carrying a rasp in the words that was never there before.

He frowned, and she could see the hard cruelty in the lines of his face. He seemed younger than he had when she'd met him. The veneer of sophistication that he had used to lure her was gone, and in its place she could see the man that he really was. Cruel, talented and hungry to succeed in this equal society. "I've made you immortal."

From the corner of her eye she saw the tour guide slip her British passport into her own bag. Her soul numb and violated; she wondered briefly how much money they would get for it. Was nothing of hers to be wasted when it could be taken and bartered and used to escape from the equal life? What extremes of theft were these?

Still carrying the doll, Gregori went through the small door leading into the shop and Anna followed him, trying to grab at him, needing more of an explanation. Panic pumped at her tired heart. She needed to know when she was going to feel normal again. When these drugs were going to wear off. She couldn't go back to the hotel and Robert just yet. She wouldn't be able to explain herself. Glancing at her wrist, there was an empty space where her Cartier watch had been, and looking at the shop window she could see it was still dark outside. Maybe she would just tell him that she'd gone for a walk and had been robbed. He wouldn't need to know everything. As soon as her body got back to normal she would go back. Go back and forget that this had ever happened.

Turning to Gregori, her heart froze and she felt the tinkling of her life and soul breaking inside. She could see a reflection in the glass of the cabinets, a disfigured stranger staring out, and it was only when she met the terrified gaze that she realised the reflection was her own. One half of her face had sagged completely as if she'd had a stroke, and a series of lumps and boils were protruding over the skin that had lost its youthful tone.

She watched in horror as her reflection raised a hand, and then her own fingers confirmed what she was seeing, navigating the new shapes of her face with trembling digits. She stared, oblivious to both Gregori and the woman now dressed in his shirt who stood in the workshop doorway.

Her head echoed with the story Gregori had told in the Armoury. The aristocratic model that had hidden out her days in a nunnery. The husband whose grief had made him a murderer. *He was rambling like a madman about magic and the Devil all the way to the executioner's block.* She stared at her stranger's face in the glass and then at herself bottled up in the vivacious doll behind it, and she knew that her beauty and sensuality were lost to her forever. What he had done, could not be undone. It was magic. Russian magic; cold and passionate and alien to her.

Watching her, the woman in the doorway laughed, the sound as thick with the Russian accent as her voice was. "If he loves you, then you can still go back to your rich husband. He'll look after you." She raised an eyebrow. "If he recognises you, of course." She'd gathered up the roubles that Anna had left on the workshop floor where they'd been thrown at her, and she now held them out with the same disdain that Anna had once felt when looking at her. "Take this."

Humiliated, Anna grabbed at the notes with her good hand and shoved them into her pocket, before Gregori grabbed her shoulders, pushing her towards the door. He opened it, releasing her when she was on the cobbles outside. Her boots wobbled; thin weak legs no longer steady in the heels. She was sobbing out loud, her vision blurring as he disappeared inside, abandoning her to the strange city. For a few seconds she banged on the door, but her own noise frightened her and she stood back, panting and lost.

The sticky air was still hot with only a slight breeze signalling that the night was nearly over, and although the streetlamps still cast their light, the walkway was deserted. Tears cast new paths in the unfamiliar contours of her face, and hunching over as she walked, she was glad that there was no longer anyone about to gasp at her body and face that made a mockery of the seductive outfit she wore.

About twenty paces from Gregori's shop, she leaned against the rough wall and slid to the ground, her spirit broken; the reality of her situation dawning on her. She was truly lost. Displaced. There was nowhere for her to go. Maybe a stronger person would have returned to the hotel and to Robert and told him the strange tale of the bohemian on the Arbat, hoping that he would still love her or at least show her pity. Maybe there would be something that plastic surgeons could do to restore some of what she had been before, making her less obscene to look at. But it would never be enough to replace what he had taken from her. That essence was gone for good. And without her beauty she was nothing. She couldn't go back to her life and be *less*.

She had been sitting there for an hour or more, curled in on herself, head buried in her arms, willing herself to die, when she felt the light touch on her shoulder and the warmth of a body huddling down beside her.

"I wanted to warn you." The voice was soft, the accent American. "I tried to catch you up, but I couldn't."

Raising her head, Anna looked into the malformed face of the cowled black figure and saw that she too was crying. A long wisp of blonde hair fell out from the hood, and for a moment Anna thought she could imagine what this shell had once been, with her head thrown back in careless laughter.

"You . . . you too?"

She nodded. "My name is Kate." She pulled Anna to her feet, before peering cautiously over her shoulder. "He called me Katya." Her sadness made the words heavy as they drifted away with her breath into the humid Moscow night. Above them the stars were starting to fade, the first hint of dawn's arrival, and the two women shuffled towards the end of the street and towards the Metro station.

"Where are we going?" Anna's body ached, its supple flexibility gone for good and she clung gratefully to the American beside her. Her words were whispered, no longer wanting to draw any attention to herself. Ignoring the main entrance to the underground, Kate led them down the side of the building, stopping at a grate.

"Under the city. Away. There are others there."

As the two women tugged the metal upwards, Anna took one long last look at the dawning sun, and then disappeared down into the safety of the invisible dark and the tribes that awaited her.

NOT OUR BROTHER

ROBERT SILVERBERG

Robert Silverberg is a multiple winner of both the Hugo and Nebula Awards and he was named a Grand Master by the Science Fiction/Fantasy Writers of America in 2004.

Silverberg began submitting stories to science fiction magazines in his early teens, and his first published novel, a children's book entitled Revolt on Alpha C, *appeared 1955. He won his first Hugo Award the following year. Always a prolific writer—for the first four years of his career he reputedly wrote a million words a year—his numerous books include such novels as* To Open the Sky, To Live Again, Dying Inside, Nightwings, *and* Lord Valentine's Castle. *The latter became the basis for his popular "Majipoor" series, set on the eponymous alien planet.*

He is married to science fiction writer Karen Haber and lives in Oakland, California.

About "Not Our Brother", he recalls: "The story itself was written after a trip to Mexico in, I think, 1982, and has some autobiographical elements, since at the time I was an avid collector of Mexican masks. (The fantastic elements of the tale, I assure you, are entirely fictional.)

"I did try to buy some masks while I was wandering around Oaxaca and neighboring territory, but very little of interest was available. As it

turned out, most of my best items were acquired right here in San Francisco."

An American collector encounters a mythic shape-changer in a small Mexican town. . . .

Halperin came into San Simón Zuluaga in late October, a couple of days before the fiesta of the local patron saint, when the men of the town would dance in masks. He wanted to see that. This part of Mexico was famous for its masks, grotesque and terrifying ones portraying devils and monsters and fiends. Halperin had been collecting them for three years. But masks on a wall are one thing, and masks on dancers in the town plaza quite another.

San Simón was a mountain town about halfway between Acapulco and Taxco. "Tourists don't go there," Guzmán López had told him. "The road is terrible and the only hotel is a Cucaracha Hilton—five rooms, straw mattresses." Guzmán ran a gallery in Acapulco where Halperin had bought a great many masks. He was a suave, cosmopolitan man from Mexico City, with smooth dark skin and a bald head that gleamed as if it had been polished. "But they still do the Bat Dance there, the Lord of the Animals Dance. It is the only place left that performs it. This is from San Simón Zuluaga," said Guzmán, and pointed to an intricate and astonishing mask in purple and yellow depicting a bat with outspread leathery wings that was at the same time somehow also a human skull and a jaguar. Halperin would have paid ten thousand pesos for it, but Guzmán was not interested in selling. "Go to San Simón," he said. "You'll see others like this."

"For sale?"

Guzmán laughed and crossed himself. "Don't suggest it. In Rome, would you make an offer for the Pope's robes? These masks are sacred."

"I want one. How did you get this one?"

"Sometimes favors are done. But not for strangers. Perhaps I'll be able to work something out for you."

"You'll be there, then?"

"I go every year for the Bat Dance," said Guzmán. "It's important to me. To touch the real Mexico, the old Mexico. I am too much a Spaniard, not enough an Aztec; so I go back and drink from the source. Do you understand?"

"I think so," Halperin said. "Yes."

"You want to see the true Mexico?"

"Do they still slice out hearts with an obsidian dagger?"

Guzmán said, chuckling, "If they do, they don't tell me about it. But they know the old gods there. You should go. You would learn much. You might even experience interesting dangers."

"Danger doesn't interest me a whole lot," said Halperin.

"Mexico interests you. If you wish to swallow Mexico, you must swallow some danger with it, like the salt with the tequila. If you want sunlight, you must have a little darkness. You should go to San Simón." Guzmán's eyes sparkled. "No one will harm you. They are very polite there. Stay away from demons and you will be fine. You should go."

Halperin arranged to keep his hotel room in Acapulco and rented a car with four-wheel drive. He invited Guzmán to ride with him, but the dealer was leaving for San Simón that afternoon, with stops en route to pick up artifacts at Chacalapa and Hueycantenango. Halperin could not go that soon. "I will reserve a room for you at the hotel," Guzmán promised, and drew a precise road map for him.

The road was rugged and winding and barely paved, and turned into a chaotic dirt-and-gravel track beyond Chichihualco. The last four kilometers were studded with boulders like the bed of a mountain stream. Halperin drove most of the way in first gear, gripping the wheel desperately, taking every jolt and jounce in his spine and kidneys. To come out of the pink-and-manicured Disneyland of plush Acapulco into this primitive wilderness was to make a journey five hundred years back in time. But the air up here was fresh and cool and clean, and the jungle was lush from recent rains, and now and then Halperin saw a mysterious little town half-buried in the heavy greenery: dogs barked, naked children ran out and waved, leathery old Nahua folk peered gravely at him and called incomprehensible greetings. Once he heard a tremendous thump against his under-carriage and was sure he had ripped out his oil pan on a rock, but when he peered below everything seemed to be intact. Two kilometers later, he veered into a giant rut and thought he had cracked an axle, but he had not. He hunched down over the wheel, aching, tense, and imagined that splendid bat mask, or its twin, spotlighted against a stark white wall in his study. Would Guzmán be able to get him one? Probably. His talk of the difficulties involved was just a way of hyping the price. But even if Halperin came back empty-handed from San Simón, it would be reward enough simply to have witnessed the dance, that bizarre, alien rite of a lost pagan civilization. There was more to collecting Mexican masks, he knew, than simply acquiring objects for the wall.

In late afternoon he entered the town just as he was beginning to think he had misread Guzmán's map. To his surprise it was quite imposing, the largest village he had seen since turning off the main highway—a great bare plaza ringed by stone benches, marketplace on one side, vast heavy-walled old church on the other, giant gnarled trees, chickens, dogs, children running about everywhere, and houses of crumbling adobe spreading up the slope of a gray flat-faced mountain to the right and down into the dense darkness of a barranca thick with ferns and elephant-ears to the left. For the last hundred meters into town an impenetrable living palisade of cactus lined the road on both sides, unbranched spiny green columns that had been planted one flush against the next. Bougainvillea in many shades of red and purple and orange cascaded like gaudy draperies over walls and rooftops.

Halperin saw a few old Volkswagens and an ancient ramshackle bus parked on the far side of the plaza and pulled his car up beside them. Everyone stared at him as he got out. Well, why not? He was big news here, maybe the first stranger in six months. But the pressure of those scores of dark amphibian eyes unnerved him. These people were all Indians, Nahuas, untouched in any important way not only by the twentieth century but by the nineteenth, the eighteenth, all the centuries back to Moctezuma. They had nice Christian names like Santiago and Francisco and Jesús, and they went obligingly to the iglesia for mass whenever they thought they should, and they knew about cars and transistor radios and Coca-Cola. But all that was on the surface. They were still Aztecs at heart, Halperin thought. Time-travelers. As alien as Martians.

He shrugged off his discomfort. Here *he* was the Martian, dropping in from a distant planet for a quick visit. Let them stare: he deserved it. They meant no harm. Halperin walked toward them and said, *"Por favor, donde está el hotel del pueblo?"*

Blank faces. *"El hotel?"* he asked, wandering around the plaza. *"Por favor. Donde?"* No one answered. That irritated him. Sure, Nahuatl was their language, but it was inconceivable that Spanish would be unknown here. Even in the most remote towns *someone* spoke Spanish. *"Por favor!"* he said, exasperated. They melted back at his approach as though he were ablaze. Halperin peered into dark cluttered shops. *"Habla usted Español?"* he asked again and again, and met only silence. He was at the edge of the marketplace, looking into a chaos of fruit stands, tacos stands, piles of brilliant scrapes and flimsy sandals and stacked sombreros, and booths where vendors were selling the toys of next week's Day of the Dead holiday, candy skeletons and green banners emblazoned with grinning red skulls. *"Por favor?"* he said loudly, feeling very foolish.

A woman in jodhpurs and an Eisenhower jacket materialized suddenly in front of him and said in English, "They don't mean to be rude. They're just very shy with strangers."

Halperin was taken aback. He realized that he had begun to think of himself as an intrepid explorer, making his way with difficulty through a mysterious primitive land. In an instant she had snatched all that from him, both the intrepidity and the difficulties.

She was about thirty, with close-cut dark hair and bright, alert eyes, attractive, obviously American. He struggled to hide the sense of letdown her advent had created in him and said, "I've been trying to find the hotel."

"Just off the plaza, three blocks behind the market. Let's go to your car and I'll ride over there with you."

"I'm from San Francisco," he said. "Tom Halperin."

"That's such a pretty city. I love San Francisco."

"And you?"

"Miami," she said. "Ellen Chambers." She seemed to be measuring him with her eyes. He noticed that she was carrying a couple of Day of the Dead trinkets—a crudely carved wooden skeleton with big eyeglasses, and a rubber snake with a gleaming human skull of white plastic, like a cue-ball, for a head. As they reached his car she said, "You came here alone?"

Halperin nodded. "Did you?"

"Yes," she said. "Came down from Taxco. How did you find this place?"

"Antiquities dealer in Acapulco told me about it. Antonio Guzmán López. I collect Mexican masks."

"Ah."

"But I've never actually seen one of the dances."

"They do an unusual one here," she said as he drove down a street of high, ragged, mud-colored walls, patched and plastered, that looked a thousand years old. "Lord of the Animals, it's called. Died out everywhere else. Pre-Hispanic shamanistic rite, invoking protective deities, fertility spirits."

"Guzmán told me a little about it. Not much. Are you an anthropologist?"

"Strictly amateur. Turn left here." There was a little street an open wrought-iron gateway, a driveway of large white gravel. Set back a considerable distance was a squat, dispiriting hovel of a hotel, one story, roof of chipped red tiles in which weeds were growing. Not even the ubiquitous bougainvillea and the great clay urns overflowing with dazzling geraniums diminished its ugliness. Cucaracha Hilton indeed, Halperin thought dourly. She said "This is the place. You can park on the side."

The parking lot was empty. "Are you and I the only guests?" he asked. "So it seems."

"Guzmán was supposed to be here. Smooth-looking man, bald shiny head, dresses like a financier."

"I haven't seen him," she said. "Maybe his car broke down."

They got out, and a slouching fourteen-year-old mozo came to get Halperin's luggage. He indicated his single bag and followed Ellen into the hotel. She moved in a sleek, graceful way that kindled in him the idea that she and he might get something going in this forlorn place. But as soon as the notion arose, he felt it fizzling: she was friendly, she was good-looking, but she radiated an offputting vibe, a noli-me-tangere sort of thing, that was unmistakable and made any approach from him inappropriate. Too bad. Halperin liked the company of women and fell easily and uncomplicatedly into liasons with them wherever he traveled, but this one puzzled him. Was she a lesbian? Usually he could tell, but he had no reading on her except that she meant him to keep his distance. At least for the time being.

The hotel was grim, a string of lopsided rooms arranged around a weedy courtyard that served as a sort of lobby. Some hens and a rooster were marching about, and a startling green iguana, enormous, like a miniature dinosaur, was sleeping on a branch of a huge yellow-flowered hibiscus just to the left of the entrance. Everything was falling apart in the usual haphazard tropical way. Nobody seemed to be in charge. The mozo put Halperin's suitcase down in front of a room on the far side of the courtyard and went away without a word. "You've got the one next to mine," Ellen said. "That's the dining room over there and the cantina next to it. There's a shower out in back and a latrine a little further into the jungle."

"Wonderful."

"The food isn't bad. You know enough to watch out for the water. There are bugs but no mosquitoes."

"How long have you been here?" Halperin asked.

"Centuries," she said. "I'll see you in an hour and we'll have dinner, okay?"

His room was a whitewashed irregular box, smelling faintly of disinfectant, that contained a lumpy narrow bed, a sink, a massive mahogany chest of drawers that could have come over with the Spaniards, and an ornate candlestick. The slatted door did not lock and the tile-rimmed window that gave him an unsettling view of thick jungle close outside was without glass, an open hole in the wall. But there was a breathtaking mask mounted above the bed, an armadillo-faced man with a great gaping mouth, and next to the chest of drawers was a weatherbeaten but extraordinary helmet mask, a long-nosed man with an owl for one ear and a coyote for another, and over the bed was a double mask, owl and pig, that was finer than anything he had seen in any museum. Halperin felt such a rush of possessive zeal that he began to sweat. The sour acrid scent of it filled the room. Could he buy these masks? From whom? The dull-eyed mozo? He had done all his collecting through galleries; he had no idea how to go about acquiring masks from natives. He remembered Guzmán's warning about not trying to buy from them. But these masks must no longer be sacred if they were mere hotel decorations. Suppose, he thought, I just *take* that owl-pig when I check out, and leave three thousand pesos on the sink. That must be a fortune here. Five thousand, maybe. Could they find me? Would there be trouble when I was leaving the country? Probably. He put the idea out of his mind. He was a collector, not a thief. But these masks were gorgeous.

He unpacked and found his way outside to the shower—a cubicle of braided ropes, a creaking pipe, yellowish tepid water—and then he put on clean clothes and knocked at Ellen's door. She was ready for dinner. "How do you like your room?" she asked.

"The masks make up for any little shortcomings. Do they have them in every room?"

"They have them all over," she said.

He peered past her shoulder into her room, which was oddly bare, no luggage or discarded clothes lying around, and saw two masks on the wall, not as fine as his but fine enough. But she did not invite him to take a close look, and closed the door behind her. She led him to the dining room. Night had fallen some time ago, and the jungle was alive with sounds, chirpings and rachetings and low thunking booms and something that sounded the way the laughter of a jaguar might sound. The dining room, oblong and lit by candles, had three tables and more masks on the wall, a devil face with a lizard for a nose, a crudely carved mermaid, and a garish tiger-hunter mask. He wandered around studying them in awe, and said to her. "These aren't local. They've been collected from all over Guerrero."

"Maybe your friend Guzmán sold them to the owner," she suggested. "Do you own many?"

"Dozens. I could bore you with them for hours. Do you know San Francisco at all? I've got a big old three-story Victorian in Noe Valley and there are masks in every room. I've collected all sorts of primitive art, but once I discovered Mexican masks they pushed everything else aside, even the Northwest Indian stuff. You collect too, don't you?"

"Not really. I'm not an acquirer. Of things, at any rate. I travel, I look, I learn, I move on. What do you do when you aren't collecting things?"

"Real estate," he said. "I buy and sell houses. And you?"

"Nothing worth talking about," she said.

The mozo appeared, silently set their table, brought them, unbidden, a bottle of red wine. Then a tureen of albóndigas soup, and afterward tortillas, tacos, a decent turkey molé. Without a word, without a change of expression.

"Is that kid the whole staff?" Halperin asked.

"His sister is the chambermaid. I guess his mother is the cook. The patrón is Filiberto, the father, but he's busy getting the fiesta set up. He's one of the important dancers. You'll meet him. Shall we get more wine?"

"I've had plenty," he said.

They went for a stroll after dinner, skirting the jungle's edge and wandering through a dilapidated residential area. He heard music and hand-clapping coming from the plaza but felt too tired to see what was happening there. In the darkness of the tropical night he might easily have reached for Ellen and drawn her against him, but he was too tired for that, too, and she was still managing to be amiable, courteous, but distant. She was a mystery to him. Moneyed, obviously. Divorced, widowed young, gay, what? He did not precisely mistrust her, but nothing about her seemed quite to connect with anything else.

About nine-thirty he went back to his room, toppled down on the ghastly bed, and dropped at once into a deep sleep that carried him well past dawn. When he woke, the hotel was deserted except for the boy. *"Cómo se llama?"* Halperin asked, and got an odd smouldering look, probably for mocking a mere mozo by employing the formal construction. *"Elustesio,"* the boy muttered. Had Elustesio seen the *Norteamericano señorita?* Elustesio hadn't seen anyone. He brought Halperin some fruit and cold tortillas for breakfast and disappeared. Afterward Halperin set out on a slow stroll into town.

Though it was early, the plaza and surrounding marketplace were already crowded. Again Halperin got the visiting-Martian treatment from the townsfolk—fishy stares, surreptitious whispers, the occasional shy and tentative grin. He did not see Ellen. Alone among these people once more, he felt awkward, intrusive, vulnerable; yet he preferred that, he realized, to the curiously unsettling companionship of the Florida woman.

The shops now seemed to be stocking little except Day of the Dead merchandise, charming and playful artifacts that Halperin found irresistible. He had long been attracted to the imagery of brave defiance of death that this Mexican version of Halloween, so powerful in the inner life of the country, called forth. Halperin bought a yellow papier-mâché skull with brilliant flower-eyes and huge teeth, an elegant little guitar-playing skeleton and a bag of grisly, morbid marzipan candies. He stared at the loaves of bread decorated with skulls and saints in a bakery window. He smiled at a row of sugar coffins with nimble skeletons clambering out of them. There was some extraordinary lacquer work on sale too, trays and gourds decorated with gleaming red-and-black patterns. By mid-morning he had bought so much that carrying it was a problem, and he returned to the hotel to drop off his purchases.

A blue Toyota van was parked next to his car and Guzmán, looking just as dapper in khakis as he always did in his charcoal grey suits, was rearranging a mound of bundles in it. "Are you enjoying yourself?" he called to Halperin.

"Very much. I thought I'd find you in town when I got here yesterday."

"I came and I went again, to Tlacotepec, and I returned. I have bought good things for the gallery." He nodded toward Halperin's armload of toy skulls and skeletons. "I see you are buying too. Good. Mexico needs your help."

"I'd rather buy one of the masks that's hanging in my room," Halperin said. "Have you seen it? Pig and owl, and carved like—"

"Patience. We will get masks for you. But think of this trip as an experience, not as a collecting expedition, and you will be happier. Acquisitions will happen of their own accord if you don't try to force them, and if you enjoy the favor of *amo tokinwan* while you are here."

Halperin was staring at some straw-wrapped wooden statuettes in the back of the van. "*Amo tokinwan?* Who's that?"

"The Lords of the Animals," said Guzmán. "The protectors of the village. Perhaps protectors is not quite the right word, for protectors are benevolent, and *amo tokinwan* often are not. Quite dangerous sometimes, indeed."

Halperin could not decide how serious Guzmán was. "How so?"

"Sometimes at fiesta time they enter the village and mingle. They look like anyone else and attract no special attention, and they have a way of making the villagers think that they belong here. Can you imagine that, seeing a stranger and believing you have known him all your life? Beyond doubt they are magical."

"And they are what? Guardians of the village?"

"In a sense. They bring the rain; they ward off the lightning; they guard the crops. But sometimes they do harm. No one can predict their whims. And so the dancing, to propitiate them. Beyond doubt they are magical. Beyond doubt they are something very other. *Amo tokinwan*."

"What does that mean?" Halperin asked.

"In Nahuatl it means, 'Not our brother,' of different substance. Alien. Supernatural. I think I have met them, do you know? You stand in the plaza watching the dancers, and there is a little old woman at your elbow or a boy or a pregnant woman wearing a fine rebozo, and everything seems all right, but you get a little too close and you feel the chill coming from them, as though they are statues of ice. So you back away and try to think good thoughts." Guzmán laughed. "Mexico! You think I am civilized because I have a Rolex on my wrist? Even I am not civilized, my friend. If you are wise you will not be too civilized while you are here, either. They are not our brother, and they do harm. I told you you will see the real Mexico here, eh?"

"I have a hard time believing in spirits," Halperin said. "Good ones and evil ones alike."

"These are both at once. But perhaps they will not bother you." Guzmán slammed shut the door of the van. "In town they are getting ready to unlock the masks and dust them and arrange them for the fiesta. Would

348

you like to be there when that is done? The mayordomo is my friend. He will admit you."

"I'd like that very much. When?"

"After lunch." Guzmán touched his hand lightly to Halperin's wrist. "One word, first. Control your desire to collect. Where we go today is not a gallery."

The masks of San Simón were kept in a locked storeroom of the municipal building. Unlocking them turned out to be a solemn and formal occasion. All the town's officials were there, Guzmán whispered: the alcalde, the five alguaciles, the regidores, and Don Luis Gutiérrez, the mayordomo, an immense mustachioed man whose responsibility it was to maintain the masks from year to year, to rehearse the dancers and to stage the fiesta. There was much bowing and embracing. Most of the conversation was in Nahuatl, which Halperin did not understand at all, and he was able to follow very little of the quick, idiosyncratic Spanish they spoke either, though he heard Guzmán introduce him as an important *Norteamericano* scholar and tried thereafter to look important and scholarly. Don Luis produced an enormous old-fashioned key, thrust it with a flourish into the door and led the way down a narrow, musty corridor to a large white-walled storeroom with a ceiling of heavy black beams. Masks were stacked everywhere, on the floor, on shelves, in cupboards. The place was a museum. Halperin, who could claim a certain legitimate scholarly expertise by now in this field, recognized many of the masks as elements in familiar dances of the region, the ghastly faces of the Diablo Macho Dance, the heavy-bearded elongated Dance of the Moors and Christians masks, the ferocious cat-faces of the Tigre Dance. But there were many that were new and astounding to him, the Bat Dance masks, terrifying bat-winged heads that all were minglings of bat characters and other animals, bat-fish, bat-coyote, bat-owl, bat-squirrel, and some that were unidentifiable except for the weird outspread rubbery wings, bats hybridized with creatures of another

349

world, perhaps. One by one the masks were lifted, blown clean of dust, admired, passed around, though not to Halperin. He trembled with amazement at the power and beauty of these bizarre wooden effigies. Don Luis drew a bottle of mescal from a niche and handed it to the alcalde, who took a swig and passed it on; the bottle came in time to Halperin, and without a thought for the caterpillar coiled in the bottom of the bottle he gulped the fiery liquor. Things were less formal now. The high officials of the town were laughing, shuffling about in clumsy little dance steps, picking up gourd rattles from the shelves and shaking them. They called out in Nahuatl, all of it lost on Halperin, though the words *amo tokinwan* at one point suddenly stood out in an unintelligible sentence, and someone shook rattles with curious vehemence. Halperin stared at the masks but did not dare go close to them or try to touch them. This is not a gallery, he reminded himself. Even when things got so uninhibited that Don Luis and a couple of the others put masks on and began to lurch about the room in a weird lumbering polka, Halperin remained tense and controlled. The mescal bottle came to him again. He drank, and this time his discipline eased; he allowed himself to pick up a wondrous bat mask, phallic and with great staring eyes. The carving was far finer than on the superb one he had seen at Guzmán's gallery. He ran his fingers lovingly over the gleaming wood, the delicately outlined ribbed wings. Guzmán said, "In some villages the Bat Dance was a Christmas dance, the animals paying homage to little Jesus. But here it is a fertility rite, and therefore the bat is phallic. You would like that mask, no?" He grinned broadly. "So would I, my friend. But it will never leave San Simón."

Just as the ceremony appeared to be getting rowdy, it came to an end: the laughter ceased, the mescal bottle went back to its niche, the officials grew solemn again and started to file out. Halperin, in schoolboy Spanish, thanked Don Luis for permitting him to attend, thanked the alcalde, thanked the alguaciles and the regidores. He felt flushed and excited as he left the building. The cache of masks mercilessly stirred his acquisitive lust. That they were unattainable made them all the more desirable, of course. It was as though the storeroom were a gallery in which the smallest trifle cost a million dollars.

Halperin caught sight of Ellen Chambers on the far side of the plaza, sitting outside a small café. He waved to her and she acknowledged it with a smile.

Guzmán said, "Your traveling companion?"

"No. She's a tourist down from Taxco. I met her yesterday."

"I did not know any other Americans were here for the fiesta. It surprises me." He was frowning. "Sometimes they come, but very rarely. I thought you would be the only *extranjero* here this year."

"It's all right," said Halperin. "We gringos get lonely for our own sort sometimes. Come on over and I'll introduce you."

Guzmán shook his head. "Another time. I have business to attend to. Commend me to your charming friend and offer my regrets."

He walked away. Halperin shrugged and crossed the plaza to Ellen, who beckoned him to the seat opposite her. He signaled the waiter. "Two margaritas," he said.

She smiled. "Thank you, no."

"All right. One."

"Have you been busy today?" she asked.

"Seeing masks. I salivate for some of the things they have in this town. I find myself actually thinking of stealing some if they won't sell to me. That's shocking. I've never stolen anything in my life. I've always paid my own way."

"This would be a bad place to begin, then."

"I know that. They'd put the curse of the mummy on me, or the black hand, or God knows what. The sign of Moctezuma. I'm not serious about stealing masks. But I do want them. Some of them."

"I can understand that," she said. "But I'm less interested in the masks than in what they represent. The magic character, the transformative power. When they put the masks on, they *become* the otherworldly beings they represent. That fascinates me. That the mask dissolves the boundary between our world and *theirs.*"

"Theirs?"

"The invisible world. The world the shaman knows, the world of the were-jaguars and were-bats. A carved and painted piece of wood becomes a gateway into that world and brings the benefits of the supernatural. That's why the masks are so marvelous, you know. It isn't just an aesthetic thing."

"You actually believe what you've just said?" Halperin asked.

"Oh, yes. Yes, definitely."

He chose not to press the point. People believed all sorts of things, pyramid power, yoghurt as a cure for cancer, making your plants grow by playing Bach to them. That was all right with him. Just now he found her warmer, more accessible, than she had been before, and he had no wish to offend her. As they strolled back to the hotel, he asked her to have dinner with him, imagining hopefully that that might lead somewhere tonight, but she said she would not be eating at the hotel this evening. That puzzled him—where else around here could she get dinner, and with whom?—but of course he did not probe.

He dined with Guzmán. The distant sound of music could be heard, shrill, alien. "They are rehearsing for the fiesta," Guzmán explained. The hotel cook outdid herself, preparing some local freshwater flatfish in a startlingly delicate sauce that would have produced applause in Paris. Filiberto, the patron, came into the dining room and greeted Guzmán with a bone-crushing *abrazo*. Guzmán introduced Halperin once again as an important *Norteamericano* scholar. Filiberto, tall and very dark-skinned, with cheekbones like blades, showered Halperin with effusive courtesies.

"I have been admiring the masks that decorate the hotel," Halperin said, and waited to be invited to buy whichever one took his fancy, but Filiberto merely offered a dignified bow of thanks. Praising individual ones, the owl-pig, the lizard-nose, also got nowhere. Filiberto presented Guzmán with a chilled bottle of a superb white wine from Michoacán, crisp and deliciously metallic on the tongue; he spoke briefly with Guzmán in Nahuatl; then, saying he was required at the rehearsal, he excused himself. The music grew more intense.

Halperin said, "Is it possible to see the rehearsal after dinner?"

"Better to wait for the actual performance," said Guzmán.

Halperin slept poorly that night. He listened for the sound of Ellen Chambers entering the room next door, but either he was asleep when she came in or she was out all night.

And now finally the fiesta was at hand. Halperin spent the day watching the preparations: the stringing of colored electric lights around the plaza, the mounting of huge papier-mâché images of monsters and gods and curious spindly-legged clowns, the closing down of the shops and the clearing away of the tables that displayed their merchandise. All day long the town grew more crowded. No doubt people were filtering in from the outlying districts, the isolated jungle farms, the little remote settlements on the crest of the sierra. Through most of the day he saw nothing of Guzmán or Ellen, but that was all right. He was quite accustomed now to being here, and the locals seemed to take him equally for granted. He drank a good deal of mescal at one cantina or another around the plaza and varied it with the occasional bottle of the excellent local beer. As the afternoon waned, the crowds in the plaza grew ever thicker and more boisterous, but nothing par-ticular seemed to be happening, and Halperin wondered whether to go back to the hotel for dinner. He had another mescal instead. Suddenly the fiesta lights were switched on, gaudy, glaring, reds and yellows and greens, turning everything into a psychedelic arena, and then at last Halperin heard music, the skreeing bagpipy sound of bamboo flutes, the thump of drums, the whispery, dry rattle of tambourines, the harsh punctuation of little clay whistles. Into the plaza came ten or fifteen boys, leaping, dancing cartwheels, forming impromptu human pyramids that promptly collapsed, to general laughter. They wore no masks. Halperin, disappointed and puzzled, looked around as though to find an explanation and discovered Guzmán, suave and elegant in charcoal gray, almost at his elbow. "No masks?" he said. "Shouldn't they be masked?"

"This is only the beginning," said Guzmán.

Yes, just the overture. The boys cavorted until they lost all discipline and went pell-mell across the plaza and out of sight. Then a little old man, also unmasked, tugged three prancing white goats caparisoned with elaborate paper decorations into the center of the plaza and made them cavort, too. Two stilt-walkers fought a mock duel. Three trumpeters played a hideous discordant fanfare and got such cheers that they played it again and again. Guzmán was among those who cheered. Halperin, who had not eaten, was suddenly captured by the aroma from a stand across the way where an old woman was grilling tacos on a brazier and a tin griddle. He headed toward her, but paused on the way for a tequila at an improvised cantina someone had set up on the streetcorner, using a big wooden box as the bar. He saw Ellen Chambers in the crowd on the far side of the plaza and waved, but she did not appear to see him, and when he looked again he could not find her.

The music grew wilder and now, at last, the first masked dancers appeared. A chill ran through him at the sight of the nightmare figures marching up the main avenue, bat-faced ones, skull-faced ones, grinning devils, horned creatures, owls, jaguars. Some of the masks were two or three feet high and turned their wearers into malproportioned dwarfs. They advanced slowly, pausing often to backtrack, circling one another, kicking their legs high, madly waving their arms. Halperin, sweating, alert, aroused, realized that the dancers must have been drinking heavily, for their movements were jerky, ragged, convulsive. As they came toward the plaza he saw that they were herding four figures in white robes and pale human-faced masks before them, and were chanting something repetitively in Nahuatl. He caught that phrase again, *amo tokinwan*. Not our brother.

To Guzmán he said, "What are they saying?"

"The prayer against the *amo tokinwan*. To protect the fiesta, in case any of the Lords of the Animals actually are in the plaza tonight." Those around Halperin had taken up the chant now. "Tell me what it means," Halperin said.

Guzmán said, chanting the translation in a rhythm that matched the voices around them: *"They eat us! They are—not our brother. They are worms, wild beasts. Yes!"*

Halperin looked at him strangely. " 'They eat us?' " he said. "Cannibal gods?"

"Not literally. Devourers of souls."

"And these are the gods of these people?"

"No, not gods. Supernatural beings. They lived here before there were people, and they naturally retain control over everything important here. But not gods as Christians understand gods. Look, here come the bats!"

They eat us, Halperin thought, shivering in the warm humid night. A new phalanx of dancers was arriving now, half a dozen bat-masked ones. He thought he recognized the long legs of Filiberto in their midst. Darkness had come and the dangling lights cast an eerier, more brilliant glow. Halperin decided he wanted another tequila, a mescal, a cold cerveza, whatever he could find quickest. *Not our brother.* He excused himself vaguely to Guzmán and started through the crowd. *They are worms, wild beasts.* They were still chanting it. The words meant nothing to him, except *amo tokinwan,* but from the spacing, the punctuation, he knew what they were saying. *They eat us.* The crowd had become something fluid now, oozing freely from place to place; the distinction between dancers and audience was hard to discern. *Not our brother.* Halperin found one of the little curbside cantinas and asked for mescal. The proprietor splashed some in a paper cup and would not take his pesos. A gulp and Halperin felt warm again. He tried to return to Guzmán but no longer saw him in the surging, frenzied mob. The music was louder. Halperin began to dance—it was easier than walking—and found himself face to face with one of the bat-dancers, a short man whose elegant mask showed a bat upside down, in its resting position, ribbed wings folded like black shrouds. Halperin and the dancer, pushed close together in the press, fell into an inadvertent pas de deux. "I wish I could buy that mask," Halperin said. "What do you want for it? Five thousand pesos? Ten thousand? *Habla usted Español?* No? Come to the hotel with the mask tomorrow. You follow? *Venga mañana.*" There was no reply. Halperin was not even certain he had spoken the words aloud.

He danced his way back across the plaza. Midway he felt a hand catch his wrist. Ellen Chambers. Her khaki blouse was open almost to the waist and she had nothing beneath it. Her skin gleamed with sweat, as if it had been oiled. Her eyes were wide and rigid. She leaned close to him and said, "Dance! Everybody dances! Where's your mask?"

"He wouldn't sell it to me. I offered him ten thousand pesos, but he wouldn't—"

"Wear a different one," she said. "Any mask you like. How do you like mine?"

"Your mask?" He was baffled. She wore no mask.

"Come! Dance!" She moved wildly. Her breasts were practically bare and now and then a nipple flashed. Halperin knew that that was wrong, that the villagers were cautious about nudity and a *gringa* especially should not be exhibiting herself. Drunkenly he reached for her blouse, hoping to button one or two of the buttons, and to his chagrin his hand grazed one of her breasts. She laughed and pushed herself against him. For an instant she was glued to him from knees to chest, with his hand wedged stupidly between their bodies. Then he pulled back, confused. An avenue seemed to have opened around them. He started to walk stumblingly to some quieter part of the plaza, but she caught his wrist again and grinned a tiger-grin, all incisors and tongue. "Come on!" she said harshly.

He let her lead him. Past the tacos stands, past the cantinas, past a little brawl of drunken boys, past the church, on whose steps the dancer in the phallic bat mask was performing, juggling pale green fruits and now and then batting one out into the night with the phallus that jutted from his chin. Then they were on one of the side streets, blind crumbling walls hemming them on both sides and cold moonlight the only illumination. Two blocks, three, his heart pounding, his lungs protesting. Into an ungated courtyard of what looked like an abandoned house, shattered tumbledown heaps of masonry everywhere and a vining night-blooming cactus growing over everything like a tangle of terrible green snakes. The cactus was in bloom and its vast white trumpetlike flowers emitted a sickly sweet perfume, overpoweringly intense. He wanted to gag and throw up, but Ellen gave him no time, for she was embracing him, pressing herself fiercely against him, forcing him back against a pile of shattered adobe bricks. In the strange moonlight her skin glistened and then seemed to become transparent, so that he could see the cage of her ribs, the flat long plate of her breastbone, the throbbing purplish heart behind it. She was all teeth and bones, a Day of the Dead totem come to life. He did not understand and he could not resist. He was without will. Her hands roamed him, so cold they burned his skin, sending up puffs of steam as her icy fingers caressed him. Something was flowing from him to her, his warmth, his essence, his vitality, and that was all right. The mescal and the beer and the tequila and the thick musky fragrance of the night-blooming cereus washed through his soul and left it tranquil. From far away came the raw dissonant music, the flutes and drums, and the laughter, the shouts, the chants. *They eat us.* Her breath was smoke in his face. *They are worms, wild beasts.* As they embraced one another, he imagined that she was insubstantial, a column of mist, and he began to feel misty himself, growing thinner and less solid as his life-force flowed toward her. Now for the first time he was seized by anguish and fright. As he felt himself being pulled from his body, his soul rushing forth and out and out and out, helpless, drawn, his drugged calm gave way to panic. *They are—not our brother.* He struggled, but it was useless. He was going out swiftly, the essence of him quitting his body as though she were reeling it in on a line. Bats fluttered above him, their faces streaked with painted patterns, yellow and green and brilliant ultramarine. The sky was a curtain of fiery bougainvillea. He was losing the struggle. He was too weak to resist or even to care. He could no longer hear himself breathe. He drifted freely, floating in the air, borne on the wings of the bats.

Then there was confusion, turmoil, struggle. Halperin heard voices speaking sharply in Spanish and in Nahuatl, but the words were incomprehensible to him. He rolled over on his side and drew his knees to his chest and lay shivering with his cheek against the warm wet soil. Someone was shaking him. A voice said in English, "Come back. Wake up. She is not here."

Halperin blinked and looked up. Guzmán was crouched above him, pale, stunned-looking, his teeth chattering. His eyes were wide and tensely fixed.

"Yes," Guzmán said. "Come back to us. Here. Sit up, let me help you."

The gallery-owner's arm was around his shoulders. Halperin was weak and trembling, and he realized Guzmán was trembling too. Halperin saw figures in the background—Filiberto from the hotel and his son Elustesio, the mayordomo Don Luis, the alcalde, one of the alguaciles.

"Ellen?" he said uncertainly.

"She is gone. *It* is gone. We have driven it away."

"It?"

"*Amo tokinwan.* Devouring your spirit."

"No," Halperin muttered. He stood up, still shaky, his knees buckling. Don Luis offered him a flask; Halperin shook it away, then changed his mind, reached for it, took a deep pull. Brandy. He walked four or five steps, getting his strength back. The reek of the cactus-flowers was nauseating. He saw the bare ribs again, the pulsating heart, the sharp white teeth. "No," he said. "It wasn't anything like that. I had too much to drink—maybe ate something that disagreed with me—the music, the scent of the flowers—"

"We saw," Guzmán said. His face was bloodless. "We were just in time. You would have been dead."

"She was from Miami—she said she knew San Francisco—"

"These days they take any form they like. The woman from Miami was here two years ago, for the fiesta. She vanished in the night, Don Luis says. And now she has come back. Perhaps next year there will be one who looks like you and talks like you and sniffs around studying the masks like you, and we will know it is not you, and we will keep watch. Eh? You should come back to the hotel now. You need to rest."

Halperin walked between them down the walled streets. The fiesta was still in full swing, masked figures capering everywhere, but Guzmán and Don Luis and Filiberto guided him around the plaza and toward the hotel. He thought about the woman from Miami, and remembered that she had had no car and there had been no luggage in her room. *They eat us.* Such things are impossible, he told himself. *They are worms, wild beasts.* And next year would there be a diabolical counterfeit Halperin haunting the fiesta? *They are—not our brother.* He did not understand.

Guzmán said, "I promised you you would see the real Mexico. I did not think you would see as much of it as this."

Halperin insisted on inspecting her hotel room. It was empty and looked as if it had not been occupied for months. He stretched out on his bed fully clothed, but he did not particularly want to be left alone in the darkness, and so Guzmán and Filiberto and the others took turns sitting up with him through the night while the sounds of the fiesta filled the air. Dawn brought a dazzling sunrise. Halperin and Guzmán stepped out into the courtyard. The world was still.

"I think I'll leave here now," Halperin said.

"Yes. That would be wise. I will stay another day, I think."

Filiberto appeared, carrying the owl-pig mask from Halperin's room. "This is for you," he said. "Because that you were troubled here, that you will think kindly of us. Please take it as our gift."

Halperin was touched by that. He made a little speech of gratitude and put the mask in his car.

Guzmán said, "Are you well enough to drive?"

"I think so. I'll be all right once I leave here." He shook hands with everyone. His fingers were quivering. At a very careful speed he drove away from the hotel, through the plaza, where sleeping figures lay sprawled like discarded dolls, and mounds of paper streamers and other trash were banked high against the curb. At an even more careful speed he negotiated the cactus-walled road out of town. When he was about a kilometer from San Simón Zuluaga he glanced to his right and saw Ellen Chambers sitting next to him in the car. If he had been traveling faster, he would have lost control of the wheel. But after the first blinding moment of terror came a rush of annoyance and anger. "No," he said. "You don't belong in here. Get the hell out of here. Leave me alone." She laughed lightly. Halperin felt like sobbing. Swiftly and unhesitatingly he seized Filiberto's owl-pig mask, which lay on the seat beside him, and scaled it with a flip of his wrist past her nose and out the open car window. Then he clung tightly to the wheel and stared forward. When he could bring himself to look to the right again, she was gone. He braked to a halt and rolled up the window and locked the car door.

It took him all day to reach Acapulco. He went to bed immediately, without eating, and slept until late the following afternoon. Then he phoned the Aeromexico office.

Two days later he was home in San Francisco. The first thing he did was call a Sacramento Street dealer and arrange for the sale of all his masks. Now he collects Japanese netsuke, Hopi kachina dolls, and Navaho rugs. He buys only through galleries and does not travel much any more.

THE SUN, THE SEA AND THE SILENT SCREAM

BRIAN LUMLEY

Brian Lumley was in his early twenties and serving with the Corps of Royal Military Police in Germany when he discovered a collection of stories by H. P. Lovecraft. After searching out every available item of the author's work, Lumley contacted Lovecraft's publisher, August Derleth, in Sauk City, Wisconsin, in order to purchase the one or two volumes still missing from his collection.

After Derleth read various fictional pieces Lumley had included in his letters, he asked if the young soldier had anything he could use in an anthology he was preparing for publication, to be entitled Tales of the Cthulhu Mythos. *Thus Lumley began writing in earnest and the rest, as they say, is history.*

While serving his full term of twenty-two years with the RMP, the author managed to produce three books for Derleth's legendary Arkham House imprint, six paperback novels in the "Titus Crow" series and the stand-alone novel, Khai of Ancient Khem. *Since then he has published many other titles, including the* Psychomech *trilogy and the groundbreaking* Necroscope *series, the latter featuring Harry Keogh, the man who can talk to dead people.*

Lumley's work has now appeared in more than thirteen countries, and his books have sold well over three million copies in the United States alone.

"Ever since I spent three years on Cyprus in the mid-1960s," the author reveals, "I've been in love with the Greek islands. There is something about the air, the light, the sea. And here we are, more than forty years later, and I still go out there at least once a year to an island similar to the one in my story—but not too similar—to enjoy the company of Greek friends, and to spear-fish and hunt octopuses. And before anyone gets upset, I never shoot anything I can't eat. Most of my catch goes into a freezer in the local taverna, ending up on a plate the same night.

"But there was one place I stayed, where I put some small fish in a wash basin to clean and scale them, and . . . and anyway, when you read the story you'll see what happened. And if it puts anyone off, well I'm sorry. . . ."

For the couple in this story, an idyllic island in the Aegean harbors something nasty in the water. . . .

This time of year, just as you're recovering from Christmas, they're wont to appear, all unsolicited, *plop* on your welcome mat. I had forgotten that fact, but yesterday I was reminded.

Julie was up first, creating great smells of coffee and frying bacon. And me still in bed, drowsy, thinking how great it was to be nearly back to normal. Three months she'd been out of *that* place, and fit enough now to be first up, running about after me for a change.

Her sweet voice calling upstairs: "Post, darling!" And her slippers flip-flopping out into the porch. Then those long moments of silence—until it dawned on me what she was doing. I knew it instinctively, the way you do about someone you love. She was screaming—but silently. A scream that came drilling into all my bones to shiver into shards right there in the marrow. Me out of bed like a puppet on some madman's strings, jerked downstairs so as to break my neck, while the silent scream went on and on.

And Julie standing there with her head thrown back and her mouth agape, and the unending scream not coming out. Her eyes staring out with their pupils rolled down, staring at the thing in her white, shuddering hand—

A travel brochure, of course . . .

Julie had done Greece fairly extensively with her first husband. That had been five or six years ago, when they'd hoped and tried for kids a lot. No kids had come; she couldn't have them; he'd gone off and found someone who could. No hard feelings. Maybe a few soft feelings.

So when we first started going back to Greece, I'd suggested places they'd explored together. Maybe I was looking for far-away expressions on her face in the sunsets, or a stray tear when a familiar *bousouki* tune drifted out on aromatic taverna exhalations. Somebody had taken a piece of my heart, too, once upon a time; maybe I wanted to know how much of Julie was really mine. As it happened, all of her was.

After we were married, we left the old trails behind and broke fresh ground. That is, we started to find new places to holiday. Twice yearly we'd pack a few things, head for the sunshine, the sea, and sometimes the sand. Sand wasn't always a part of the package, not in Greece. Not the golden or pure white varieties, anyway. But pebbles, marble chips, great brown and black slabs of volcanic rock sloping into the sea—what odds? The sun was always the same, and the sea . . .

The sea. Anyone who knows the Aegean, the Ionian, the Mediterranean in general, in between and around Turkey and Greece, knows what I mean when I describe those seas as indescribable. Blue, green, mother-of-pearl, turquoise in that narrow band where the sea meets the land: fantastic! Myself, I've always liked the colours *under* the sea the best. That's the big bonus I get, or got, out of the islands: the swimming, the amazing submarine world just beyond the glass of my face mask, the spearfishing.

And this time—last time, the very last time—we settled for Makelos. But don't go looking for it on any maps. You won't find it; much too small, and I'm assured that the British don't go there anymore. As a holiday venue, it's been written off. I'd like to think I had something, everything, to do with that, which is why I'm writing this. But a warning: if you're stuck on Greece anyway, and willing to take your chances come what may, read no further. I'd hate to spoil it all for you.

So . . . what am I talking about? Political troubles, unfinished hotel apartments, polluted swimming pools? No, nothing like that. We didn't take that sort of holiday, anyway. We were strictly "off-the-beaten-track" types. Hence Makelos.

We couldn't fly there direct; the island was mainly a flat-topped mountain climbing right out of the water, with a dirt landing strip on the plateau suitable only for Skyvans. So it was a packed jet to Athens, a night on the town, and in the mid-morning a flying Greek matchbox the rest of the way. Less than an hour out of Athens and into the Cyclades, descending through a handful of cotton-wool clouds, that was our first sight of our destination.

Less than three miles long, a mile wide—that was it. Makelos. There was a "town", also called Makelos, at one end of the island where twin spurs formed something of a harbour, and the rest of the place around the central plateau was rock and scrub and tiny bays, olive groves galore, almonds and some walnuts, prickly pears and a few lonely lemons. Oh, and lots of wildflowers, so that the air seemed scented.

The year before, there'd been a few apartments available in Makelos town. But towns weren't our scene. This time, however, the island had something new to offer: a lone taverna catering for just three detached, cabin-style apartments, or "villas", all nestling in a valley two miles down the coast from Makelos town itself. Only one or two taxis on the entire island (the coastal road was little more than a track), no fast-food stands, and no packed shingle beaches where the tideless sea would be one-third sun oil and two-thirds tourist pee!

We came down gentle as a feather, taxied up to a windblown shack that turned out to be the airport, deplaned and passed in the front of the shack and out the back, and boarded our transport. There were other holiday makers; but we were too excited to pay them much attention; also a handful of dour-faced island Greeks—Makelosians, we guessed. Dour, yes. Maybe that should have told us something about their island.

Our passports had been stamped over the Athens stamp with a local variety as we passed through the airport shack, and the official doing the job turned out to be our driver. A busy man, he also introduced himself as the mayor of Makelos! The traction end of our "transport" was a three-wheeler: literally a converted tractor, hauling a four-wheeled trolley with bucket seats bolted to its sides. On the way down from the plateau, I remember thinking we'd never make it; Julie kept her eyes closed for most of the trip; I gave everyone aboard As for nerve. And the driver-mayor sang a doleful Greek number all the way down.

The town was very old, with nowhere the whitewashed walls you become accustomed to in the islands. Instead, there was an air of desolation about the place. Throw in a few tumbleweeds, and you could shoot a Western there. But fishing boats bobbed in the harbour, leathery Greeks mended nets along the quayside; old men drank muddy coffee at wooden tables outside the tavernas, and bottles of Metaxa and ouzo were very much in evidence. Crumbling fortified walls of massive thickness proclaimed, however inarticulately, a one-time Crusader occupation.

Once we'd trundled to a halt in the town's square, the rest of the passengers were home and dry; Julie and I still had a mile and a half to go. Our taxi driver (transfer charges both ways, six pounds sterling: I'd wondered why it was so cheap!) collected our luggage from the tractor's trolley, stowed it away, waited for us while we dusted ourselves down and stretched our legs. Then we got into his "taxi".

I won't impugn anyone's reputation by remarking on the make of that old bus; come to think of it, I could possibly *make* someone's name, for anywhere else in the world this beauty would have been off the road in the late sixties! Inside—it was a shrine, of course. The Greek sort, with good-luck charms, pictures of the saints, photos of Mum and Dad, and icon-like miniatures in silver frames, hanging and jangling everywhere. And even enough room for the driver to see through his windscreen.

"Nichos," he introduced himself, grave-faced, trying to loosen my arm in its socket with his handshake where he reached back from the driver's seat. And to Julie, seated beside him up front: "Nick!" and he took her hand and bowed his head to kiss it. Fine, except we were already mobile and leaving the town, and holiday makers and villagers alike scattering like clucking hens in all directions in our heavy blue exhaust smoke.

Nichos was maybe fifty, hard to tell: bright brown eyes, hair greying, upward-turned moustache, skin brown as old leather. His nicotine-stained teeth and ouzo breath were pretty standard. "A fine old car," I opened, as he jarred us mercilessly on non-existent suspension down the patchy, pot-holed tarmacadam street.

"Eh?" He raised an eyebrow.

"The car," I answered. "She goes, er, well!"

"Very well, thank you. The car," he apparently agreed.

"Maybe he doesn't speak it too well, darling." Julie was straight-faced.

"Speaks it," Nichos agreed with a nod. Then, registering understanding: "Ah—*speak* it! I am speaking it, yes, only slowly. Very *slooowly!* Then is understanding. Good morning, good evening, welcome to my house— exactly! I am in Athens. Three years. Speaks it much, in Athens."

"Great!" I enthused, without malice. After all, I couldn't speak any Greek.

"You stay at Villas Dimitrios, yes?" He was just passing the time; of course we were staying there; he'd been paid to take us there, hadn't he? And yet at the same time, I'd picked up a note of genuine enquiry, even some-thing of concern in his voice, as if our choice surprised or dismayed him. "Is it a nice place?" Julie asked.

"Nice?" he repeated her. "Beautiful!" He blew a kiss. "Beautiful sea—for swim, *beautiful!* Then he shrugged, said: "All Makelos same. But Dimitrios water—water for drink—him not so good. You drinking? Okay—you drink Coke. You drink beer. Drinking water in bottle. Drinking wine— very cheap! Not drinking water. Is big hole in Dimitrios. Deep, er—well? Yes? Water in well bad. All around Dimitrios bad. Good for olives, lemons, no good for the people."

We just about made sense of everything he said, which wasn't quite as easy as I've made it sound here. As for the water situation: that was standard, too. We never drank the local water anyway. "So it's a beautiful place," I said. "Good."

Again he glanced at me over his shoulder, offered another shrug. "Er, beautiful, yes." He didn't seem very sure about it now. The Greeks are notoriously vague.

We were out of Makelos, heading south round the central plateau, kicking up the dust of a narrow road where it had been cut through steep, seaward-sloping strata of yellow-banded, dazzling white rock to run parallel with the sea on our left. We were maybe thirty or forty feet above sea level, and down there through bites in the shallow sea cliffs, we were allowed tantalizing glimpses of white pebble beaches scalloping an ocean flat as a millpond. The fishing would be good. Nothing like the south coast of England (no Dover sole basking on a muddy bottom here), but that made it more of a challenge. You had to be *good* to shoot fish here!

I took out a small paper parcel from my pocket and unwrapped it: a pair of gleaming trident spearheads purchased in Athens. With luck these heads should fit my spears. Nichos turned his head. "You like to fish? I catch plenty! *Big* fisherman!" Then that look was back on his face. "You fish in Dimitrios? No eat. You like the fishing—good! Chase him, the fish—shoot, maybe kill—but no eat. Okay?"

I began to feel worried. Julie, too. She turned to stare at me. I leaned forward, said: "Nichos, what do you mean? Why shouldn't we eat what I catch?"

"My house!" he answered as we turned a bend through a stand of stunted trees. He grinned, pointed.

Above us, the compacted scree slope was green with shrubs and Mediterranean pines. There was a garden set back in ancient, gnarled olives, behind which a row of white-framed windows reflected the late-morning sunlight. The house matched the slope rising around and beyond it, its ochre-tiled roof seeming to melt into the hillside. Higher up there were walled, terraced enclosures; higher still, where the mountain's spur met the sky, goats made gravity-defying silhouettes against the dazzle.

"I show you!" said Nichos, turning right onto a track that wound dizzily through a series of hairpins to the house. We hung on as he drove with practised ease almost to the front door, parking his taxi in the shade of an olive tree heavy with fruit. Then he was opening doors for us, calling out to his wife: "Katrin—hey, Katrin!"

We stayed an hour. We drank cold beer, ate a delicious sandwich of salami, sliced tomatoes, and goat's milk cheese. We admired the kids, the goats and chickens, the little house. It had been an effective way of changing the subject. And we didn't give Nichos's reticence (was that what it had been, or just poor communications?) another thought until he dropped us off at Villas Dimitrios.

The place was only another mile down the road, as the crow flies. But that coastal road knew how to wind. Still, we could probably have walked it while Katrin made us our sandwiches. And yet the island's natural contours kept it hidden from sight until the last moment.

We'd climbed up from the sea by then, maybe a hundred feet, and the road had petered out to little more than a track as we crested the final rise and Nichos applied his brakes. And there we sat in that oven of a car, looking down through its dusty, fly-specked windows on Villas Dimitrios. It was . . . idyllic!

Across the spur where we were parked, the ground dipped fairly steeply to a bay maybe a third of a mile point to point. The bay arms were rocky, formed of the tips of spurs sloping into the sea, but the beach between them was sand. *White* sand, Julie's favourite sort. Give her a book, a white beach, and a little shade, and I could swim all day. The taverna stood almost at the water's edge: a long, low house with a red-tiled roof, fronted by a wooden framework supporting heavy grapevines and masses of bougainvillaea. Hazy blue woodsmoke curled up from its chimney, and there was a garden to its rear. Behind the house, separate from it and each other and made private by screening groves of olives, three blobs of shimmering white stone were almost painful to look at. The chalets or "villas".

Nichos merely glanced at it; nothing new to him. He pointed across the tiny valley to its far side. Over there, the scree base went up brown and yellow to the foot of sheer cliffs, where beneath a jutting overhang the shadows were so dark as to be black. It had to be a cave. Something of a track had been worn into the scree, leading to the place under the cliff.

"In there," said Nichos with one of his customary shrugs, "the well. Water, him no good . . ." His face was very grave.

"The water was poisoned?" Julie prompted him.

"Eh?" he cocked his head, then gave a nod. "Now is poison!"

"I don't understand," I said. "What is it—" I indicated the dark blot under the cliff "—over there?"

"The well," he said again. "Down inside the cave. But the water, he had, er—like the crabs, you know? You understand the crabs, in the sea?"

"Of course," Julie told him. "In England we eat them."

He shook his head, looked frustrated. "Here, too," he said. "But this thing not crab. Very small." He measured an inch between thumb and forefinger. "And no eat him. Very bad! People were . . . sick. They died. Men came from the government in Athens. They bring, er, chemicals? They put in well. Poison for the crabs." Again his shrug. "Now is okay—maybe. But I say, no drink the water."

Before we could respond, he got out of the car, unloaded our luggage onto the dusty track. I followed him. "You're not taking us down?"

"Going down okay," he shrugged, this time apologetically. "Come up again—difficult! Too—how you say?" He made an incline with his hand.

"Too steep?"

"Is right. My car very nice—also very old! I sorry." I picked up the cases; Julie joined us and took the travel bags. Nichos made no attempt to help; instead, he gave a small, awkward bow, said: "You see my house? Got the problem, come speak. Good morning." Then he was into his car. He backed off, turned around, stopped, and leaned out his window. "Hey, mister, lady!"

We looked at him.

He pointed. "Follow road is long way. Go straight down, very easy. Er, how you say—short-cut? So, I go. See you in two weeks."

We watched his tyres kicking up dust and grit until he was out of sight. Then:

Taking a closer look at the terrain, I could see he was right. The track followed the ridge of the spur down to a sharp right turn, then down a hard-packed dirt ramp to the floor of the valley. It was steep, but a decent car should make it—even Nichos's taxi, I thought. But if we left the track here and climbed straight down the side of the spur, we'd cut two or three hundred yards off the distance. And actually, even the spur wasn't all that steep. We made it without any fuss, and I sat down only once when my feet shot out from under me.

As we got down onto the level, our host for the next fortnight came banging and clattering from the direction of the taverna, bumping over the rough scrub in a Greek three-wheeler with a cart at the back. Dimitrios wore a wide-brimmed hat against the sun, but still he was sweating just as badly as we were. He wiped his brow as he dumped our luggage into his open-ended cart. We hitched ourselves up at the rear and sat with our feet dangling. And he drove us to our chalet.

We were hot and sticky, all three of us, and maybe it wasn't so strange we didn't talk. Or perhaps he could see our discomfort and preferred that we get settled in before turning on the old Greek charm. Anyway, we said nothing as he opened the door for us, gave me the key, helped me carry our bags into the cool interior. I followed him back outside again while Julie got to the ritual unpacking.

"Hot," he said then. "Hot, the sun . . ." Greeks have this capacity for stating the obvious. Then, carrying it to extreme degrees, he waved an arm in the direction of the beach, the sea, and the taverna. "Beach. Sea. Taverna. For swimming. Eating. I have the food, drinks. I also selling the food for you the cooking . . ." The chalet came with its own self-catering kit.

"Fine," I smiled. "See you later."

He stared at me a moment, his eyes like dull lights in the dark shadow of his hat, then made a vague sort of motion halfway between a shrug and a nod. He got back aboard his vehicle and started her up, and as his clatter died away, I went back inside and had a look around.

Julie was filling a pair of drawers with spare clothing, at the same time building a teetering pyramid of reading material on a chair. Where books were concerned, she was voracious. She was like that about me, too. No complaints here.

Greek island accommodation varies from abominable to half decent. Or, if you're willing to shell out, you might be lucky enough to get good— but rarely better than that. The Villas Dimitrios chalets were . . . well, OK. But we'd paid for it, so it was what we expected.

I checked the plumbing first. Greek island plumbing is never better than basic. The bathroom was tastefully but totally tiled, even the ceiling! No bathtub, but a good shower and, at the other end of the small room, the toilet and washbasin. Enclosed in tiles, you could shower and let the water spray where-the-heck; if it didn't end up in the shower basin, it would end up on the floor, which sloped gently from all directions to one corner where there was a hole going—where? That's the other thing about Greek plumbing: I've never been able to figure out where everything goes.

But the bathroom did have its faults: like, there were no plugs for the washbasin and shower drainage, and no grilles in the plugholes. I suppose I'm quirky, but I like to see a grille in there, not just a black hole gurgling away to nowhere. It was the same in the little "kitchen" (an alcove under an arch, really, with a sink and drainer unit, a two-ring gas stove, a cupboard containing the cylinder, and a wall-mounted rack for crockery and cutlery; all very nice and serviceable and equipped with a concealed overhead fan-extractor): no plug in the sink and no grille in the plughole.

I complained loudly to Julie about it.

"Don't put your toe down and you won't get stuck!" was her advice from the bedroom.

"Toe down?" I was already miles away, looking for the shaver socket.

"Down the shower plughole," she answered. And she came out of the bedroom wearing sandals and the bottom half of her bikini. I made slavering noises, and she turned coyly, tossed back her bra straps for me to fasten. "Do me up."

"You were quick off the mark," I told her.

"All packed away, too," she said with some satisfaction. "And the big white hunter's kit neatly laid out for him. And all performed free of charge—while he examines plugholes!" Then she picked up a towel and tube of lotion and headed for the door. "Last one in the sea's a pervert!"

Five minutes later I followed her. She'd picked a spot halfway between the chalet and the most northerly bay arm. Her red towel was like a splash of blood on the white sand two hundred yards north of the taverna. I carried my mask, snorkel, flippers, some strong string, and a tatty old blanket with torn corners; that was all. No spear gun. First I'd take a look-see, and the serious stuff could come later. Julie obviously felt the same as I did about it: no book, just a slim, pale white body on the red towel, green eyes three-quarters shuttered behind huge sunglasses. She was still wet from the sea, but that wouldn't last long. The sun was a furnace, steaming the water off her body.

On my way to her, I'd picked up some long, thin, thorny branches from the scrub; when I got there, I broke off the thorns and fixed up a sunshade. The old blanket's torn corners showed how often we'd done this before. Then I took my kit to the water's edge and dropped it, and ran gasping, pell-mell into the shallows until I toppled over! My way of getting into the sea quickly. Following which I outfitted myself and finned for the rocks where the spur dipped below the water.

As I've intimated, the Mediterranean around the Greek islands is short on fish. You'll find red mullet on the bottom, plenty of them, but you need half a dozen to make a decent meal. And grey mullet on top, which move like lightning and cause you to use up more energy than eating them provides; great sport, but you couldn't live on it. But there's at least one fish of note in the Med, and that's the grouper.

Groupers are territorial; a family will mark out its own patch, usually in deep water where there's plenty of cover, which is to say rock or weeds. And they love caves. Where there are plenty of rocks and caves, there'll also be groupers. Here, where the spur crumbled into the sea, this was ideal grouper ground. So I wasn't surprised to see this one—especially since I didn't have my gun! Isn't that always the way of it?

He was all of twenty-four inches long, maybe seven across his back, mottled red and brown to match his cave. When he saw me, he headed straight for home, and I made a mental note to mark the spot. Next time I came out here, I'd have my gun with me, armed with a single flap-nosed spear. The spear goes into the fish, the flap opens, and he's hooked, can't slip off. Tridents are fine for small fish, but not for this bloke. And don't talk to me about cruel; if I'm cruel, so is every fisherman in the world, and at least I eat what I catch. But it was then, while I was thinking these things, that I noticed something was wrong.

The fish had homed in on his cave all right, but as his initial reaction to my presence wore off, so his spurt of speed diminished. Now he seemed merely to drift toward the dark hole in the rock, lolling from side to side like some strange, crippled sub, actually missing his target to strike *against* the weedy stone! It was the first time I'd ever seen a fish collide with something underwater. This was one very sick grouper.

I went down to have a closer look. He was maybe ten feet down, just lolling against the rock face. His huge gill flaps pulsed open and closed, open and closed. I could have reached out and touched him. Then, as he rolled a little on one side, I saw—

I backed off, felt a little sick—felt sorry for him. And I wished I had my gun with me, if only to put him out of his misery. Under his great head, wedging his gill slits half open, a nest of fish lice or parasites of some sort were plainly visible. Not lampreys or remora or the like, for they were too small, only as big as my thumbs. Crustaceans, I thought—a good dozen of them—and they were hooked into him, leeching on the raw red flesh under his gills.

God, I have a *loathing* of this sort of thing! Once in Crete I'd come out of the sea with a suckerfish in my armpit. I hadn't noticed it until I was towelling myself dry and it fell off me. It was only three or four inches long but I'd reacted like I was covered with leeches! I had that same feeling now.

Skin crawling, I drifted up and away from the stricken fish, and for the first time got a good look at his eyes. They were dull, glazed, bubbly as the eyes of fatally diseased goldfish. And they followed me. And then *he* followed me!

As I floated feet first for the surface, that damned grouper finned lethargically from the rocks and began drifting up after me. Several of his parasites had detached themselves from him and floated alongside him, gravitating like small satellites about his greater mass. I pictured one of them with its hooked feet fastened in my groin, or over one of my eyes. I mean, I knew they couldn't do that—their natural hosts are fish—but the thoughts made me feel vulnerable as hell.

I took off like Tarzan for the beach twenty-five yards away, climbed shivering out of the water in the shadow of the declining spur. As soon as I was out, the shudders left me. Along the beach my sunshade landmark was still there, flapping a little in a light breeze come up suddenly off the sea; but no red towel, no Julie. She could be swimming. Or maybe she'd felt thirsty and gone for a drink under the vines where the taverna fronted onto the sea.

Kit in hand, I padded along the sand at the dark rim of the ocean, past the old blanket tied with string to its frame of branches, all the way to the taverna. The area under the vines was maybe fifty feet along the front by thirty deep, a concrete base set out with a dozen small tables and chairs. Dimitrios was being a bit optimistic here, I thought. After all, it was the first season his place had been in the brochures. But . . . maybe next year there'd be more chalets, and the canny Greek owner was simply thinking well ahead.

I gave the place the once-over. Julie wasn't there, but at least I was able to get my first real look at our handful of fellow holiday makers.

A fat woman in a glaring yellow one-piece splashed in eighteen inches of water a few yards out. She kept calling to her husband, one George, to come on in. George sat half in, half out of the shade; he was a thin, middle-aged, balding man not much browner than myself, wearing specs about an inch thick that made his eyes look like marbles. "No, no, dear," he called back. "I'm fine watching you." He looked frail, timid, tired—and I thought: *Where the hell are marriages like this made?* They were like characters off a seaside postcard, except he didn't even seem to have the strength to ogle the girls—if there'd been any! His wife was twice his size.

George was drinking beer from a glass. A bottle, three-quarters empty and beaded with droplets of moisture, stood on his table. I fancied a drink but had no money on me. Then I saw that George was looking at me, and I felt that he'd caught me spying on him or something. "I was wondering," I said, covering up my rudeness, "if you'd seen my wife? She was on the beach there, and—"

"Gone back to your chalet," he said, sitting up a bit in his chair. "The girl with the red towel?" And suddenly he looked just a bit embarrassed. So he was an ogler after all. "Er, while you were in the sea . . . ." He took off his specs and rubbed gingerly at a large red bump on the lid of his right eye. Then he put his glasses on again, blinked at me, held out the beer bottle. "Fancy a mouthful? To wash the sea out of your throat? I've had all I want."

I took the bottle, drained it, said: "Thanks! Bite?"

"Eh?" He cocked his head on one side.

"Your eye," I said. "Mosquito, was it? Horsefly or something?"

"Dunno." He shook his head. "We got here Wednesday, and by Thursday night this was coming up. Yesterday morning it was like this. Doesn't hurt so much as irritates. There's another back of my knee, not fully in bloom yet."

"Do you have stuff to dab on?"

He nodded in the direction of his wallowing wife and sighed, "She has *gallons* of it! Useless stuff! It will just have to take its own time."

"Look, I'll see you later," I said. "Right now I have to go and see what's up with Julie." I excused myself.

Leaving the place, I nodded to a trio of spinsterish types relaxing in summer frocks at one of the tables farther back. They looked like sisters, and the one in the middle might just be a little retarded. She kept lolling first one way, then the other, while her companions propped her up. I caught a few snatches of disjointed, broad Yorkshire conversation:

"Doctor? . . . sunstroke, I reckon. Or maybe that melon? . . . taxi into town will fix her up . . . bit of shopping . . . pull her out of it . . . Kalamari?—

yechhh! Don't know what decent grub is, these foreign folks . . ." They were so wrapped up in each other, or in complaint of the one in the middle, that they scarcely noticed me at all.

On the way back to our chalet, at the back of the house/taverna, I looked across low walls and a row of exotic potted plants to see an old Greek (male or female I couldn't determine, because of the almost obligatory floppy black hat tilted forward, and flowing black peasant clothes) sitting in a cane chair in one corner of the garden. He or she sat dozing in the shade of an olive tree, chin on chest, all oblivious of the world outside the tree's sun-dappled perimeter. A pure white goat, just a kid, was tethered to the tree; it nuzzled the oldster's dangling fingers like they were teats. Julie was daft for young animals, and I'd have to tell her about it. As for the figure in the cane chair: he/she had been there when Julie and I went down to the beach. Well, getting old in this climate had to be better than doing it in some climates I could mention. . . .

I found Julie in bed, shivering for all she was worth! She was patchy red where the sun had caught her, cold to the touch but filmed with perspiration. I took one look, recognized the symptoms, said: "Oh-oh! Last night's moussaka, eh? You should have had the chicken!" Her tummy *always* fell prey to moussaka, be it good or bad. But she usually recovered quickly, too.

"Came on when I was on the beach," she said. "I left the blanket . . ."

"I saw it," I told her. "I'll go get it." I gave her a kiss.

"Just let me lie here and close my eyes for a minute or two, and I'll be okay," she mumbled. "An *hour* or two, anyway." And as I was going out the door: "Jim, this isn't Nichos's bad water, is it?"

I turned back. "Did you drink any?"

She shook her head.

"Got crabs?"

She was too poorly to laugh, so merely snorted.

I pocketed some money. "I'll get the blanket, buy some bottled drinks. You'll have something to sip. And then . . . will you be okay if I go fishing?"

She nodded. "Of course. You'll see; I'll be on my feet again tonight."

"Anyway, you should see the rest of them here," I told her. "Three old sisters, and one of 'em not all there—a little man and fat woman straight off a postcard! Oh, and I've a surprise for you."

"Oh?"

"When you're up," I smiled. I was talking about the white kid. Tonight or tomorrow morning I'd show it to her.

Feeling a bit let down—not by Julie but by circumstances in general, even by the atmosphere of this place, which was somehow odd—I collected the sunscreen blanket and poles, marched resolutely back to the taverna. Dimitrios was serving drinks to the spinsters. The "sunstruck" one had recovered a little, sipped Coke through a straw. George and his burden were nowhere to be seen. I sat down at one of the tables, and in a little while Dimitrios came over. This time I studied him more closely.

He was youngish, maybe thirty, thirty-five, tall if a little stooped. He was more swarthy peasant Greek than classical or cosmopolitan; his natural darkness, coupled with the shadow of his hat (which he wore even here in the shade), hid his face from any really close inspection. The one very noticeable thing about that face, however, was this: it didn't smile. That's something you get to expect in the islands, the flash of teeth. Even badly stained ones. But not Dimitrios's teeth.

His hands were burned brown, lean, almost scrawny. Be that as it may, I felt sure they'd be strong hands. As for his eyes: they were the sort that make you look away. I tried to stare at his face a little while, then looked away. I wasn't afraid, just concerned. But I didn't know what about.

"Drink?" he said, making it sound like "dring". "Melon? The melon he is free. I give. I grow plenty. You like him? And water? I bring half-melon and water."

He turned to go, but I stopped him. "Er, no!" I remembered the conversation of the spinsters, about the melon. "No melon, no water, thank you." I tried to smile at him, found it difficult. "I'll have a cold beer. Do you have bottled water? You know, in the big plastic bottles? And Coke? Two of each, for the refrigerator. Okay?"

He shrugged, went off. There was this lethargy about him, almost a malaise. No, I didn't much care for him at all . . .

"Swim!" the excited voice of one of the spinsters reached me. "Right along there, at the end of the beach. Like yesterday. Where there's no one to peep."

God! You'll be lucky, I thought.

"Shh!" one of her sisters hushed her, as if a crowd of rapacious men were listening to every word. "Don't tell the whole world, Betty!"

A Greek girl, Dimitrios's sister or wife, came out of the house carrying a plastic bag. She came to my table, smiled at me—a little nervously, I thought. "The water, the Coke," she said, making each definite article sound like "thee" *But at least she can speak my language,* I had to keep reminding myself. "Four hundred drachmas, please," she said. I nodded and paid up. About two pounds sterling. Cheap, considering it all had to be brought here from the mainland. The bag and the bottles inside it were tingling cold in my hand.

I stood up—and the girl was still there, barring my way. The three sisters made off down the beach, and there was no one else about. The girl glanced over her shoulder toward the house. The hand she put on my arm was trembling and now I could see that it wasn't just nervousness. She was afraid.

"Mister," she said, the word very nearly sticking in her dry throat. She swallowed and tried again. "Mister, please. I—"

"Elli!" a low voice called. In the doorway to the house, dappled by splashes of sunlight through the vines, Dimitrios.

"Yes?" I answered her. "Is there—?"

"Elli!" he called again, an unspoken warning turning the word to a growl.

"Is all right," she whispered, her pretty face suddenly thin and pale. "Is—nothing!" And then she almost ran back to the house.

Weirder and weirder! But if they had some husband-and-wife thing going, it was no business of mine. I'm no Clint Eastwood—and they're a funny lot, the Greeks, in an argument.

On my way back to the chalet, I looked again into the garden. The figure in black, head slumped on chest, sat there as before; it hadn't moved an inch. The sun had, though, and was burning more fiercely down on the drowsing figure in black. The white kid had got loose from its tether and was on its hind legs, eating amazing scarlet flowers out of their tub. "You'll get hell, mate," I muttered, "when he/she wakes up!"

There were a lot of flies about. I swatted at a cloud of the ugly, buzzing little bastards as I hurried, dripping perspiration, back to the chalet.

Inside, I took a long drink myself, then poured ice-cold water into one glass, Coke into another. I put both glasses on a bedside table within easy reach of Julie, stored the rest of the stuff in the fridge. She was asleep: bad belly complicated by a mild attack of sunstroke. I should have insisted that Nichos bring us right to the door. He could have, I was sure. Maybe he and Dimitrios had a feud or something going. But . . . Julie was sleeping peacefully enough, and the sweat was off her brow.

Someone tut-tutted, and I was surprised to find it was I. Hey!—this was supposed to be a holiday, wasn't it?

I sighed, took up my kit—including the gun—went back into the sun. On impulse I'd picked up the key. I turned it in the lock, withdrew it, stooped, and slid it under the door. She could come out, but no one could go in. If she wasn't awake when I got back, I'd simply hook the key out again with a twig.

But right now it was time for some serious fishing!

There was a lot of uneasiness building up inside me, but I put it all out of my head (what was it anyway but a set of unsettling events and queer coincidence?) and marched straight down to the sea. The beach was empty here, not a soul in sight. No, wrong: at the far end, near the foot of the

second spur, two of the sisters splashed in the shallows in faded bathing costumes twenty years out of date, while the third one sat on the sand
watching them. They were all of two or three hundred yards away, however,
so I wouldn't be accused of ogling them.

In a little while I was outfitted, in the water, heading straight out to
where the sandy bottom sloped off a little more steeply. At about eight or
nine feet, I saw an octopus in his house of shells—a big one, too, all coiled
pink tentacles and cat eyes wary—but in a little while I moved on. Normally I'd have taken him, gutted him and beaten the grease out of him,
then handed him in to the local taverna for goodwill. But on this occasion
that would be Dimitrios. Sod Dimitrios!

At about twelve feet the bottom levelled out. In all directions I saw an
even expanse of golden, gently rippled sand stretching away: beautiful but
boring. And not a fish in sight! Then . . . the silvery flash of a belly turned
side-on—no, two of them, three!—caught my eye. Not on the bottom but
on the surface. Grey mullet, and of course they'd seen me before I saw
them. I followed their darting shapes anyway, straight out to sea as before.

In a little while a reef of dark, fretted rocks came in view. It seemed fairly
extensive, ran parallel to the beach. There was some weed but not enough
to interfere with visibility. And the water still only twelve to fifteen feet
deep. Things were looking up.

If a man knows the habits of his prey, he can catch him, and I knew my
business. The grey mullet will usually run, but if you can surprise him,
startle him, he'll take cover. If no cover's available, then he just keeps on
running, and he'll very quickly outpace any man. But here in this pockmarked reef, there *was* cover. To the fish, it would seem that the holes in
the rocks were a refuge, but in fact they'd be a trap. I went after them with
a will, putting everything I'd got into the chase.

Coming up fast behind the fish, and making all the noise I could, I saw
a central school of maybe a dozen small ones, patrolled by three or four

full-grown outriders. The latter had to be two-pounders if they were an ounce. They panicked, scattered; the smaller fish shot off in all directions, and their big brothers went to ground! Exactly as I'd hoped they would. Two into one outcrop of honeycombed rock, and two into another.

I trod water on the surface, getting my breath, making sure the rubbers of my gun weren't tangled with the loose line from the spear, keeping my eyes glued to the silvery grey shapes finning nervously to and fro in the hollow rocks. I picked my target, turned on end, thrust my legs up, and let my own weight drive me to the bottom; and as my impetus slowed, so I lined up on one of the two holes. Right on cue, one of the fish appeared. He never knew what hit him.

I surfaced, freed my vibrating prize from the trident where two of the tines had taken him behind the gills, hung him from a gill ring on my belt. By now his partner had made off, but the other pair of fish was still there in the second hole. I quickly reloaded, made a repeat performance. My first hunt of the season, and already I had two fine fish! I couldn't wait to get back and show them to Julie.

I was fifty yards out. Easing the strain on muscles that were a whole year out of practice, I swam lazily back to the beach and came ashore close to the taverna. Way along the beach, two of the sisters were putting their dresses on over their ancient costumes, while the third sat on the sand with her head lolling. Other than these three, no one else was in sight.

I made for the chalet. As I went, the sun steamed the water off me and I began to itch; it was time I took a shower, and I might try a little protective after-sun lotion, too. Already my calves were turning red, and I supposed my back must be in the same condition. Ugly now, but in just a few day's time . . .

Passing the garden behind the house, this time I didn't look in. The elderly person under the tree would be gone by now, I was sure; but I did hear the lonely bleating of the kid.

Then I saw Dimitrios. He was up on the roof of the central chalet, and from where I padded silently between the olives, I could see him lifting a metal hatch on a square water tank. The roofs were also equipped with solar panels. So the sun heated the water, but . . . where did the water come from? Idiot question, even to oneself! From a well, obviously. But which well?

I passed under the cover of a clump of trees, and the Greek was lost to sight. When I came out again into the open, I saw him descending a ladder propped against the chalet's wall. He carried a large galvanized bucket—empty, to judge from its swing and bounce. He hadn't seen me, and for some hard-to-define reason, I didn't want him to. I ran the rest of the way to our chalet.

The door was open; Julie was up and about in shorts and a halter. She greeted me with a kiss, *oohed* and *aahed* at my catch. "Supper," I told her with something of pride. "No moussaka tonight. Fresh fish done over charcoal, with a little Greek salad and a filthy great bottle of retsina—or maybe two filthy great bottles!"

I cleaned the fish into the toilet, flushed their guts away. Then I washed them, tossed some ice into the sink unit, and put the fish in the ice. I didn't want them to stiffen up in the fridge, and they'd keep well enough in the sink for a couple of hours.

"Now you stink of fish," Julie told me without ceremony. "Your forearms are covered in scales. Take a shower and you'll feel great. I did."

"Are you okay?" I held her with my eyes.

"Fine now, yes," she said. "System flushed while you were out—you don't wish to know that—and now the old tum's settled down nicely, thank you. It was just the travel, the sun—"

"The moussaka?"

"That, too, probably." She sighed. "I just wish I didn't love it so!"

I stripped and stepped into the shower basin, fiddled with the knobs. "What'll you do while I shower?"

"Turn 'em both on full," she instructed. "Hot and cold both. Then the temperature's just right. Me? I'll go and sit in the shade by the sea, start a book."

"In the taverna?" Maybe there was something in the tone of my voice.

"Yes. Is that okay?"

"Fine," I told her, steeling myself and spinning the taps on. I didn't want to pass my apprehension on to her. "I'll see you there—*ahh!*—shortly." And after that, for the next ten minutes, it was hissing, stinging jets of water and blinding streams of medicated shampoo . . .

Towelling myself dry, I heard the clattering on the roof. Maintenance? Dimitrios and his galvanized bucket? I dressed quickly in lightweight flannels and a shirt, flip-flops on my feet, went out, and locked the door. Other places like this, we'd left the door open. Here I locked it. At the back of the chalet, Dimitrios was coming down his ladder. I came round the corner as he stepped down. If anything, he'd pulled his hat even lower over his eyes, so that his face was just a blot of shadow with two faint smudges of light for eyes. He was lethargic as ever, possibly even more so. We stood looking at each other.

"Trouble?" I eventually ventured.

Almost imperceptibly, he shook his head. "No troubles," he said, his voice a gurgle. "I just see all okay." He put his bucket down, wiped his hands on his trousers.

"And is it?" I took a step closer. "I mean, is it all okay?"

He nodded and at last grinned. Briefly a bar of whiteness opened in the shadow of his hat. "Now is okay," he said. And he picked up his bucket and moved off away from me.

Surly bastard! I thought. And: *What a dump! God, but we've slipped up this time, Julie, my love!*

I started toward the taverna, remembered I had no cigarettes with me, and returned to the chalet. Inside, in the cool and shade, I wondered what

Dimitrios had been putting in the water tanks. Some chemical solution, maybe? To purify or purge the system? Well, I didn't want my system purified, not by Dimitrios. I flushed the toilet again. And I left the shower running full blast for all of five minutes before spinning the taps back to the off position. I would have done the same to the sink unit, but my fish were in there, the ice almost completely melted away. And emptying another tray of ice into the sink, I snapped my fingers: *Hah!* A blow for British eccentricity!

By the time I got to the taverna, Dimitrios had disappeared, probably inside the house. He'd left his bucket standing on the garden wall. Maybe it was simple curiosity, maybe something else; I don't know—but I looked into the bucket. Empty. I began to turn away, looked again. No, not empty, but almost. Only a residue remained. At the bottom of the bucket, a thin film of . . . jelly? That's what it looked like: grey jelly.

I began to dip a finger. Hesitated, thought: *What the hell! It's nothing harmful.* It couldn't be, or he wouldn't be putting it in the water tanks. Would he? I snorted at my mind's morbid fancies. Surly was one thing, but homicidal—?

I dipped, held my finger up to the sun where that great blazing orb slipped down toward the plateau's rim. Squinting, I saw . . . just a blob of goo. Except—black dots were moving in it, like microscopic tadpoles.

Urgh! I wiped the slime off my finger onto the rough concrete of the wall. Wrong bucket, obviously, for something had gone decidedly wrong in this one. Backing uncertainly away, I heard the doleful bleating of the white kid.

Across the garden, he was chewing on the frayed end of a rope hanging from the corner of a tarpaulin where it had been thrown roughly over the chair under the olive tree. The canvas had peaked in the middle, so that it seemed someone with a pointed head was still sitting there. I stared hard, felt a tic starting up at the corner of my eye. And suddenly I knew that I didn't want to be here. I didn't want it one little bit. And I wanted Julie to be here even less.

Coming round the house to the seating area under the vines, it became noisily apparent that I wasn't the only disenchanted guest around here. An angry, booming female voice, English, seemed matched against a chattering wall of machine-gun-fire Greek. I stepped quickly in under the vines and saw Julie sitting in the shade at the ocean's edge, facing the sea. A book lay open on her table. She looked back over her shoulder, saw me, and even though she wasn't involved in the exchange, still relief flooded over her face.

I went to her, said, "What's up?" She looked past me, directing her gaze toward the rear of the seating area.

In the open door of the house, Dimitrios made a hunched silhouette, stiff as a petrified tree stump; his wife was a pale shadow behind him, in what must be the kitchen. Facing the Greek, George's wife stood with her fists on her hips, jaw jutting. "How *dare* you?" she cried, outraged at something or other. "What do you mean, you can't help? No phone? Are you actually telling me there's no telephone? Then how are we to contact civilization? I have to speak to someone in the town, find a doctor. My husband, George, *needs* a doctor! Can't you understand that? His lumps are moving. *Things are alive under his skin!*"

I heard all of this, but failed to take it in at once. George's lumps moving? Did she mean they were spreading? And still, Dimitros stood there, while his wife squalled shrilly at him (at *him*, yes, not at George's wife as I'd first thought) and tried to squeeze by him. Whatever was going on here, someone had to do something, and it looked like I was the one.

"Sit tight," I told Julie, and I walked up behind the furious fat lady. "Something's wrong with George?" I said.

All eyes turned in my direction. I still couldn't see Dimitros's face too clearly, but I sensed a sudden wariness in him. George's wife pounced on me. "Do you know George?" she said, grasping my arm. "Oh, of course! I saw you talking to him when I was in the sea."

I gently prized her sweaty, iron-band fingers from my arm. "His lumps," I pressed. "Do you mean those swollen stings of his? Are they worse?"

"Stings?" I could see now that her hysteria had brought her close to the point of tears. "Is that what they are? Well, God only knows what stung him! Some of them are opening, and there's movement in the wounds! And George just lies there, without the will to do anything. He must be in agony, but he says he can't feel a thing. There's something terribly wrong. . . ."

"Can I see him?"

"Are you a doctor?" She grabbed me again.

"No, but if I could see how bad it is—"

"—A waste of *time!*" she cut me off. "He needs a doctor now!"

"I take you to Makelos." Dimitrios had apparently snapped out of his rigor mortis mode, taken a jerky step toward us. "I take, find doctor, come back in taxi."

She turned to him. "Will you? Oh, *will* you, really? Thank you, oh, thank you! But . . . *how* will you take me?"

"Come," he said. They walked round the building to the rear, followed the wall until it ended, crossed the scrub to a clump of olives, and disappeared into the trees. I went with them part of the way, then watched them out of sight: Dimitrios stiff as a robot, never looking back, and Mrs George rumbling along massively behind him. A moment later there came the clattering and banging of an engine, and his three-wheeler bumped into view. It made for the packed-dirt incline to the road where it wound up the spur. Inside, Dimitrios at the wheel behind a flyspecked windscreen, almost squeezed into the corner of the tiny cab by the fat lady where she hunched beside him.

Julie had come up silently behind me. I gave a start when she said: "Do you think we should maybe go and see if this George is okay?"

I took a grip of myself, shrugged, said: "I was speaking to him just—oh,

387

an hour and a half ago. He can't have got really bad in so short a time, can he? A few horsefly bites, he had. Nasty enough, but you'd hardly consider them as serious as all that. She's just got herself a bit hot and bothered, that's all."

Quite suddenly, shadows reached down to us from the high brown and purple walls of the plateau. The sun had commenced to sink behind the island's central hump. In a moment it was degrees cooler, so that I found myself shivering. In that same moment the cicadas stopped their frying-fat onslaught of sound, and a strange silence fell over the whole place. On impulse, quietly, I said: "We're out of here tomorrow."

That was probably a mistake. I hadn't wanted to get Julie going. She'd been in bed most of the time; she hadn't experienced the things I had, hadn't felt so much of the strangeness here. Or maybe she had, for now she said: "Good," and gave a little shudder of her own. "I was going to suggest just that. I'm sure we can find cheap lodging in Makelos. And this place is such—I don't know—such a dead and alive hole! I mean, it's beautiful—but it's also very ugly. There's just something morbid about it."

"Listen," I said, deciding to lighten the atmosphere if I could. "I'll tell you what we'll do. You go back to the taverna, and I'll go get the fish. We'll have the Greek girl cook them for us and dish them up with a little salad—and a bottle of retsina, as we'd planned. Maybe things will look better after a bite to eat, eh? Is your tummy up to it?"

She smiled faintly in the false dusk, leaned forward, and gave me a kiss. "You know," she said, "whenever you start worrying about me—and using that tone of voice—I always know that there's something you're worrying about yourself. But actually, you know, I do feel quite hungry!"

The shadows had already reached the taverna. Just shadows—in no way night, for it wasn't properly evening yet, though certainly the contrast was a sort of darkness—and beyond them the vast expanse of the sea was blue as ever, sparkling silver at its rim in the brilliant sunlight still striking there. The strangeness of the place seemed emphasized, enlarged . . .

I watched Julie turn right and disappear into the shade of the vines, and then I went for our fish.

The real nightmare began when I let myself into the chalet and went to the sink unit. Doubly shaded, the interior really was quite dark. I put on the light in the arched-over alcove that was the kitchen, and picked up the two fish, one in each hand—and dropped them, or rather tossed them back into the sink! The ice was all melted; the live-looking glisten of the scales had disappeared with the ice, and the mullets themselves had been—infected!

Attached to the gill flap of one of them, I'd seen a parasite exactly like the ones on the big grouper; the second fish had had one of the filthy things clamped half over a filmed eye. My hair actually prickled on my head; my scalp tingled; my lips drew back from my teeth in a silent snarl. The things were something like sheep ticks, in design if not in dimension, but they were pale, blind, spiky, and hooked, infinitely more loathsome. They were only—crustaceans? Insects? I couldn't be sure—but there was that about them which made them more horrific to me than any creature has a right to be.

Anyone who believes you can't go cold, break out in gooseflesh, on a hot, late afternoon in the Mediterranean is mistaken. I went so cold I was shaking, and I kept on shaking for long moments, until it dawned on me that just a few seconds ago, I'd actually handled these fish!

Christ!

I turned on the hot tap, thrust my hands forward to receive the cleansing stream, snatched them back again. God, no! I couldn't wash them, for Dimitrios had been up there putting something in the tank! Some kind of spawn. But that didn't make sense: hot water would surely kill the things. If there was any hot water . . .

The plumbing rattled, but no hot water came. Not only had Dimitrios interfered with the water, introduced something into it, but he'd also made sure that from now we could use only the *cold* water!

I wiped my trembling hands thoroughly on sheets from a roll of paper towel, filled the kettle with water from a refrigerated bottle, quickly brought the water toward boiling. Before it became unbearable, I gritted my teeth, poured a little hot water first over one hand, then the other. It stung like hell, and the flesh of my hands went red at once, but I just hugged them and let them sting. Then, when the water was really boiling, I poured the rest of the contents of the kettle over the fish in the sink.

By that time the parasites had really dug themselves in. The one attached to the gill flap had worked its way under the gill, making it bulge; the other had dislodged its host's eye and was half-way into the skull. Worse, another had clawed its way up the plughole and was just now emerging into the light! The newcomer was white, whereas the others were now turning pink from the ingestion of fish juices.

But up from the plughole! This set me shuddering again; and again I wondered: *what's down there, down in the slop under the ground? Where does everything go?*

These fish had been clean when I caught them; I'd gutted them, and so I ought to know. But their scent had drawn these things up to the feast. Would the scent of human flesh attract them the same way?

As the boiling water hit them, the things popped like crabs tossed into a cooking pot. They seemed to hiss and scream, but it was just the rapid expansion and explosion of their tissues. And the stench that rose up from the sink was nauseating. God!—would I ever eat fish again?

And the thought kept repeating over and over in my head: what was down below?

I went to the shower recess, put on the light, looked in, and at once shrank back. The sunken bowl of the shower was crawling with them! Two, three dozen of them at least. And the toilet? And the cold-water system? And all the rest of the bloody plumbing? There'd be a cesspit down there, and these things were alive in it in their thousands! And the maniac Dimitrios had been putting their eggs in the water tanks!

But what about the spinsters? They had been here before us, probably for the past three or four days at least. And what about George? George and his lumps! And Julie: she wouldn't have ordered anything yet, would she! She wouldn't have *eaten* anything!

I left the door of the chalet slamming behind me, raced for the taverna.

The sun was well down now, with the bulk of the central mountain throwing all of the eastern coastline into shadow; halfway to the horizon, way out to sea, the sun's light was a line ruled across the ocean, beyond which silver-flecked blueness seemed to reach up to the sky. And moment by moment the ruled line of deeper blue flowed eastward as the unseen sun dipped even lower. On the other side of the island, the west coast, it would still be sweltering hot, but here it was already noticeably cooler. Or maybe it was just my blood.

As I drew level with the garden at the back of the house, something came flopping over the wall at me. I hadn't been looking in that direction or I'd have seen her: Julie, panic-stricken, her face a white mask of horror. She'd seemed to fly over the wall—jumped or simply bundled herself over I couldn't say—and came hurtling into my arms. Nor had she seen me, and she fought with me a moment when I held her. Then we both caught our breath, or at least I did. Julie had a harder time of it. Even though I'd never heard her scream before, there was one building up in her, and I knew it.

I shook her, which served to shake me a little, too, then hugged her close. "What were you doing in the garden?" I asked, when she'd started to breathe again. I spoke in a whisper, and that was how she answered me, but drawing breath raggedly between each burst of words:

"The little goat . . . he was bleating . . . so pitifully . . . frightened! I heard him . . . went to see . . . got in through a gate on the other side." She paused and took a deep breath. "Oh *God*, Jim!"

I knew without asking. A picture of the slumped figure in the chair, under the olive tree, had flashed momentarily on my mind's eye. But I asked anyway: "The tarpaulin?"

She nodded, gulped. "Something had to be dead under there. I had no idea it would be a . . . a . . . a man!"

"English?" That was a stupid question, so I tried again: "I mean, did he look like a tourist, a holiday maker?"

She shook her head. "An old Greek, I think. But there are—*ugh!*—these things all over him. Like . . . like—"

"Like crabs?"

She drew back from me, her eyes wide, terror replaced by astonishment. "How did you know that?"

Quickly, I related all I knew. As I was finishing, her hand flew to her mouth. "Dimitrios? Putting their eggs in the tanks? But Jim, we've taken showers—both of us!"

"Calm down," I told her. "We had our showers *before* I saw him up there. And we haven't eaten here, or drunk any of the water."

"Eaten?" her eyes opened wider still. "But if I hadn't heard the kid bleating, I might have eaten!"

"What?"

She nodded. "I ordered wine and . . . some melon. I thought we'd have it before the fish. But the Greek girl dropped it, and—"

She was rapidly becoming incoherent. I grabbed her again, held her tightly. "Dropped it? You mean she dropped the food?"

"She dropped the melon, yes." She nodded jerkily. "The bottle of wine, too. She came out of the kitchen and just let everything drop. It all smashed on the floor. And she stood there wringing her hands for a moment. Then she ran off. She was crying: "Oh Dimitrios, Dimitrios!""

"I think he's crazy," I told her. "He has to be. And his wife—or sister, or whatever she is—she's scared to death of him. You say she ran off? Which way?"

"Toward the town, the way we came. I saw her climbing the spur."

I hazarded a guess: "He's pushed her to the edge, and she's slipped over. Come on, let's go and have a look at Dimitrios's kitchen."

We went to the front of the building, to the kitchen door. There on the floor by one of the tables, I saw a broken wine bottle, its dark red contents spilled. Also a half-melon, lying in several softly jagged chunks. And in the melon, crawling in its scattered seeds and pulp red juices—

"Where are the others?" I said, wanting to speak first before Julie could cry out, trying to forestall her.

"Others?" she whispered. She hadn't really heard me, hadn't even been listening; she was concentrating on backing away from the half-dozen crawling things that moved blindly on the floor.

I stamped on them, crushed them in a frenzy of loathing, then scuffed the soles of my flip-flops on the dusty concrete floor as if I'd stepped in something nasty—which is one hell of an understatement. "The other people," I said. "The three sisters and . . . and George." I was talking more to myself than to Julie, and my voice was hoarse.

My fear transferred itself instantly. "Oh Jim, Jim!" she cried. She threw herself into my arms, shivering as if in a fever. And I felt utterly useless—no, defenceless—a sensation I'd occasionally known in deep water, without my gun, when the shadow of a rock might suddenly take on the aspect of a great, menacing fish.

Then there came one of the most dreadful sounds I've ever heard in my life: the banging and clattering of Dimitrios's three-wheeler on the road cut into the spur, echoing down to us from the rocks of the mountainside. "My spear gun," I said. "Come on, quickly!"

She followed at arm's length, half running, half dragged. "We're too vulnerable," I gasped as we reached the chalet. "Put clothes on, anything. Cover up your skin."

"What?" She was still dazed. "What?"

"*Cover yourself!*" I snapped. Then I regained control. "Look, he tried to give us these things. He gave them to George, and to the sisters for all I know. And he may try again. Do you want one of those things on your flesh, maybe laying its eggs in you?"

She emptied a drawer onto the floor, found slacks, and pulled them on; good shoes, too, to cover her feet. I did much the same: pulled on a long-sleeved pullover, rammed my feet into decent shoes. And all in a sort of frenzied blur, fingers all thumbs, heart thumping. And: "*Oh shit!*" she sobbed. Which wasn't really my Julie at all.

"Eh?" She was heading for the small room at the back.

"Toilet!" she said. "I have to."

"*No!*" I jumped across the space between, dragged her away from the door to the toilet-*cum*-shower unit. "It's crawling with them in there. They come up the plugholes." In my arms, I could feel that she was also crawling. Her flesh. Mine, too. "If you must go, go outside. But first let's get away from here." I picked up my gun, loaded it with a single flap-nosed spear.

Leaving the chalet, I looked across at the ramp coming down from the rocky spur. The clatter of Dimitrios's three-wheeler was louder, it was there, headlight beams bobbing as the vehicle trundled lurchingly down the rough decline. "Where are we going?" Julie gasped, following me at a run across the scrub between clumps of olives. I headed for the other chalets.

"Safety in numbers," I answered. "Anyway, I want to know about George, and those three old spinsters."

"What good will they be, if they're old?" She was too logical by half.

"They're not that old." Mainly, I wanted to see if they were all right. Apart from the near-distant racket Dimitrios's vehicle was making, the whole valley was quiet as a tomb. Unnaturally quiet. It had to be a damned funny place in Greece where the cicadas keep their mouths shut.

Julie had noticed that, too. "They're not singing," she said. And I knew what she meant.

"Rubbing," I answered. "They rub their legs together or something."

"Well," she panted, "whatever it is they do, they're not."

It was true evening now, and a half-moon had come up over the central mountain's southern extreme. Its light silvered our way through thorny shrubs and tall, spiked grasses, under the low grey branches of olives and across their tangled, groping roots.

We came to the first chalet. Its lights were out, but the door stood ajar. "I think this is where George is staying," I said. And calling ahead: "George, are you in?", I entered and switched on the light. He was in—in the big double bed, stretched out on his back. But he turned his head toward us as we entered. He blinked in the sudden, painful light. One of his eyes did, anyway. The other couldn't. . . .

He stirred himself, tried to sit up. I think he was grinning. I can't be sure, because one of the things, a big one, was inside the corner of his mouth. They were hatching from fresh lumps down his neck and in the bend of his elbow. God knows what the rest of his body was like. He managed to prop himself up, hold out a hand to me—and I almost took it. And it was then that I began to understand something of the nature of these things. For there was one of them in his open palm, its barbed feet seeming poised, waiting.

I snatched back my hand, heard Julie's gasp. And there she was, backed up against the wall, screaming her silent scream. I grabbed her, hugged her, dragged her outside. For of course there was nothing we could do for George. And, afraid she would scream, and maybe start *me* going, I slapped her. And off we went again, reeling in the direction of the third and last chalet.

Down by the taverna, Dimitrios's three-wheeler had come to a halt, its engine stilled, its beams dim, reaching like pallid hands along the sand. But I didn't think it would be long before he was on the move again. And the nightmare was expanding, growing vaster with every beat of my thundering heart.

In the third chalet . . . it's hard to describe all I saw. Maybe there's no real need. The spinster I'd thought was maybe missing something was in much the same state as George; she, too, was in bed, with those god-awful things hatching in her. Her sisters . . . at first I thought they were both dead, and . . . But there, I've gone ahead of myself. That's how it always happens when I think about it, try to reconstruct it again in my own mind: it speeds up until I've outstripped myself. You have to understand that the whole thing was kaleidoscopic.

I went inside ahead of Julie, got a quick glimpse, an indistinct picture of the state of things fixed in my brain—then turned and kept Julie from coming in. "Watch for him." I forced the words around my bobbing Adam's apple and returned to take another look. I didn't want to, but I thought the more we knew about this monster, the better we'd know how to deal with him. Except that in a little while, I guessed there would be only one possible way to deal with him.

The sister in the bed moved and lolled her head a little; I was wary, suspicious of her, and left her strictly alone. The other two had been attacked. With an axe or a machete or something. One of them lay behind the door, the other on the floor on the near side of the bed. The one behind the door had been sliced twice, deeply, across the neck and chest and lay in a pool of her own blood, which was already congealing. Tick-things, coming from the bathroom, had got themselves stuck in the darkening pool, their barbed legs twitching when they tried to extricate themselves. The other sister. . . .

Senses swimming, throat bobbing, I stepped closer to the bed with its grimacing, hag-ridden occupant, and I bent over the one on the floor. She was still alive, barely. Her green dress was a sodden red under the rib cage, torn open in a jagged flap to reveal her gaping wound. And Dimitrios had dropped several of his damned pets onto her, which were burrowing in the raw, dark flesh.

She saw me through eyes already filming over, whispered something. I got down on one knee beside her, wanted to hold her hand, stroke her hair, do something. But I couldn't. I didn't want those bloody things on me. "It's all right," I said. "It's all right." But we both knew it wasn't.

"The . . . the Greek," she said, her voice so small I could scarcely hear it.

"I know, I know," I told her.

"We wanted to . . . to take Flo into town. She was . . . was so *ill!* He said to wait here. We waited, and . . . and . . . ." She gave a deep sigh. Her eyes rolled up, and her mouth fell open.

Something touched my shoulder where I knelt, and I leapt erect, flesh tingling. The one on the bed, Flo, had flopped an arm in my direction—deliberately! Her hand had touched me. Crawling slowly down her arm, a trio of the nightmare ticks or crabs had been making for me. They'd been homing in on me like a bee targeting a flower. But more slowly, thank God, far more slowly.

Horror froze me rigid; but in the next moment, Julie's sobbing cry—"Jim, he's coming!"—unfroze me at once.

I staggered outside. A dim, slender, dark and reeling shape was making its way along the rough track between the chalets. Something glinted dully in his hand. Terror galvanized me. "Head for the high ground," I said. I took Julie's hand, began to run.

"High ground?" she panted. "Why?" She was holding together pretty well. I thanked God I hadn't let her see inside the chalet.

"Because then we'll have the advantage. He'll have to come up at us. Maybe I can roll rocks down on him or something."

"You have your gun," she said.

"As a last resort," I told her, "yes. But this isn't a John Wayne Western, Julie. This is real! Shooting a man isn't the same as shooting a fish . . ." And we scrambled across the rough scrubland toward the goat track up the far spur. Maybe ten minutes later and halfway up that track, suddenly it dawned on both of us just where we were heading. Julie dug in her heels and dragged me to a halt.

"But the cave's up there!" she panted. "The well!"

I looked all about. The light was difficult, made everything seem vague and unreal. Dusk is the same the world over: it confuses shapes, distances, colours and textures. On our right, scree rising steeply all the way to the plateau: too dangerous by far. And on our left a steep, in places sheer, decline to the valley's floor. All you had to do was stumble once, and you wouldn't stop sliding and tumbling and bouncing till you hit the bottom. Up ahead the track was moon-silvered, to the place where the cliff over-hung, where the shadows were black and blacker than night. And behind . . . behind us came Dimitrios, his presence made clear by the sound his boots made shoving rocks and pebbles out of his way.

"Come on," I said, starting on up again.

"But where to?" Hysteria was in her whisper.

"That clump of rocks there." Ahead, on the right, weathered out of the scree, a row of long boulders like leaning graveyard slabs tilted at the moon. I got between two of them, pulled Julie off the track, and jammed her behind me. It was last-ditch stuff; there was no way out other than the way we'd come in. I loaded my gun, hauling on the propulsive rubbers until the spear was engaged. And then there was nothing else to do but wait.

"Now be quiet," I hissed, crouching down. "He may not see us, go straight on by."

Across the little valley, headlights blazed. Then came the echoing roar of revving engines. A moment more, and I could identify humped silhouettes making their way like beetles down the ridge of the far spur toward the indigo sea, then slicing the gloom with scythes of light as they turned onto the dirt ramp. Two cars and a motorcycle. Down on the valley's floor, they raced for the taverna.

Dimitrios came struggling out of the dusk, up out of the darkness, his breathing loud, laboured, gasping as he climbed in our tracks. His silhou-ette where he paused for breath was scarecrow-lean, and he'd lost his floppy, wide-brimmed hat. But I suspected a strength in him that wasn't entirely his own. From where she peered over my shoulder Julie had spotted him, too. I heard her sharp intake of breath, breathed, *"Shh!"* so faintly I wasn't even sure she'd hear me.

He came on, the thin moonlight turning his eyes yellow, and turning his machete silver. Level with the boulders he drew, and almost level with our hiding place, and paused again. He looked this way and that, cocked his head, and listened. Behind me, Julie was trembling. She trembled so hard I was sure it was coming right through me, through the rocks, too, and the earth, and right through the soles of his boots to Dimitrios.

He took another two paces up the track, came level with us. Now he stood out against the sea and the sky, where the first pale stars were beginning to switch themselves on. He stood there, looking up the slope toward the cave under the cliff, and small, dark silhouettes were falling from the large blot of his head. Not droplets of sweat, no, for they were far too big, and too brittle-sounding where they landed on the loose scree.

Again Julie snatched a breath, and Dimitrios's head slowly came round until he seemed to be staring right at us.

Down in the valley the cars and the motorcycle were on the move again, engines revving, headlight beams slashing here and there. There was some shouting. Lights began to blaze in the taverna, the chalets. Flashlights cut narrow searchlights swaths in the darkness.

Dimitrios seemed oblivious to all this; still looking in our direction, he scratched at himself under his right armpit. His action rapidly became frantic, until with a soft, gurgling cry, he tore open his shirt. He let his machete fall clatteringly to the track and clawed wildly at himself with both hands! He was shedding tick-things as a dog sheds fleas. He tore open his trousers, dropped them, staggered as he stepped out of them. Agonized sulphur eyes burned yellow in his blot of a face as he tore at his thighs.

I saw all of this, every slightest action. And so did Julie. I felt her swell up behind me, scooping in air until she must surely burst—and then she let it out again. But silently, screaming like a maniac in the night—and nothing but air escaping her!

A rock slid away from under my foot, its scrape a deafening clatter to my petrified mind. The sound froze Dimitrios, too—but only for a moment. Then he stooped, regained his machete. He took a pace toward us, inclined his head. He couldn't see us yet, but he knew we were there. Then—*God*, I shall dream of this for the rest of my life!—

He reached down a hand and stripped a handful of living, crawling filth from his loins, and lobbed it in our direction as casually as tossing crumbs to starveling birds!

The next five seconds were madness.

I stumbled out from cover, lifted my gun, and triggered it. The spear struck him just below the rib cage, went deep into him. He cried out, reeled back, and yanked the gun from my hand. I'd forgotten to unfasten the nylon cord from the spear. Behind me, Julie was crumpling to the ground; I was aware of the latter, turned to grab her before she could sprawl. There were tick-things crawling about, and I mustn't let her fall on them.

I got her over my shoulder in a fireman's lift, went charging out onto the track, skipping and stamping my feet, roaring like a maddened bull. And I was mad: mad with shock, terror, loathing. I stamped and kicked and danced, never letting my feet stay in one place for more than a fraction of a second, afraid something would climb up onto me. And the wonder is I didn't carry both of us flying down the steep scree slope to the valley's floor.

Dimitrios was halfway down the track when finally I got myself under a semblance of control. Bouncing toward our end of the valley, a car came crunching and lurching across the scrub. I fancied it was Nichos's taxi. And sure enough, when the car stopped and its headlight beams were still, Nichos's voice came echoing up, full of concerned enquiry:

"Mister, lady—you okay?"

"Look out!" I shouted at the top of my voice, but only at the second attempt. "He's coming down! Dimitrios is coming down!"

And now I went more carefully, as in my mind the danger receded, and in my veins the adrenalin raced less rapidly. Julie moaned where she flopped loosely across my shoulder, and I knew she'd be all right.

The valley seemed alight with torches now, and not only the electric sort. Considering these people were Greeks, they seemed remarkably well organized. That was a thought I'd keep in mind, something else I would have to ask about. There was some shouting down there, too, and flaring torches began to converge on the area at the foot of the goat track.

Then there echoed up to me a weird, gurgled cry: a cry of fear, protestation—relief? A haunting, sobbing shriek—cut off at highest pitch by the dull boom of a shot fired, and a moment later by a blast that was the twin of the first. From twin barrels, no doubt.

When I got down, Julie was still out of it, for which I was glad. They'd poured gasoline over Dimitrios's body and set fire to it. Fires were burning everywhere: the chalets, taverna, gardens. Cleansing flames leaping. Figures moved in the smoke and against a yellow roaring background, searching, burning. And I sat in the back of Nichos's taxi, cradling Julie's head. Mercifully, she remained unconscious right through it.

Even with the windows rolled up, I could smell something of the smoke, and something that wasn't smoke . . .

In Makelos town, Julie began to stir, I asked for her to be sedated, kept down for the night. Then, when she was sleeping soundly and safely in a room at the mayor's house, I began asking questions. I was furious at the beginning, growing more furious as I started to get the answers.

I couldn't be sorry for the people of Makelos, though I did feel something for Elli, Dimitrios's wife. She'd run to Nichos, told him what was happening. And he'd alerted the townspeople. Elli had been a sort of prisoner at the taverna for the past ten days or so, after her husband had "gone funny". Then, when she'd started to notice things, he'd told her to keep quiet and carry on as normal, or she'd be the loser. And he meant she'd lose all the way. She reckoned he'd got the parasites off the goats, accidentally, and she was probably right, for the goats had been the first to die. Her explanation was likely because the goats used to go up there sometimes, to the cave under the mountain. And that was where the things bred, in that cave and in the well it contained, which now and then overflowed, and found its way to the sea.

But Elli, poor peasant that she was: on her way to alert Nichos, she'd seen her husband kill George's wife and push her over the cliffs into the sea. Then she'd hid herself off the road until he'd turned his three-wheeler round and started back toward the taverna.

As for the corpse under the tarpaulin: that was Dimitrios's grandfather, who along with his grandson had been a survivor of the first outbreak. He'd been lucky that time, not so lucky this time.

And the tick-things? They were . . . a *disease,* but they could never be a plague. The men from Athens had taken some of them away with them that first time. But away from their well, away from the little shaded valley and from Makelos, they'd quickly died. This was their place, and they could exist nowhere else. Thank God!

Last time the chemicals hadn't killed them off, obviously, or maybe a handful of eggs had survived to hatch out when the poisons had dissolved away. For they *were* survivors, these creatures, the last of their species, and when they went, their secret would go with them. But a disease? I believe so, yes.

Like the common cold, or rabies, or any other disease, but far worse because they're visible, apparent. The common cold makes you sneeze, so that the disease is propagated, and hydrophobia makes it victims claw and bite, gets passed on in their saliva. The secret of the tick-things was much the same sort of thing: they made their hosts pass them on. It was the way their intelligent human hosts did it that made them so much more terrible.

In the last outbreak, only Greeks—Makelosians—had been involved; this time it was different. This time, too, the people would take care of the problem themselves: they'd pour hundreds of gallons of gasoline and fuel oil into the well, set the place on fire. And then they'd dynamite the cliff, bring it down to choke the well for ever, and they'd never, *ever,* let people go into that little valley again. That was their promise, but I'd made myself a couple of promises, too. I was angry and frightened, and I knew I was going to stay that way for a long time to come.

We were out of there first thing in the morning, on the first boat to the mainland. There were smart-looking men to meet us at the airport in Athens, Greek officials from some ministry or other. They had interpreters with them, and nothing was too much trouble. They, too, made promises, offers of compensation, anything our hearts desired. We nodded and smiled wearily, said yes to this, that, and the other, anything so that we could just get aboard that plane. It had been our shortest holiday ever: we'd been in Greece just forty-eight hours, and all we wanted now was to be out of it as quickly as possible. But when we were back home again—*that* was when we told our story!

It was played down, of course: the Common Market, international tensions, a thousand other economic and diplomatic reasons. Which is why I'm now telling it all over again. I don't want anybody to suffer what we went through, what we're still going through. And so if you happen to be mad on the Mediterranean islands . . . well, I'm sorry, but that's the way it was.

As for Julie and me: we've moved away from the sea, and come summer, we won't be going out in the sun too much or for too long. That helps a little. But every now and then, I'll wake up in the night, in a cold sweat, and find Julie doing her horrible thing: nightmaring about Dimitrios, hiding from him, holding her breath so that he won't hear her—

—And sometimes screaming her silent screams . . .

BEING RIGHT

Michael Marshall Smith

*Michael Marshall Smith is a winner of the Philip K. Dick, August Der-
leth, British Fantasy, and International Horror Guild awards for his
horror and science fiction stories, and he was a Guest of Honor at the
World Horror Convention 2007 in Toronto, Canada.*

He is also the author of the internationally best-selling Straw Men
thriller trilogy, under the name "Michael Marshall". A new novel, The
Intruders, *is to be published in 2007. He is currently writer/producer on
a feature adaptation of one of his own short stories, and working on his
eighth novel. He lives in London with his wife, son, and two cats.*

*"The odd thing about this story is that, although it's about a couple
on vacation, it's set in the city where I live," observes Smith. "Something
I love about going on holiday to cities is the feeling of being at a skewed
angle to the locals, walking the same streets, and inhabiting the same
spaces, while having a totally different relationship to them: like being a
ghost, or being surrounded by them.*

*"Also that cities, however much they may tout their attractions, were
never designed to be tourist destinations. They grew up for other reasons,
and have a hidden life of their own. I always wonder what's happening
there in the cracks, what things and places a resident like myself may
never chance upon. . . ."*

For a discontented husband, a divine encounter in London changes everything. . . .

I t was monday, the fourth day of their vacation, and the fourth solid day of rain. That didn't bother Dan unduly—you didn't come to London, London in February, moreover, if you were looking to work on your tan. The city was full of museums, galleries, stores. It had history up the wazzoo and nearly as many Starbucks as at home. If you could bear to get a little damp in between stops, there was a good time to be had whatever the weather. The forecast—which Dan knew all about, having been woken by it at five-thirty that morning—said it was going to get better as the week went on. Either way, the weather was something you couldn't do anything about. It was simply there. You had to just accept it, change your plans accordingly, move on. There was no point complaining.

No point going on and on and *on*.

What you *could* affect, of course, was jetlag. If you were flying to Europe—which they had done many times since the kids left home—there was a simple procedure to follow. You were going to land in the early morning, so it made sense to catch some sleep on the plane. From the minute you arrived you locked yourself mentally to the new time, and you stayed awake until you would normally at home. That way your body got itself into some new kind of understanding, and you were so bushed by the time it came to turn in that you'd sleep regardless. Might be a couple of days where you felt draggy late afternoon, but otherwise you'd be okay.

This is what Dan had done. This is what he always did. Marcia, she did it different.

Despite the fact they'd discussed it, she stayed awake the whole flight. Said she'd found it impossible to sleep, though Dan had managed to catch an hour or two—not much, but enough to make a difference, to con the body into believing it had been through a night. Then when they'd gotten to the hotel just before lunch, she'd started yawning, muttering about a nap. Dan told her to keep going—but mid-afternoon still found her spark out on the bed. Dan left her there and went for a stroll around the surrounding blocks. Sure, he felt a little spacey and weird, but he kind of enjoyed the feeling, and the walk. It served as a first recon of the neighbourhood, informing him where the cafés where, the nearest bookstore, all of that. It reminded you too that you'd done a strange thing, travelled a long way, and that you weren't at home any more. For Dan, this walk was the opening ceremony of the vacation.

When he got back to the hotel, Marcia was in the shower. They went out, had another little walk, and then dinner in the nearest restaurant. By ten o'clock Dan was utterly beat, and ready for bed. Marcia was speeding by now, however, and wanted to talk up the issues around Proposition 7, the *cause de jour* back home in Oregon. Dan hadn't much cared about P7 when on his own turf (it was going to be defeated, which was a shame, but that's what people are like), and sure as hell didn't care about it now. What was the point of coming to another country if you were going to mire yourself in the same old crap?

When he eventually said this, yawning massively, Marcia led the discussion into a playful analysis of why he was apparently unable to enter into any kind of intellectual dialogue that wasn't about books, and then deftly turned back to Proposition 7. This lasted a further twenty-five minutes. When Dan finally said he was just going to have to go to bed, she shook her head and stood up. First evening of the holiday ruined, her body language said: thank you once again, my brutish husband.

Dan slept like a baby that night. Marcia, not so well.

They spent the next couple of days getting some tourism done, seeing the big sights, ticking them off the list. Dan was happy to do this, knowing they'd relax by the weekend, be able to kick back and do their own thing.

By Saturday he was locked on GMT, the late-afternoon slump nothing an extra-shot latté couldn't shake off. Marcia meanwhile was getting further and further out of sync. She was waking at six, five, four: sitting up in bed reading (and reading a novel set in America, naturally, or else one of the magazines she'd brought from home); alternatively, as on the Monday morning, turning the television on—quietly, of course, but you could still hear the tube crackle—and obsessing about the rain.

The real problem wasn't the jetlag, annoying though it was when it could been avoided. Dan could sympathise with jetlag. Not sleeping, it's no fun. You lie there on your back staring up at an unfamiliar ceiling and your brain goes round and round and round. The problem was the *mentioning* of it, the endless fricking . . . It was the same when Marcia had a cold. Dan got a cold, he took some tablets, waited for it to go away. He'd snuffle and wheeze a little, but that was physical. You couldn't do anything about that. With Dan, a cold lasted four days, tops, soup to nuts. With Marcia it was a two week miniseries, an HBO big season event. The first signs would be noted, discussed, held up for scrutiny. The danger of an approaching malaise would be flagged, and the particular inconvenience of its timing loudly mourned. Nine times out of ten this phase would last a single evening—and then the symptoms would disappear for good, having never been anything more than two sneezes, or a mild headache. But sometimes the cold would arrive for real—and she would wander down the next morning wrapped in a blanket, face crumpled, nose red, hair mad as you like. And then, for at least a week, the *mentioning of it*. The constant updates—as if, twenty times a day, he'd said to her "Now, darling, tell me *exactly* how every single little bit of your body feels, and don't stint on the detail." The sinus report. The lower back state-of-play. The throat film-at-eleven—but first here's a message from our sponsor, Runny Noses R Us.

The cold would go away, eventually. Two days of noting its passing, and she'd be fine—would return, in fact, to the woman who said she never got colds, not ever. That's when Dan knew he was in trouble. Ten days of reduced conversation would mean she was full up to the brim with observations of pith and moment, stuff that simply *had* to get out of her head before it popped. Any chat, no matter how formerly relaxed, could get suddenly derailed into a long discussion of the major or minor issues of the day/year/century, with Marcia being firm but fair, subtle but strident, as if performing to a sizeable radio audience. His participation was allowed once in a while, as a foil, a sentence thrown in as by an interviewer. Other than that, she'd just roll. Any suggestion that the length and depth of discussion was inappropriate to a dinner out at a local restaurant, to Sunday breakfast, or when he was trying to have a quiet bath, would be met with the masterfully oblique suggestion that he just hadn't thought about the issues enough, and that he'd had his say and it was her turn now.

Followed by more discussion.

It was on one of these occasions, a romantic supper that had turned into a two-hour debate on their town's zoning regulations, that Dan had first fantasised about the possibility of some kind of independent adjudication. The idea that there might be some agency to which he could appeal, not with ill-will, but just so he could be proved right—so that it could be established, once and for all, that she hogged discussions, cheated in arguments, and got mini-colds once a month. He loved his wife and wouldn't want her any different. But just once in a while he wished there were some way of proving *he was right*.

No-one was more surprised than him to find out that actually, there was.

The bookstore was in a side street halfway down Charring Cross Road. When they'd last been to London, back in the early 1990s, the area had been wall-to-wall books. Like everywhere else in the world, it was now feeling the dual pinch of the megastores and on-line auction sites. The speciality shops were still in place, but the second-hand and antiquarian had closed or gone to seed. Having left Marcia back at the hotel in the health spa for the morning, Dan was mildly ticked to find he'd done the street with an hour-and-a-half to spare. He didn't want to go back early, kick his heels in the hotel. Marcia had been her most jetlagged yet that morning, and very down about the weather. He'd been unsympathetic on two subjects he considered himself powerless over, and words had been spoken.

On a whim, he started poking around the uncharted streets just behind the main road, and it was here he found Pandora's Books. A little wooden shop front, the name appropriately picked out in faded gold paint. The window was littered with a random selection of ancient-looking volumes, none of which he'd heard of. Perfect. Especially as it was beginning to drizzle. Again.

The smell made him smile as soon as he was inside. Old, forgotten paper, paper foxed and creased and bumped. The scent of old bookcases and venerable dust added their own welcome notes. It was the way these places should smell, the smell of peace and quiet and your own thoughts. The room wasn't too big—probably only twenty feet by fifteen—but the high shelves packed into it, along with the dim light, made it seem larger. In the back there were wooden staircases leading up and down, neither marked PRIVATE, promising more of the same. There was a little desk over on the right, piled high with books waiting categorisation, but nobody in sight. Dan dithered, then propped his bag against the desk. Usually bookstores preferred it that way, and it would leave both hands free.

He worked his way down from the top. They had a whole lot of books, that was for sure. Most of the stuff on the upper level was modern and of no interest, though he did find a pulp paperback worth keeping in his hand. He thought he heard someone coming up the stairs while he turned this book over, debating the couple of pounds, but when he looked up no-one was there. By the time he got back to street level they'd evidently gone down to the basement.

He took his time around these shelves, as many were dedicated to local history. In the end he found one thing he thought was a definite, plus a couple of maybes. Depended on whether they shipped. The book he wanted was heavy—a vast Victorian facsimile of an older history of London—and he went over to prop it up against his bag. As he did so he thought he heard someone coming into the room from the back, but when he turned there was no-one. Evidently just a noise from upstairs. Booksellers creep in mysterious ways, their alphabetising to perform.

It was in the basement that he found the book.

At first he thought there was nothing for him down there: the room was only half the size of those on the higher floors, and had none of their sense of order. Tomes of all ages and conditions were piled onto cases in danger of imminent collapse. There was a strong smell of damp too, doubtless caused or at least enhanced by the grim-looking patches on the walls. The plaster had come away in many places, revealing seeping brickwork behind. He poked around for a while, shoving aside piles of bashed-up book-length ephemera (do your own accounts, learn Spanish in twenty seconds, find your inner you and dream your inner dream), finding and rejecting a few older tomes.

He was about to give up and go pay for what he'd already put aside, when a bookcase right at the end caught his eye. He went and had a look. There was no hurry, after all.

He'd thought these books were much older than the rest, but he soon saw they were not. Most were Everyman Editions, leather-bound and quite attractive, but not worth the carrying. He had already turned away when something made him turn back and look again. He stood square onto the case and ran his eyes over it. He'd evidently glimpsed something without really seeing it. He wasn't expecting much, but it would be mildly interesting to see what had caught his eye.

Eventually he found it, a book whose spine was much more scuffed up than the rest. He gently eased it out. It was called *Hopes of a Lesser Demon, Part II,* which was odd, for a start. It was a small, chunky thing with battered boards and old leather covers; about an inch thick, six high, and four deep. The title on the spine seemed to have been hand-written in ink. When Dan turned to the front the indicia claimed the book had been published in Rome in 1641, but that couldn't be right. For a start, it should have been in Latin, or Italian at the very least. It wasn't. It was in English, for the most part.

As he leafed through the book it also seemed clear that it could never have been published in this form at all. Chunks of it did look old, the paper spotted and towelly, the text in languages he didn't understand and typefaces that were hard to read. Others had been printed far more recently; the paper fresh and glossy, the subjects contemporary. Though there were sections in French and German—and something he guessed was Korean from its similarity to the signs on a food market he sometimes walked by back home.

It was also far from clear what the book was *about.*

There was a sermon on chastity, a few pages on deciduous trees. Part seemed to be a travel guide to Bavaria, with spotty black and white plates that must have been taken before the First World War. A polemic on some obscure Middle-Eastern sect was followed by a stretch of love poetry, and proceeded by two hand-written pages of what looked like the accounts of a sugar plantation in the eighteenth century. There was no sense to it whatsoever, and yet at the bottom of each page was a folio—a page number—and the ordering of these numerals was consistent from front to back, regardless of subject change or whether they were printed in decaying hand-plated Gothic type or super-crisp computer-generated Gill Sans.

Dan flipped back to the front, and saw a price written there in pencil. Five pounds. Eight-nine bucks. Hmm. He already wanted the book, without really knowing why.

He glanced through the pages a little further, looking for an excuse,

finding further pockets of unrelated non-information. A handful of reproductions of watercolours, none by artists he recognised, and few of them
any good. A list of popular meadows in Armenia. A section on electronic
engineering, a Da Vinci-like ink sketch of a man holding an axe, and then
a long portion of an illustrated children's book, about a happy dog.

And then there were the invocations.

The paper of this section was very, very old, and the writing had been
entered by hand. Portions had faded back to nothing, and those that were
strong weren't very easy to read. The first page seemed to be a kind of index.

Item one read: *The Vision of Love's Arc invocation—for to glimpse what
man or woman (or both) shall when come into your life, hopefully.*

Item eleven: *The Sadness of Cattle invocation—the purpose being to make
less gloomy your livestock in the night.*

Item twenty-two: *The Regeneration of Heat invocation—a most useful gesture for the revitalisation of a time-soured hot beverage.*

What? A spell to warm up a cup of coffee? That was silly. The whole
index was dumb, in fact, the most stupid section of what was evidently a
very stupid book. Dan had more-or-less changed his mind about buying
it—five pounds was five pounds, after all, and the book was surprisingly
heavy for its size—when he caught sight of the last entry in the index.

Item thirty-eight: *The Listening Angel invocation—for to prove whether
you are right.*

Frowning, Dan flicked to the indicated page and read just enough to
establish that yes, this meant exactly what he thought it did. He seemed
suddenly to hear a rushing noise, quite loud, like the tread of a hundred
feet, or the beat of thousands of tiny wings.

He closed the book and hurried up the stairs.

There was still no-one at the desk, though he saw the explanation for the
sound he'd heard. It was raining properly now outside, and raining hard.
The store's dim lamps struggled against the lowering darkness. Dan waited

for a few moments, moving impatiently from foot to foot, and then ventured to call out. There was no response. He waited a little longer, then strode to the back of the store and hiked up the stairs. There was no-one up there. No-one in the basement, either, when he went back down to look. He found himself back at street level, standing again in front of a desk that was still deserted.

Dan dug in his wallet and took out a five pound note. He put it on the desk and picked up his bag. He left the big Victorian book behind.

It no longer seemed very interesting.

When he got back to the hotel he was soaked, and surprised to discover he was late. Somehow it had become three o'clock. He was half-expecting to find Marcia waiting huffily in the lobby, but she wasn't there. He took the elevator up to the room. It was empty. Baffled, he called the spa—and was relieved to find that a woman of his wife's description was fast asleep on one of the loungers around the pool. Relieved and, of course, irritated. He left the book on the bed and wandering around the room, drying his hair with a towel. He *could* go down and wake Marcia, remind her they were supposed to be . . . but what was the point? By the time she was dressed it would be too late to get the Tate. And he would also, he realise, have to account for the fact he'd returned well after he'd said he would. It was not the first time, and "looking at books" never seemed to be a good enough explanation.

He set up the room's coffee machine and waited for it to do its thing. Meanwhile he sat in the chair at the desk, and watched the book on the bed. It wasn't moving, naturally, and there was no danger that it would.

But it didn't feel as if he was just looking at it.

When he had a coffee he went and picked the book up. At first he thought he must have been mistaken, because he couldn't find the 'Index of Invocations'. After dipping into the book at random he started at the beginning and rigorously leafed through from front to back. He saw a lot of odd things, but not the index. His heart, which had been beating rather faster that usual, gradually returned to normal. He flicked through the book again, more slowly, obscurely relieved. He had imagined it, that was all. Perhaps it had just been a kind of jetlag fever: annoyance at the crossed words that morning, a fantasy born of the dust and damp of the shop . . .

Then he found it. The Invocations, sandwiched between two sections he *knew* he'd seen on the front-to-back pass. Whatever. He scanned a few of the other entries—

Item twenty-four: *The Strengthening of Bark—a whisper for aiding a tree or bush (of considerable size) that is under attack.*

Item six: *The Flattening Stroke—for to redress a planet that has become mistakenly round. Use only once.*

But they were just diversions. Very quickly he made it down to item thirty-eight, then flicked through pages until he again found the one the entry referred to. As he opened the page he heard the sound again, the beating of wings.

A glimpse out of the window confirmed that this was, for a second time, merely an increase in the volume of rain outside. Odd how it kept happening, though. And how dark it had become.

The instructions on the page were short, and the ingredients it called for were not unduly hard to come by. Marcia still hadn't returned.

Dan didn't see how he had much choice.

Half-an-hour later he was standing on the roof of the hotel. This hadn't been easy to achieve, but the recipe stipulated that the invoker must be both outside and at the highest place available within one hundred horizontal feet of his or her position when the book had been most recently opened. Dan took the elevator to the highest floor of the hotel—the twelfth—but knew somehow this wouldn't be enough. Plus, if something was going to happen, he didn't want to be interrupted by another guest heading back to their room. A certain amount of poking around led him to a door around a corner, which was marked STORES. There were indeed stores inside, and Dan helped himself to a bath towel, but at the back was another door. Opening this led to a dark interior staircase that led upwards.

At the top was a metal door. It was locked. Of course. Dan kicked at it, impotently. He could hear the sound of rain beyond it. He was so close. He kicked again, the lock clicked, and the door swung open a foot.

The sound of rain was suddenly far louder, and Dan saw it was now pelting down outside. Putting aside the question of why the door was now unlocked, he wrapped the towel around his head, left the book on the floor where it wouldn't get wet, and stepped outside.

A large, flat area lay in front of him, the roof of the hotel. Various protuberances stuck up here and there, some disgorging steam or smoke. Piles of forgotten wood lay against the low wall that went right around the edges. The grey surface of the roof was hidden in places by sizeable pools of water, which reflected a blackening sky which seemed to be getting lower and lower.

Dan walked right out in the centre of the roof and stopped. London was spread around him, albeit obscured by sheets of rain and gathering gloom. The towel was soon soaked, and he took it off. Evidently you just had to take this experience as it came. He had memorised the invocation. It wasn't hard. It was so straightforward, in fact, that it was ludicrous to believe it would achieve anything. Nonetheless he unwrapped the hand towel he'd brought up from the room. Inside were three things. A small sample of his saliva, in one of the room's water glasses: a "secretion" had been called for, and saliva was as far as he was prepared to go. A few strands of Marcia's hair, easily gleaned from her brush, wrapped in a piece of toilet tissue, and also put into the glass. Rather more trickily, a postcard to Marcia's sister. The recipe called for a sample of both their words, and didn't explain it any more than that. This defeated Dan until he noticed the postcard, written the previous evening and now lying on the desk awaiting a stamp. Most of it was in Marcia's hand, but he'd added a cheery sentence at the bottom. Would it do? Dan supposed he was about to find out.

He rolled the postcard and put it into the glass too. He straightened, and quickly threw his hand up into the air. He was a fool, he knew, and braced himself the immediate return of the glass.

It didn't come back down.

After a second he looked up, and saw that the glass had disappeared. The rain had started falling harder too, and now it really did sound like wings.

Parts of the sky seemed to detach themselves from the rest, patches of darkness gathering as if a cloud was settling over the hotel, wisps of it catching on the buildings across the street like the ghosts of future fires. The sound of traffic seemed to get both louder and further away. Dan listened to it, and to the rain as it fell, until the two noises became one and entered his head, and disappeared.

"Seventy eight percent," said a voice.

Dan turned. Behind him, something was sitting on the low wall at the edge of the roof. It was about twelve feet tall, the white of old, tarnished marble, and difficult to see. It seemed to sit hunched on the wall, huge wings hanging off its shoulders. It appeared a little uncomfortable, as if finding itself in the wrong place, somewhere either too hot or too cold.

"Are you the angel?" Dan said.

"Over the length of the marriage, you have spoken twenty two percent of the time," the figure said. Its face was turned away from him, hidden behind long wet hair. Its voice was cold, dry, and seemed to come to Dan both via his ears and up through his legs. "If you limit the enquiry to periods of discussion of issues that could be considered academic or of purely hypothetical interest, her contribution rises to eighty-six percent. This peaks, under the influence of alcohol, at ninety-four percent."

"Then I am right," Dan said. "I knew it."

The angel gave no indication it had heard. "If considered in terms of total words uttered, rather than time spent speaking, the breakdown is about the same. The shortness and lack of fluidity of your sentences is generally counterbalanced by your attempts to pack them in the short intervals available."

"Now hold on," Dan said. He started to walk forward, but a loud, heavy movement of the angel's wings warned him to stay where he was. Somewhere, far away, there was the rumble of thunder. "What do you mean, lack of 'fluidity'?"

"Caused merely by lack of opportunity to get into your stride," the angel said. "Of course."

Dan nodded, mollified. "Thank you," he said. "Now. How do I . . ."

"Sometimes she even talks when you're not there," the angel said. "Quite often, in fact."

"And you listen?"

"Of course. It's what I do."

Dan frowned. "What kind of things does she say?"

"She hopes your kids are safe."

"Well, so do I."

"Yes, But she says it out loud. And her words are heard."

"Okay," Dan said. He was cold. Unbelievably, it was starting to rain harder, the sky pressing closer down. His hair was plastered to his skull, water running down his face. "What else does she say?"

It seemed like the angel was turning to look at him, but when the movement was finished it was still looking another way.

"She says it makes her sad when the children call and you hand the phone straight to her, after just grunting hello. She tries not to resent the fact you make no effort with her friends, though—and these are my figures, not hers—you are on average responsible for less than four percent of the conversation when they're around. She has issues with the fact that you seem to believe her having a massage once in a while is a huge indulgence, when you spend three times as much every month on books which you'll mostly never read and often don't even *open* again. She feels hurt when you look at her as if wondering what she is harping on about, and why. She also wishes that once in a while you would handle her in the way you do an interesting book—and says you used to, once."

Dan smiled tightly. "Well, that's very interesting. Thanks for your time. And your unbiased opinion."

The angel rolled its shoulders, as if preparing to leave. "She cares about things. Who do you think we're in favour of, those who do, or those who don't?"

Dan said nothing.

"And the colds," the angel added. "Who do you think they're worse for, her or you?"

"I've got to go," Dan said. "I assume you will let yourself out."

He headed back toward the metal door, sloshing straight through the puddles. He didn't want this any more. Sometimes the person you love is a pain in the ass. He wished he could have left it that. The rain drummed on the roof like the turning of a million dusty pages. He felt tired suddenly, fifty years of coffee gone sour. With each step it became harder to remember what had just happened, or to believe it, or to remember why he'd wanted to know.

He was reaching for the handle on the door when the angel spoke again. It sounded different, quieter, further away. "When she cannot sleep she lies awake and hopes you still love her."

Dan stopped dead in his tracks, and turned.

"Of course I do," he said, stricken. "She must know that."

The angel was fading now, the steady flap of its wings turning back to rain, the grey of its skin becoming cloud once more. As it stood it blew slowly into rising mist in front of his eyes, its words coming to him as cold wind, blown his way by the beating of those wings.

It said: "For her, the sound of the two of you talking together is like the smell of books for you. Do you think she doesn't *notice*, when you believe you're being good about being bored? Sometimes that's *why* she keeps talking, because she panics when she fears you might not find her interesting any more."

It said: "This 'peace and quiet' you think you want: what is it for? What thoughts do you harbour, so valuable they are worth wishing someone to be quiet? Meanwhile she fears for all the ways that things can go wrong in the world, and become still, and lose strength and fall apart."

It said: "If she dies before you, which she might, will you then wish you'd spent more time in silence? When you live in that endless quiet after, in those years of deadening cloud and solitude, what might you be prepared to promise, to hear just one word more from her?"

Then the wind dropped and it was gone.

Dan stood on the roof a full five minutes longer. When he stepped back through the metal door into the hotel, he found the book was gone. He hurried down the stairs, through the store cupboard, ran to the elevator and stabbed at the button.

When he let himself back into the room he heard the sound of Marcia in the bath.

"Dan?" she said quickly, "Is that you?"

"Yes," he said.

"Where have you *been?*"

"Got caught out in the rain," he said, carefully, not yet wanting to go in, not yet ready to see her face. "I'm sorry. Had to hunker down and wait inside somewhere while it passed over. I called the room. You weren't here,"

"Fell asleep," she said, sheepishly. There was silence for a moment. Then she said: "I missed you."

"I missed you too." He took his jacket off and hung it up in the wardrobe to dry. "You okay?"

"You know, I think I'm going down with a cold."

Dan rolled his eyes, but called room service to bring up tea, lemon and honey, before going to help her wash her hair. She told him about the spa in the hotel. He told her about his walk, leaving out Pandora's Books. The two of them sat with their words in the warm bathroom, the world cold and wet outside. They decided to order room service. They watched TV, read a little, went to bed.

In the small hours of the night, while Marcia fitfully dozed, the listening angel came into the room and touched her brow, whispered to her to worry no more for a while. When Dan woke in the morning, she was asleep next to him.

It rained a little again as they ate breakfast together, but after that the day was fine.

IN THE HILLS, THE CITIES

CLIVE BARKER

Clive Barker was born in Liverpool, England, but relocated to Holly-wood, California, in the early 1990s.

An author, playwright, film director, and visual artist, he exploded upon the horror scene in the mid-1980s with his six-volume collection of stories, Books of Blood, *and the novel,* The Damnation Game. *Since then he has published such international best-sellers as* Weaveworld, The Great and Secret Show, Imajica, The Thief of Always, Everville, Sacrament, Galilee, Coldheart Canyon: A Hollywood Ghost Story, *and the illustrated* Abarat *series. Forthcoming is* The Scarlet Gospels, *which features his signature characters Pinhead and Harry D'Amour.*

Following a career in the theatre, Barker made his film directorial debut in 1987 with the influential Hellraiser, *based on his novella* The Hellbound Heart. *He followed that with* Nightbreed *and* Lord of Illusions, *and he was executive producer on the Oscar-winning* Gods and Monsters. Hellraiser *has spawned a number of sequels, and the* Candyman *trilogy is inspired by his short story "The Forbidden."*

"I've always felt that the imagination was the way that you dealt with things in the real world that were perhaps impossible to deal with in any other way," reveals Barker. "To give a direct example, I published a story

called 'In the Hills, the Cities', which had two gay men as its heroes who made love, and there was a fairly graphic reference to that.

"I was urged by both my agent, who was gay, and my editor not to publish the story—that I would be revealing, at the beginning of my career, my sexuality and that it was not a clever thing to do—that I would alienate people. There was a suggestion that I simply change the gender of one of the characters, that it be a boyfriend and a girlfriend, but I wasn't going to go for that."

In the following story, a couple find themselves caught up in a bizarre tradition between two warring cities. . . .

It wasn't until the first week of the Yugoslavian trip that Mick discovered what a political bigot he'd chosen as a lover. Certainly, he'd been warned. One of the queens at the Baths had told him Judd was to the Right of Attila the Hun, but the man had been one of Judd's ex-affairs, and Mick had presumed there was more spite than perception in the character assassination.

If only he'd listened. Then he wouldn't be driving along an interminable road in a Volkswagen that suddenly seemed the size of a coffin, listening to Judd's views on Soviet expansionism. Jesus, he was so boring. He didn't converse, he lectured, and endlessly. In Italy the sermon had been on the way the Communists had exploited the peasant vote. Now, in Yugoslavia, Judd had really warmed to his theme, and Mick was just about ready to take a hammer to his self-opinionated head.

It wasn't that he disagreed with everything Judd said. Some of the arguments (the ones Mick understood) seemed quite sensible. But then, what did he know? He was a dance teacher. Judd was a journalist, a professional pundit. He felt, like most journalists Mick had encountered, that he was obliged to have an opinion on everything under the sun. Especially politics; that was the best trough to wallow in. You could get your snout, eyes, head and front hooves in that mess of muck and have a fine old time splashing around. It was an inexhaustible subject to devour, a swill with a little of everything in it, because everything, according to Judd, was political. The arts were political. Sex was political. Religion, commerce, gardening, eating, drinking and farting—all political.

Jesus, it was mind-blowingly boring; killingly, love-deadeningly boring.

Worse still, Judd didn't seem to notice how bored Mick had become, or if he noticed, he didn't care. He just rambled on, his arguments getting windier and windier, his sentences lengthening with every mile they drove.

Judd, Mick had decided, was a selfish bastard, and as soon as their honeymoon was over he'd part with the guy.

It was not until their trip, that endless, motiveless caravan through the graveyards of mid-European culture, that Judd realized what a political lightweight he had in Mick. The guy showed precious little interest in the economics or the politics of the countries they passed through. He registered indifference to the full facts behind the Italian situation, and yawned, yes, yawned when he tried (and failed) to debate the Russian threat to world peace. He had to face the bitter truth: Mick was a queen; there was no other word for him; All right, perhaps he didn't mince or wear jewellery to excess, but he was a queen nevertheless, happy to wallow in a dream-world of early Renaissance frescoes and Yugoslavian icons. The complexities, the contradictions, even the agonies that made those cultures blossom and wither were just tiresome to him. His mind was no deeper than his looks; he was a well-groomed nobody.

Some honeymoon.

The road south from Belgrade to Novi Pazar was, by Yugoslavian standards, a good one. There were fewer pot-holes than on many of the roads they'd travelled, and it was relatively straight. The town of Novi Pazar lay in the valley of the River Raska, south of the city named after the river. It wasn't an area particularly popular with the tourists. Despite the good road it was still inaccessible, and lacked sophisticated amenities; but Mick was determined to see the monastery at Sopocani, to the west of the town and after some bitter argument, he'd won.

The journey had proved uninspiring. On either side of the road the cultivated fields looked parched and dusty. The summer had been unusually hot, and droughts were affecting many of the villages. Crops had failed, and livestock had been prematurely slaughtered to prevent them dying of malnutrition. There was a defeated look about the few faces they glimpsed at the roadside. Even the children had dour expressions; brows as heavy as the stale heat that hung over the valley.

Now, with the cards on the table after a row at Belgrade, they drove in silence most of the time; but the straight road, like most straight roads, invited dispute. When the driving was easy, the mind rooted for something to keep it engaged. What better than a fight?

"Why the hell do you want to see this damn monastery?" Judd demanded.

It was an unmistakable invitation.

"We've come all this way . . ." Mick tried to keep the tone conversational. He wasn't in the mood for an argument.

"More fucking Virgins, is it?"

Keeping his voice as even as he could, Mick picked up the Guide and read aloud from it: ". . . there, some of the greatest works of Serbian painting can still be seen and enjoyed, including what many commentators agree to be the enduring masterpiece of the Raska school: 'The Dormition of the Virgin'."

Silence.

Then Judd: "I'm up to here with churches."

"It's a masterpiece."

"They're all masterpieces according to that bloody book."

426

Mick felt his control slipping.

"Two and a half hours at most—"

"I told you, I don't want to see another church; the smell of the places makes me sick. Stale incense, old sweat and lies . . ."

"It's a short detour; then we can get back on to the road and you can give me another lecture on farming subsidies in the Sandzak."

"I'm just trying to get some decent conversation going instead of this endless tripe about Serbian fucking masterpieces—"

"Stop the car!"

"What?"

"Stop the car!"

Judd pulled the Volkswagen into the side of the road. Mick got out.

The road was hot, but there was a slight breeze. He took a deep breath, and wandered into the middle of the road. Empty of traffic and of pedestrians in both directions. In every direction, empty. The hills shimmered in the heat off the fields. There were wild poppies growing in the ditches. Mick crossed the road, squatted on his haunches and picked one.

Behind him he heard the VW's door slam.

"What did you stop us for?" Judd said. His voice was edgy, still hoping for that argument, begging for it.

Mick stood up, playing with the poppy. It was close to seeding, late in the season. The petals fell from the receptacle as soon as he touched them, little splashes of red fluttering down on to the grey tarmac.

"I asked you a question," Judd said again.

Mick looked round. Judd was standing the far side of the car, his brows a knitted line of burgeoning anger. But handsome; oh yes; a face that made women weep with frustration that he was gay. A heavy black moustache (perfectly trimmed) and eyes you could watch forever, and never see the same light in them twice. Why in God's name, thought Mick, does a man as fine as that have to be such an insensitive little shit?

427

Judd returned the look of contemptuous appraisal, staring at the pouting pretty boy across the road. It made him want to puke, seeing the little act Mick was performing for his benefit. It might just have been plausible in a sixteen-year-old virgin. In a twenty-five-year-old, it lacked credibility.

Mick dropped the flower, and untucked his T-shirt from his jeans. A tight stomach, then a slim, smooth chest were revealed as he pulled it off. His hair was ruffled when his head re-appeared, and his face wore a broad grin. Judd looked at the torso. Neat, not too muscular. An appendix scar peering over his faded jeans. A gold chain, small but catching the sun, dipped in the hollow of his throat. Without meaning to, he returned Mick's grin, and a kind of peace was made between them.

Mick was unbuckling his belt.

"Want to fuck?" he said, the grin not faltering.

"It's no use," came an answer, though not to that question.

"What isn't?"

"We're not compatible."

"Want a bet?"

Now he was unzipped, and turning away towards the wheat-field that bordered the road.

Judd watched as Mick cut a swathe through the swaying sea, his back the colour of the grain, so that he was almost camouflaged by it. It was a dangerous game, screwing in the open air—this wasn't San Francisco, or even Hampstead Heath. Nervously, Judd glanced along the road. Still empty in both directions. And Mick was turning, deep in the field, turning and smiling and waving like a swimmer buoyed up in a golden surf. What the hell . . . there was nobody to see, nobody to know. Just the hills, liquid in the heat-haze, their forested backs bent to the business of the earth, and a lost dog, sitting at the edge of the road, waiting for some lost master.

Judd followed Mick's path through the wheat, unbuttoning his shirt as he walked. Field-mice ran ahead of him, scurrying through the stalks as the giant came their way, his feet like thunder. Judd saw their panic, and smiled. He meant no harm to them, but then how were they to know that? Maybe he'd put out a hundred lives, mice, beetles, worms, before he reached the spot where Mick was lying, stark bollock naked, on a bed of trampled grain, still grinning.

It was good love they made, good, strong love, equal in pleasure for both; there was a precision to their passion, sensing the moment when effortless delight became urgent, when desire became necessity. They locked together, limb around limb, tongue around tongue, in a knot only orgasm could untie, their backs alternately scorched and scratched as they rolled around exchanging blows and kisses. In the thick of it, creaming together, they heard the phut-phut-phut of a tractor passing by; but they were past caring.

They made their way back to the Volkswagen with body-threshed wheat in their hair and their ears, in their socks and between their toes. Their grins had been replaced with easy smiles: the truce, if not permanent, would last a few hours at least.

The car was baking hot, and they had to open all the windows and doors to let the breeze cool it before they started towards Novi Pazar. It was four o'clock, and there was still an hour's driving ahead.

As they got into the car Mick said, "We'll forget the monastery, eh?"

Judd gaped.

"I thought—"

"I couldn't bear another fucking Virgin—"

They laughed lightly together, then kissed, tasting each other and themselves, a mingling of saliva, and the aftertaste of salt semen.

The following day was bright, but not particularly warm. No blue skies: just an even layer of white cloud. The morning air was sharp in the lining of the nostrils, like ether, or peppermint.

Vaslav Jelovsek watched the pigeons in the main square of Popolac courting death as they skipped and fluttered ahead of the vehicles that were buzzing around. Some about military business, some civilian. An air of sober intention barely suppressed the excitement he felt on this day, an excitement he knew was shared by every man, woman and child in Popolac. Shared by the pigeons too for all he knew. Maybe that was why they played under the wheels with such dexterity, knowing that on this day of days no harm could come to them.

He scanned the sky again, that same white sky he'd been peering at since dawn. The cloud-layer was low; not ideal for the celebrations. A phrase passed through his mind, an English phrase he'd heard from a friend, "to have your head in the clouds". It meant, he gathered, to be lost in a reverie, in a white, sightless dream. That, he thought wryly, was all the West knew about clouds, that they stood for dreams. It took a vision they lacked to make a truth out of that casual turn of phrase. Here, in these secret hills, wouldn't they create a spectacular reality from those idle words? A living proverb.

A head in the clouds.

Already the first contingent was assembling in the square. There were one or two absentees owing to illness, but the auxiliaries were ready and waiting to take their places. Such eagerness! Such wide smiles when an auxiliary heard his or her name and number called and was taken out of line to join the limb that was already taking shape. On every side, miracles of organization. Everyone with a job to do and a place to go. There was no shouting or pushing: indeed, voices were scarcely raised above an eager whisper. He watched in admiration as the work of positioning and buckling and roping went on.

It was going to be a long and arduous day. Vaslav had been in the square since an hour before dawn, drinking coffee from imported plastic cups, discussing the half-hourly meteorological reports coming in from Pristina and

Mitrovica, and watching the starless sky as the grey light of morning crept across it. Now he was drinking his sixth coffee of the day, and it was still barely seven o'clock. Across the square Metzinger looked as tired and as anxious as Vaslav felt.

They'd watched the dawn seep out of the east together, Metzinger and he. But now they had separated, forgetting previous companionship, and would not speak until the contest was over. After all Metzinger was from Podujevo. He had his own city to support in the coming battle. Tomorrow they'd exchange tales of their adventures, but for today they must behave as if they didn't know each other, not even to exchange a smile. For today they had to be utterly partisan, caring only for the victory of their own city over the opposition.

Now the first leg of Popolac was erected, to the mutual satisfaction of Metzinger and Vaslav. All the safety checks had been meticulously made, and the leg left the square, its shadow falling hugely across the face of the Town Hall.

Vaslav sipped his sweet, sweet coffee and allowed himself a little grunt of satisfaction. Such days, such days. Days filled with glory, with snapping flags and high, stomach-turning sights, enough to last a man a lifetime. It was a golden foretaste of Heaven.

Let America have its simple pleasures, its cartoon mice, its candy-coated castles, its cults and its technologies, he wanted none of it. The greatest wonder of the world was here, hidden in the hills.

Ah, such days.

In the main square of Podujevo the scene was no less animated, and no less inspiring. Perhaps there was a muted sense of sadness underlying this year's celebration, but that was understandable. Nita Obrenovic, Podujevo's loved and respected organizer, was no longer living. The previous winter had claimed her at the age of ninety-four, leaving the city bereft of her fierce opinions and her fiercer proportions. For sixty years Nita had worked with the citizens of Podujevo, always planning for the next contest and improving on the designs, her energies spent on making the next creation more ambitious and more life-like than the last.

Now she was dead, and sorely missed. There was no disorganization in the streets without her, the people were far too disciplined for that, but they were already falling behind schedule, and it was almost seven-twenty-five. Nita's daughter had taken over in her mother's stead, but she lacked Nita's power to galvanize the people into action. She was, in a word, too gentle for the job in hand. It required a leader who was part prophet and part ring-master, to coax and bully and inspire the citizens into their places. Maybe, after two or three decades, and with a few more contests under her belt, Nita Obrenovic's daughter would make the grade. But for today Podujevo was behindhand; safety-checks were being overlooked; nervous looks replaced the confidence of earlier years.

Nevertheless, at six minutes before eight the first limb of Podujevo made its way out of the city to the assembly point, to wait for its fellow.

By that time the flanks were already lashed together in Popolac, and armed contingents were awaiting orders in the Town Square.

Mick woke promptly at seven, though there was no alarm clock in their simply furnished room at the Hotel Beograd. He lay in his bed and listened to Judd's regular breathing from the twin bed across the room. A dull morning light whimpered through the thin curtains, not encouraging an early departure. After a few minutes' staring at the cracked paintwork on the ceiling, and a while longer at the crudely carved crucifix on the oppo-site wall, Mick got up and went to the window. It was a dull day, as he had guessed. The sky was overcast, and the roofs of Novi Pazar were grey and featureless in the flat morning light. But beyond the roofs, to the east, he could see the hills. There was sun there. He could see shafts of light catching the blue-green of the forest, inviting a visit to their slopes.

Today maybe they would go south to Kosovska Mitrovica. There was a market there, wasn't there, and a museum? And they could drive down the valley of the Ibar, following the road beside the river, where the hills rose wild and shining on either side. The hills, yes; today he decided they would see the hills.

It was eight-fifteen.

By nine the main bodies of Popolac and Podujevo were substantially assembled. In their allotted districts the limbs of both cities were ready and waiting to join their expectant torsos.

Vaslav Jelovsek capped his gloved hands over his eyes and surveyed the sky. The cloud-base had risen in the last hour, no doubt of it, and there were breaks in the clouds to the west; even, on occasion, a few glimpses of the sun. It wouldn't be a perfect day for the contest perhaps, but certainly adequate.

Mick and Judd breakfasted late on hemendeks—roughly translated as ham and eggs—and several cups of good black coffee. It was brightening up, even in Novi Pazar, and their ambitions were set high. Kosovska Mitrovica by lunch time, and maybe a visit to the hill-castle of Zvecan in the afternoon.

About nine-thirty they motored out of Novi Pazar and took the Srbovac road south to the Ibar valley. Not a good road, but the bumps and pot-holes couldn't spoil the new day.

The road was empty, except for the occasional pedestrian; and in place of the maize and corn fields they'd passed on the previous day the road was flanked by undulating hills, whose sides were thickly and darkly forested. Apart from a few birds, they saw no wildlife. Even their infrequent travelling companions petered out altogether after a few miles, and the occasional farmhouse they drove by appeared locked and shuttered up. Black pigs ran unattended in the yard, with no child to feed them. Washing snapped and billowed on a sagging line, with no washerwoman in sight.

At first this solitary journey through the hills was refreshing in its lack of human contact, but as the morning drew on, an uneasiness grew on them.

"Shouldn't we have seen a signpost to Mitrovica, Mick?"

He peered at the map.

"Maybe . . ."

"—we've taken the wrong road."

"If there'd been a sign, I'd have seen it. I think we should try and get off this road, bear south a bit more—meet the valley closer to Mitrovica than we'd planned."

"How do we get off this bloody road?"

"There've been a couple of turnings . . ."

"Dirt-tracks."

"Well it's either that or going on the way we are."

Judd pursed his lips.

"Cigarette?" he asked.

"Finished them miles back."

In front of them, the hills formed an impenetrable line. There was no sign of life ahead; no frail wisp of chimney smoke, no sound of voice or vehicle.

"All right," said Judd, "we take the next turning. Anything's better than this."

They drove on. The road was deteriorating rapidly, the pot-holes becoming craters, the hummocks feeling like bodies beneath the wheels.

Then:

"There!"

A turning: a palpable turning. Not a major road, certainly. In fact barely the dirt-track Judd had described the other roads as being, but it was an escape from the endless perspective of the road they were trapped on.

"This is becoming a bloody safari," said Judd as the VW began to bump and grind its way along the doleful little track.

"Where's your sense of adventure?"

"I forgot to pack it."

They were beginning to climb now, as the track wound its way up into the hills. The forest closed over them, blotting out the sky, so a shifting patchwork of light and shadow scooted over the bonnet as they drove. There was birdsong suddenly, vacuous and optimistic, and a smell of new pine and undug earth. A fox crossed the track, up ahead, and watched a long moment as the car grumbled up towards it. Then, with the leisurely stride of a fearless prince, it sauntered away into the trees.

Wherever they were going, Mick thought, this was better than the road they'd left. Soon maybe they'd stop, and walk a while, to find a promontory from which they could see the valley, even Novi Pazar, nestled behind them.

The two men were still an hour's drive from Popolac when the head of the contingent at last marched out of the Town Square and took up its position with the main body.

This last exit left the city completely deserted. Not even the sick or the old were neglected on this day; no-one was to be denied the spectacle and the triumph of the contest. Every single citizen, however young or infirm, the blind, the crippled, babes in arms, pregnant women—all made their way up from their proud city to the stamping ground. It was the law that they should attend: but it needed no enforcing. No citizen of either city would have missed the chance to see that sight—to experience the thrill of that contest.

The confrontation had to be total, city against city. This was the way it had always been.

So the cities went up into the hills. By noon they were gathered, the citizens of Popolac and Podujevo, in the secret well of the hills, hidden from civilized eyes, to do ancient and ceremonial battle.

Tens of thousands of hearts beat faster. Tens of thousands of bodies stretched and strained and sweated as the twin cities took their positions.

The shadows of the bodies darkened tracts of land the size of small towns; the weight of their feet trampled the grass to a green milk; their movement killed animals, crushed bushes and threw down trees. The earth literally reverberated with their passage, the hills echoing with the booming din of their steps.

In the towering body of Podujevo, a few technical hitches were becoming apparent. A slight flaw in the knitting of the left flank had resulted in a weakness there: and there were consequent problems in the swivelling mechanism of the hips. It was stiffer than it should be, and the movements were not smooth. As a result there was considerable strain being put upon that region of the city. It was being dealt with bravely; after all, the contest was intended to press the contestants to their limits. But breaking point was closer than anyone would have dared to admit. The citizens were not as resilient as they had been in previous contests. A bad decade for crops had produced bodies less well-nourished, spines less supple, wills less resolute. The badly knitted flank might not have caused an accident in itself, but further weakened by the frailty of the competitors it set a scene for death on an unprecedented scale.

They stopped the car.

"Hear that?"

Mick shook his head. His hearing hadn't been good since he was an adolescent. Too many rock shows had blown his eardrums to hell.

Judd got out of the car.

The birds were quieter now. The noise he'd heard as they drove came again. It wasn't simply a noise: it was almost a motion in the earth, a roar that seemed seated in the substance of the hills.

Thunder, was it?

No, too rhythmical. It came again, through the soles of the feet—

Boom.

Mick heard it this time. He leaned out of the car window.

"It's up ahead somewhere. I hear it now."

Judd nodded.

Boom.

The earth-thunder sounded again.

"What the hell is it?" said Mick.

"Whatever it is, I want to see it—"

Judd got back into the Volkswagen, smiling.

"Sounds almost like guns," he said, starting the car. "Big guns."

Through his Russian-made binoculars Vaslav Jelovsek watched the starting-official raise his pistol. He saw the feather of white smoke rise from the barrel, and a second later heard the sound of the shot across the valley.

The contest had begun.

He looked up at twin towers of Popolac and Podujevo. Heads in the clouds—well almost. They practically stretched to touch the sky. It was an awesome sight, a breath-stopping, sleep-stabbing sight. Two cities swaying and writhing and preparing to take their first steps towards each other in this ritual battle.

Of the two, Podujevo seemed the less stable. There was a slight hesitation as the city raised its left leg to begin its march. Nothing serious, just a little difficulty in co-ordinating hip and thigh muscles. A couple of steps and the city would find its rhythm; a couple more and its inhabitants would be moving as one creature, one perfect giant set to match its grace and power against its mirror-image.

The gunshot had sent flurries of birds up from the trees that banked the hidden valley. They rose up in celebration of the great contest, chattering their excitement as they swooped over the stamping-ground.

"Did you hear a shot?" asked Judd.

Mick nodded.

"Military exercises . . . ?" Judd's smile had broadened. He could see the headlines already—exclusive reports of secret manouevres in the depths of the Yugoslavian countryside. Russian tanks perhaps, tactical exercises being held out of the West's prying sight. With luck, he would be the carrier of this news.

Boom.

Boom.

There were birds in the air. The thunder was louder now.

It did sound like guns.

"It's over the next ridge . . ." said Judd.

"I don't think we should go any further."

"I have to see."

"I don't. We're not supposed to be here."

"I don't see any signs."

"They'll cart us away; deport us—I don't know—I just think—"

Boom.

"I've got to see."

The words were scarcely out of his mouth when the screaming started.

Podujevo was screaming: a death-cry. Someone buried in the weak flank had died of the strain, and had begun a chain of decay in the system. One man loosed his neighbour and that neighbour loosed his, spreading a cancer of chaos through the body of the city. The coherence of the towering structure deteriorated with terrifying rapidity as the failure of one part of the anatomy put unendurable pressure on the other.

The masterpiece that the good citizens of Podujevo had constructed of their own flesh and blood tottered and then—a dynamited skyscraper, it began to fall.

The broken flank spewed citizens like a slashed artery spitting blood.

Then, with a graceful sloth that made the agonies of the citizens all the more horrible, it bowed towards the earth, all its limbs dissembling as it fell.

The huge head, that had brushed the clouds so recently, was flung back on its thick neck. Ten thousand mouths spoke a single scream for its vast mouth, a wordless, infinitely pitiable appeal to the sky. A howl of loss, a howl of anticipation, a howl of puzzlement. How, that scream demanded, could the day of days end like this, in a welter of falling bodies?

"Did you hear that?"

It was unmistakably human, though almost deafeningly loud. Judd's stomach convulsed. He looked across at Mick, who was as white as a sheet.

Judd stopped the car.

"No," said Mick.

"Listen—for Christ's sake—"

The din of dying moans, appeals and imprecations flooded the air. It was very close.

"We've got to go on now," Mick implored.

Judd shook his head. He was prepared for some military spectacle—all the Russian army massed over the next hill—but that noise in his ears was the noise of human flesh—too human for words. It reminded him of his childhood imaginings of Hell; the endless, unspeakable torments his mother had threatened him with if he failed to embrace Christ. It was a terror he'd forgotten for twenty years. But suddenly, here it was again, fresh-faced. Maybe the pit itself gaped just over the next horizon, with his mother standing at its lip, inviting him to taste its punishments.

"If you won't drive, I will."

Mick got out of the car and crossed in front of it, glancing up the track as he did so. There was a moment's hesitation, no more than a moment's, when his eyes flickered with disbelief, before he turned towards the wind-

439

screen, his face even paler than it had been previously and said: "Jesus Christ . . ." in a voice that was thick with suppressed nausea.

His lover was still sitting behind the wheel, his head in his hands, trying to blot out memories.

"Judd . . ."

Judd looked up, slowly. Mick was staring at him like a wildman, his face shining with a sudden, icy sweat. Judd looked past him. A few metres ahead the track had mysteriously darkened, as a tide edged towards the car, a thick, deep tide of blood. Judd's reason twisted and turned to make any other sense of the sight than that inevitable conclusion. But there was no saner explanation. It was blood, in unendurable abundance, blood without end—

And now, in the breeze, there was the flavour of freshly-opened carcasses: the smell out of the depths of the human body, part sweet, part savoury.

Mick stumbled back to the passenger's side of the VW and fumbled weakly at the handle. The door opened suddenly and he lurched inside, his eyes glazed.

"Back up," he said.

Judd reached for the ignition. The tide of blood was already sloshing against the front wheels. Ahead, the world had been painted red.

"Drive, for fuck's sake, drive!"

Judd was making no attempt to start the car.

"We must look," he said, without conviction, "we have to."

"We don't have to do anything," said Mick, "but get the hell out of here. It's not our business . . ."

"Plane-crash—"

"There's no smoke."

"Those are human voices."

Mick's instinct was to leave well alone. He could read about the tragedy

440

in a newspaper—he could see the pictures tomorrow when they were grey and grainy. Today it was too fresh, too unpredictable—

Anything could be at the end of that track, bleeding—

"We must—"

Judd started the car, while beside him Mick began to moan quietly. The VW began to edge forward, nosing through the river of blood, its wheels spinning in the queasy, foaming tide. "No," said Mick, very quietly, "Please, no . . ."

"We must," was Judd's reply. "We must. We must."

Only a few yards away the surviving city of Popolac was recovering from its first convulsions. It stared, with a thousand eyes, at the ruins of its ritual enemy, now spread in a tangle of rope and bodies over the impacted ground, shattered forever. Popolac staggered back from the sight, its vast legs flattening the forest that bounded the stamping-ground, its arms flailing the air. But it kept its balance, even as a common insanity, woken by the horror at its feet, surged through its sinews and curdled its brain. The order went out: the body thrashed and twisted and turned from the grisly carpet of Podujevo, and fled into the hills.

As it headed into oblivion, its towering form passed between the car and the sun, throwing its cold shadow over the bloody road. Mick saw nothing through his tears, and Judd, his eyes narrowed against the sight he feared seeing around the next bend, only dimly registered that something had blotted the light for a minute. A cloud, perhaps. A flock of birds.

Had he looked up at that moment, just stolen a glance out towards the north-east, he would have seen Popolac's head, the vast, swarming head of a maddened city, disappearing below his line of vision, as it marched into the hills. He would have known that this territory was beyond his comprehension; and that there was no healing to be done in this corner of Hell. But he didn't see the city, and he and Mick's last turning-point had passed.

From now on, like Popolac and its dead twin, they were lost to sanity, and to all hope of life.

They rounded the bend, and the ruins of Podujevo came into sight.

Their domesticated imaginations had never conceived of a sight so unspeakably brutal.

Perhaps in the battlefields of Europe as many corpses had been heaped together: but had so many of them been women and children, locked together with the corpses of men? There had been piles of dead as high, but ever so many so recently abundant with life? There had been cities laid waste as quickly, but ever an entire city lost to the simple dictate of gravity?

It was a sight beyond sickness. In the face of it the mind slowed to a snail's pace, the forces of reason picked over the evidence with meticulous hands, searching for a flaw in it, a place where it could say:

This is not happening. This is a dream of death, not death itself.

But reason could find no weakness in the wall. This was true. It was death indeed.

Podujevo had fallen.

Thirty-eight thousand, seven hundred and sixty-five citizens were spread on the ground, or rather flung in ungainly, seeping piles. Those who had not died of the fall, or of suffocation, were dying. There would be no survivors from that city except that bundle of onlookers that had traipsed out of their homes to watch the contest. Those few Podujevians, the crippled, the sick, the ancient few, were now staring, like Mick and Judd, at the carnage, trying not to believe.

Judd was first out of the car. The ground beneath his suedes was sticky with coagulating gore. He surveyed the carnage. There was no wreckage: no sign of a plane crash, no fire, no smell of fuel. Just tens of thousands of fresh bodies, all either naked or dressed in an identical grey serge, men, women and children alike. Some of them, he could see, wore leather harnesses, tightly buckled around their upper chests, and snaking out from these contraptions were lengths of rope, miles and miles of it. The closer he looked, the more he saw of the extraordinary system of knots and lashings that still held the bodies together. For some reason these people had been tied together, side by side. Some were yoked on their neighbours' shoulders, straddling them like boys playing at horse back riding. Others were locked arm in arm, knitted together with threads of rope in a wall of muscle and bone. Yet others were trussed in a ball, with their heads tucked between their knees. All were in some way connected up with their fellows, tied together as though in some insane collective bondage game.

Another shot.

Mick looked up.

Across the field a solitary man, dressed in a drab overcoat, was walking amongst the bodies with a revolver, dispatching the dying. It was a pitifully inadequate act of mercy, but he went on nevertheless, choosing the suffering children first. Emptying the revolver, filling it again, emptying it, filling it, emptying it—

Mick let go.

He yelled at the top of his voice over the moans of the injured.

"What is this?"

The man looked up from his appalling duty, his face as dead-grey as his coat.

"Uh?" he grunted, frowning at the two interlopers through his thick spectacles.

"What's happened here?" Mick shouted across at him. It felt good to shout, it felt good to sound angry at the man. Maybe he was to blame. It would be a fine thing, just to have someone to blame.

"Tell us—" Mick said. He could hear the tears throbbing in his voice. "Tell us, for God's sake. Explain."

Grey-coat shook his head. He didn't understand a word this young idiot was saying. It was English he spoke, but that's all he knew. Mick began to walk towards him, feeling all the time the eyes of the dead on him. Eyes like black, shining gems set in broken faces: eyes looking at him upside down, on heads severed from their seating. Eyes in heads that had solid howls for voices. Eyes in heads beyond howls, beyond breath.

Thousands of eyes.

He reached Grey-coat, whose gun was almost empty. He had taken off his spectacles and thrown them aside. He too was weeping, little jerks ran through his big, ungainly body.

At Mick's feet, somebody was reaching for him. He didn't want to look, but the hand touched his shoe and he had no choice but to see its owner. A young man, lying like a flesh swastika, every joint smashed. A child lay under him, her bloody legs poking out like two pink sticks.

He wanted the man's revolver, to stop the hand from touching him. Better still he wanted a machine-gun, a flame-thrower, anything to wipe the agony away.

As he looked up from the broken body, Mick saw Grey-coat raise the revolver.

"Judd—" he said, but as the word left his lips the muzzle of the revolver was slipped into Grey-coat's mouth and the trigger was pulled.

Grey-coat had saved the last bullet for himself. The back of his head opened like a dropped egg, the shell of his skull flying off. His body went limp and sank to the ground, the revolver still between his lips.

"We must—" began Mick, saying the words to nobody. "We must . . ."

What was the imperative? In this situation, what *must* they do?

"We must—"

Judd was behind him.

"Help—" he said to Mick.

"Yes. We must get help. We must—"

"Go."

444

Go! That was what they must do. On any pretext, for any fragile, cowardly reason, they must go. Get out of the battlefield, get out of the reach of a dying hand with a wound in place of a body.

"We have to tell the authorities. Find a town. Get help—"

"Priests," said Mick. "They need priests."

It was absurd, to think of giving the Last Rites to so many people. It would take an army of priests, a water cannon filled with holy water, a loudspeaker to pronounce the benedictions.

They turned away, together, from the horror, and wrapped their arms around each other, then picked their way through the carnage to the car.

It was occupied.

Vaslav Jelovsek was sitting behind the wheel, and trying to start the Volkswagen. He turned the ignition key once. Twice. Third time the engine caught and the wheels span in the crimson mud as he put her into reverse and backed down the track. Vaslav saw the Englishmen running towards the car, cursing him. There was no help for it—he didn't want to steal the vehicle, but he had work to do. He had been a referee, he had been responsible for the contest, and the safety of the contestants. One of the heroic cities had already fallen. He must do everything in his power to prevent Popolac from following its twin. He must chase Popolac, and reason with it. Talk it down out of its terrors with quiet words and promises. If he failed there would be another disaster the equal of the one in front of him, and his conscience was already broken enough.

Mick was still chasing the VW, shouting at Jelovsek. The thief took no notice, concentrating on manouevering the car back down the narrow, slippery track. Mick was losing the chase rapidly. The car had begun to pick up speed. Furious, but without the breath to speak his fury, Mick stood in the road, hands on his knees, heaving and sobbing.

"Bastard!" said Judd.

Mick looked down the track. Their car had already disappeared.

"Fucker couldn't even drive properly."

"We have . . . we have . . . to catch . . . up . . ." said Mick through gulps of breath.

"How?"

"On foot . . ."

"We haven't even got a map . . . it's in the car."

"Jesus . . . Christ . . . Almighty."

They walked down the track together, away from the field.

After a few metres the tide of blood began to peter out. Just a few congealing rivulets dribbled on towards the main road. Mick and Judd followed the bloody tyremarks to the junction.

The Srbovac road was empty in both directions. The tyremarks showed a left turn. "He's gone deeper into the hills," said Judd, staring along the lovely road towards the blue-green distance. "He's out of his mind!"

"Do we go back the way we came?"

"It'll take us all night on foot."

"We'll hop a lift."

Judd shook his head: his face was slack and his look lost. "Don't you see, Mick, they all knew this was happening. The people in the farms—they got the hell out while those people went crazy up there. There'll be no cars along this road, I'll lay you anything—except maybe a couple of shit-dumb tourists like us—and no tourist would stop for the likes of us."

He was right. They looked like butchers—splattered with blood. Their faces were shining with grease, their eyes maddened.

"We'll have to walk," said Judd, "the way he went."

He pointed along the road. The hills were darker now; the sun had suddenly gone out on their slopes.

Mick shrugged. Either way he could see they had a night on the road ahead of them. But he wanted to walk somewhere—anywhere—as long as he put distance between him and the dead.

• • •

In Popolac a kind of peace reigned. Instead of a frenzy of panic there was a numbness, a sheep-like acceptance of the world as it was. Locked in their positions, strapped, roped and harnessed to each other in a living system that allowed for no single voice to be louder than any other, nor any back to labour less than its neighbour's, they let an insane consensus replace the tranquil voice of reason. They were convulsed into one mind, one thought, one ambition. They became, in the space of a few moments, the single-minded giant whose image they had so brilliantly re-created. The illusion of petty individuality was swept away in an irresistible tide of collective feeling—not a mob's passion, but a telepathic surge that dissolved the voices of thousands into one irresistible command.

And the voice said: Go!

The voice said: take this horrible sight away, where I need never see it again.

Popolac turned away into the hills, its legs taking strides half a mile long. Each man, woman and child in that seething tower was sightless. They saw only through the eyes of the city. They were thoughtless, but to think the city's thoughts. And they believed themselves deathless, in their lumbering, relentless strength. Vast and mad and deathless.

Two miles along the road Mick and Judd smelt petrol in the air, and a little further along they came upon the VW. It had overturned in the reed-clogged drainage ditch at the side of the road. It had not caught fire.

The driver's door was open, and the body of Vaslav Jelovsek had tumbled out. His face was calm in unconsciousness. There seemed to be no sign of injury, except for a small cut or two on his sober face. They gently pulled the thief out of the wreckage and up out of the filth of the ditch on to the road. He moaned a little as they fussed about him, rolling Mick's sweater up to pillow his head and removing the man's jacket and tie.

447

Quite suddenly, he opened his eyes.

He stared at them both.

"Are you all right?" Mick asked.

The man said nothing for a moment. He seemed not to understand. Then:

"English?" he said. His accent was thick, but the question was quite clear.

"Yes."

"I heard your voices. English."

He frowned and winced.

"Are you in pain?" said Judd.

The man seemed to find this amusing.

"Am I in pain?" he repeated, his face screwed up in a mixture of agony and delight.

"I shall die," he said, through gritted teeth.

"No," said Mick, "You're all right—"

The man shook his head, his authority absolute.

"I shall die," he said again, the voice full of determination, "I want to die."

Judd crouched closer to him. His voice was weaker by the moment.

"Tell us what to do," he said. The man had closed his eyes. Judd shook him awake, roughly.

"Tell us," he said again, his show of compassion rapidly disappearing. "Tell us what this is all about."

"About?" said the man, his eyes still closed. "It was a fall, that's all. Just a fall . . ."

"What fell?"

"The city. Podujevo. My city."

"What did it fall from?"

"Itself, of course."

The man was explaining nothing; just answering one riddle with another.

"Where were you going?" Mick inquired, trying to sound as unaggressive as possible.

"After Popolac," said the man.

"Popolac?" said Judd.

Mick began to see some sense in the story.

"Popolac is another city. Like Podujevo. Twin cities. They're on the map—"

"Where's the city now?" said Judd.

Vaslav Jelovsek seemed to choose to tell the truth. There was a moment when he hovered between dying with a riddle on his lips, and living long enough to unburden his story. What did it matter if the tale was told now? There could never be another contest: all that was over.

"They came to fight," he said, his voice now very soft, "Popolac and Podujevo. They come every ten years—"

"Fight?" said Judd, "You mean all those people were slaughtered?"

Vaslav shook his head.

"No, no. They fell. I told you."

"Well how do they fight?" Mick said.

"Go into the hills," was the only reply.

Vaslav opened his eyes a little. The faces that loomed over him were exhausted and sick. They had suffered, these innocents. They deserved some explanation.

"As giants," he said. "They fought as giants. They made a body out of their bodies, do you understand? The frame, the muscles, the bone, the eyes, nose, teeth all made of men and women."

"He's delirious," said Judd.

"You go into the hills," the man repeated. "See for yourselves how true it is."

"Even supposing—" Mick began.

Vaslav interrupted him, eager to be finished. "They were good at the game of giants. It took many centuries of practice: every ten years making the figure larger and larger. One always ambitious to be larger than the

other. Ropes to tie them all together, flawlessly. Sinews . . . ligaments . . .
There was food in its belly . . . there were pipes from the loins, to take away
the waste. The best-sighted sat in the eye-sockets, the best voiced in the
mouth and throat. You wouldn't believe the engineering of it."

"I don't," said Judd, and stood up.

"It is the body of the state," said Vaslav, so softly his voice was barely
above a whisper, "it is the shape of our lives."

There was a silence. Small clouds passed over the road, soundlessly shedding their mass to the air.

"It was a miracle," he said. It was as if he realized the true enormity of
the fact for the first time. "It was a miracle."

It was enough. Yes. It was quite enough.

His mouth closed, the words said, and he died.

Mick felt this death more acutely than the thousands they had fled from;
or rather this death was the key to unlock the anguish he felt for them all.

Whether the man had chosen to tell a fantastic lie as he died, or whether
this story was in some way true, Mick felt useless in the face of it. His
imagination was too narrow to encompass the idea. His brain ached with
the thought of it, and his compassion cracked under the weight of misery
he felt.

They stood on the road, while the clouds scudded by, their vague, grey
shadows passing over them towards the enigmatic hills.

It was twilight.

Popolac could stride no further. It felt exhaustion in every muscle. Here
and there in its huge anatomy deaths had occurred; but there was no
grieving in the city for its deceased cells. If the dead were in the interior, the
corpses were allowed to hang from their harnesses. If they formed the skin
of the city they were unbuckled from their positions and released, to plunge
into the forest below.

The giant was not capable of pity. It had no ambition but to continue until it ceased.

As the sun slunk out of sight Popolac rested, sitting on a small hillock, nursing its huge head in its huge hands.

The stars were coming out, with their familiar caution. Night was approaching, mercifully bandaging up the wounds of the day, blinding eyes that had seen too much.

Popolac rose to its feet again, and began to move, step by booming step. It would not be long surely, before fatigue overcame it: before it could lie down in the tomb of some lost valley and die.

But for a space yet it must walk on, each step more agonizingly slow than the last, while the night bloomed black around its head.

Mick wanted to bury the car-thief, somewhere on the edge of the forest. Judd, however, pointed out that burying a body might seem, in tomorrow's saner light, a little suspicious. And besides, wasn't it absurd to concern themselves with one corpse when there were literally thousands of them lying a few miles from where they stood?

The body was left to lie, therefore, and the car to sink deeper into the ditch.

They began to walk again.

It was cold, and colder by the moment, and they were hungry. But the few houses they passed were all deserted, locked and shuttered, every one.

"What did he mean?" said Mick, as they stood looking at another locked door.

"He was talking metaphor—"

"All that stuff about giants?"

"It was some Trotskyist tripe—" Judd insisted.

"I don't think so."

"I know so. It was his deathbed speech, he'd probably been preparing for years."

"I don't think so," Mick said again, and began walking back towards the road.

"Oh, how's that?" Judd was at his back.

"He wasn't towing some party line."

"Are you saying you think there's some giant around here someplace? For God's sake!"

Mick turned to Judd. His face was difficult to see the twilight. But his voice was sober with belief.

"Yes. I think he was telling the truth."

"That's absurd. That's ridiculous. No."

Judd hated Mick that moment. Hated his naïvete, his passion to believe any half-witted story if it had a whiff of romance about it. And this? This was the worst, the most preposterous . . .

"No," he said again. "No. No. No."

The sky was porcelain smooth, and the outline of the hills black as pitch.

"I'm fucking freezing," said Mick out of the ink. "Are you staying here or walking with me?"

Judd shouted: "We're not going to find anything this way."

"Well it's a long way back."

"We're just going deeper into the hills."

"Do what you like—I'm walking."

His footsteps receded: the dark encased him.

After a minute, Judd followed.

The night was cloudless and bitter. They walked on, their collars up against the chill, their feet swollen in their shoes. Above them the whole sky had become a parade of stars. A triumph of spilled light, from which the eye could make as many patterns as it had patience for. After a while, they slung their tired arms around each other, for comfort and warmth.

About eleven o'clock, they saw the glow of a window in the distance.

The woman at the door of the stone cottage didn't smile, but she understood their condition, and let them in. There seemed to be no purpose in trying to explain to either the woman or her crippled husband what they had seen. The cottage had no telephone, and there was no sign of a vehicle, so even had they found some way to express themselves, nothing could be done.

With mimes and face-pullings they explained that they were hungry and exhausted. They tried further to explain they were lost, cursing themselves for leaving their phrasebook in the VW. She didn't seem to understand very much of what they said, but sat them down beside a blazing fire and put a pan of food on the stove to heat.

They ate thick unsalted pea soup and eggs, and occasionally smiled their thanks at the woman. Her husband sat beside the fire, making no attempt to talk, or even look at the visitors.

The food was good. It buoyed their spirits.

They would sleep until morning and then begin the long trek back. By dawn the bodies in the field would be being quantified, identified, parcelled up and dispatched to their families. The air would be full of reassuring noises, cancelling out the moans that still rang in their ears. There would be helicopters, lorry loads of men organizing the clearing-up operations. All the rites and paraphernalia of a civilized disaster.

And in a while, it would be palatable. It would become part of their history: a tragedy, of course, but one they could explain, classify and learn to live with. All would be well, yes, all would be well. Come morning.

The sleep of sheer fatigue came on them suddenly. They lay where they had fallen, still sitting at the table, their heads on their crossed arms. A litter of empty bowls and bread crusts surrounded them.

They knew nothing. Dreamt nothing. Felt nothing.

Then the thunder began.

In the earth, in the deep earth, a rhythmical tread, as of a titan, that came, by degrees, closer and closer.

The woman woke her husband. She blew out the lamp and went to the door. The night sky was luminous with stars: the hills black on every side.

The thunder still sounded: a full half minute between every boom, but louder now. And louder with every new step.

They stood at the door together, husband and wife, and listened to the night-hills echo back and forth with the sound. There was no lightning to accompany the thunder.

Just the boom—

Boom—

Boom—

It made the ground shake: it threw dust down from the door-lintel, and rattled the window-latches.

Boom—

Boom—

They didn't know what approached, but whatever shape it took, and whatever it intended, there seemed no sense in running from it. Where they stood, in the pitiful shelter of their cottage, was as safe as any nook of the forest. How could they choose, out of a hundred thousand trees, which would be standing when the thunder had passed? Better to wait: and watch.

The wife's eyes were not good, and she doubted what she saw when the blackness of the hill changed shape and reared up to block the stars. But her husband had seen it too: the unimaginably huge head, vaster in the deceiving darkness, looming up and up, dwarfing the hills themselves with its ambition.

He fell to his knees, babbling a prayer, his arthritic legs twisted beneath him.

His wife screamed: no words she knew could keep this monster at bay— no prayer, no plea, had power over it.

In the cottage, Mick woke and his outstretched arm, twitching with a sudden cramp, wiped the plate and the lamp off the table.

They smashed. Judd woke.

The screaming outside had stopped. The woman had disappeared from the doorway into the forest. Any tree, any tree at all, was better than this sight. Her husband still let a string of prayers dribble from his slack mouth, as the great leg of the giant rose to take another step—

Boom—

The cottage shook. Plates danced and smashed off the dresser. A clay pipe rolled from the mantelpiece and shattered in the ashes of the hearth.

The lovers knew the noise that sounded in their substance: that earth-thunder.

Mick reached for Judd, and took him by the shoulder.

"You see," he said, his teeth blue-grey in the darkness of the cottage. "See? See?"

There was a kind of hysteria bubbling behind his words. He ran to the door, stumbling over a chair in the dark. Cursing and bruised he staggered out into the night—

Boom—

The thunder was deafening. This time it broke all the windows in the cottage. In the bedroom one of the roof-joists cracked and flung debris downstairs.

Judd joined his lover at the door. The old man was now face down on the ground, his sick and swollen fingers curled, his begging lips pressed to the damp soil.

Mick was looking up, towards the sky. Judd followed his gaze.

There was a place that showed no stars. It was a darkness in the shape of a man, a vast, broad human frame, a colossus that soared up to meet heaven. It was not quite a perfect giant. Its outline was not tidy; it seethed and swarmed.

He seemed broader too, this giant, than any real man. His legs were abnormally thick and stumpy, and his arms were not long. The hands, as they clenched and unclenched, seemed oddly-jointed and over-delicate for its torso.

Then it raised one huge, flat foot and placed it on the earth, taking a stride towards them.

Boom—

The step brought the roof collapsing in on the cottage. Everything that the car-thief had said was true. Popolac was a city and a giant; and it had gone into the hills . . .

Now their eyes were becoming accustomed to the night light. They could see in ever more horrible detail the way this monster was constructed. It was a masterpiece of human engineering: a man made entirely of men. Or rather, a sexless giant, made of men and women and children. All the citizens of Popolac writhed and strained in the body of this flesh-knitted giant, their muscles stretched to breaking point, their bones close to snapping.

They could see how the architects of Popolac had subtly altered the proportions of the human body; how the thing had been made squatter to lower its centre of gravity; how its legs had been made elephantine to bear the weight of the torso; how the head was sunk low on to the wide shoulders, so that the problems of a weak neck had been minimized.

Despite these malformations, it was horribly life-like. The bodies that were bound together to make its surface were naked but for their harnesses, so that its surface glistened in the starlight, like one vast human torso. Even the muscles were well copied, though simplified. They could see the way the roped bodies pushed and pulled against each other in solid cords of flesh and bone. They could see the intertwined people that made up the body: the backs like turtles packed together to offer the sweep of the pectorals; the lashed and knotted acrobats at the joints of the arms and the legs alike, rolling and unwinding to articulate the city.

But surely the most amazing sight of all was the face.

Cheeks of bodies; cavenous eye-sockets in which heads stared, five bound together for each eyeball; a broad, flat nose and a mouth that opened and closed, as the muscles of the jaw bunched and hollowed rhythmically. And from that mouth, lined with teeth of bald children, the voice of the giant, now only a weak copy of its former powers, spoke a single note of idiot music.

Popolac walked and Popolac sang.

Was there ever a sight in Europe the equal of it?

They watched, Mick and Judd, as it took another step towards them.

The old man had wet his pants. Blubbering and begging, he dragged himself away from the ruined cottage into the surrounding trees, dragging his dead legs after him.

The Englishmen remained where they stood, watching the spectacle as it approached. Neither dread nor horror touched them now, just an awe that rooted them to the spot. They knew this was a sight they could never hope to see again; this was the apex—after this there was only common experience. Better to stay then, though every step brought death nearer, better to stay and see the sight while it was still there to be seen. And if it killed them, this monster, then at least they would have glimpsed a miracle, known this terrible majesty for a brief moment. It seemed a fair exchange.

Popolac was within two steps of the cottage. They could see the complexities of its structure quite clearly. The faces of the citizens were becoming detailed: white, sweat-wet, and content in their weariness. Some hung dead from their harnesses, their legs swinging back and forth like the hanged. Others, children particularly, had ceased to obey their training, and had relaxed their positions, so that the form of the body was degenerating, beginning to seethe with the boils of rebellious cells.

Yet it still walked, each step an incalculable effort of coordination and strength.

Boom—

The step that trod the cottage came sooner than they thought.

457

Mick saw the leg raised; saw the faces of the people in the shin and ankle and foot—they were as big as he was now—all huge men chosen to take the full weight of this great creation. Many were dead. The bottom of the foot, he could see, was a jigsaw of crushed and bloody bodies, pressed to death under the weight of their fellow citizens.

The foot descended with a roar.

In a matter of seconds the cottage was reduced to splinters and dust.

Popolac blotted the sky utterly. It was, for a moment, the whole world, heaven and earth, its presence filled the senses to overflowing. At this proximity one look could not encompass it, the eye had to range backwards and forwards over its mass to take it all in, and even then the mind refused to accept the whole truth.

A whirling fragment of stone, flung off from the cottage as it collapsed, struck Judd full in the face. In his head he heard the killing stroke like a ball hitting a wall: a play-yard death. No pain: no remorse. Out like a light, a tiny, insignificant light; his death-cry lost in the pandemonium, his body hidden in the smoke and darkness. Mick neither saw nor heard Judd die.

He was too busy staring at the foot as it settled for a moment in the ruins of the cottage, while the other leg mustered the will to move.

Mick took his chance. Howling like a banshee, he ran towards the leg, longing to embrace the monster. He stumbled in the wreckage, and stood again, bloodied, to reach for the foot before it was lifted and he was left behind. There was a clamour of agonized breath as the message came to the foot that it must move; Mick saw the muscles of the shin bunch and marry as the leg began to lift. He made one last lunge at the limb as it began to leave the ground, snatching a harness or a rope, or human hair, or flesh itself—anything to catch this passing miracle and be part of it. Better to go with it wherever it was going, serve it in its purpose, whatever that might be; better to die with it than live without it.

He caught the foot, and found a safe purchase on its ankle. Screaming his sheer ecstasy at his success he felt the great leg raised, and glanced down through the swirling dust to the spot where he had stood, already receding as the limb climbed.

The earth was gone from beneath him. He was a hitchhiker with a god: the mere life he had left was nothing to him now, or ever. He would live with this thing, yes, he would live with it—seeing it and seeing it and eating it with his eyes until he died of sheer gluttony.

He screamed and howled and swang on the ropes, drinking up his triumph. Below, far below, he glimpsed Judd's body, curled up pale on the dark ground, irretrievable. Love and life and sanity were gone, gone like the memory of his name, or his sex, or his ambition.

It all meant nothing. Nothing at all.

Boom—

Boom—

Popolac walked, the noise of its steps receding to the east. Popolac walked, the hum of its voice lost in the night.

After a day, birds came, foxes came, flies, butterflies, wasps came, Judd moved, Judd shifted, Judd gave birth. In his belly maggots warmed themselves, in a vixen's den the good flesh of his thigh was fought over. After that, it was quick. The bones yellowing, the bones crumbling: soon, an empty space which he had once filled with breath and opinions.

Darkness, light, darkness, light. He interrupted neither with his name.

INCOGNITA, INC.

HARLAN ELLISON

Harlan Ellison has written or edited more than seventy-five books; over 1,700 stories, essays, articles, and newspaper columns; two dozen teleplays—for which he received the Writers Guild of America most outstanding teleplay award for solo work an unprecedented four times—and a dozen movie scripts.

He has won numerous other awards throughout his career, including the Mystery Writers of America Edgar Allan Poe Award twice, the Horror Writers Association Bram Stoker Award six times (including the Lifetime Achievement Award in 1996), the Nebula Award of the Science Fiction Writers of America three times, the Hugo Award, the World Fantasy Award, the British Fantasy Award and the Silver Pen for Journalism from P.E.N. In 2006 Ellison was named a Grand Master by the Science Fiction/Fantasy Writers of America.

"I refuse to write the same story twice," Ellison explains. "I keep experimenting. I keep learning how to work. I've been at it pretty much fifty years, and I'm now beginning to learn how to do the job well. I'm not like Robert Silverberg, who came full-blown out of the egg. The man wrote brilliantly right from the git-go. I had to learn. My earliest stuff is painful to read! Now, fifty years later, I'm at a point where I write pretty damn okay. I need to keep learning, and I need to keep pushing the envelope.

"The most perfectly written story I've done in years is 'Incognita, Inc.'
I finally got a glimmering of what I was capable of producing when I
wrote that story. But because it isn't mean and because it isn't screaming,
I'll bet most readers will discount it as an aberration by the otherwise stri-
dent, rabid Ellison."
    If you've ever wondered where all these imaginary lands come from,
you're about to discover the answer. . . .

You've asked me to file the report, so that's what I'm doing. But
this is also my resignation notice. It was a miserable, meanspirited
job you stuck me with, and I hated even the *idea* of doing it. But I
did it. I did as I was told, I suppose, because I've been with WorldSpan
(formerly Blackstar Holdings [Pty.] [Ltd.]) since you recruited me out of
the U. of Chicago twenty years ago, and like a good obedient dog I was
part of that generation between the Baby Boomers and GenX that
believed Daddy Corporation would take care of me all the way to senes-
cence. And I *was* your good little running dog, did whatever you asked,
didn't weigh the ethical freight, swallowed hard sometimes as I watched
the knives go in, but I just intoned the mantra *I don't want to get involved,*
it ain't none of my business. I ate those fat paychecks and never got bulimic.

But this time, oh boy *this* time it couldn't be swallowed. I particularly
hated it, Howard, when you gave me the assignment and said it was apropos
that *I* be the one to carry it out, seeing as how my name is Charles Trimbach.
You laughed at that. You and Barry, both of you thought it was hilarious:
"trim back" was a terrific play on words for such a puke job you wanted
done. I couldn't swallow hard this time; it made my gorge buoyant. And the
lesson I learned, if it's a lesson at all, is what prompts my resignation,

I quit, WorldSpan. Howard, Tom Jr., Kincaid, all the rest of you up on
the 44th floor. I'm done. Take the fat paycheck and stuff it. Done, fellahs.
But I'm dogtrot trained; a lot of years; so here's my last piece of work. The
report. Pardon the casual tone.

• • •

The flight was late coming into Chicago Midway; and by the time the cab dropped me off in Old Town on the corner of N. Wells and Wieland it was coming up on late afternoon, early evening. Even with all the gentrification, it was still a sweetly raffish part of town. Jammed crisscross at the proper hemlines of Lincoln Park and the Gold Coast, what was left of Old Town still sucked up all the light and breathed back disturbing shadows. In a few more years everything between N. La Salle and Larrabee would be so squeaky clean you'd have to clear it with the condo committee to import even a tiny sinful act. But on this bitter cold February afternoon, with the blade of wind slicing in off the lake, turning my bones to tundra, it was the old vengeful Chicago I'd grown up in.

And I got lost.

I *always* got lost in Old Town. Somewhere near Elm and Hill I turned the wrong way, got twisted, and wandered for the better part of an hour. Then, some dim memory of my childhood kicked in, and as I passed a sweep of vacant shops with the blind eyes of upstairs apartments reflecting the last tremor of setting sunlight. I saw the mouth of the dark alleyway that was my landing site. How I'd recalled it, over decades, I don't know. But there it was; and I crossed the street and stepped into dim shadowed yesterday.

There was a paper flower shoppe, and a guitar repair joint, and an antiques/collectibles store; and wedged in between the guitar emporium— with a really cherry 1947 Les Paul "Broadcaster" hanging in the fly-specked front window—and the scentless dried brayera trying to look brave like a Victorian ruined garden . . .

There was the map shop. As neat and clean and brightly painted as a little red wagon on Christmas morning. The shop of maps in which labored a man named Abner Wonacott. The old guy you had sent me to fire. Charlie Trimbach, come to "trim back" that old cartographer in a store that shouldn't have existed, but did. Maybe it always had.

• • •

In hundreds of adventure movies, there's always a map of some strange, lost land. In Muslim mythology it's Kaf, the mountain range that circles the Earth. In *The Odyssey* it was Ogygia, the island where Calypso kept Odysseus a captive. If you went looking for King Kong it was "2 south, 90 east, latitudes way west of Sumatra, southwest to Skull Island." The Garden of Eden, Barsoom, Asgard and Midgard, Atlantis and Avalon, the Catacombs of Rome, Mount Olympus, Oz, Nepenthe, Lilliput, Islandia, Hi-Brasil, Lemuria.

Did you never wonder: where do these maps come from?

Who makes these maps?

By what arcane mappery do these cartographs come to be? What nameless Mercator or Henry the Navigator, what astonishing Ptolemy or Kropotkin, beat the paths to Narnia and lost Hyperborea and the Fountain of Youth?

Who, did you ever ask yourself, who? What mapmaker sat and actually drew the lines and shapes? To all those *terra incognita* venues.

One of those things no one really thinks about. You hear a story about some expedition going to Mount Everest—"chomolungma" the Mother Goddess of the Earth—because they've got a highly reliable map of the terrain where the *yeti* mates; or Sotheby's has auctioned off for two million five a map—highly reliable—that locates El Dorado; or the Seven Cities of Cíbola; or the fabulous sunken islands of Gunnbjorn Ulfson between Iceland and Greenland; the *real* Yoknapatawpha County; the *real* Graver's Mill that changed its name and altered its city limits after that Sunday night radio broadcast on CBS in October of 1938; the *real* location of Noah's ark at 17,000 feet above the Aras River plain but *not* atop Mount Ararat; you hear these stones, and you may wonder for an instant . . .

Where did such a map come from?

The last survivor of a Norwegian barque. The rambling mad foot-soldier who emerged from the jungle after six months' missing. The withered septua-generic Cree sitting by the side of the road selling potions and talismans. The gypsy fortune teller. The speaking-in-tongues child who has been blind since birth.

There's always a chain of provenance; and it's always bogus. Comes to as dead an end as *terra incognita* itself. Yet the maps do exist. They come into the hands of the L. Frank Baums and the Edgar Rice Burroughses and the Ponce de Leons, the Samuel Butlers and St. Thomas Aqumases. But, do you ever ask yourself, where did *they* . . . how did *they* . . . come by these amazing—highly reliable—charts? Who draws the map that shows the entrance to the mountain where the children of Hamelin disappeared? Who describes latitude and longitude of the tropical island beyond Anacapa where Amelia Earhart came down safely and hid from the Japanese fleet? How does the singular cartographer get a highly reliable tracing of the rocky battered shore of Lemuria and the Kingdom of Prester John and the Well of Souls?

Did you ever ask that kind of question?

I never did, Howard, till that shadowy alleyway in Old Town on a bitter chill late afternoon in February.

What inferior landscape I could see through the elegant gray-glass of the central pane of the ornately carved teak front door of the map shop was inchoate, indeterminate, yes a *terra incognita*. Absolutely appropriate. The handsomely whittled wooden sign that hung by brass chains at 90° to the storefront read:

INCOGNITA, INC.
A. Wonacott, Prop.

I turned the bright shining gold handle of the front door, the handle in the shape of a sextant, and let the warmth from within flow out around me in the dark alley.

Then I stepped inside the curious map shop.

Understand something: I had been born and raised in Chicago, I had been away a long time, I had been married and widowed, I had a grown son and daughter who no longer needed my daily attention and who lived half a continent away, I had been a loyal corporate tool for most of my adult life, and I was solidly grounded in the pragmatic world, what they call the Real World, the continuum as received safely and sanely by those who renew their drivers' licenses regularly and who watch their saturated fat intake. I do not go off on flights of fancy.

Now let me describe Incognita, Inc. to you.

All I knew was that WorldSpan had acquired this enterprise, this supposedly "mom'n'pop" shop, line-item-buried on a Schedule of Assets & Liabilities, on the second-to-the-last page of a thick sheaf of wholly owned subsidiaries of the mega-conglomerate WorldSpan had murdered in the takeover. Then had begun the pogrom, the flensing, the "de-accessioning" of properties that did not breathlessly contribute to the bottom line. The memo you e-mailed me, if you recall, Howard, used the phrase *cease and terminate this operation.*

But there had been no phone number, no fax number, no e-mail address, nothing but the shop number in a tiny commercial alleyway I couldn't find on the most detailed city map of Chicago. And so you had me fly to Old Town.

To trim back one Abner Wonacott, who apparently had been the owner and sole employee of Incognita, Inc., at this odd location, for what seemed to be—in spotty records—sixty-five years. And now I stood inside the door, and now I looked upward, and now I looked around, and now I found myself unable to grasp what I was seeing, here, inside this tiny shop.

Outside. Very small.

INCOGNITA, INC.

Inside. Vast.

I don't mean to tell you it was large. Large is the rotunda of Grand Central Station. Large is the basilica of St. Peter's. Large is Hanging Rock in Australia. This was vast. Narrow, but vast. It stretched out beyond the logical, codifiable, eyesight-correct limit that Euclidean space acknowledged. The horizon line was invisible. There was no back wall to the shop. It all just stretched on out of sight, vast and deep, and going on and on till it came to a blurred point somewhere a million or so miles back there at the rear of the shop. On either side of me the walls rose straight up without break, and both walls were nothing but deep cubbyholes, hundreds of them, thousands of them, uncountable perhaps *millions* of them. Up and up and up into some sort of inexplicable ceilingless ionosphere, where clouds and chirruping creatures moved lazily. And in every cubbyhole there was a rolled map, or a group of rolled maps. Hundreds of maps, thousands of maps, uncountable perhaps . . .

And clambering all over chose two walls of cubbyholes, were the tendrils of the most luxurious liana vines I've ever seen. Dark green and lustrous, the vines writhed upward and downward and from side to side, wrapping themselves about a map roll here, a pair of papyrus charts there, then extricating their tendril ends from the cubby and slithering swiftly across the face of the wall—sometimes hurling themselves full across the shop to the wall opposite—and then fled rearward, to extend their length to an unknown destination far away in the cloudy foggy misty backland of Incognita. Inc.

It was, truly, the jungle telegraph. Possibly a kind of fern FedEx. Delivery by botanical messenger.

And right in front of me, not ten steps inside the front door, was the (apparently) sole living employee of this soon-to-be-terminated establishment, Abner Wonacott. Prop.

He sat high up on a bookkeepers stool, something hugely Dickensian in appearance, like one of those old woodcuts by "Phiz" or Cruikshank from *Dombey and Son* or *A Christmas Carol.* The desk at which he worked was a

467

very tall slant-top, tulip stenciled with tapering legs framed with cross stretchers. The grain identified it as a very old mahogany.

He wore a full day-coat with short tails, striped trousers, wing-collar shirt with a plum-colored cravat, and a diamond stickpin glistening between the trisail lapels. He wore a pince-nez that perched securely at the bridge of his aquiline nose, his hair was thick and pure white, and it hung over his forehead with an abundant curl like a dollop of whipped cream.

His eyes were the most revelatory shade of almond I've ever seen, with very black pupils, like a pair of well-ensconced beetles frozen in hundred-million-year-old Baltic amber. It was enigmatic trying to ascertain his age. He might have been sixty, less likely a weathered fifty, perhaps much older.

He had the kindest face ever gifted by the cruel and mostly uncaring world. He wore it without affectation.

"Excuse me," I said. "Mr. Wonacott?"

"Be with you in a spot, young man. Having a nip of a mean time with one of these isogrivs." He was working on a line, on a map he was drawing, up there on his high stool. "Grivation has never been my strong suit." He scratched quickly with the nib of a crowquill pen. "Look around. Amuse yourself. Be with you in two shakes of a lamb's tail."

I turned to look at the wall on my right. I walked across the pleasantly springy, mist-shrouded floor to the cubbyholes and marveled at what they held. Not just maps to Happy Valley and Rumania and Lyonesse and Shangri-La; to Zothique and Ur and Erewhon and Pellucidar; but the route Verne parodied to reach the center of the Earth; a sad-looking graph locating the mass grave of the original colonists of the Lost Roanoke Colony (with a triptych map to the gravesite of Virginia Dare, first queen of the Croatan Indians); a large scroll map of "The Dark Continent" with an identifying Gothic cross marking the locale of The Elephants' Graveyard. It was somewhere near Mali.

There was a recently configured map of the shoreline of Lake Michigan indicating where to dredge to find the Bowie knife O.J. Simpson had thrown away.

"Would you like to know what our most requested item is?" I turned at his voice. He was sitting now with hands folded decently on the slant-top of the desk, I walked back to him and looked up into the kindest face in the world.

"Yes."

"Well now, you would think, wouldn't you, that it would be something like Atlantis or Camelot or an underwater configuration for Spanish treasure galleons, yes?" I smiled agreement. But no, he indicated with a waggle of a finger, "Five to one, our best seller is a personal site location map to the original *and translated into spoken English* lyrics to the song 'Louie Louie.' Isn't that remarkable?"

I stared up into his amber eyes. "Remarkable," I said, in a soft voice. "Like this shop. It's, uh, it's improbable." I felt my cheeks burning with embarrassment: "improbable." What the hell kind of a stupid word was that to use?! "It's very big. Inside."

"Oh, this is cramped quarters, I fear." He waved a hand above his head, diminishing the ascendant abyss that rose high and away over us. "You should have seen the absolutely imperial spaces accorded me when I worked for Khufu. Pyramid, it was. Very nice. And there was a canyon in Mesopo—"

I cut him off. "I've come to close you down, sir."

I couldn't help myself. I had to stop him. I felt so awful, like some sleazy server of subpoenas pretending to be an interested bypasser. "I've come from corporate headquarters to . . . I have a very generous severance check here in my . . . how is it you've worked for this company for, what is it, *sixty-five* years, can that be accurate, we don't seem to have much paper-work on all this, uh . . ."

I ground to a halt. I felt just awful.

"Look," I said, "you won't remember me, but I came here, I think, once before; a long time ago; thirty-something years ago. To get a map. I'd lost something . . ."

He smiled down at me. "A bronze medal you had won, third prize in a kite flying contest in grade school."

"Yes! Yes, that was it, exactly! You remember. I'd lost it. Your map . . ."

"To be sure. My map. It's an all-purpose item, we sell quite a lot of them. I call it the Map to Your Heart's Desire. Do you still have that medal?"

"Migod yes!" I pulled our my pocket watch, and showed him the bronze fob. "It's the only thing I've ever won in my life. Not so much as ten bucks on a lottery, but I have the bronze medal. You found it for me."

"And now you've come to put me out of business."

"Believe me, it's not my idea. They gave me this lousy job because I mentioned one day, just idly, mentioned I was from around here . . . and they thought it would be . . ."

He looked sad. "I've been expecting something like this. There was a letter from . . . what's the name of the new company that bought up the old one . . . ?"

Now here among the million conundra that scintillated and sang within the vast, questioning mind of the very old man who now called himself Abner Wonacott, like a heavenly chorus of inebriated lightning bugs, was there even one that wondered by whom Abner had been employed, now going on sixty-six years. If it wasn't a Pharaoh, it was a Doge, if it wasn't a Khan it was a Demiurge. The shop, and Abner under other names, had gone on for centuries. Every Friday by 5 P.M. the cashier's check appeared in a late post, signed in pen in an unintelligible hand, for that weeks labors. Abner was only human, after all, and he did require food and shelter. And so it had been for now going on sixty-six years at this current location. Periodically, every sixteen months by rough estimation, Abner's check was nine percent greater than those that had preceded it. On his birthday—June 11th usually—and at holidaytime—he had never known if the impetus was Chanukah, Ramadan, or Christmas—the check included a crisp new one hundred dollar bill as bonus. And so, without wondering, because he loved his work of a lifetime, of many lifetimes, Abner worked with serenity and satisfaction in the vast tiny narrow and limitless cartography shop in the shadowy, dismal, perfectly pleasant narrow alley three streets off the bustling thoroughfares of that immense metropolitan nexus that might, at other times, have been Avalon or Tyre or Carthage, might have been Marrakech or Constantinople or Vienna, but was only, in truth, for going on sixty-six years, at this location, the hamlet of Chicago.

"I will, I must say, hate to see me go. Abandoning the work to Replogle and Rand McNally will be . . . well, of course, they're very fine people, and they try to do their best, but I think they still use that silly *Here There Be Dragons* at the edge of the drop-off."

I stammered and heard myself babbling. "We, that is to say, WorldSpan, has just completed on-orbit checkout and synchronization of our three geodetic polar orbital satellites, all of which are in geosynchronous configurations 22,300 miles above the planet, all with completely automated computer-driven cartography programs." His eyes were wide as I gibbered, unable to stop myself: I'd rehearsed all this, straight from the tech memoranda, on the plane, not knowing who or what Abner Wonacott was going to be. And now I couldn't shut up. "These are electro-optical imaging satellites. We now have a multi-planar, LEO, MEO, and GEO corporate capability to provide under-an-hour mapping and geospatial products to our worldwide customers. We can 'direct-task' both an electro-optical and hyperspectral satellite to image any 100 x 100 kilometer swath on Earth. We can employ our highly refined processing algorithms which allow us to . . . levels of reflectance . . . hundreds of spectral bands . . ."

I ran down. So ashamed of myself. Just so damned, damned *ashamed* of what I'd let you make of me. Howard. I wanted to sink through the unseen, misty floor. I felt like a giant gobbet of crap. And Abner Wonacott just stared at me.

"So I am the relic from an earlier time," he said. "I seem to be, as they put it, redundant. Well, that must be it, then, of course." He slid off his high perch and put his hands on my shoulders. He was taller than I'd thought.

"What is your name, young man?"

"Charlie Trimbach, sir."

"Ah. Yes, of course. I do indeed remember the bronze medal and how you cried. Well, let me say this. Master Charles Trimbach: you are a very nice young man. You need not be so unforgiving, of yourself, and of those for whom you labor. You have turned out to be an absolutely imperial young man, and I hold no bad cess for your having come to deliver this nasty news."

I handed him the envelope containing the severance check. Though how you could pay him for what must have been hundreds of years of maps, well, I don't know; I just don't know.

He reached into a shelf beneath the slant-top of his desk and removed a derby hat. He placed it carefully on his head at a rakish angle, took one last look around the shop—the greenery seemed to rustle a farewell—and he walked me to the door.

We stepped out into the Chicago night. It was lit by a full moon. He closed the door behind us, and turned to me as he locked up. "But with all your capacity for producing a map down to the last grain of sand in the Gobi, Charlie, the sad thing is that now and forevermore no one will be able to provide the questing customer with a route to Baskerville Hall, or Riallaro, or Nimmr in the Valley of the Sepulchre. With the closing of this little oasis, Charlie, your little civilization loses for all time to come. There is no Charta Caelestis for the improbable."

And when I turned back to see, the shop was gone. It was now a boarded-up derelict, what had once been a deli or a place where they sold banded 12-packs of socks. Seconds.

Abner Wonacott and I walked out into the street, left the alley, and headed toward the city lights. It was terribly cold, that special awful Chicago cold that makes you think of the end of the world. He held his derby on with one hand and hunched deeper inside his jacket. I wished I'd brought a heavier topcoat. It hadn't been supposed to get this cold, this soon.

"What will you do now?" I asked him.

He shrugged. "Perhaps I'll retire somewhere nice and warm. I hear Boca is pleasant."

I wanted to cry. Just like that, so damned casually, I'd made everything go sour in the world. I fingered the bronze medal fob on my watch chain. I was a bad person, no matter what the old mapmaker said to ease my guilt. A bad person. I told him that. He smiled wryly and said, "Most of us think we're more important than we really are, Charlie. The universe isn't watching. It mostly, for the most part, doesn't care."

And at that moment, before I could wallow much more in adolescent self-pity, a stout lady with one of those wire shopping baskets on wheels came up to us, and she looked at Abner Wonacott, the one man who could actually tell you where King Kong resided, and she said, "Excuse me, mister, is there a Dominick's around here?"

"No, not too close," he said. "There *was* an A&P for a long time, but it's gone. I think there's a Jewel Supermarket about a mile toward Lincoln Park, but . . . oh, wait a moment . . . yes, now that I recall, yes indeed there *is* a Dominick's.

"You'll have to go over three blocks that way, and then go left for two more blocks to . . ."

He paused, looked thoughtful for a moment, then reached into his inside jacket pocket and brought out a lovely fountain pen and a pad. "Here," he said, "let me draw you a map."

And all at once, the wind wasn't nearly as cold as it had been; and the night was not nearly as empty.

ABOUT THE EDITOR

STEPHEN JONES lives in London, England. He is the winner of three World Fantasy Awards, four Horror Writers Association Bram Stoker Awards and three International Horror Guild Awards, as well as being a seventeen-time recipient of the British Fantasy Award and a Hugo Award nominee. A former television producer/director and genre movie publicist and consultant (the first three *Hellraiser* movies, *Night Life, Nightbreed, Split Second, Mind Ripper, Last Gasp,* etc.), he is the co-editor of *Horror: 100 Best Books, Horror: Another 100 Best Books, The Best Horror from Fantasy Tales, Gaslight & Ghosts, Now We Are Sick, H. P. Lovecraft's Book of Horror, The Anthology of Fantasy & the Supernatural, Secret City: Strange Tales of London, Great Ghost Stories, Tales to Freeze the Blood: More Great Ghost Stories and the Dark Terrors, Dark Voices,* and *Fantasy Tales* series. He has written *Stardust: The Film Companion, Creepshows: The Illustrated Stephen King Movie Guide, The Essential Monster Movie Guide, The Illustrated Vampire Movie Guide, The Illustrated Dinosaur Movie Guide, The Illustrated Frankenstein Movie Guide and The Illustrated Werewolf Movie Guide,* and compiled *The*

Mammoth Book of Best New Horror series, *The Mammoth Book of Terror, The Mammoth Book of Vampires, The Mammoth Book of Zombies, The Mammoth Book of Werewolves, The Mammoth Book of Frankenstein, The Mammoth Book of Dracula, The Mammoth Book of Vampire Stories By Women, The Mammoth Book of New Terror, The Mammoth Book of Monsters, Shadows Over Innsmouth, Weird Shadows Over Innsmouth, Dark Detectives, Dancing with the Dark, Dark of the Night, White of the Moon, Keep Out the Night, By Moonlight Only, Don't Turn Out the Light, H. P. Lovecraft's Book of the Supernatural, Travellers in Darkness, Summer Chills, Exorcisms and Ecstasies* by Karl Edward Wagner, *The Vampire Stories of R. Chetwynd-Hayes, Phantoms and Fiends* and *Frights and Fancies* by R. Chetwynd-Hayes, *James Herbert: By Horror Haunted, The Complete Chronicles of Conan* by Robert E. Howard, *The Emperor of Dreams: The Lost Worlds of Clark Ashton Smith, Sea-Kings of Mars and Otherworldly Stories* by Leigh Brackett, *The Mark of the Beast and Other Fantastical Tales* by Rudyard Kipling, *Clive Barker's A-Z of Horror, Clive Barker's Shadows in Eden, Clive Barker's The Nightbreed Chronicles,* and the *Hellraiser Chronicles.* He was a Guest of Honor at the 2002 World Fantasy Convention in Minneapolis, Minnesota, and the 2004 World Horror Convention in Phoenix, Arizona. You can visit his web site at www.herebedragons.co.uk/jones.